Never the
Same Again

Also by Jesse Sublett

Fiction

Rock Critic Murders
Tough Baby
Boiled in Concrete
The Teflon Babe
Deader Than Hell
I Love My Gun

Nonfiction

History of the Texas Turnpike Authority

Never the Same Again

A rock 'n' roll gothic

Jesse Sublett

BOAZ Publishing Company
Berkeley, California

 BOAZ Publishing Company
1111 Eighth Street
Berkeley, California 94710

Distributed by Ten Speed Press
www.tenspeed.com

Distributed in the United States of America by Ten Speed Press, in
Australia by Simon and Schuster Australia, in Canada by Ten Speed Press
Canada, in New Zealand by Southern Publishing Group, in South Africa
by Real Books, and in the United Kingdom and Europe by Airlift Book
Company.

Designed by E. Vahlsing

Library of Congress Control Number: 2004103990

ISBN 1-58008-598-9
Printed in Canada
April 2004
05 04 03 02 01

~ to Lois and Dashiell ~

Contents

PART 1.
NEVER THE
SAME AGAIN

1. WHITE ROOM
November 17, 1997

I'm lying inside a CAT scan tube in a bright white room at a radiological lab in Austin, Texas. It's night outside, about 10:30 p.m. Time seems to stand still in here, even when you have to hold your breath. It's not especially uncomfortable, except when my thoughts race ahead to why I'm here and the isolation starts to bug me. I remember hearing my mother tell people how I was always happy playing alone. Later, on the road with the band, I loved driving all night, the other guys sleeping or lost in their private reveries. Just me and my thoughts, and the gray twilight world caught in the low glare of my headlights.

They've got me trussed up tight so I won't move and spoil the pictures—one giant elastic band around my ankles and another pulling my shoulders down, masking tape holding my head in position. Maybe this is what a caterpillar feels like inside its cocoon.

I've been playing songs in my head. "White Room" by Cream is good, the wah-wah guitar sounding no less exotically weird than it did thirty years ago, blasting out of the dashboard radio. Segue to "Frankenstein" by the New York Dolls, which helped me get through the ugly parts of the seventies. In the eighties, nothing was nearly as fine as "Avalon" by Roxy Music, coasting through the ether like a cloud-surfing limousine. Wish I could ride it out of here.

The machine starts whirring again, spinning like a roulette wheel as its

3

trio of electromagnetic eyes slice through me from teeth to throat, then down through chest and abdomen. Someday they'll have a scanner so powerful it searches through every cell and fiber of your body to reveal your past and all your secrets. Its report will be the ultimate home video, complete with a forensic diagnostic critique that enumerates the crucial mistakes you made in life, especially the ones that trapped you inside the future equivalent of this white cocoon. We're all prisoners of our past.

When I first walked in, the technician said I looked familiar.

"I used to have a band called the Skunks," I said. "Maybe that's it."

"Oh yeah," he said, grinning. "I used to see you guys in high school. You were great."

"Thanks," I said.

People here seem pretty cool—at least, they do until the weirdness starts to sink in. Like when the tech took a closer look at my file and his grin disappeared. What did that mean? Try not to think about it.

"You guys stay open pretty late," I said.

"It's convenient for people who can't get off work during the day."

Since I'm my own boss, I could've come down here anytime, but my doctor said it would be a good idea to get this done right away. "Maybe you could go tonight," she said. So here I am.

Once in a while the tech says, "How you doing in there?" or gives me an update on how much longer it's going to take.

"I'm fine," I tell him. Which is only half true. Outwardly, I'm calm, but as I stare fish-eyed at the whiteness in front of my nose, I'm mentally screening a film noir called *The Big C*, starring yours truly. *He's got nowhere to run, nowhere to hide, because the enemy is right where it's always been—inside him—and the only thing taller than the odds stacked against him is his own sense of guilt. Because of his own foolish past, he knows he's got it coming.*

Reminds me of my favorite line in *Unforgiven: We've all got it comin', kid.*

"Excuse me?" says the tech. "You OK?"

"Nothing. I'm fine."

I'm not supposed to talk, or move, or even breathe while the machine is scanning me. I give a Clint Eastwood squint anyway. I'm a hunk of heavy metal destiny inside a gunfighter's bullet. *We've all got it comin'.*

I've got a lump in my throat about the size of a .45 caliber slug, tucked just beneath my lower right jaw. By now it seems familiar, almost like an old friend. I had another one very much like it, in exactly the same place, when we lived in Los Angeles. In January 1994, the lump was surgically removed by Dr. Nixon, a specialist in otolaryngology, what they used to call ENT, for ear, nose and throat.

"Don't worry about it," Dr. Nixon told me after the surgery. "It was really ugly, and it turned out to be bigger than I thought it was, but it wasn't cancer."

Talk about relief! Happy new year, 1994. Lois gave me a kiss so big it penetrated my Demerol haze. Besides our love affair and partnership of sixteen years (nine as husband and wife), we had a four-month-old boy—Dashiell, named after the great American writer Dashiell Hammett. The idea of checking out on them, Dashiell growing up without any memory of his father, was severely depressing.

Over the months, before the first surgery, Dr. Nixon had repeatedly assured me that the lump was probably benign. He said it before and after the X rays, the blood tests, the CAT scan, the biopsy. Despite the negative test results, despite Dr. Nixon's assurances, despite the air of steely confidence and casual unconcern I carefully maintained, every passing week marked a growing conviction that the lump in my throat really was cancer. That it would be terminal. I didn't envision a debilitating battle for survival against the exquisite tortures of surgery, radiation and chemotherapy. All I saw was death.

Mostly, I forced myself not to think about it. That's how I made it through the months between that first appointment with Dr. Nixon in August 1993 and the surgery the following January. In between came the drama and celebrations of Dashiell's birth, Thanksgiving and Christmas. All that time I held my fear like a scream in my fist. I swaggered with phony courage and confidence. It's probably nothing. Sometimes I even believed myself.

But now it appeared that I was only being paranoid. "It wasn't cancer," he said. "Nothing to worry about." No shit? I'd been reprieved! Why the hell had I been so scared? Of course it wasn't cancer. Not me, cancer is something other people get.

Skies were blue again. Lois was overjoyed, her face flushed with relief, her big brown eyes full of light. My heart thumped the bass line to "Love and Happiness."

Three days later they sent me home. In the wee hours of the morning of the fifth day, the Northridge earthquake threw us out of bed, the bedrock below growling the end of the world, our apartment creaking, things crashing to the floor. It seemed like the punch line of a very strange joke.

But our apartment building did not do a pancake collapse, unlike many in adjacent neighborhoods, and after the rumbling stopped, Dashiell was still asleep. Lois was seriously rattled, and she had a big bruise where she'd been knocked into the wall by the dancing floor. The cats were seriously rattled. More of our belongings would've been damaged, but most were already packed in boxes for our move back to Austin. I loved L.A., but our families were in Texas, and Lois, an air force brat whose father was transferred to a different base—often, in a new part of the world—every three years, strongly felt that it was time for a change. If nothing else, Austin would be a safer place to raise our son. Now she pointed out that this earthquake might be a sign, just in case we were having second thoughts about leaving. Maybe it was just that, a kick in the ass on our way out of town.

I still didn't want to leave, but Lois was usually right about these things, so off we went. After all, it was her idea to move to L.A. in the first place.

I'm not sure when the lump came back, but it's definitely there now, in the same place as the first one. There are several smaller lumps, too, about the size of BBs, near the front of my throat. The back of my neck feels hard and knotty. I asked my new otolaryngologist if this might have anything to do with all those years of hard singing. After a beat of silence, she shook her head and said no, it wouldn't. I didn't think so, I said, but my mother wanted to know.

Finally the tech says, "We're done."

He presses a button and a motor conveys me back into the bright room. Another button lowers me. The tech unfastens all those ridiculous straps, then offers to help me up. I decline. Whatever it is I've got, I'm not that far gone yet.

The tech is avoiding eye contact. Maybe he's just bored. I gather my keys and wallet and stand there. He still won't look at me.

The door is open. I walk out.

"Good luck," he calls. To my back.

The waiting room is empty. On the other side of the sign-in window is the girl who was so friendly when I came in to fill out my forms. She doesn't seem to notice me. I watch her carry some files into the next room. The only light comes from the big monitor screens displaying black and white images. Another tech is staring at one of the monitors. The Skunks fan is looking over his shoulder. No one speaks. The girl puts the files down and stands next to them. The monitor paints their faces an eerie grayish blue. If you wanted to convey foreboding and dread in a low-budget science fiction movie, this scene would do the trick.

It's chilly outside. My Karmann Ghia looks lonely in the empty parking lot. Moths and bats swirl around the lights in tight orbits, reminding me of the atomic energy icon. I suppose those were my images on those monitors.

I don't like the way the guy said "Good luck." It didn't sound right.

They were all so friendly at first. But a freak accident seems to have occurred while I was under the machine's electromagnetic gaze. It must've altered my molecular structure and made me invisible. I've disappeared.

Yes, it feels a little like an episode of *The Twilight Zone*. Rod Serling died of cancer, didn't he?

A few days later my otolaryngologist, Dr. Melba Lewis, tells me I have a type of head and neck cancer called squamous cell carcinoma. She says it's a life-threatening situation, that I need major surgery, maybe radiation and chemotherapy. And she can't say it, but the truth behind the maybe part of the scenario is this: The cancer is so advanced and aggressive, there's a good chance I'll die no matter what last-ditch slash-and-burn-and-poison they attack it with. *Thank you and goodnight, ladies and gentlemen. Your favorite bass player is about to leave the building.*

What scares me more than death is the possibility that I'll lose the ability to speak. That they might have to cut out my tongue or voice box or that I'll be disfigured in some other way too grotesque to imagine. That I'll live out my life as the ugly secret behind the curtains at the Sublett house. A real *Frankenstein* rocker. Lois will never confess that she finds my appearance repulsive, although nothing she can say will convince me otherwise. Dashiell won't be able to lie as well as his mom, and how could I even expect him to try? His friends at school will tease him cruelly, the kid with the monster dad.

Maybe I'll die and maybe I won't, but it's for real this time. Unlike four years ago, I force myself to contemplate Lois and Dashiell without me.

And what about the big record deal I never got? The novels that didn't hit the bestseller list, the ones I abandoned, the screenplays that didn't get made? I've had some good luck in my forty-three years on the planet, just not enough of it.

I'm staring death in the face, and I probably was in 1994, too. Then there was the time way before that, when I was a hot-shit twenty-something rocker all set to take over the world and boom, I had a head-on collision at the crossroads. Bad as this is, that time was worse. Back then I wasn't afraid to die. I felt dead already. What scared me was the idea that I might go on living.

Her name was Dianne Roberts. She was a long-legged brunette, just a few inches shorter than me, and I'm six-foot-three. Her eyes were big, brown and dreamy, her hair luxuriously long, swaying with the rest of her when she walked. A pretty and sophisticated girl from Houston, an art major and rock 'n' roller who had me spellbound from the moment I laid eyes on her in the fall of 1972, our first semester in college in San Marcos, Texas.

I was a longhair in Levi bellbottoms and boots, an English major working hard at being a hipster. I was from Johnson City, Texas, a town with fewer people than Dianne's senior class. English major, poet, Rolling Stones fanatic on an Alice Cooper kick.

I was shy with girls, and even though I felt sure the attraction was mutual, I let her get away the first time. After being in agony for several days, I chased after her and caught her and didn't let go. And then finally, one night after a rock concert, on the heels of twelve straight nights of making out, with me too afraid to go further, with Led Zeppelin on the radio, we consummated our love in the front seat of my '64 Mercury Comet.

We were inseparable after that, like two mice in a sock. Necks perpetually splattered with vampire bites. Having her as my girlfriend boosted my confidence and broadened my experience. She made me feel gallant just for who I was, and for whatever I might aspire to be.

Dianne's artistic impulses, plus our constant immersion in music, stoked my ambition to play rock 'n' roll for real, not just in shitty garage bands with my friends. After two years together, we bailed out of college and moved to Austin so I could start a band there. I was gonna be a rock star, no doubt about it. It might take a year or two, three at the outside. Dianne got a job at a credit bureau, I worked in a mailroom, crummy jobs to subsidize a rock 'n' roll life. We were happy. We assumed we'd be together forever. Everyone else thought so, too.

I can see her now, on the dance floor, tall and sexy, grooving and toasting the flash debut of our hot new band, cheering us on. After a gig, she's waiting in the wings to give me a sweaty hug and a big kiss. She's dressed to the nines in a shiny blouse, bangle bracelets, feather boa. A girl out of a T Rex song.

Except it's just an illusion, a dream. She wasn't there. Not at our debut or any gig I played from then on. Not in the flesh, anyway. She wasn't there because one night she was murdered by a savage monster who broke into our house and left her there for me to find when I came home.

The world came skidding to a stop. I thought I would die, but didn't. Wanted to die, but didn't. Tried to forget that last sight of her, but never will.

Twenty-one years ago.

I had a music career. Played and recorded my songs, had lots of fun, saw my name in the headlines and strutted in the spotlights, put a million miles on the road in smelly band vans, saw America one Motel 6 at a time. Musicians have thanked me for inspiring them to start their own bands. Regular people tell me they met their spouse at one of my gigs.

I owe a lot of people for helping me along the way, particularly Lois, who pulled me back from the darkness and pushed me in new directions and who continues to do so. But none of it would've happened the way it did without Dianne.

Except for my rock 'n' roll dreams, she was everything to me. I might've curled up in a dark closet or a ditch and cried myself to death, or floated away on a sea of booze and pills, or slashed my wrists in a hot bath, but there were gigs to play, rehearsals, other band business. Rock 'n' roll juiced my pulse, my bass guitar became my heartbeat, and every hour onstage was one I didn't spend wrestling with the horror of what had happened. Rock 'n' roll saved my life, Dianne remained in my heart. And that's how, one gig at a time, one virtual snakeskin boot in front of the other, life went on.

So did the nightmares and flashbacks. Today they just got a lot bigger.

2. CROSSROADS

The date was August 16, 1976. On this day in 1938, Mississippi bluesman Robert Johnson, who wrote "Cross Road Blues," was murdered with a dose of poisoned whiskey. They say Johnson sold his soul to the devil at a Mississippi crossroads in exchange for his musical talent.

As the Austin city limits sign came into view, Eddie and I grinned at each other and did high fives for about the hundredth time. We were unwashed and hung over, but we felt beautiful. In our minds at least, we were the very image of morning-after rock stars: artfully disheveled Keith Richards–style rooster shag haircuts, facial stubble, and bloodshot eyes ringed with smears of last night's eyeliner and mascara. Savoring the sweet taste of the day's first Budweiser and the obligatory cigarette, we were as cocky and self-assured as conquering generals.

It was almost three in the afternoon. Neither of us could say what time we'd gotten to bed that morning, but it must've been almost three a.m. when we played the last chord and called out *Thank you very much, we love you, good night!* to the diehard rockers in that dusty field outside San Antonio. We were supposed to go on at eleven, but the show ran late. Technical problems, heatstroke, and the tantrums of certain musicians with delusions of stardom made a joke of the original schedule. Midnight came and went, but we remained cool despite the godawful heat and completely flaked-out situation. All those ice-cold Budweisers backstage helped a lot. We were still ready to rock when we went on at two.

At the post-gig party, we did plenty of backslapping, beer slurping, joking and clowning. A few girls were there, enough to flirt and tease and remind us that we were fabulous. With power chords still ringing in our ears, we finally crashed at George's house at some unknown hour.

Slept until noon, grabbed a Tex-Mex lunch, hit the road. All the way home, we replayed every high point like sports analysts after a game. What a night. The first time Eddie and I played onstage together—and we rocked. Before long we'd be trading in our Converse All-Stars for snakeskin boots.

"Fazz" Eddie Muñoz and I had only known each other for a few months, but you'd think we'd been copping each other's riffs forever. We were so much alike that when I looked at him it was like looking in the mirror, except I played bass and he played guitar. He was a light-skinned Hispanic, I was an angular-faced German, but we had the same height, same build, similar hair, same hipster poise. Thrift shop clotheshorses with a license to be cool.

When we first met, we each had a band. By late May Eddie's band had fallen apart, as bands will do, and I'd left mine for dead, so we got together over a couple of budweisers and sniffed each other out. The Stones were a big topic. Of course they were our favorite band, and *Exile on Main Street* was the ultimate rock album. The Who were obvious role models, too, especially for their ferocious live sound. We both loved Pete Townsend, while I did my best to cop John Entwhistle's monster bass attack. Then there were Iggy Pop, New York Dolls, Lou Reed, Yardbirds, Kinks, Freddie King, Howlin' Wolf and Muddy Waters.

"What a drag about Krackerjack breaking up," I said. "Did you like them?"

"What, are you kidding, man?" Eddie said. "Fucking great band." And he segued straight into "Chicken Slacks," one of their best songs, popping his fingers, wailing into an invisible microphone. Shaking his ass for imaginary groupies.

That moment I was sold on Eddie. Krackerjack was probably the main reason I quit college and got serious about starting a band. When you love a band that much, you don't just watch them play; you fantasize about being one of them. You see yourself playing those songs, living that life.

Krackerjack looked like a glam rock band, but instead of playing retro-styled rock at a frenetic pace like the Dolls or futuristic glam ballads like Bowie, they played bump-and-grind tempo hard-rock blues. Music with metal-rock muscle and deep blues roots—a band that sounded a little like ZZ Top but looked more like the Stones and Aerosmith.

"That's more or less the kind of band I want," I said.

"Me, too."

"Yeah?"

"Yeah," he said.

"Cool, let's just do it," I said.

A short jam followed at my house. Eddie staggered the rhythm just right on "Sweet Jane," slashed rude chords on "My Generation" while my fingers ran down the fretboard like a monkey skipping over hot coals. On Stones songs, he seemed to know every special tuning Keith used, and all the cool inversions of Chuck Berry riffs that gave those songs their sexual thrust. When he played a sequence of power chords I'd never heard before, my fingers danced down my fretboard and instinctively resolved the sequence on the tonic note of his last open chord; then I blew it by slipping in a major third instead of a minor.

"You dipshit!" he said, laughing. I repaid the compliment and flipped him the bird.

Yeah, playing together was gonna be a blast.

We hooked up with a singer named Danny Coulson and started a band, recruiting another guitarist, Robin Detlefsen, and a drummer, Ron Dixon. Danny wanted to call the band Jellyroll, an old blues term with a sexual connotation. Cool. Rehearsed a dozen or so times, and we were more than ready. Gigs were lined up; then we had to wait a whole month. Eddie and I were antsy.

Two weeks went by. A call came from Eddie's friend George in San Antonio: Did Eddie and I want to play a gig that weekend? Sunday night only, backing up a glam singer who went by the name of Queen Bee at an outdoor festival. The pay was fifty bucks apiece plus free beer. Hell, yes, we'd do it.

"But what about learning the songs?" I asked Eddie.

"No sweat," he said, snapping bubblegum and smirking. "It's just some Stones covers, some Beatles, Little Richard, and some other shit. It's only rock 'n' roll, man."

"Yeah, cool," I said. "We can handle that. So is he sending a tape or what?"

"No, man. We'll just drive down Sunday afternoon and learn the songs before the gig. Don't worry about it, it'll be great!"

I didn't worry, not much. It's not that I wasn't confident about my bass playing. If anything, I was probably a little too confident. Only more experience would hone my skills. I was plagued by fear of the unknown. What if the other guys were far better musicians and I couldn't keep up? What if we didn't get along? But I didn't want to blow it—I'd been in garage band hell for too long. I was twenty-two years old, and it felt like I'd been wanting this forever.

"Don't worry about any of that," Dianne said. "Eddie thinks you're a great bass player, and they're friends of his, so I'm sure you'll blow them away."

"Yeah, OK," I said. "Everything will be cool."

She'd been boosting my ego since the first time she smiled at me, almost four years ago.

"Bogey says so, too," she said. She picked up the beautiful tabby Manx and nuzzled him with her cheek. Bogey was the favorite of our four cats.

She loved animals and nature. The first time I met her, she told me about the baby elephant she cared for when she worked for the zoo one summer. She fed him milk from a bottle and sang him lullabies. "He was the sweetest little baby," she said. That was back in high school, and she still missed that baby.

Whenever we were apart for more than half an hour, I missed her, too. When I was onstage that night, I longed to see her face in the audience. This was her dream almost as much as it was mine. Until recently she'd gone to almost every crummy gig I'd played, to almost every rehearsal and jam session. Some of them were pretty dismal, too.

I was packed and ready on Sunday when I heard Eddie's VW bus in the drive. Not quite noon and Dianne was still asleep, her long legs almost reaching the foot of the bed. Her brown hair spilling over the leopard print pillowcase, a half smile on her lips.

The sun burned through the oak trees outside. The room was an addition, adjoining a sunken den and the rehearsal room. We slept on a simple mattress on the floor with lots of pillows. The windows had no curtains or blinds. You could imagine you were in a tree house, treetops above you, your walls decorated with favorite album posters—Lou Reed, *Rock and Roll Animal*; David Bowie, *The Man Who Sold the World*; and T Rex, *The Slider*. There was also one of Dianne's watercolors, an impressionistic cityscape.

Eddie tapped a double beep on the horn.

I kneeled down to kiss her. She had a sweet, sleepy look on her face, the sheet falling away and exposing her breasts and pale skin as she raised up and cradled my head in one hand and said, "Bye, sweetie."

We kissed good-bye.

"Bye, sweetie," I said, and I left.

The other guys were cool. George also played guitar, a Ron Wood to Eddie's Keith Richards. They looked practically like twins, and their riffs and rhythm chords slid together like greased gears. They even knew the same jokes and dirty limericks. The drummer, Urban Urbano, was seasoned and hard hitting. We locked into a groove. There were two girl back-up singers, too, a girl whose name I could never remember and George's girlfriend, Dianne with two *n*'s just like my own Dianne.

Queen Bee, once known as Jay Hoyer, was a flamboyant wreck with a substance-abuse problem. He was funny, he was tragic. Something about him was seriously cracked, but after a small dose of his gravelly singing and his constant stream of scatological x-rated asides, I had no doubt he'd put on a hell of a show—if he didn't walk in front of a speeding car before we got there.

At first glance, the set list seemed strange. There were a couple of Stones songs, a couple of Beatles songs. Then there was "My Boyfriend's Back" by the Shirelles and "Good Lovin'" by the Young Rascals. I liked the latter two songs, but I'd never considered playing them. Never been a big Beatles fan, either.

All doubts vanished once we blasted through the first song. With Queen Bee's gritty voice and twisted phrasing, Urban pummeling his drums, and Eddie and George blasting their guitar artillery, it was the high-energy, no-bullshit racket and roll I craved. I cranked the volume on my bass and boosted the treble and hammered each note. This produced my ideal bass tone: the sound of piano strings being hit by falling anvils.

We even covered "Boom, Boom (Gonna Shoot You Right Down)" by John Lee Hooker. With its menacing lyrics and great walking bass line, it had always been one of my favorite songs to play. I felt at ease rehearsing with these guys. It was as if my coolness quotient had shot up several points.

It took us two and a half hours to get the set down. After taking a break and drinking a beer, we loaded up and left for sound check.

Almost show time: big stage, big lights, open field. Mouth full of dust when the wind blows. Glitches, delays, waiting backstage. Budweiser, yucks. Dig the other bands: some good, some not so good. More Budweiser. Mosquitoes, dust, heat. I'm not nervous; I'm psyched. Beer goes through me like water. I've pissed a hundred times. The band before us plays their last song. We're next.

I check the tuning on my bass. In this weather, a guitar or bass heats up and your tuning can go completely out of whack. But it's fine, right on A 440. We do high fives behind the amp line, all set. Looking out into the darkness of the dusty field where people are waiting to hear us play. And finally, it's time. The stage is dark, amp lights glowing like red eyes in the jungle, and we follow the roadies' flashlight beams to our places. There's the usual crackle and zap from our amps as we plug in. Test, one, two. . . feedback *squeeeeal.* . . Check, mic check, test. There goes the *thrap-thrap* . . . *bim-bam-boom-boom,* Urban checking his drum kit. He tightens the lugs on a ride tom and messes with his snare, but the last lug twist and rap on the head puts a big smile on his face, and he's ready. I give him a smile of reassurance, but it's a lie, because nothing onstage sounds the way it did during sound check. It would be so easy to screw up. I'm shaking like a leaf at a bonfire. I can't even feel my fingertips.

The stage reeks of beer and sweat, dust and smoldering electronics. The light man brings up the side spots. Red gels on Klieg lights make the people in the front row look like they're enveloped in red mist. Some of them have been here for almost twelve hours. Whistles and hollers. The stage manager gives the thumbs-up and we nod, and the emcee announces, "Ladies and gentlemen, will you please welcome THE QUEEN BEE REVUE!"

Urban clicks off a four-count and we launch into "Day Tripper." The sound mix is a weird roar. *Where's the kick drum, where's the one?* But then I realize I'm playing along with it and it sounds pretty good. People are grooving, smiling. Queen Bee growls the lyrics, twisting them as he goes, prancing like he just popped out of a jukebox from hell.

"Twist & Shout," "Tutti Frutti," "I Ain't Got You." We sound like a mid-sixties sock-hop band on speed and cheap whiskey. There are a few catcalls from guys who think Queen Bee is too weird, but mostly the crowd seems to be into it.

My bass notes are thrumming from toes to teeth. My Rickenbacker and Eddie's Les Paul sound great together. It's a hot-rod sound, blasting through the main speaker towers, bouncing around the Hill Country. What a kick! We're supercool: Eddie's got a 100-watt Marshall double stack, and it's red. I've got a 300-watt Acoustic amp, two cabinets with horn-loaded eighteen-inch speakers that go *boom* like battleship guns. Our sense of timing clicks, tones blend, poses complement. When we sing on a chorus, we sidle at the microphone, like Mick and Keith.

On lead guitar, George serves as musical conductor, cueing breaks and making sure no one gets lost. Queen Bee's up front and over the top, taunting and teasing, shaking his ass and humping the mic stand, camping it up, boogying down. It's high-energy fluid, but it veers close to pandemonium. There's a false start on "Boom, Boom," but the second attempt is close enough and off we go, my bass rumbling like a freight train. Queen Bee's voice has true blues grit. After all, he's got his own version of the blues life. During rehearsal, he told us all about his electroshock treatments, between popping pills and guzzling beers.

Last song: We finish it off with an avalanche of heavy power chords, stretching it out another two minutes, then *Thank-you-thank-you-very-much-we-love-you-good-night*. We leave the stage.

The audience musters just enough noise to call us back for an encore. What the hell, we're easy. We go back out and give them "Good Lovin'" by the Rascals, unleashing a rocket-powered roller coaster. Awesome. We slash out the last chords, then end with another avalanche of heavy metal, not for any reason except that it's fun to bash the hell out of your instrument.

Backstage we grab ice-cold beers and dry towels for blotting sweat. It's gotta be 130 degrees under those lights. We're slapping each other on the back and exchanging understated compliments like *Not bad, not bad at all. . . Yeah, man, we actually pulled it off.*

It felt so good playing tonight, and I know it's only the beginning. I'll probably remember this gig for a long time.

By the time we pull up in front of the house at 2109 Glendale, we've catalogued every riff and nuance, every solo that was sloppy but cool, every groove that was right in the pocket, plus all the fun we're gonna have when Jellyroll gets rolling.

Eddie leaves the van running while I pull my bass and amp head from the back.

"See ya later, Eddie."

"See ya, Jesse." He drives away.

Walking up to the front door with my bass, shoulder bag and amp head, I can hear the whine of the VW engine as Eddie rounds the corner. I can't wait to tell Dianne about last night. I can see her smile already.

I set the amp head down, fish out my keys, open the screen door. Before inserting my house key, my fingers brush against the doorknob. The door swings open.

I carry my things inside. House silent. The front room with its stucco walls and tile floor. Bogey enters the room, glances at me and runs. That's odd.

"Sweetie?" I call out. No answer.

No other cats come out. Where are they?

I glance right. The front bedroom empty. One detail: a pane of glass missing from the window.

"Sweetie, I'm home."

My ears are still ringing. The only sound.

The house is full of cops. They seem to think I murdered my girlfriend. I'm at the crossroads and I'm sinking down.

An hour might have passed, but who can say? I have no sense of time. I feel like a grain of sand in outer space. I'm sinking fast.

All I know for sure is this: Nothing will ever be the same.

3. FINGERPRINTS

I didn't mind the ride in the police car. I'd only been taken downtown a couple of times before, but there was a comforting familiarity about it. My heart was racing, but the movement was soothing. So was the idea that these people needed my help. Not that I knew what happened. I couldn't have told you what day it was. I stared at the floorboard. Were these my feet? Fingers to fingers, hands to face. Were these my hands?

Into the parking garage, through the back door. Just like on *Kojak* and *Police Story*, men in blue with Sam Browne belts weighing down their hips, the coiled authoritative tone of everything they did.

Never had a serious run-in with the police. In high school and college, redneck cops hassled us on general principle: we had long hair. A peace sign sticker like the one on my '64 Comet guaranteed you'd get pulled over. If you smelled like patchouli oil, and I always did, your car would get searched, too. *I know you been smoking pot 'cause I can smell it. You can't fool me, son.* It was scary, but it was funny-scary, too. Sometimes I brought it on myself. The week before Christmas 1972, Dianne and I were walking around the San Marcos town square. We stopped to make out against the *coming soon* poster in front of the movie theater. A cop appeared. *Let's see some ID.* Dianne resented it but complied politely. *What's the problem, man?* I said. The bad attitude dude. We'd been drinking a little. The legal age was twenty-one; we were eighteen. Things could've gone the other way, but the cop let us go. He was getting in his car when Dianne called out, *Merry Christmas!* He was caught off balance. *Thanks. Merry Christmas to you, too,* he said, smiling. *But we don't mean it, man!* I yelled. *All right, you're going to jail, boy.* Off we went, not so merrily, either. Just me. Dianne's pleas for mercy went unheeded. She stood on the sidewalk, her eyes full of worry. If she was pissed at me for being an idiot, she never said so.

I was booked for being drunk in public, locked in a cell just big enough for a double bunk. It smelled like a zoo cage. My teeth chattered from the cold. My Mexican cellmate, who spoke little English, was puzzled as to why he'd been arrested. Something about a car they said was stolen. An hour later I was still trying to decipher the rest of his story when the jailer came and said one of my teachers was there to see me. A teacher?

Miss Priscilla Simmons, he said. *Math teacher.*

Waiting for me was a prim-looking female in a conservative plaid suit with her hair pulled back into a bun and a pair of oversized glasses. Dianne in disguise. Next to her was another familiar face—cat's eye glasses and a preppy sweater. Her best friend and roommate, Mary McGee, in disguise. They glared at me as Miss Simmons paid my fine and walked me out of there. Nobody burst out giggling until we were almost at the car.

On the way home, Dianne reminded me that Miss Priscilla Simmons was one of her alter egos. She said she figured her schoolteacher persona would have better luck convincing them to spring me than the cool-chickie girlfriend I'd been busted with. Sounded logical to me. I'd gotten the impression they wanted to keep me for several days. No one said a word about paying a fine. No one found the hit of acid in my pocket, either.

The elevator doors opened, and I was taken into the brightly lit robbery-homicide division. Someone introduced me to Sgt. James Beck, the bald one they called Curly. He asked me to sit down for a minute. Unlike the uniformed cops who'd come to the house, Curly didn't frown at my rooster hair, the smudged eye makeup, the pajama top I wore as a shirt. He seemed sympathetic.

"Would you mind if I take a look at your driver's license, Jesse?" he asked.

My hands shook so badly I almost couldn't get it out of my wallet. He pretended not to notice. "Jesse, what's your relationship to Miss Roberts?" he said.

"She's my . . . girlfriend," I said, voice quavering. What an inadequate word. I had to say more, explain somehow, but it was hard to speak. "We've been together for—four years, well—" Throat spasm, dry mouth. From now on, it's *were together.*

He nodded. "Would you mind coming with me?"

I nodded and stood, swaying unsteadily.

He led me to the fingerprint room. Black ink pads and blocked cards, a thick-browed guy who took my elbow and guided each digit onto the pad and the card like he'd done it ten thousand times before.

"But why? Am I a suspect?" I said.

"It's so we can eliminate any prints that belong there," Curly said.

Right, they have to do these things. I was still in a fog. Maybe Dianne's death had been the result of some freak accident, a ruptured blood vessel or something. The black ink pads turned my fingers black as cat's paws. No, this stuff says *murder.* That's why we're here.

Almost done. They brought in Eddie with his hip girlfriend, Carla. With her wan looks and blonde hair nearly down to her belt, she resembled a better-looking, more streetwise Joni Mitchell.

"Hey, Jesse," she said in a nonchalant, upbeat voice. "I heard San Antonio was pretty good."

Eddie nodded at me and said, "Hey, man, how's it goin'?"

I was startled. Did they think we were backstage at a gig? Later I decided they were trying to take my mind off the reason I was there.

Curly nodded at me. Time to go.

Eddie gave me a hang-tough nod. Carla waved good-bye. Their turn.

Next stop, a small white room, one chair, one table. Some paper and a pencil. Curly wanted me to write down everything I'd done in the last two days. My hands were shaking so badly I doubted I could shape the letters, even after I sorted out what day it was. Pencil to paper, heart hammering my rib cage, head full of bad pictures, I held my breath and watched the twiggy shapes form one word, then another, following each other like crippled bugs across the page. Like the ride in the cop car, the sense of doing something was good.

> *Today is Monday, August 16, 1976. My name is Jesse Sublett and I'm a musician. Dianne Roberts, my girlfriend of four years, is an artist.*

First came the astonishment that I was able to do it, then the realization that I had to keep going. Whenever I stopped, the pictures started coming back. Can't face them. Just keep the pencil moving across the page.

> *Dianne and I have lived together since the beginning of 1973. We met in the fall of '72, during our first semester at SWTSU.*

Those words led to nice memories. An October night, when Gary Guthrie and I were sitting on the grass. Dianne and Mary were famous on campus. Sighting them was something we looked forward to. Our friends talked about them, but no one knew their names. Hip huggers and halter tops seemed to have been invented for them. Slender, tall, pretty. Half the time they were decked out with scarves or hats, sometimes feathers, sometimes face paint or glitter. You never knew what to expect.

We were sure we'd meet them sooner or later. If growing up in a forlorn little town like Johnson City had taught Gary and me anything, it was patience. Stake out a spot and keep hanging there; something's bound to happen.

Gary had contracted polio when he was two. Despite being paraplegic, he got around a lot more and had more fun than most people I knew. He was outgoing to the extreme, and perhaps his challenged mobility had forced him to learn to make things happen. A lot of girls seemed to like flirting with him. Some did a lot more than that.

"Hey, look," Gary said. "Play it cool, they're coming."

The dynamic duo, the blonde and brunette, detouring off the sidewalk and coming toward us. To my astonishment, they stopped, made small talk, bummed cigarettes. Soon they were sitting with us, laughing and telling stories. They were from Houston, both art majors.

Dianne was sitting next to me, her leg nearly touching mine, practically the same length as mine, too. Her hair was almost to her elbows, with skinny braids tied in back. Her nickname was Willow, she said.

"Why Willow?" I said.

"I just think they're so cool, you know?" she said. "They live next to the water, they love water. Their branches, they're so long and they hang down so low, down in the water. They're so graceful and sad-looking. I talk to them sometimes."

"What do they say?"

She gave me a smile full of mischief and intrigue. "Whatever they're thinking. It depends."

I'd never met anyone like her. She loved nature. She spoke rapturously about animals she loved and adventures she'd had in the bayous and parks of Houston. Not that she looked anything like a backpacker or mountain climber. Not in those platform shoes, not with those long fingernails, each one painted with a moon and star.

Sometimes, she said, she fantasized about being a wood nymph, living naked in the woods.

I told her I used to have seventeen cats. She liked that. I didn't tell her about all the deer I'd killed. Where I grew up, hunting was something you did. You started off going with your dad when you were five or six, just like him and his father before that.

She was a Tarot card reader, a spell caster. I told her that was so cool, because I was interested in that stuff, too. My senior term paper was on lycanthropy. I'd read tons of stuff on werewolves and vampires.

"Well, actually, I'm a witch," she said.

Until that moment I hadn't even dared to wonder if she was interested in me. Now I got nervous. Maybe I was doing OK so far, but I didn't know.

She touched my hand when I lit her cigarette. Her eyes sparkled. I wanted her to be mine. I had a feeling I could make it happen right then, but when she finally sighed and said, *Well, I guess we'd better go*, I just let her walk away.

Seconds later, I was cursing myself. The next few days I seesawed between confidence and doubt. I thought of her constantly, but she was nowhere to be seen. Finally I ran into Mary, who gave me their phone number. I managed to ask Dianne out, and she accepted. We went to a party and immediately gravitated to a dark corner. Finally, after some foolish preliminaries, we kissed. We didn't stop kissing until our lips were bruised and our necks thoroughly bitten. For the rest of the semester, we were one of those couples you get sick of seeing making out in public wherever they go. Mary said we always had sock monkey mouths.

The depth of my feelings scared me, like a pilgrim's first gasp at the Grand Canyon. We were together for twelve nights, making out and doing almost everything two people can do shy of having actual intercourse. I was scared. I'd only had one steady girlfriend, and although sex with Debbie had been frequent and satisfactory, it had been unimaginative. I felt unprepared for someone as obviously sophisticated as Dianne.

By the night of the Uriah Heep/Savoy Brown concert in San Antonio, holding back had become unbearable for both of us. We drank too much tequila, but somehow we made it back to San Marcos in one piece. It was way past curfew, and we couldn't afford motel rooms. We made out in the front seat of my Comet, and finally Dianne climbed onto my lap and wrapped her legs around me and bit me on the ear. "If you don't make love to me," she said, "I think I'm gonna die."

"I've been thinking the same thing," I told her. Everything was new with her, everything was deeper, grander, more exciting. "Whole Lotta Love" was blasting from the radio, and as we made love behind the steering wheel, I drank in the sight of her long, lean body, painted silver blue by the street lights. We were face to face, eyes wide open, and I knew what she was looking for. Often when kissing, one of us would peer into the other's eye, delighting in the reflection there—a tiny face with a blissful smile, trapped in the gleaming eye of our love. She was everything to me, day and night.

I kissed her eyes, and pulled her down on the car seat and lay on top of her so that every bit of our nakedness was pressed together. Heartbeat to heartbeat. I'd never felt remotely like this before.

Later, after we made love again, she stroked my face and my hair and told me, "You must be part rabbit." Rabbits were her favorite animals.

We spent the last hours before dawn locked together in my sleeping bag at the foot of a willow tree near the drama building.

Our love was awesome, deep, crazy. We wrote each other poems when we were apart, hungrily devoured each other when we were together, which was most of the time. We scammed permission to move off campus the next semester, and rented a duplex with Gary and Dan, my other best friend from high school. Now we could have cats, too. We got some right away.

We became part of a merry band who partied together every weekend and frequently on weeknights. Either as a couple or with the gang, we rocked out in nightclubs and at concerts, and sought adventure in the city and country, at lakes and beaches. She showed me around Houston, introduced me to her dad and her friends, took me to her favorite places on the bayou and in Memorial Park. Sometimes we drove all the way to Port Isabel on South Padre Island, at the tip of Texas, then went across the border to Matamoros, Mexico, where we pretended to be outlaws on the run.

Sometimes, just for fun and because it was free, we hitchhiked. We'd thumb rides to Austin or San Antonio to concerts, and sometimes to Houston for the holidays—with both cats in our arms! Although we ran into the occasional weirdo, we never gave serious thought to what might happen if we took a ride with the wrong party. The Charles Manson murders happened in 1969, just three years before Dianne and I met, but we never worried. We thought we were invincible.

My pencil stops moving. Cops are talking outside the door. The smell of burnt coffee stings my nose. I wonder how much longer I'll be able to hold on.

4. LBJ COUNTRY

Dianne snuggled next to me, squeezing my thigh to the throbbing pulse of the legendarily wicked Rolling Stones thumping from the eight-track. We were off on another one of our gonzo adventures. Gary, Dan, and a friend named Robert from Brownsville were along, too. Passing a joint and giggling, and it smelled as though someone had spilled their beer again. Lyndon Johnson was dead, and on this cold, gray afternoon, legions of family, friends and admirers were planting the old lion in his beloved Hill Country ground. I'd convinced my pals that we had to be there.

At the time I was in a period of caustic rebellion. I spoke to my parents infrequently and Johnson City could kiss my ass, but I still prized my associations with Lyndon Johnson. Despite the war (which he'd inherited from Kennedy and Eisenhower, and which I really didn't care much about anyway), LBJ was one of the few things about my roots that wasn't a source of alienation or conflicted feelings. I thought LBJ was cool.

I was in first grade when Lyndon Johnson became vice president, in fourth grade when John Kennedy was shot and Johnson took over as leader of the free world. I remember thinking how lucky I was to be growing up in the same town the president had lived in when he was a boy. People all over the world were talking about Johnson City and the Hill Country. We were in newspapers and glossy magazines and on TV.

The school I attended was named after Lyndon B. Johnson; the town itself was named after his grandfather. LBJ visited us at school a few times and shook everybody's hand. Lots of my friends were children of Secret Service agents, including Nancy Knetsch, who had a crush on me. I would've liked Nancy even if her dad was a poor dirt farmer, but Mr. Knetsch was the president's top agent, and I didn't mind that at all.

Johnson also attended our church, Trinity Lutheran, which was in Stonewall, right next to Johnson's ranch. I loved watching the man in person. He glowed with power and magnetism. He reminded me of a lion, confident and full of coiled energy. During the Sunday sermon, he'd lean back, cross his legs and drape his arm on the back of the pew, like he was sitting in the parlor with an old friend.

Rev. Truesdell was cool, too. His Sunday morning themes were often the evils of prejudice and racism, and the righteousness of the civil rights movement and the war on poverty—cornerstones of LBJ's vision for a Great Society. Truesdell also shared stories of being jailed and harassed in civil rights marches before becoming our pastor.

I was an eleven-year-old kid, and except for Sunday school and church and vacation Bible school every summer, I didn't think much about religion. Outside of history class, I didn't think much about politics. But I knew that Johnson and Truesdell were righteous men. I still think so.

I liked Nancy a lot but I was too shy to do anything about it, and I was just working up my courage to make my move when she was killed in a gruesome riding incident with a horse she'd gotten for her birthday. I was devastated. I moped for weeks, fantasizing about the love we might have had. I sang along with the morbid teen death anthem "Last Kiss" every time it came on the radio. I also wrote a poem about her. My mother sent it to the weekly paper and they published it. Nancy's family sent heart-felt words of appreciation. My own family treated me like a child prodigy. My first taste of fame.

I liked it.

A Saturday afternoon, sounds: Farfisa organ, the "96 Tears" riff? Electric guitar, drums. . . BASS! Thunder in my chest. Pulling me outside, what the heck? Coming from somewhere, but where? Definitely not from a record player or radio. This is live rock 'n' roll—unheard of in Johnson City in 1967.

Most of the kids I know listen to their parents' music, which means C&W or hillbilly. My brother, James, and I listen to KTSA-AM, a powerful San Antonio station that plays Top 40 and a lot of regional rock 'n' roll bands, like Mouse and the Traps, Zakary Thaks, the Chains, Sir Douglas Quintet. For about a year now, I've been buying records with the money I make mowing lawns. My first LP was *96 Tears* by ? and the Mysterians, but I mostly buy singles.

This is way different. The sounds are bouncing down the street from the amps and drums and hitting me in the chest. Giving me goose bumps.

I get on my bike and pedal toward the music. I find the source a half mile away. In the city park, five guys from my brother's class, all friends of his. The Vibrations. The repertoire is sixties garage band boilerplate: "Dirty Water," "House of the Rising Sun," "Louie Louie," "Hanky Panky," "Midnight Hour," "Gloria," "Knock on Wood." Across the state and around the nation, a thousand—maybe ten thousand—other bands are playing the same songs, playing them just as well or better. But right now, and the handful of times I see them later on, the Vibrations are the greatest rock 'n' roll band in the world. Good enough to change my life.

Soon after this incident, my parents take me to the Sears in Austin, the same source of my Nehru jackets and Beatle boots, wide-wale cord pants, and navy pea coat. I find an aqua green Silvertone electric guitar, $38.95 on sale, matching vinyl bag. Walking out of the store with it a few minutes later, I know I'm on my way to Coolsville. The world already looks shinier. I start wearing my hair floppy. I start taking guitar lessons at $5 an hour from Boots Mauldin, a busty C&W singer with a beehive hairdo who once played on the famed Louisiana Hay Ride, nowadays busy raising her kids. Boots teaches me basic chords, some scales, and a handful of songs. It was the only musical instruction I ever got.

James, who is adept at reading schematics and using a soldering gun, helps me assemble a tiny amp from Heathkit. He builds a fuzz tone pedal for me, too: $5 in parts, from plans in *Popular Science*. James also lets me ride along to rock concerts in Austin and San Antonio.

A rock concert means two or three hours in a room full of people I long to associate with—longhaired guys and enticingly exotic girls drenched in patchouli and marijuana smoke, braless in peasant blouses or crushed velvet, their hair impossibly long and straight, sometimes an afro. Anything but the goofy bobs and teased styles of small-town girls with their turquoise eye shadow, gobby mascara and clothes from JCPenney and Sears. Combined with the sounds and sights onstage, amplified with colored and strobe lights, fog machines and the occasional flash pot—stone-age stage craft by later standards—the experience is total sensory overload, even without benefit of drugs, which will come soon enough.

Nearly every concert is a mind-blower: Steppenwolf, Deep Purple, Spirit, Canned Heat, Iron Butterfly, Jethro Tull, Fleetwood Mac (the early, bluesy version), Johnny Winter, Traffic, Jefferson Airplane, Jimi Hendrix, Black Sabbath, Mountain, and many others, including, eventually, the Stones. Sometimes we spend the evening in the black-light haze of the Vulcan Gas Company, Austin's first psychedelic night club. Although, tragically, we miss the Velvet Underground's appearance there, we see numerous local hard rock and blues bands, including Fred McDowell, Big Joe Williams, and Mance Lipscomb, one of Texas' great treasures.

As I watch the guys in those bands, I fantasize that I'm one of them, living the kind of life they live instead of my own, which seems increasingly bleak by comparison. The more I'm drawn into this new world, the more insufferable Johnson City becomes.

Dianne had been to Johnson City a couple of times before, but Gary and Dan convinced me to make a loop through town anyway so that Dianne and Robert could get a good look at the incredibly hokey place we'd escaped from.

Gary pointed out his favorite landmarks using an exaggerated drawl he'd inherited from his father Albert, a long-haul truck driver. "Check this out," he said, pointing to the big sign trumpeting Johnson City as "The Home Town of Lyndon B. Johnson," with a giant cut-out of his hat. I slowed down as we rolled past Red's Place, a seedy beer joint on the square facing the county courthouse. Red's Place was the only business in town that defiantly remained open on the day of Lyndon Johnson's funeral.

Dan filled in an occasional colorful detail about the sights. His father was our high school chemistry teacher, a crusty little redneck with caved-in cheekbones from playing football in the days before helmets had face guards. Mr. G, as we called him, was especially mean when drunk or hungover and perpetually disappointed in Dan, his only son from a previous marriage, despite Dan's genius-level intelligence and his creative abilities. Not surprisingly, Dan managed to avoid looking, acting or sounding anything like his father.

Dan pointed out the movie theater, which had closed just before we started high school. I told Dianne I remembered seeing *Charade* and *Gypsy* there, and learning the art of getting your arm into position around your seventh grade girlfriend, and almost, but not quite, cupping her breast. Demonstrating my command of the craft, I pulled Dianne close, caressed her right breast, and playfully fingered the nipple. She responded by grabbling my crotch and grinning.

Next on the tour was one of my favorite landmarks, the old drive-in, closed down even longer than the indoor movie house. The movie screen was on the back side of a house built expressly for that purpose. The Barrows family, who owned the drive-in and the indoor theater, lived there. I always used to wonder, I said to Dianne, what it was like living inside a movie screen.

Gary's legs had atrophied to the point they looked like a scrawny ten-year-old's, but he had sinewy arms, big hands and huge, piercing blue eyes. He could be arrogant, but it's hard to be mellow when you're smarter than the next ten guys in the room. Wherever he went, he'd create an island of activity—conversation, jokes, smoke, laughter, debate—as he popped wheelies, pontificated, and held court. Although I never heard him mention it to anyone, Gary was the March of Dimes poster boy of 1967.

Being a longhaired rocker in Johnson City was tough. The worst rednecks in school called us *faggot, homo, queer, commie, hippie* and a variety of hyphenates. At least they didn't physically harass Gary, but the fact that they couldn't increased their resentment of us both. In my case, the taunts often escalated into scuffles and worse. I rarely fought back, preferring to step back after having my nose bloodied and laugh in their faces, flashing a peace sign and sending their taunts boomeranging back. *Takes a sissie to know one*, or *If I'm a faggot, then come over here and blow me*. Usually, instead of prompting a renewed attack, my ant-brained antagonists would back off, shaking their heads.

In restaurant parking lots, and much worse, on lonely country roads, grown men frequently threatened to hurt me just because I had long hair. On some occasions, they'd have a rifle in their hands.

My parents didn't like my hair or the music I listened to and gave no indication that they derived any pleasure from the sounds I was learning to make on my guitar. But when they realized the abuse I was taking, they were on my side and that was that. They also couldn't help noticing that while I was consistently at the head of my class without putting much effort into it, the kids who bullied me struggled to maintain a B or C average. I never told them about the men with guns.

When I first started playing guitar, Mom and Dad said it was OK as long as it was just a hobby. "That kind of life is no good," said my mother. I knew what she was thinking. It wasn't just the horror stories they'd heard about decadent rock stars like the Stones and Beatles. A former coworker of my dad's had been a promising honky-tonk singer in the vein of Hank Williams, but he ended up pissing it away in jails and neighborhood ditches. My dad used to take him fishing until he got tired of pulling him out of the river.

When I was fifteen, progress on my inevitable course gained new momentum with the acquisition of a cheap bass guitar and amplifier. Bass was my heartbeat, I realized, and I made more musical progress in a few weeks of thumping along to records in my room than I had in two years of playing six-string guitars.

My junior year in high school was such a drag I started scheming to leave home and finish high school in Austin, but James, who'd dropped out of college and was running a head shop in Austin with his pals, poured cold water on these romantic plans. Resigned to my fate, I sought distraction instead, delving even more deeply into rock 'n' roll, pot and the occasional acid trip, and reaping inevitable consequences both good and bad. The emerging thunder of heavy metal, spearheaded by Led Zeppelin, Deep Purple and Black Sabbath (which seemed as fresh and radical at the time as punk rock in 1977), was grand, but it made my world seem even more dismal. Drugs aggravated tensions with my parents, especially when they came across my poorly hidden stashes, which exposed all my exclamations of innocence (*What do you mean, what's wrong with my eyes?*) as the lame fictions they were.

I retreated to my bedroom to play my bass with the volume cranked or immersed myself in sci-fi, Tolkien, Hermann Hesse and books on witchcraft and the occult. I'd rejected organized religion, but Mom kept making me go to church. Otherwise I couldn't use the car. I loved reading about witchcraft and witch trials, paganism and occult phenomena. Bram Stoker's *Dracula* blew my mind, and Colin Wilson's *Space Vampires* thrilled me so much I read it twice. These interests angered my mother. The posters I made for my room, emblazoned with yippie slogans like "Smash the Fascist State!" and "Down with Amerika!" puzzled and perturbed my father, but I wasn't really interested in overturning the government. I just wanted all the grownups thrown in jail so I wouldn't have to get my hair cut.

At least I had a girlfriend. Debbie, a hippie chick from Eureka, California. A pretty, voluptuous blonde, hair as straight as falling water, down to her waist. She was neurotic, but I didn't care. As inexperienced with life as I was, I knew that things could always be worse.

"That's how it was," I said to Dianne. "The usual teen experience, out-in-the-sticks style. Pretty different from Houston, huh?"

"No kidding," she said. Deep down I realized that, in my self-deprecating way, I was trying to impress her and Robert. Especially her.

She told me about herself and Mary riding their bikes along the bayou on LSD, about a cool art teacher at Bellaire who gave them passes to smoke a joint where they wouldn't get caught, about seeing bands at a famously psychedelic club called Love Street. The usual teen experience, Houston style.

"Wow," I said. "Pretty different."

We looked so much alike that people sometimes assumed we were sister and brother. Yet in some ways we seemed like opposite sides of a coin. She grew up in the big badass city of Houston, I was from a town so small it came out like a punch line. Her father was an oil company executive with a degree from Harvard. Mine was a linesman for Pedernales Electric Co-op with a sixth-grade education.

We were both born in 1954, the year Elvis released his first single, "That's All Right, Mama," and the Soviets exploded their first H-bomb. Warped by the sixties, graduated high school in 1972. Went to the polls together, voted for George McGovern, the first year eighteen-year-olds had the right to vote. Our picture was in the paper. We look confused, possibly high. Nixon won.

She came from Shawnee Mission, Kansas, where an Indian school was established in 1839 for native children in the area. Her parents met at the University of Kansas.

"Kansas?" I said when she told me. I envisioned prairie fields, white farmhouses. I said my mom and dad grew up on farms, too, and when we went to visit Grandma and Grandpa Duecker, they let us feed the sheep and chickens and gather the eggs. Dianne was smiling, pretty as a dream.

"They made their own soap," I said. "They wore underwear they made out of flour bags."

"Shawnee Mission is just south of Kansas City," she said. "It's actually kind of a suburb."

What did I know? Never been out of Texas.

Her father, gregarious Earl Roberts, broad shoulders and a midwestern baritone, a guy who can fill up a room. Her mother, Mary Ann, a math teacher at Bellaire, strict and proper. Maybe just the kind you'd expect to produce an artist/poet daughter compelled toward nature worship. Dianne's older brother Gary was the one who loved numbers, required less discipline and tended not to talk to trees.

They came to Houston in 1959, Earl moving up the corporate ladder at Continental Oil Company. Middle-class home in a predominantly Jewish area known as Meyerland. The Roberts were Presbyterian; so were the McGees. Dianne and Mary McGee—blonde, artistic, and mischievous—met at the Presbyterian church Sunday school when they were in junior high.

"Our moms enrolled us," Mary told me. "They thought it was the thing to do, to get us into church. Mary Ann in particular was always trying to make Dianne do things that were so unDiannelike. Anyway, Sunday school didn't take, but Dianne and I became best friends instantly."

Dianne and Mary painted during sleepovers. They loved T Rex, *Electric Warrior*, and Donovan, *Cosmic Wheels*, and cried along with Joni Mitchell's soaring sadness on *Blue*. But during the Monkees' heyday, Dianne was crazy about Mickey Dolenz. She had a poster above her bed and gave him a good-night kiss every night. Mary gave her shit about it.

Once when they were stoned they bought a can of chicken fat, mistaking it for some new kind of dip. *Yuck.* From then on, they were *chickies.*

I graduated valedictorian at Lyndon B. Johnson High School, but big deal, there were only eighteen students in our class. Going to a humongous school like Bellaire had to be infinitely more cool. But it didn't always seem so cool to Dianne, especially with her mom being a teacher there. Mary Ann Roberts was always stalking the halls, looking for scofflaws. The chickies, smoking cigarettes in their secret hiding place under the stairs, could hear this *tap-tap-tapping.* Dianne's eyes would get big and she'd say, *Oh my God, that's Mary Ann!* She could recognize the sound of her high heels. The chickies would laugh when they told this story, but there'd be a faraway look in Dianne's eyes.

Earl and Mary Ann divorced in 1971, waiting until the kids were old enough to understand, as they put it. Earl married a prettier, much younger woman named Kathleen at a swanky wedding in Acapulco that year.

Dianne had a hard time adjusting to having a stepmother who could easily pass for her sister. She went on a shoplifting spree, and got caught. She spent lots of time in the bayou and Memorial Park, hanging out, communing with nature and spirits. She got some books of spells, burned candles, tried incantations and writing runes. She got pregnant and didn't know what to do about it. Her mother was a lot more simpatico with equations and detention rules than the mother-daughter thing, but Dianne finally told her about the pregnancy. She took Dianne to have the abortion. The experience did nothing to improve their bond. Afterward,

Dianne felt sad and conflicted. She fantasized: What if she'd kept the baby? She missed him. She couldn't stop thinking about it.

I didn't know what to do about that memory, but I did my best to distract her and keep us warm during our first winter in our funky off-campus duplex. We were still getting settled during the first week of January 1973 when an unusually potent ice storm shut down San Marcos for almost a week, delaying the start of the semester. We cozied up at night, finding new intimate corners of each other to explore. During the day we huddled around a dinky space heater and entertained guests. Friends would come by to drink a beer or smoke a joint and end up staying the night because the streets were too hazardous to navigate. Occasionally we ventured out for beer and cigarettes, or to go ice sledding on cafeteria trays down the campus hills.

The ice retreated and the semester got under way, though the partying in San Marcos never stopped. I was glad school was back on because that's when the checks started coming in, like my so-called pusher fee. There were few handicap ramps back then, so the Texas Rehabilitation Commission paid me $120 to push Gary to and from his classes. They called it a *pusher fee*. Gary and I were taking most of the same classes, so helping him manage stairs and uphill grades (then riding on the back on the way down) was something I would've done anyway. I was receiving another $120 from the agency for being what I considered an average eighteen-year-old. Who just happened to know, thanks to Gary, how to qualify for the money. Go to the office and say you have mental or emotional problems. Fill out a few forms, take a couple of screening tests, talk to an examiner, answer a bunch of questions.

It couldn't have been easier. *Are you happy? Do you get along with your parents?* I didn't know a single eighteen-year-old who would've answered yes. *Have you experimented with drugs? If so, which ones?* Gimme a few minutes to make a list. *Do you drink any alcoholic beverages and if so, how much?* Another truthful answer: "A six-pack or so every night during the week, sometimes more, and at least twice that much on the weekend." When I saw the counselor write down *drinks to excess,* and underline it twice, I knew I had the money.

With the $240 a month I received for being an emotionally disturbed pusher, plus funds from a few other sources, I managed to scrape by without getting a part-time job until my third semester. The other sources included a couple of small scholarships I received after graduation, a little grocery money from my parents, and the proceeds from occasionally selling a little pot. Ironically, the state never offered me any assistance for my so-called problems, only the monthly check.

On January 22, it was announced that Lyndon Johnson had died of heart failure at home on his ranch. Formal services were to be held in Washington, D.C., but afterward, his body would be flown to Texas to be interred in the small family cemetery at his ranch. The graveside services would be open to the public. Mary McGee already had plans, but Gary, Dan and Robert were up for it.

A half dozen of us partied hard the night before, drinking pitchers of Budweiser in a black light disco room, where we met up with a rodeo cowboy on acid named Buck, just in from San Francisco. He regaled us with wild tales about bad bulls, great drugs and the reckless heroism of rodeo clowns. During his bull-riding career he'd incurred a number of painful injuries. Fortunately, doctors kept him well supplied with prescription painkillers. He was generous, and over the course of the evening he shared his pharmaceutical wealth. He ended up crashing on our couch.

Morning struck back at us like a jackhammer. It was so cold you could see your breath inside the duplex. Outside, ominous gray clouds swirled overhead. Buck needed a ride home and it was on the way, so he piled in my Comet with everyone else. When he was saying good-bye, he thanked us again for our hospitality by giving us all more pills. We already had some in our pockets from the night before.

We hadn't gotten very far before I got pulled over by a cop. He claimed I was weaving all over the road. I never expected to talk my way out of the situation, but somehow I did. He let me go with a stern warning, and off we went. But our worries weren't over. When the patrol car first appeared in the rearview, we fully expected to be searched, so we swallowed every pill we had. None of us had ever taken that many pills before.

The narrow road kept disappearing playfully around the next bend. Those weren't necessarily drug-induced impressions; back roads are like that in the Hill Country. The drive kept reminding me of Sunday dinners at my grandparents' place after church. The Duecker farm where my mother grew up was located just a few miles from the LBJ ranch, down a tangle of increasingly narrow roads that serve a sparsely populated rural community called Nebgen, after one of the area's original German settlers. It's the same dry, rugged landscape that Robert Caro wrote about so eloquently in *Means of Ascent*.

It's white-tailed deer country, full of armadillos, cedar breaks and mesquite pastures, rolling hills studded with shin oak, burr oak and live oak. In places the ground seems to be rockier than the moon. German immigrants, including my ancestors, crossed the Atlantic to build homesteads here, but they found out the hard way that it didn't rain enough to support traditional farming methods. Tough lessons were learned. My great-great grandfather, Johann Casper Danz, arrived in Central Texas in 1845. By 1848, he'd been widowed twice. Hard times.

My mother was one of four girls and two boys born to Walter and Katy Duecker. Her youngest brother died of diphtheria before his second birthday. They lived on a modest 200-acre farm. During the war the family moved to Fort Worth because they could make more money working in meatpacking plants. German was their first language. My mother didn't learn English until she started school.

We loved visiting the farm when I was kid, even though Grandpa and Grandma had no television, telephone or indoor bathroom. Trips to the outhouse meant running the gauntlet with a homicidal rooster who seemed to have a grudge against children. On overnight stays, we prayed for rain just so we could go to sleep with the sound of it falling on the tin roof. Deer hunting was good.

Walter Duecker was a short, skinny man. He had an impish grin and his eyes sparkled with mischief. He was full of jokes and tricks. I used to bring him pill bottles that I'd filled with pill bugs. He'd get a glass of water and pretend to swallow every one. We did this every visit. He drank whisky by the pint, slurped his coffee from a saucer and refused to eat his vegetables. "Don't give me any of those damn vegetables," he'd say at dinner. "I don't like vegetables, I like meat."

For deer hunting, Grandpa used an old Winchester 30-30 with an octagonal barrel. He was a crack shot, too. The kids were fascinated by him. I remember predawn mornings when my brother and I would walk out to our assigned deer blinds with Walter, just as the horizon beyond the cedar breaks was beginning to show pink, trying to match his silent footfalls on the rocky trail. Later, on the way back, we were amazed at his ability to roll and light a Bull Durham without breaking his stride.

Katie Duecker had crinkly pale skin and blued hair and a low tolerance for Catholicism. She favored simple dresses with tiny flower prints, and when she was outside nurturing the Eden of flowers that dominated the front yard, or in her garden growing giant squash that won blue ribbons at the Gillespie County fair, she wore a sunbonnet the size of a mailbox. She used to tell us about going to school with Lyndon Johnson. When Lyndon was a first-grader, she said, he refused to read unless his teacher, Miss Kate, held him on her lap. Grandma would take me in her lap and say, "Just think, your grandma went to school with the president. You could be president someday, too, my Jesse. Someday some little girl who goes to school with you could say to her grandson, 'Just think, I went to school with him, and now he's the president.'"

At family dinners, the men sat on the porch and talked about the weather and livestock and deer hunting and smoked and drank beer while the women commandeered the kitchen and cooked and spoke in rapid-fire German. After dinner the women cleaned up the kitchen and the men played poker and smoked and drank beer or whiskey.

"Promise me you won't ever take up smoking and drinking," Grandma would say. "What terrible habits they are"—never once casting an eye toward Grandpa, as if he wasn't even in the room.

My father, Jesse "Jake" Sublett, Jr., met Elizabeth Duecker at a dance at the Nebgen school. He was working on a nearby farm when someone told him about a pretty teenage girl named Elizabeth, a slender thing with long, curly brown hair. Jake went to the dance, found the right girl. They danced, hit it off, started going steady. He grew up on a farm in a rural community called Henly, located roughly halfway between Johnson City and Austin. He turned eighteen three weeks after Pearl Harbor, but a mild case of diabetes kept him out of the army until 1946. After his discharge, he went to work for the Pedernales Electric Co-op and married Elizabeth on July 16, 1950.

Somehow we made it to the Johnson ranch without further incident. It was a long walk to the cemetery on our rubbery legs (and Gary's wobbly wheels), and our little group stood out in that sea of people. Thousands of people, including politicians and journalists. None of us wore funeral attire. I had on my big coat and heavy boots, Dianne wore a suede jacket and boots and a big feather boa.

Famous and weighty personages were everywhere. Walter Cronkite was there. So were Rev. Billy Graham, the Kennedys, John Connally, Anita Bryant, Jack Valenti, Liz Carpenter, and of course Lady Bird, Luci and Lynda.

The cold sobered us up a bit. The emotional atmosphere, too, kept us from bowling over and completely blowing it. Dan fell down a few times and Gary rolled over someone's foot while I was pushing. Robert paused to light a cigarette and a joint fell out of the pack onto the ground. Probably no one would've noticed if he hadn't scrambled so frantically to pick it up.

I started feeling overcome with sadness, though I couldn't say why. I put my arms around Dianne and we held each other tight. It wasn't grief, although I regretted the fact that the great man had left us. It wasn't shame for showing up at his funeral socked full of pills and Budweiser— I thought that was cool. And even though everything from the sound of pecans crunching underfoot to the foggy silhouette of the hills and the constant jittering mockingbirds was as familiar to me as my own face, I doubted this melancholy could be homesickness. I hadn't gone very far, for one thing, and it had been too many years since I felt at home in this place.

I did know that the girl in my arms made me feel so warm and alive that nothing else seemed to matter. I looked at her and she smiled and it was like the sun burning through the mist in the morning. I wasn't worried about the future. I didn't give a damn about the past.

The people were arrayed in concentric circles around the grave. The inner circle consisted of family and close friends, then old friends and business associates. Outside of that circle were politicians who'd worked with Johnson, from the beginning on up to the White House years. The press made up a fifth circle, wedging themselves as close to the family as the Secret Service would allow. We, the common people Johnson loved the most, made up the thickest of all the circles.

The traditional homilies about the cycles of life and death meant nothing to us. Allusions to bible verses left us cold. Johnson was quoted as having said he loved the Hill Country because "it's a place where they love you while you're alive, they care when you're sick and they miss you when you die." We were stoned and our attitude was vaguely nihilistic. Still, we never giggled or snorted. For our gang, it was a remarkable display of restraint and respect.

The Hill Country was a place I liked when I was a kid. The last few years I lived there, I resented it because I had to live there, and because it was anything but New York City or Los Angeles or even Austin. Now it was a goofy place where I took my girlfriend and said, Look, I grew up here, isn't it weird and stupid? At least LBJ was from here.

The prayers and eulogies focused on simple things, trying to bring Johnson down to life size. This land, this stingy, clayey soil, these limestone rocks, this river, these hills, these simple people—they said the Hill Country made him what he was.

They lowered his casket into the ground. Rev. Billy Graham said a prayer. "He was a mountain of a man with a whirlwind for a heart," he said. A Catholic priest offered prayers, too. Anita Bryant sang "The Battle Hymn of the Republic."

Military bugles blew taps with such gray solemnity the sound seemed to suck the breath right out of my lungs.

5. RABBIT TRICK

I'm trying to remember some other important details. One thing is that Dianne and I both quit college in the summer of 1974 and moved to Austin so I could concentrate on my music career, and I already knew some musicians here. Some of the names you asked for —

Easy decision. Being a musician had become infinitely more important to me than getting a degree. I played a few gigs in a band called Nasty Habit. Mary McGee's ex-boyfriend Stan Gilbert was the guitarist and bandleader. At gigs I liked the way girls looked at me, as if I had a shiny aura and a license to be cool, but the music was too slow, the image wasn't right. It was like listening to ZZ Top when you're thinking T Rex and New York Dolls. We made a studio demo and I hated the way it sounded. Afterward I packed up my bass and told Stan I was off to play in a band called the Piranhas.

"Piranhas?" he said, scratching his beard. "I've never heard of that band."

"That's because I haven't started it yet," I said. "But you'll hear all about us soon enough."

By the summer of 1974, though, going to school had become very hard work, and it was interfering with my efforts to pursue my music career. Gary and I had a falling out, and afterward he moved in with Stan, who also took over my job as pusher. Mysteriously, my emotional problems subsidy was cut off, too. Pushing pot was out of the question, since

I'd developed a strong aversion to the stuff, even when it was being smoked by people around me. My grant money had also run out. Dianne's father paid her college expenses, but my parents could only send grocery money now and then and I wasn't about to ask them for more. That left the pizza restaurant, where I started as delivery boy and within six months was promoted to manager. Being a restaurant boss was OK for a couple of months, but it was too much responsibility, and too many of our employees were lying scammers like myself. The job was like a license to steal.

I had assembled a loose configuration of musicians and called it the Piranhas, but it was hard to tell when we'd be good enough to play in public. Too many times band rehearsal was interrupted by a crisis at the restaurant. And the neighbors called the cops whenever we played. Between school, the pizza business, cranky neighbors and the police, the Piranhas were floundering.

Then one day the San Marcos cops came to the restaurant and hauled me down to the justice of the peace. He told me in no uncertain terms that if my neighbors filed one more complaint about my band, or even if we played our TV too loud, he'd have me locked up. That was the last straw.

Austin had the clubs, the bands and the musicians, and it had been the center of my rock 'n' roll universe since I was fifteen. Dianne and I were already going there several nights a week to see bands. It was just a thirty-mile trip, but after drinking and dancing for several hours, we often had to pull over at the halfway mark for a nap. We were young and dumb and felt indestructible, but we had to admit that the odds might turn against us.

Dianne wanted a break from school anyway, and she was confident that Austin would work its magic for us. The first place we lived with our three cats and my big bass amp was a small apartment off Barton Springs Road. The neighbors frequently called the cops when I played my bass. I found a job at a state agency working in the mailroom. Dianne hired on at a credit bureau. I started jamming with some people I met. My chops improved and it felt like progress. As far as I knew, this was how you started a band. Dianne came along every time. After almost a year of jamming and daydreaming about the band I wanted, there was another configuration of musicians who called themselves the Piranhas, but we still had a long way to go before we would be a real band. Finding a place to rehearse was a never-ending hassle, just like in San Marcos.

Dianne found a house in the classifieds. It seemed ideal. Three bed-rooms. A little work and one could be made into a rehearsal studio. We figured the stucco walls were probably almost soundproof. With any luck, the neighbors wouldn't send for the S.W.A.T. team every time we tried to rehearse. Rent was steep, but with that third bedroom, Dean could move in and share the rent. At that point, I wasn't certain he'd work out as the Piranhas' permanent drummer, but having a drummer in the house, whether he was technically in the band or not, would make it easier for me to write songs. Nobody had drum machines in 1975.

Besides being old pals from Johnson City, Dean was the first drum-mer I'd ever played with. Come to think of it, Dean was the second musi-cian I'd ever played with. Dan and I had been jamming together since I got my first electric guitar. Without a single drummer in town, or any other rock musicians, for that matter (the Vibrations having scattered sev-eral years earlier), there didn't seem much point in even fantasizing about starting a band. Then Dean moved to town. He heard Dan and me play and said it would be really cool if we started a band. Claimed he used to play drums back in San Antonio. Too bad his drums had gotten stolen. If he only had a drum kit, man, we could start a killer band. We'd blow people's minds.

One day after school Dean called and told me to pick him up and bring my bass and my amp. Why? I asked. He'd just bought a Ludwig drum kit, he said. Now we could start that band. Dan wasn't available, so Dean and I took our gear out to an airplane hangar at an airstrip on the edge of town. I got my equipment ready and watched and listened as Dean set up the kit and started banging around on it. I tried playing some bass patterns as he hammered and flailed, but it was hard to follow his beats. Finally he suggested we play "Wipe Out," so we did. He played so furiously that within a minute's time, a lot of the kit's hardware—the drum stands, cymbal stands, the lugs on the heads—had come loose, the various components falling into disarray or apart. When we came to the drum solo, Dean played with an awesome ferocity that impressed the hell out of me, and by the end of the song his kit was completely wrecked. He tried getting it back together again, but it wasn't the same. So we called it a day.

Dan was ecstatic that Dean had gotten a drum kit. We got together and tried to bash out some songs. After a while, it became apparent that "Wipe Out" was the only song Dean could play. The existence of his band in San Antonio was never mentioned again. We started jamming semiregularly, hoping for rapid progress. Practices usually petered out early because Dean would wear himself out and make a shambles of his kit long before we were done. In our situation though, just getting together and making noise gave us enormous relief. It created camaraderie between us, and enhanced my own sense of identity.

Dan graduated a year ahead of me and registered for college at SWTSU (now Texas State University) in San Marcos as an English major. He and I vowed to pick up again where we'd left off when I registered for school the following fall. Dean was a year behind me. It was hard to predict what he was going to do. A big, rangy guy with blue eyes and a shock of wavy blond hair, he expended a lot of manic energy in almost everything he did—drumming, football and other sports, getting high, pulling practical jokes, even working summer jobs. Everything, that is, except school. His grades were poor, which didn't help his adversarial relationship with his parents. He was always dreaming up grandiose plans for getting even with them and running away. He had a great imagination, and I thought his plots were harmless fantasies to blow off steam. For some reason, he had a lot of steam to blow off. That made him fun to hang around with. At least in high school it did. Once we kidnapped a Santa Claus dummy from someone's front yard. We wrote a ransom note to send to the owners, but finally chickened out and threw it over the bridge into the Pedernales River. Thought it was funny as hell.

One summer Dean and I worked for a crazy Polish housepainter named Don Tomazewski. Driving down the road in his beat up Chevy pickup, he'd yell, "I'm a crazy fucking Polack!" and sing profane songs though a mouth full of jagged teeth. He looked like a rat: big ears, beady gray eyes, broken nose spiked with hairs. Don Tomazewski told vile war stories about killing Germans and screwing French girls. He was a strange and sometimes scary person, but we needed the money, and our parents just didn't allow their sons to lie around all summer.

The crazy housepainter paid cash and made every job seem like a caper, but he sometimes made egregious mistakes that eradicated his profit margin. Sometimes we left a home or ranch improvement project worse off than before. On occasion, he'd fly into a psychotic rage, screaming curses at the person who hired us, stomping around, throwing tools and busting up the place. Then, while driving us away from the scene of the crime, he'd laugh maniacally and scream, "I'm a crazy fucking Polack!"

On rainy days when outside jobs had to wait, we'd drive through the country and find houses to break into. Call me naive, but the first time we did it, I didn't quite snap to what was going on. Crazy Don said the owner left some tools for him to pick up, but we took a portable TV and radio, too. He kept everything we took, except for the odd tool or trinket, which he bestowed on us like golden trinkets. A screwdriver, vise grips, putty knife, broken flashlight.

I didn't really want the loot, and my total haul was probably no more than $20. The adrenaline rush was the main thing—going into people's houses and seeing how they lived, touching their stuff and trying out their furniture, like Goldilocks, keeping an eye on the window to see if the bears were coming. But who knows where it might've led, because I did resent being poor, and Dean and I believed in the yippie aesthetic of liberating goods from the Establishment.

In August my dad got a call from the sheriff. A rancher we'd worked for had reported the theft of a chain saw. Neither Dean nor I knew anything about it. Crazy Don fingered us for the heist, then left town in the middle of the night owing me $180, which seemed like a small fortune. I couldn't believe he'd ripped me off.

The last house I broke into with Dean was an old two-story ranch house that had been boarded up for twenty years or more. Everything in it was faded by time and covered in dust, as if the color pigments had expired. The cupboard held bottles with exotic labels, the contents long since desiccated. One closet held ancient suits and dresses; another held a band uniform. On the top shelf was a violin case. I held my breath as I opened it. The instrument was still inside. Old and faded, like everything else in the place, but I'd never even touched a violin before. Maybe it was valuable. When I tried to lift it out of the case, the thing disintegrated in my hands, like a prize in a dream, dust and bones. For a long time afterward I felt sick about it, as though I'd hurt someone in a way that would never heal. I never did anything like that again.

I was young and bored and stupid. Dean really hated his parents. I never figured out why, but he did say they told him his birth had been an accident. They did seem to show a preference for his brothers and sisters. Though his father seemed distant, he was likeable and intelligent. His mother struck me as cold and abrasive. I never thought a lot about why Dean drank so much or put so much effort into getting high. I never stopped to think about how many times he screwed up something other people might consider important—like dropping out of high school to marry a pregnant girlfriend, the same girl later divorcing him for being a screw-up, or joining the army and going AWOL, or losing job after job after job.

When being around him became too obnoxious, we began to grow apart. For a brief time, he worked in the mailroom with me. A few times, on his suggestion, we split a six-pack during our lunch break. One day when neither of us felt like going back to work, he called in a bomb threat, which gave all 400 employees in the building the afternoon off.

A lot of Dean's schemes hinged on acquiring a big sum of money somehow, for example, by robbing a bank or kidnapping someone, then splitting for Europe or South America or Alaska. These plans had one element in common: he'd also have to murder his parents.

Our new house had large expanses of wall that Dianne could fill with new paintings. She was feeling inspired. Our cats had a lush green yard to romp around in. We loved the place. It suited us to a T. Coming home put a smile on our faces. We felt lucky.

I started off 1976 determined to kick the Piranhas into shape. I was trying hard to write more songs. With a collection of great material, I could recruit new musicians in case the current band didn't work out.

Saturday, the 14th, Dianne and I slept till about noon. . .

We lived for the weekend. Our jobs were a drag. The nine-to-five grind sapped your energy, tempted you to give up your dreams. This band was going to break us out of that. We knew it. Once Jellyroll started gigging regularly, I'd be sleeping until noon every day. When we were making real money, Dianne could quit her job and do her art all the time, too.

In May, when I turned twenty-two, it had become obvious that the Piranhas were a dead issue. The name was the only together thing about it. Two or three joke gigs, nothing more, and a good thing, too. We sucked. The guitarist was a flake. Dean was drinking too much. I probably wasn't ready to be a bandleader anyway. My dream of having a super-cool band was nothing but sand through my fingers.

Then I ran into Eddie. He was available, and he was ready, too. We hooked up with Danny and the other guys, and now we were on our way. Cool. Finding the right musical partners is like true love. When it's right, you just know. The guys I'd been playing with were never going to cut it. When I met Eddie, I knew.

Later we ate lunch at a Mexican restaurant downtown. . .

Dianne let me ramble on while we ate cheese enchiladas and drank cold Budweisers. About the band, the new songs we'd worked up at the last rehearsal. Which ones were my favorites, the ones with bass parts that let me show off the most.

It was obvious to Dianne that Eddie was in a different class from my old bandmates. She laughed when Eddie did his Iggy Pop and Mick Jagger imitations in our kitchen. She didn't seem to mind the late hours I spent rehearsing at Jellyroll's studio or when Eddie and I went to Mother Earth to check out other bands. She was just as excited as I was when the Queen Bee gig popped up out of the blue. I didn't invite her along. Carla wasn't coming, either, and we were going in Eddie's van. I didn't think he wanted any girls along.

We talked about Mary McGee a little, recalling some of the crazy things they used to do. Mary was back in Houston now. She'd been planning to spend the weekend, but something came up. Dianne was disappointed.

At least she wasn't working at the credit bureau anymore. That had sucked. A room full of office drones at computer terminals, taking calls from merchants, reading them data, while the fat, ugly boss sat up front scowling. All she lacked was a bullwhip. You had to raise your hand to use the rest room.

She was looking for something else, but not too strenuously. She deserved a break. Maybe she'd collect unemployment and do some painting.

"You're an artist," I said. "Fuck the credit bureau."

She smiled and raised her glass. "Fuck 'em. Here's to Jellyroll."

We clinked glasses. Everything was gonna be cool.

Saturday afternoon, Dianne and I went to some thrift shops, St. Vincent de Paul and. . .

We didn't have much luck this time out. Sometimes you score, sometimes you don't. I did buy some cool earrings, and thought I might wear one at the gig. That night we stayed in and watched TV. There was a Bogart and Bacall movie. Every summer we would go see *The Big Sleep* and *To Have and Have Not* at the Paramount, the great old movie palace downtown. Once you saw Bogey and Bacall on the big screen, Bacall's nostrils flaring and Bogey's lip curling, passion sparks flying between faces the size of a billboard, you were hooked for good. We were, anyway.

The house was quiet, just the two of us and the four cats. If Dean's drinking hadn't gotten so out of hand, we might have let him stay, even though he hadn't paid the rent for months. He'd promised to move his stuff soon.

Sunday morning I got up at ten-thirty or so. I took a shower and got my stuff together. . .

That meant my bass guitar, amp, cords and stage clothes. I was taking my silver Lurex T-shirt and some light yellow pants, plus a long silver scarf.

Dianne was still in bed when I left. . .

I fed the cats and entered the bedroom from the rehearsal room, stepping down onto the dark plank floor. We loved that bedroom. It was as cozy as a pocket in a favorite coat. I remember seeing the pillows all around her, the cats lounging at her feet. The sun on her pale skin. A little smile forming as her eyes opened.

I knelt down. I remember the sleepy-cute look on her face, her head still full of dreams. She guided my face to hers for a kiss. "Bye, Sweetie," she said.

We kissed.

"Bye, Sweetie," I said, and I left.

We were supposed to play at 11:30, but it kept getting pushed back. We finally went on at two in the morning. We slept at George Callins' house. Eddie can give you the number. We got up about noon and bought some tacos and stuff to go at a place on San Pedro before we left. . .

We talked about the gig, how great it was, how fabulous Jellyroll was going to be. I felt damn good. From now on, I'd be playing gigs at least once a week. Kiss the mailroom job goodbye. Cool, cool, cool.

Eddie dropped me off at our house Monday about three in the afternoon. When I got to the front door I started to unlock it but it came open when I touched it, which surprised me. I carried my stuff in. There was only one cat and he seemed to be acting strangely.

It was Bogey. With his longer hind legs and nub of a tail, he always reminded us of a rabbit. There was a thing Dianne used to do, her rabbit trick. She did it for me that first night, out on the grass outside the dorm. "I can make you feel like a rabbit," she said. "Wanna see?" Of course I did. She closed her hands and softly pressed them on my cheeks. I could barely see them in my lower peripheral vision. With her face so close I could see my reflection in her eyes, she said, "See? Doesn't that make you feel like a rabbit?"

I would've cut off my right arm to be with her forever.

When we were apart I'd think about the rabbit trick. I didn't even have to do it to feel the warmth through my body, the electrical charge that bound us together.

I called out for Dianne, but she didn't answer. I went into the rehearsal room and put my things down and called out for her again, but she still didn't answer.

Then I went to the bedroom. And I . . .

I couldn't write the words. I tried, but I couldn't. I wanted to jab the pencil into my eye and drive it into my brain.

Think of the rabbit trick instead. Just think about the rabbit trick. . .

6. TAPE LOOP

It's like a tape loop in my head. Ringing in my ears, the only sound. Went into our bedroom. Dianne was lying on her stomach, sprawled on the sheets. Naked, but we always slept that way.

"Sweetie," I said. On my knees, leaned close, said, "Sweetie, I'm home." Putting my hand on her shoulder, tugging gently. Her skin cold to the touch. Her body rolled over. Like a plank of wood.

Her eyes were open, ringed with purple and black. *She doesn't see me.*

Dark blood clogging her nostrils. I wouldn't remember seeing the leopard print pillowcase tight around her throat. Not until later. Something inside me imploded. No more sound. No sense of place or time. As in a dream, familiar objects seemed foreign. Things near looked far away. My feet were down there, touching the floor, but the floor was tilted. Reached for the wall, a chair, surprised that they didn't disintegrate.

Den empty and silent. This used to be our home. Now just a shell. No one has ever lived here.

Alone now. A grain of sand in outer space.

In the kitchen, water dripping. Bottom of sink, ashtray with cigarette butts, full of water. She wouldn't have done that. Different brands of cigarettes, underwater.

Living room. There's the phone. Call the police.

An orange sticker listed emergency numbers. No 911 service in 1976. Studied the sticker. Hands like butterfly wings, fingers found numbers, pressed buttons, no results. *If you need help, hang up and dial the operator.* Tried again, same thing. Something wrong with the phone. Body shaking all over, almost out of control. Studied the orange sticker. Stabbed numbers again. *If you need help. . .*

Finally called the operator. I need the police, I said. I think my girlfriend's dead. Something happened. I need help. My phone won't work.

Stay on the line, she said. Another voice answered, Austin Police Department.

I need help. I think my girlfriend's dead.

They were on their way.

Sat there, careening through emptiness. Maybe I was wrong. Maybe I'd gotten the wrong impression. Maybe she's just sick. The ambulance will come and take her to the hospital and she'll be OK. Maybe. . . maybe. . . oh, God, maybe. . . Should go back there, see if I can wake her up. Something happened, she contracted some weird disease and—

The police wouldn't let me go back to the bedroom. They asked questions. I said I just got home, I played a gig in San Antonio last night. I said, Maybe she's not dead, she's just really sick? They gave me that cop look, that dead eyes look.

What happened? I said. What could've happened?

They wouldn't say. A lot of cops in the house. More cop cars pulled up outside.

Yeah, I live here. Thinking, once I leave, I'll never come back.

The cats came out of hiding. I saw them in my peripheral vision only. Whenever cats disappeared and we couldn't find them, we said they'd gone to the moon.

One of the cops said, You oughta take them outside. Cats aren't cool around dead people.

Dead people. Ears ringing louder now.

They asked questions. I said I just got home, I'd been in San Antonio playing a gig. I said that already, didn't I? Maybe they didn't hear me.

They didn't nod as if they'd heard me this time, either. Like they were watching my lips move to see what would come out. What were they thinking? What really happened?

They said I should ride to the police station with them. Sure, I said. Can't dial a phone, can't drive a car.

On the way out, I noticed some pictures on the coffee table, snapshot size. They weren't there before. This could be important. Weird pictures, fanned out. I leaned closer, trying to figure out what they were. I said, Look, what's this? These weren't here before.

Then my eyes focused, receptors worked, zapped info to brain: Polaroid shots, close up, various angles, naked female. Porno shots, I thought. They're lurid and strange, zoomed in close, weird angles, too close. Someone left these here, they don't belong, this is—

No—That's Dianne's body. Look, somebody took these and. . .

They just looked at me.

You guys took them.

I wanted to gouge out my eyes, peel my face off my skull. You guys wanted me to see those. You guys wanted me to see. You must think—

The one with the camera was looking at my shirt. I was wearing a pajama top. Cool designs on it. A musician could dress this way. They snapped chewing gum. They looked at the weird stuff in our house. The antique photo of a bearded man over Dean's bed. We stuck a bayonet in his forehead. Dianne painted a dribble of red from the wound. Some people didn't get it, but we thought it was funny.

A wooden box in the corner, lid shaped like a pyramid, painted in wild colors, eyeballs and other witchy designs. Inside were incense and herbs, candles, vials of dirt, leaves, a knife, some scrolls of paper with spells written on them. No embalmed rats or anything like that.

Uh oh, look at this, one of them said.

A noose dangled by the door to the rehearsal room. We'd learned how to tie the knot from a crazy dude in San Marcos. Gave great parties, was a big disappointment to his dad, the football coach. Once he ran away in the family RV, living it up on Dad's credit cards. The RV was totaled, Dad's credit was wrecked, and the bad boy had to go away for a while. The doctors put him on Thorazine, but he somehow managed to party down on that, too. I tried it once. Terrible stuff.

The noose was a reminder. We'd laugh and say, Can you believe Mike

57

stole his parents' RV? What a trip. But after a while it was like wall-paper. I'd forgotten it was there. I could sure see it now. I felt one around my own neck. I couldn't breathe without her. I couldn't live. Didn't want to. I got what I wanted most—my life as a musician—for this, this nothingness.

Someone dropped me at the crossroads. I didn't ask for this. This wasn't supposed to be the deal. When I got my new life, we were supposed to be together.

I'm sinking down. . . Just like on TV, they told me to watch my head when I got in the car.

Behind the cluttered desk was a big man with a jowly face and dark, tired eyes, Lt. Colon Jordan. He weighed 350 pounds. No surprise to learn he played tackle in high school football.

He had my statement. He turned the pages gingerly as he read. Curly sat in a swivel chair on the left side of Jordan's desk, but Jordan did all the talking.

"Johnson City, that right?" said Jordan.

"Yes."

"Your dad works for Pedernales Electric Co-op?"

"Yes."

Talking was still difficult, but I wanted to help. Whatever they needed. But the tenor of the questions changed as he took four Big Chief tablets from a box behind his desk. The box had been hidden until now. Was that intentional? Dianne recorded the most intimate parts of her life in Big Chief tablets, in prose, drawings and poems.

"I've got her diary here," he said, stretching the word to its full three syllables.

A new layer of sadness enveloped me. Big Chief was never intended for the eyes of some fat cop with a doughy face and lazy drawl.

"Here we go," he said, clearing his throat. "Apparently this is called 'Sea Girl.' 'Tears of salt scraping the green, Thoughts of blue, linking dreams. Will we unlock her soul?'"

He paused and nodded at me, as if it was an indictment of some kind. The poem was something she'd written in high school, probably when her parents divorced.

Jordan flipped to another page marked with a paper clip. Lots of other pages were marked that way.

"Here's a longer one," he said. "It's about somebody by the name of Seth—"

"A teddy bear," I said.

"Oh, teddy bear, huh?" he said in his flat voice. "OK." He made a mark on a notepad. Curly leaned over and said something in his ear. The lieutenant opened the diary to another section. After skimming the page, he asked me about a guy named Keith. Who was he, friend, boyfriend? Just a friend from college, I said. He flipped to another page and asked about some other names. Friend or boyfriend?

Things got worse. He would read a few lines, then ask what I thought about it. Sometimes he'd just leaf through the pages, pausing now and then to make a face at something, like a guy going through his refrigerator, sorting out rotten food.

"I need to know something, Jesse," he said. "What kind of drugs did you and your girlfriend use?"

"Budweiser and cheap brandy, mostly," I said. "I haven't smoked pot in two years. Dianne smoked a little but she was bored with it, too."

Of course they didn't believe me. Their smugness was ugly, but I was used to that from Texas cops.

"What about other drugs?" Curly said.

"I don't take any drugs. They're a waste of time. Dianne probably hasn't taken any since college. We did get high in high school and college, but everybody did, except for geeks and rednecks, and that was years ago." In my teens and twenties, two years seemed like a long time.

"On what? What drugs were they?" said the lieutenant.

"Occasionally, hash and speed," I said. "Acid, a few times, mescaline, and downers. Let me think." If they pored over Big Chief long enough, they'd find a complete inventory, so no sense holding back.

"Mushrooms and coke, a few times each, and THC a few times," I added. "Probably a couple of other things, too, but like I said, in the last year or so she rarely even smoked pot anymore, and I haven't at all."

Jordan shook his head. He didn't seem to believe me. Curly was harder to read. "What about this witchcraft stuff?" said Jordan. "Were y'all in some kind of cult?"

"No, of course not."

"Dianne wasn't into witchcraft?"

"Witchcraft? Yeah, sure. She was a nature lover. She burned a lot of candles and sometimes she said incantations and did little spells from a spell book. There wasn't anything sinister about it."

He sneered at me. This was bad. What kind of parties did you have? Why'd you have a noose over the door jamb? What about that picture with a bayonet through a guy's head? I said it was just art, and they gave me that blank look, and I just shrugged. Fuck 'em if they don't get it. Then it came back to drugs again: What kind of drugs did you say y'all took? Hoping to trip me up this time.

"Did Dianne usually sleep in the nude?"

Now that seemed like a weird question. "Sure," I said. "We both did."

"Did you have orgies or other kinds of kinky sex?"

"No, we sure as hell didn't," I said. I was disgusted. "We didn't have orgies or three-ways or anything like that. You may think we're really depraved, but we were just two normal people who were in love with each other. We had a very normal monogamous relationship."

"Uh-huh," Jordan said, nodding as he flipped to another section in the tablet. He took a deep breath and started reading aloud.

It was an entry I didn't think I'd seen. The date was about two years ago, when Dianne and I were separated temporarily, after I told her I needed some space to think about things—a lame cliché which meant I wanted to sleep with some other girls but couldn't stand the idea of breaking up with her. The separation lasted all of two weeks. I couldn't stand being without her. It made me crazy. I begged her to forgive me, and that ended my experiment. In the passage the lieutenant selected, Dianne referred to me as "shithead" in passing as she chronicled a night of lust with a mutual friend. How could I begrudge her that, especially now?

In the middle of a couple of lines that were vaguely pornographic, the fat cop looked at me with a raised eyebrow. "And what do you think about that?" he said.

"What do I think about what?"

"What she wrote."

I explained about the breakup. How stupid I'd been, and what was the point here, anyway?

Then, as if a light switched on, I realized they were trying to provoke me. *They think I murdered my girlfriend.*

No wonder all the bizarre questions. If I hadn't been in shock, I might've realized it sooner. What a waste of time, but I was the obvious suspect, wasn't I? The jealous boyfriend, a cult and drug thing that got out of hand.

Once they got a peek at the Big Chiefs, they thought they'd hit the jackpot. Look at these kooky, kinky poems and stuff. Drug tales, sex chronicles, magic spells. . .

"Look," I told them, "I didn't kill my girlfriend. I loved her more than anything. Sure, we had problems now and then, but it was because of my own immaturity, and that was a long time ago. Things were good between us."

The lieutenant nodded and snuck a skeptical look at Curly. They really pissed me off.

"I don't know what else to tell you," I said, "except she did not have other boyfriends. We did not have orgies. We are not drug addicts. We were not in some weird cult. I guess we seem pretty strange to you, and I'm not saying we were perfect, but whatever happened, it wasn't our fault."

Jordan stared at me. The phone rang. Curly answered it, then nodded at Jordan and handed it to him. Jordan thanked me and said that would be all for now and took the call.

Curly took me to another place to sit for a while. Walking past a room where the other detectives were drinking coffee, I heard them kicking wisecracks back and forth. My blood began to boil. They were talking about Dianne.

She didn't deserve this. I should be dead instead. She was better than me.

I found myself thinking about what I'd trade to have her back. Hack off an arm, hack off my legs. Gladly do it. Gimme the knife right now. I'd give my life. Kill me now, I don't care, just bring her back.

I had to call my friends and say that homicide detectives wanted to talk to them, could they come down to APD tonight? I had to repeat the reason over and over again. *No, it's not a joke.* Over and over and over. Every person I called. I've pulled some strange pranks before, but never anything that dark.

It was after midnight when I decided to call Dianne's father. From the sound of his voice, the phone had awakened him from a deep sleep.

"I thought you'd be awake," I said.

"No, no," he said. "What's going on, Jesse? Is everything OK there in Austin?"

"No one called you?"

"Called about what?"

"The police. I thought the police were going to call you. They told me—"

"What's this about, Jesse? Are you in trouble or something?"

"It's about Dianne. She's—she was killed."

"What do you mean?" At first he was off balance; now he was getting annoyed.

"She was killed. Murdered. Someone broke into the house and killed her."

"Now, come on, Jesse. That's not really funny. Why don't you let me talk to Dianne? Put Dianne on the phone."

Nothing I said could convince him. Nothing. I could hear Kathleen in the background, asking what was going on, Earl telling her. She took the phone, so I tried explaining to her, *No, it's not a joke, please believe me.* Then Earl got on again, and I tried with him again, but he just kept insisting that I stop kidding around. *Are you drunk or something, Jesse?*

Finally Curly took the phone, identified himself, and told Earl to call him back. He gave him the number and added, "Ask for Sergeant Beck in homicide."

The tape loop: Front doorstep, keys out, door swings open. Walk inside. "Sweetie?" Living room, look right, missing pane. Band room, bass down, "Sweetie?" Bedroom, she's naked on her stomach, "Sweetie?" Kneel, "Sweetie, I'm home," touch arm, she rolls over. Face purple, dried blood. Her eyes don't see me.

I was in the bright room again, but they left the door open this time. I was doubled over, biting my lip so I wouldn't scream. The tape loop played again and again. Sometimes when I banged my head on the table it would stop, but not always. There was blood on the table. Maybe I should stop biting my lip.

I was still absorbing reality slowly and intermittently. She was dead. I was alone. Someone murdered her. Why? A burglar, maybe. But guitars and amps looked untouched, the stereo and TV were still there. What other scenario could lead to murder? I fantasized on a drug deal gone bad, but shut it off. That would be absurd. Dianne hadn't bought so much as a pill or a joint in years.

The tape loop started again. I banged my head on the table until it stopped. An image floated back. The window pane. The tape loop rolled again. I banged my head. I heard the lieutenant say, *Did Dianne usually sleep in the nude?*

Why did he want to know that? Another bit of reality seeped in. It should've been apparent, but the layers of shock gradually peeling away now were that thick. Oh, she was raped. It was that kind of murder. I saw it: *the missing window pane. . . someone's face. . . rape. . . murder.*

I went to find Curly.

"I know who killed her," I said.

I can't say exactly when I gave up on Dean. He used to be a guy with a wild imagination and energy to burn, fun to be around precisely because he was so unpredictable. That was in high school. His loose cannon act had long since lost its charm. When did his drinking get so out of hand? At some point, whenever Dean and I split a fifth of booze, I'd end up getting three or four drinks at the most, while he plowed through the rest, all in one sitting. He was getting too drunk to rehearse, too hung over to work, too broke to buy sticks and drum heads because he lost his job, too broke to pay the rent. I never tried to stop him drinking. I just stopped taking him seriously.

He offered to move out, and we accepted his offer. He mooched off his girlfriend, Candy. I saw him maybe once a week. When I wasn't working or with Dianne, I was hanging out with Eddie or rehearsing with

Jellyroll. The last month he was our roommate, he lost his house key for the second or third time. Instead of getting a new one, he'd come in through his bedroom window, removing a loose pane of glass to reach the window lock. That was typical Dean behavior.

I kept thinking he might turn around. He got a job on a construction site. When he came by a couple of days later, he was filthy and completely wiped out—from working like a mule in the hot sun all day long, not from drinking. He seemed happy. I thought, maybe this is what he needed, something as hardcore as busting rocks in prison.

The next time he came by, he brought a guy named Lyle, a friend from work. Lyle had empty eyes. When he looked at you, his lip curled funny, a sneer. I suspected he might be a speed freak and disliked him instantly. So did Dianne.

"That guy Lyle is creepy," I said. "What's his problem?"

Dean just shrugged. I let him know that his new friend wasn't welcome at our house, but beyond that I didn't worry about it. Once Dean cleared out his stuff, I didn't expect to see him much anymore. When I did see Dean again, he said, "You know what? I just found out Lyle is out on bail for rape in Kerrville." Apparently that was all he knew. He seemed shocked by the revelation. I told him not to bring Lyle around anymore. He said not to worry about it. He'd be steering clear of him.

I thought that was the end of it. But one evening two weeks later, Dean came by with Lyle after work, both of them loaded to the gills. Dean wanted to see if a check had come in the mail. They only stayed a few minutes. As they were leaving, Dean lingered for a minute. He knew I was pissed. "Candy needed the car, so Lyle offered me a ride," he explained.

"You still haven't moved your stuff," I said.

"Maybe next week, OK? By the way, Lyle and I came by during lunch to pick up a few things. Hope you don't mind, man."

I already knew he'd been there because he forgot to put the window pane back. I didn't say anything about it. My feelings for him were complicated. I was annoyed with him, but I'd known him so long I felt partially responsible for him. I didn't like Lyle. I didn't like Dean coming and going through the bedroom window. It was like he'd never left.

But I didn't do anything about it.

"I feel worse than stupid," I told Curly. "He knew exactly how to get into our house without a key. His fingerprints are probably on that window pane, aren't they?"

He shrugged. "The problem is, there'll be other fingerprints on it. Your roommate's, and didn't you say you handled it, too?"

"Yeah, I did," I said, feeling even worse. "I wish I knew Lyle's last name, but I remember Dean said he was from Kerrville."

He looked at me for a second, then crossed the room to talk to one of the other detectives who'd just come on shift. His name was Manley Stephens. A flurry of activity followed, but I wasn't part of it, and no one told me anything until much later on.

Lyle Richard Brummett was his name, they said. He was arrested at 1:50 that morning.

They let me go around the same time. We might have passed each other in the hall.

Move the clock back twenty-four hours, to two a.m. Monday: I'm going onstage to play what I consider to be the first important gig of my music career. Back in Austin, Lyle Brummett is climbing through the bedroom window of our little house.

7. DOUBLE LIFE

In retrospect, it must have taken Dean a lot of courage to offer me a ride from police headquarters. He and Candy had been summoned earlier to give their statements. Candy insisted that I come home with them. I had nowhere else to go. I welcomed the beer they offered me.

Dean drove, gulping beer and crying. He sped through stop signs and screeched around corners, a sputtering meteor of grief and guilt. Candy pleaded with him to slow down, finally shouting, "Just because you want to kill yourself doesn't mean Jesse and I want to die, too!"

I did want to die, but I didn't say anything.

Dean ignored her. It was her car, a little red Chevy Vega. He made turns in front of oncoming traffic. "Oh, God, goddamn it, Jesse, I'm sorry," he said. "Oh, fuck, I'm sorry. I'm so sorry, goddamn, goddamn it. I loved Dianne, too. Everybody loved her, man."

Never in a million years could he expect me to forgive him, he said. He kept ripping his guts out. He careened into ditches and over curbs. He was gonna kill Lyle, then kill himself. He swore it. Goddamn, he was sorry.

"I know you'll never forgive me," he said. "There's no way."

What a grueling night for Candy. I remember her touching me, her small hands on the back of my neck. Wispy blonde hair, birdlike face. A tiny woman with a toddler (not Dean's, thank goodness) and two big, fucked-up guys. Things would get better somehow, she said, and whatever I needed, just say so, they loved me. Then she'd scream at Dean, "Slow down, goddamn it! Please, please, slow down."

Why would I get in a car with the person who'd brought the killer to my house?

"I didn't know you weren't gonna be home," Dean said. "Fuck, man. I'm so sorry."

Sunday night, Dean and Brummett got some beer and came by for a while. Dianne was there. Of course she let Dean in. He was one of my oldest friends. She'd known him almost four years.

Dianne made it clear that she disliked Brummett, Dean said. She made it painfully obvious he wasn't welcome there. Dean said they stayed a little while, then went to Mother Earth. Afterward, Dean went back to Candy's apartment. But Lyle came back to our house. Now we knew.

I didn't forgive Dean. I shared his guilt and a good portion of his fathomless stupidity, too. Why didn't I keep Lyle away? Why didn't I bar the door when I saw the two of them coming?

Dean was a drunk, but I never thought that deeply about it. Maybe he never saw the warning signs about Brummett, or maybe he just blurred them with alcohol. I should've known better. Instincts tried to warn me, but I did nothing. I'd hardly given it a thought.

Brummett had a wife. Once I saw the two of them together at the convenience store on Oltorf Street where she worked, less than a mile from our house. Her name was Laurie. Blonde, small-boned. A scar on her mouth, like from a cleft palate. Brummett introduced us. She was pregnant.

He had a job. The landlady at their apartment would tell a reporter that Lyle was the nicest tenant she had.

Even though Lyle Brummett fooled other people, I couldn't let Dean off the hook. I couldn't let myself off the hook, either.

Earl picked me up at seven. He and Kathleen had driven in from Houston after I called him. Kathleen met us in the hotel restaurant. We hugged. She and Earl were there for me, she said.

They had breakfast, I had coffee. Earl and I went to APD afterward, leaving Kathleen at the hotel. Curly met us on the robbery/homicide floor. He said Brummett would be charged any minute now. After he met with Earl privately for a few minutes, our business there was concluded.

Next stop, the funeral home. Dianne's body had been taken there for the autopsy. In keeping with Dianne's wishes, her remains would be cremated. Earl had to see her for himself, but I couldn't do it again. There was no point. The brutalized body I'd found in our bedroom wasn't her anymore. It was just tissue and bone.

The memorial services would be in Houston. Earl wanted me to go with him and Kathleen and stay a few days. Sure, that would be good, I said.

I'd called my parents before leaving the hotel. They'd seen the story on the local news the night before. I gave my mother the basics in a flurry of sobs, and told her I was going to Houston with Kathleen and Earl. I didn't know any details about the services, she made no inquiries, and that was it. My parents didn't come, and as far as I knew, made no effort.

I wasn't close to my parents then. In their eyes, Dianne and I had been living in sin. I felt the weight of my mother's disapproval in particular. This attitude didn't help our relationship any, especially now.

I felt very warmly toward Earl and Kathleen. Earl's strength and grace under pressure was an awesome thing to see. He never cried, never asked questions that were too difficult to answer. He seemed fearless. Was that from his experience in the corporate world, or Harvard? Maybe it was midwestern forbearance. Something in the soil or wind.

Once we got to Houston, Earl doled out Valium pills the vet had prescribed for their Lhasa apso, who got nervous on airplane trips. The tranks helped us all feel less frantic, but even taken by the handful they couldn't help me sleep that night.

Earl took me to Neiman-Marcus and stuck a $100 bill in my pocket to buy a dress shirt and tie. He and Kathleen tried to force me to eat something. Finally, after being well plied with Scotch, I had a few bites Wednesday night.

The memorial service was Thursday. I wore my new tie and shirt. Mary Ann was there, Dianne's brother Gary, Mary McGee and other friends from Houston, a few friends from Austin, and lots of relatives whose names I never absorbed. A pastor conducted the service. I'd registered a stiff protest with Earl when he told me about the arrangements. Dianne wasn't a Christian; she was a pagan, I said, and to pretend otherwise would be hypocritical and insulting to her. Earl nodded and said I was right. When you think about it, though, he said, if we held an unconventional service like the thing I envisioned, it would be intensely disturbing to people like Dianne's grandmother, and Dianne wouldn't want that. Besides, he said, after this service, you and Mary and everybody can go out to the bayou in Memorial Park and do the thing your way, and I know Dianne will be right there with you.

Cool and calm and diplomatic, Earl was one broad-shouldered guy. No wonder Dianne was a daddy's girl.

The service was bearable, but just barely. The pastor delivered the usual bland homilies. He also worked in the usual sales pitch for coming to Jesus with your cares. Jesus died for us but now he lives forever, and we can liver forever, too, if we just sign up for his program. God loves us, and we're all in his hands, even though his grasp seems awfully slippery sometimes.

She wouldn't be there anymore, in the audience when I was playing onstage, after the gig to tell me how fine we sounded, by my side when we drove home.

Why didn't God do anything? What kind of a god lets this happen? Why would I get on my knees for a god like that?

I didn't feel inclined to humor him or flatter him. I especially felt disinclined to worship him. And if he was that kind of god, he had no reason to care what I thought. So much for eighteen years of religious indoctrination.

Sitting with our friends, I bit back my bitterness and cried, tears running off my face onto my shirt and tie. I imagined Dianne's arms around me. I held onto that fantasy for as long as I could.

The music was good. Earl had arranged for me to meet the pianist the day before. I gave her the names of three Neil Young songs and "Angie" by the Stones. To my surprise, she played them with beauty and feeling. "Only Love Can Break Your Heart" and "Tell Me Why" transported me, and I was surprised that Neil's songs could be so powerful stripped of his emotive whine and stabbing one-note guitar solos.

"Angie," with its pleading grace like a painful letter home, was full of regret but laced with a little hope. *When will those clouds all disappear?* But the beauty in Neil's "Words Between the Lines of Age" was all pain and sorrow, and I found myself falling through the stops in the chorus. It was a wrenching three minutes, but it belonged to me and me alone, a space where no one could intrude.

After the service, a bunch of us took some beer out to Memorial Park. Mary led us to one of Dianne's favorite spots, and we drank and cried. This was the real memorial. This was where we felt her presence, under the trees, by the water, in the wind.

As we were leaving, I walked under the canopy of a willow tree, the air cool and fragrant in its shadow. Going out into the sun again, I felt the soft touch of a long slender branch sweep across my shoulders and neck.

The landlord, or maybe one of the neighbors, had mowed the yard and hauled away the toilet we used as a flowerpot by the front door. Obviously, there'd been some embarrassment over these things when the house appeared in the newspapers and TV news. We'd allowed the St. Augustine grass to grow into a luxurious green shag carpet over a foot in height. We thought it looked cool. Now it had a regulation buzz cut.

I went back to the house twice, both times with friends. We had to cut the yellow crime-scene tape. Black fingerprint powder smudges covered every surface like bruises and burn marks.

I'd recently bought a new Toyota Corolla. My first car that cost over $300. I'd only made a few payments. Next week I would go to the bank and plead with them to repossess it. The bank president, a friend of my father's, would urge me to keep up the payments or find someone to buy it from me so I could repay the loan. A repossession would be a bad bargain. It would ruin my credit, he said. I would thank him and leave without telling him that a dead man loses no sleep over a bad credit rating.

I couldn't go in the bedroom. Friends did that for me. The house had a disembodied feeling, like an old refrigerator sitting empty. It seemed to have little to do with me anymore.

Earl gathered up some things from Dianne's childhood—pictures and stuff. I kept her large artworks, her magic box, the lapis lazuli ring I'd had made for her, the pocket-sized teddy bear named Seth, the last pair of jeans she bought. We used to wear each other's jeans. She wore my hip huggers with the Star Trek patch she sewed on the thigh.

Earl and I packed up the rest of the things for Goodwill. Her green velvet platform shoes with four-inch soles, her scarves, feather boas, hats and other things. All in boxes, going away.

I left the furniture, dishes and kitchen utensils, beds and bedding, everything else.

Two suitcases and a couple of boxes were sufficient to carry the things I took with me, except for her art, which I'd have to put in storage. I had no plans except finding somewhere to sleep that night. I had no place to live, no plans to look for one.

When we were leaving, I caught a glimpse of the longhaired tabby named Mickey. He came through the bushes bordering the yard, just far enough to spy on me. Then he disappeared. A friend from Houston had taken Roxy, the silver Manx. Dean and Candy had one of her kittens.

I stood there, feeling something like remorse for abandoning my cats. This was what I had come to, the kind of person I would despise. A person with no heart left for his animals, a person with no heart.

I could only bleed so much.

I got in the car and we drove away.

The next time Earl came to town, I met him at APD to pick up Dianne's personal items, including the Big Chiefs. While we were there, I spoke to one of the detectives. I'd remembered something, a detail that might help. When I found Dianne I noticed that the pillowcase was missing from one of the large pillows at the foot of the bed.

"What did it look like?" he said.

"It was leopard print," I said.

"Oh, you mean the one that was wrapped around her neck?" he said.

"Oh," I said.

I saw the pillowcase. Saw her face. The blood, the black and purple.

Outside APD, Earl was getting into his Cadillac. "I think I should take the Big Chiefs," I said. He had them in the trunk.

"No, Jesse," he said, some of the warmth fading from his voice. Maybe it was weariness. "I let you have her paintings and other things, and that's enough. I don't want to quarrel with you about this."

"I really think I should have those," I said. "They mean a lot to me."

"No," he said. "I'm not going to discuss it any further. I want to leave it there, and that's final. In fact, I want to forget about Austin and this whole part of Dianne's life."

That was that. The end of Earl's diplomacy. He drove away.

In my hands, folded into a neat rectangle, was the pillowcase. I couldn't believe they'd given it to me. My hands were shaking. I found a dumpster and threw it in and walked away as quickly as I could.

The murder was big news. In the Tuesday morning edition of the *Austin American-Statesman*, the story ran on the front page above the masthead, accompanied by Dianne's photo and the headline: "Suspect Jailed In Woman's Strangling." The lead paragraph started off just like my tape loop: "Jesse Sublett knew something was wrong when he walked inside the small South Austin house at 2109 Glendale and noticed the cats were missing. . ." The evening edition gave more details of the crime, plus a photo of the house with a forlorn-looking cat at the foot of the walk.

I didn't see these stories. I avoided newspapers and TV news as much as possible. I knew everything I needed to know, or I thought I did. I relived the murder every waking hour. Saw it in my dreams. Saw endless replays of the crime.

I picked up two bits of news by accident. Less than a month after the murder, a station interrupted its programming to report a daring escape from APD. During a follow-up interrogation there, Brummett was left alone in a room and simply walked out. His mug shot was flashed repeatedly on TV until he turned himself in the next day. APD had egg on its face. A week or so later, I glanced at a newspaper and saw Brummett's name. He had been charged with sexual assault for his role in the gang rape of another prisoner at the county jail. After that, I avoided the news even more scrupulously.

I knew I'd have to find some way to deal with it during the trial. I was confident that Lyle Brummett would be convicted and then executed. It was one of the things I lived for. I was all for the death penalty. Execution was society's remedy for certain varieties of evil. Society had to take a stand: Certain crimes were unforgivable, and anyone found guilty of them should be put to death. I knew there were problems in ensuring that the system was justly applied. But that didn't mean the system should be junked. It was a moral issue. There were problems in the public schools, too, but that didn't mean we should abolish the school system, did it?

I couldn't brush off the arguments against capital punishment, but I did close my mind to them, if only so that Brummett could be executed. He had forfeited his right to live on this planet, and now society had a responsibility to rub him out. No argument could change my mind.

Months later, I was sitting behind a polished oak table at the Travis County Courthouse. I had played a gig the night before and probably smelled like smoke and alcohol. The man across the table wore a dark suit with a wide tie that was a funky shade of lime green. I'll refer to him as Limey because of the ugly tie, even though I never forgot his real name. He was with the Travis County district attorney's office.

After some cordial preliminaries, Limey asked me a few questions. How long had Dianne and I been together, were we married, other background questions. Then he asked me to tell the story from my perspective. My pulse raced, my voice broke, my throat spasmed, and I cried, but I got through it.

"Jesse," he said, "do you know what happened after Brummett was arrested?"

"I've tried to avoid the papers and TV," I said. "But I know he was charged with rape and murder. Will he get the death penalty? When is the trial?"

"The thing is, Brummett confessed. He made a plea bargain."

"He confessed?" I said.

Limey nodded.

"So will there be a trial?"

"No," he said. "You see, Brummett confessed that he killed Dianne, and he also confessed to some other murders."

Good. Brummett would definitely be executed now. There'd be more publicity, and everyone would know that the monster who murdered Dianne got what he deserved.

But it wasn't that simple. He mentioned there was a case that involved a second murderer, a friend of Brummett's. He and the friend murdered two girls. After his confession, Brummett took a group of lawmen to the murder site. Only the girls' bones were left.

The D.A.'s man offered no other details. "That was his end of the plea bargain," he said. "In exchange for his cooperation, the county gave him some special consideration."

"Are you trying to say he won't be executed?" I said.

"Well, even if he was convicted of capital murder, he couldn't get the death penalty."

"Why?"

"The U.S. Supreme Court ruled it unconstitutional. There's a moratorium on executions."

"But what did you mean by that part, 'Even if he was convicted of capital murder'? I thought he confessed."

"Well, first of all, a capital murder charge means the homicide was committed in conjunction with another felony crime, such as rape. In this case, Brummett confessed to murder. He admits he killed Dianne but denies the charge of rape. He claims that the act of intercourse was consensual."

"That's bullshit. That's a lie. It's ridiculous."

He nodded. "I'm sorry. He's a pretty scummy character."

"This really sucks," I said. "It's just ridiculous."

"I can imagine how you feel about it."

"What did he say? No, wait. I don't want to hear it." I was torn. I didn't want to know, but I couldn't stand not knowing, either. "Can you sort of summarize it?"

"Look, why don't I just read you that part of his statement? It's not graphic. In fact, there's not much to it."

I thought a moment, then nodded.

He flipped a page and skipped to the part where Brummett related how he broke in by removing a pane of glass in the window and found his way back to the bedroom. Limey looked at me cautiously before reading the next line: "I sat down on the bed, and nature took its course." Then he stopped.

I was seething. It wasn't graphic, but it was stupid. The phrase "nature took its course," obviously dictated by an attorney, didn't soften the blow much, but it could've been worse. "It's ridiculous," I said. "It's crazy. There's got to be enough evidence that he raped her. He hurt her. I saw it. He beat her up. I mean, I found her, goddamn it."

"Let me explain a couple of things, Jesse," he said. "The DA's office doesn't want to try the case in front of a jury. The defense would make things as ugly as possible. All they have to do to get Brummett off is create reasonable doubt in the minds of the jurors. See? They would question witnesses about Dianne's sex life, did she use drugs, other things about her past. And your private life, too."

That was all I needed to hear, especially after my experience with Jordan and Beck. I knew enough about people to realize that Dianne and I would be put on trial, and Brummett might win.

It was outrageous and depressing, but there was no use screaming about it. We were beaten. In exchange for Brummett's confessions, the state sentenced him to two life terms. I thought that meant he would stay in prison the rest of his life, but I learned that, with time off for good behavior, a prisoner serving a life sentence might be eligible for parole after only seventeen years.

I took some solace in the assumption, then, that double life would mean at least thirty-four years, but I was wrong about that, too. The two terms would be served concurrently, which meant that, theoretically, Brummett might be eligible for parole in seventeen years.

"Seventeen years? What kind of a goddamn sentence is that?"

"That probably won't happen," he said. "I mean, this is a bad character. You heard what happened when he was in jail?"

I nodded.

"All those things will be taken into consideration, along with the seriousness of his crimes. He's going to be in jail a long, long time."

That was all he could promise me, and it wasn't even a promise.

The D.A.'s office had done me a courtesy, I supposed, by having someone tell me about the cynical bargain they made with Brummett, but it would've been nicer if they'd consulted with me first. At least Brummett and his friend, whatever his name was, were no longer free to rape and kill women. I told myself Brummett would never be paroled, that he would stay in prison until his miserable life expired. Maybe he'd be killed in prison. Maybe he'd realize what a monster he was and commit suicide.

I wanted to stop thinking of him, but I could never forget his name. I had to keep tabs on this monster.

On August 18, when I was in Houston making preparations for the memorial service, people in Austin and Kerrville were learning gruesome new details about Brummett's violent life. In Kerrville, the parents of two teenage girls learned the grim truth about what happened the night they disappeared.

Carol Ann London, eighteen, and Beth Pearson, fifteen, were driving around on the night of September 17, 1975, when they had car trouble. The car was found in the courthouse parking lot the next day, but there was no sign of the girls.

Kerrville was a rural town deep in the Hill Country about an hour and a half west of Austin. The landscape around Kerrville is like all the rural spots I haunted as a kid—rocky and dry, with oak- and cedar-studded rolling hills and cypress-lined creeks, limestone sticking out everywhere you look. White-tailed deer and armadillo country. A pasture near Cypress Creek is where they found the skeletal remains of Carol Ann and Beth, under a large live oak tree.

According to Brummett, on the night of September 17, he and his friend, Allen Ladd Woody, picked up Carol Ann London and Beth Pearson and took them to that cow pasture and strangled them during sexual intercourse. Eleven months later, on August 17, 1976, Brummett was arrested by APD on information from me. Later that day he made a confession about his guilt in all three murders. Later that night, he led some lawmen to the cow pasture near Cypress Creek.

Carol Ann and Beth's parents finally found out what happened to their daughters. The mother of Lyle Brummett, who was known as Lyle Stone in Kerrville, found out her son was in trouble again, and this time there'd be no squirming out of it. Woody's mother also learned that her son was in trouble again, but she rushed to Texas Department of Public Safety headquarters in Austin, where he was being questioned, in time to warn him to shut up.

Woody denied his part in the rape murders. The state would have to take him to trial. He entered a plea of not guilty, and in April 1977 a jury found him guilty of murder, rejecting the more serious charge of capital murder, and sentenced him to ninety-nine years in prison.

I never knew about the Woody trial and its connection to Brummett, his plea bargain deals or his sentencing. I stayed away from crime coverage, and no one ever told me about it. I didn't know how badly the state needed Brummett to convict his accomplice in that crime. Didn't know the other rapist-murderer's name. Didn't know the names of the girls.

I guess my friends thought it was pretty obvious that I couldn't handle any new information. So I wouldn't learn anything more about the case for twenty-five years. By then, I had suppressed the story long enough to cause myself serious damage.

On April 27, 1977, Brummett was transferred to the Walls Unit of the Texas Department of Criminal Justice penitentiary in Huntsville to begin his double term on two counts of homicide, to run concurrently.

I'd already begun serving my own double life term. I had to live without Dianne, and I had to live with the fact that I was partially responsible for her death.

PART 2.
SHOOTING
BOTTLE ROCKETS
at the MOON

8. EMOTIONAL VAMPIRE

Up in the dressing room, Eddie asked if he could borrow my eyeliner and should he wear the green scarf or blue. Blue, I said, and hang on, I'm gonna touch up my eye shadow, then the eyeliner again. I glanced up in time to see Eddie's reflection in the mirror. He wiggled his shoulders and bopped around the room in a Mick Jagger impersonation. That was Eddie, always in motion. A moment of repose would've been death.

The Austin hard blues rockers the Fools were finishing their set with a high-decibel boogie that sounded like early ZZ Top. We were on next, then the Fools would come on again for the last set. They pulled a large crowd, so it was great exposure for Jellyroll's first gig.

Touching up the eyeliner, then a little lipstick. Stage makeup wasn't unusual—all my favorite bands wore it. Makeup also made it easier to be around people, almost like wearing sunglasses or a weird hat. Or a black veil. I was wearing a lot more makeup since Dianne's death.

"Two minutes," the sound man said.

I checked the tuning on my bass one last time. Danny warmed up his voice. Eddie bopped over, said: "How 'bout that eyeliner, man? You done yet?"

"Yeah." Thump, thump on my Fender Precision bass.

He found the eyeliner in my shoulder bag and inscribed both eyes quick, an old pro. We did high fives. "We're gonna set the stage on fire, right?"

"You bet," I said.

"Hey, nice bass, man," he said, winking.

As if he'd never seen it before. Just to make him happy, I kissed the neck for luck. Thanks to Eddie, I had discovered one of the essential truths of the universe: the Fender bass was the icon of cool. Rock 'n' roll was a quirky little edge kind of music until Leo Fender invented the first practical electric bass guitar, an instrument you could throw in the trunk of a car instead of having to rent a bus or trailer. The upright bass was cool, but rock 'n' roll needed something whose booming heartbeat rattled the bedrock, tickled the inner ear, and was audible on recordings, too.

My first bass was a cheap, no-name piece of shit. The second wasn't much better. My third was the Dan Armstrong, which looked cool with its see-through body; its tone was as clear as mud, though. I could play fast on my fourth, a Rickenbacker, and the tone was crisp and trebly, but when I plugged in a Fender Precision, there was no comparison. It was love at first thump. The lows had much more definition, the highs had character and color. The neck had an intuitive feel. A Fender P-bass fit in my grasp, as familiar as an old lover, as dependable as a cop's revolver. *Boom-boom-boom-boom*, man. I had my anchor, my electric heartbeat.

Eddie kept saying, "Man, get rid of that Rickenbacker piece of shit. Get yourself a real bass. Get a Fender." We'd only been playing together a month when I saw the light. Eddie found my dream axe in a pawnshop on Red River Street. A black Fender Precision with a '63 neck on a later body. At $250, it was an awesome bargain, one that changed my outlook as a bass player.

Now I said, "Thanks, bro."

"You got the boss tone now, brother," Eddie said.

When I came back from Houston, Eddie was the one who checked on me every day. Did I have a place to stay? Did I want to do something tonight? But he never asked how I was doing, if I missed Dianne, if I could sleep at night, did I want to talk about it. Maybe he thought those were stupid questions.

He was like my right arm. Around each other all day in the mailroom, lunch together for cheap Mexican food or cheeseburgers. Nights, if we didn't have a gig or rehearsal, he'd say, "Hey, let's go down to Mother Earth, check it out. Have a couple of beers."

Danny asked if I was OK. Ron the drummer, too. But we didn't talk about it. None of the other guys I knew asked about it at all.

Eddie strutted into the glare of a red-filtered Klieg light and started ripping into the twelve-bar intro of the Stones' "Flight 505," his gold-top Les Paul cranked. A sound loud enough to flutter the fillings in your teeth.

At the crack of Ron's snare, the rest of us came in, tight and heavy, vocals and all, and rocked. The stage was a good ten feet above the dance floor, almost eye level with people in the balcony. Almost everywhere I looked, people were watching us, girls smiling, guys nodding as they sipped their drinks, puffed on cigarettes and maybe moved out to the dance floor. This was it, the thing I craved. My bass so loud the room shook with every thump of my fingers.

Our second song was "I'm Ready," the Willie Dixon tune about getting drunk and hoping "some screwball starts a fight." You couldn't help but nod to the jumping bass line, and I enjoyed watching people quickly make up their minds to dance to it. Dianne and I met Willie Dixon after his gig at Antone's one night. I shook his hand, my own hand disappearing in the amazingly callused grip of that gentle giant.

The club, the Too Bitter, was in San Marcos, just off the town square where I was arrested for smarting off to a cop, in the same block as the Nickel Keg where we spent countless nights dancing to Crackerjack. Despite that, I felt fine onstage. The tape loop didn't roll. I didn't cry. I played my bass and disappeared into the music.

It was always that way when I played, even in our dank rehearsal room in East Austin. The times in between were tougher.

I was a semi-elegant mess after gigs, a pill-munching rock 'n' roll gigolo in mourning. I took Librium and Valium to take the edge off the nightmares and the tape loop. I drank Budweiser at gigs, cocktails too, and kept a bottle of cheap brandy by the bed for nightly emergencies.

Lots of guys, it's true, start playing in bands so they can get girls. A boring guy can pretend to be interesting if he's in a band, a shy one can pretend to be deep and mysterious. You don't have to try as hard. Girls come to you.

Meeting girls the easy way is nice, but it was never at the top of my list. Yet within a few months of Jellyroll's first gig, I'd slept with over a dozen girls, and that was without trying. I enjoyed the sex. I liked being around women. Being pampered in the morning by a beautiful stranger was nice. Some had interesting pets. I savored the variety in their faces and bodies, their aromas, the way they kissed. But the only reason I had the freedom to sleep with other girls was that the one I wanted was dead. Sleeping with other women, and enjoying it, also reminded me of the times I'd been unfaithful to Dianne. What a shithead I'd been.

Once I was alone with a woman, I had to share my darkness. I would cry, she would comfort me, we'd make out, have sex. A cynical person might suspect I was doing the whole grief routine to get laid. I can relate to that kind of cynicism. I don't mind admitting that there were times when I wasn't above it. But this wasn't a routine; it was a compulsion.

A few of the girls were already friends, and some became friends as well as lovers. First I slept with a friend's girlfriend. She was tall and slender like Dianne, with long black hair and oversized lips. Her name was Dianne, too. She took me home, and at first I actually resisted. She gently persisted and my resistance melted. It was good medicine. For the first time since August 16, I slept through the rest of the night.

After her came strangers, groupies, friends and acquaintances, as well as more friends' girlfriends and wives. Borrowing someone else's lover didn't bother me; my need was too great. I told them I'd never love anyone else. I tried not to be a jerk. I admired their beauty, kindness, strength and generosity, and I never wanted them to feel used. But some did, and some probably were. I took all they had to give and gave little in return. I wrote a song that was an unflattering portrait of people like me called "Emotional Vampire."

Pattie was one of the girls I liked best, so sweet to me I sometimes felt guilty. She looked like a rock star's girlfriend but loved to cook and decorate. She would've made a great mother. Her generosity seemed boundless. She even bought my Toyota so the bank wouldn't repossess it.

We had only one fight, over the love question. I don't remember if she used the word, but I thought she was leading up to commitment, suggesting that I maybe let go of Dianne a little. The answer was no. I could see that it hurt her, but I told her I was surprised at her. Didn't she know better than to ask?

"You know I grew up in Kerrville, right?" she said.

I nodded. I'd never thought about it much.

"I knew Lyle Brummett," she said. "We were in the same class at Tivy High."

"Really?" I said. "That's weird." I didn't want to know more.

"We even went out on a date."

I could hardly blame her. I was glad she'd told me, but I didn't want to hear any more about it. Staring at the space between us, I made a silent plea. No more. Can't you see I'm bleeding?

"You probably wish it was me he killed instead of Dianne, don't you?" she said.

"Don't say that," I said. "Please don't." But how could I make it sound convincing?

Sometimes there seemed to be minefields everywhere. Three weeks after the murder, Melissa, my boss, convinced me to come back to work at the mailroom. Any longer and she might have to fire me, she said, and besides, it would be good for me. Maybe she was right. I resumed sorting and delivering mail to all the offices in that four-story building. Over four hundred people. Aside from Melissa, Eddie and a few other friends in the mailroom, no one could bring themselves to acknowledge what had happened. I felt like a leper.

Melissa was two or three years older than me. She was pretty and trim with an eye-catching chest, and she had an endearing Lubbock drawl. I'd always known I was lucky to have such a cool boss, and now she became one of my best friends. She even let me move into her apartment. One night her sister-in-law, Becky, came over to have a few drinks with us. Eddie was there, too. Becky dropped a few acid remarks about her husband, Chris. Melissa agreed that her brother was a jerk. As the night wore on, Eddie ended up in bed with Melissa. I went to bed with Becky, who made love like a newly unleashed force of nature. She moved in a few days later and shared my bedroom, though I kept going home with other women, too.

Everyone who knew Chris said he and I were doubles. Becky and Melissa said so, and Melissa and Chris' parents said so. I saw their jaws drop when they met me. Chris was a bass player, too.

Becky was a friend and she was outrageously fun in bed, but I never saw our relationship as anything more than that. She did a few things that told me she was starting to see it differently. One was a phony pregnancy. She even fooled herself. Luckily, her doctor confirmed that it was a false alarm, a case of hysterical pregnancy, he called it. One night she told me to look under the bed. I pulled up the sheet and saw a long guitar case, Fender logo. Inside was a fine Fender Precision with a sunburst finish. The action was almost as nice as my '63. "You can have it," she said. "To hell with Chris. If you want it, it's yours."

It was a terrible temptation. With a lump in my throat, I said, "No thanks." I slid the bass back under the bed. I would borrow a bass player's wife, but I wouldn't take his bass.

I continued to have the tape-loop flashback, nightmares, panic attacks. One afternoon I walked up the front steps of Melissa's apartment and took out my key. I was about to touch the doorknob when the door became invisible and I could see inside. It was a bloodbath. The bodies of those closest to me, hacked apart, gutted and hung from meat hooks. The floor a sea of blood. Gore and organ parts everywhere. Variations of this hallucination would strike wherever I lived, wherever I went, for many years. Time heals all wounds is bullshit.

I'd been staying with Melissa for a couple of months when she found a two-bedroom house. She took me to look at it. The extra bedroom was mine for as long as I wanted it. I lived there through Christmas and a few months afterward. It was cozy, but I was still in bad shape a lot of the time. Flashbacks and nightmares and lots of crying.

The front door had a small window. One night I came home to find a face looking out: Humphrey Bogart, with his sad dog eyes and melancholy toughness, keeping guard for me. Melissa had tacked a *Casablanca* poster on the other side to give me a distraction. What a sweetheart.

Some of my best friends came in pill form. I took a lot of them, but never enough to kill myself. At first I just assumed I would die, of heartbreak or self-neglect. I didn't want to live, but I didn't like the idea of suicide. Maybe it was one of the last shreds of my Christian upbringing.

And I hated the idea of leaving a mess for someone else. It's inconsiderate to leave your crusted brains on the wall, the bloody bathtub, the sour smell of your despair and selfishness.

I started writing again. First it was free-form prose, stream-of-consciousness misery and agony, letters, poems about her, poems about me and my pain. Mary McGee wrote me long letters, and I wrote her even longer ones. Our rapport was practically telepathic.

Letters helped, poems helped. Pills, brandy and Budweiser, too. But playing in the band was the main thing. When I was onstage, I never thought about it. The tape loop was off. Somehow I was able to govern my consumption of pills and booze so that it didn't interfere with my performance. I didn't need them while I was playing. I needed them afterward, though. The nightmares were always waiting to pounce.

Rare nights spent alone were the worst.

The world of a struggling rock band was a scruffily exotic existence. Late nights and all-nights, smoky bars, recording studios, long rides in a cramped van, road food, groupies, roadies, club owners, promoters, managers, unusual people of all stripes. Being in a band put a little extra spring in your walk. Beer tasted better, girls kissed better. When a cop pulled you over to give you a ticket and asked your occupation, you said "musician," and you gave him a smirk as he filled in the blank. Little things like that meant a lot to me.

There was more to it than ego and meeting girls. At the core was the notion of brotherhood. You saw another musician, and even if you didn't know the guy you might greet him with the little nod of recognition you reserved for a brother rocker. That nod meant something, especially now.

Eddie and I assumed that once we started the band, we'd have to play a handful of gigs before we could tell our day jobs to kiss our asses goodbye. The weeks and months rolled by, and Jellyroll gigged a lot, but we weren't making much money and we saw the day we planned to moon our beloved mailroom boss receding into the ether.

One morning the agency director happened to walk through the mail-room while Eddie and I were playing free throw with wadded paper balls. Our target was the mouth of Godzilla, a six-foot stack of boxes on which we'd sketched the Japanese monster's features. A spur-of-the-moment detail: the abbreviated nickname "God" emblazoned on his chest in large block letters. The director was a born-again Christian, an unfriendly prig who wore cheap suits and reeked of sweet cologne.

Normally it took months to terminate a state employee in a complex process of evaluations, probationary periods and procedures, all recorded in quadruplicate and distributed by mailroom employees like Eddie and me, but they made an exception for us. The director walked over to Melissa's desk, spoke a few words and left in a red-faced huff.

Ten seconds later we stood in front of her desk, summoned there by her intercom. "Jesse and Eddie," she said in a terse, authoritative tone, "you've been terminated. You have to be out of the building in thirty minutes."

It was a bit odd being fired by a woman you'd seen stoned silly on half a joint the night before. After a moment of stunned disbelief, Eddie and I whooped and did high fives. Seeing the frown on Melissa's face, we resisted any further displays. After all, she had to maintain appearances. However, on our way out of the building, we ducked into the direc-tor's office for an unscheduled exit interview. Although we didn't moon him, we did call him a few choice names you never hear in Sunday school, then thanked him for doing us such a swell favor, told him to kiss our asses and strutted out, free at last.

We partied late that night with Melissa and Becky and rose at the crack of noon to go down to the unemployment office. Since we'd been justifiably terminated, they said, we would be penalized with a two-week delay in our weekly rock 'n' roll subsidy checks. Big deal, we said. This was our first big break in the music biz!

There was an art to getting by for guys like us, and no better place to practice it than the sunny, slacker wonderland of seventies Austin. Even though Austin was a musician's haven, we had to resort to some gypsy tricks. Once Jellyroll started gigging, I usually made around $50 to $100 a week. At times it was only half that, sometimes nothing at all. We got $64 a week for unemployment, but that could be stretched a long way. I happened to like Top Ramen noodles. Four-for-a-dollar frozen potpies made fine dining. Slide one out of the oven onto a nickel's worth of rice, wash it down with a quart of iced tea. On the way to rehearsal stop at 7-Eleven for a Bruce's cherry fried pie or Baby Ruth bar, either of which cost less than a quarter, and I had change left for a couple of Budweisers at Mother Earth. I never ate breakfast, unless it was after a gig and I'd just gotten paid. Lunch was PBJ or bologna and Velveeta on Branola, or a $1.25 Mexican dinner at Tamale House, or a $3.25 splurge for a cheeseburger and onion rings at a great east side joint called Hamburger Haven.

We got by on free cover charges, $300 cars, couch crashing and the kindness of women who loved rock 'n' roll enough to put up with the men who made it. We got our rock-star duds at Goodwill and other thrift shops where you could snag a shiny Japanese smoking jacket for a buck, retro rayon shirts for a quarter. Groovy hairdressers adjusted our rooster cuts for free. Friendly waitresses lost our tickets or looked the other way when we walked the tab. Being a musician was like a life of crime. Every dollar we scammed was better than ten or twenty in a paycheck from a day job.

There were lots of trade secrets. A new set of bass strings cost a whopping $16. But if you took them off and boiled them you could make them last twice as long. At least I was never so hard up that I drank the broth.

Months went by. Not much changed, except I bought a '63 Karmann Ghia for $300 that I drove from girlfriend to girlfriend. I loved that car. I took pills, drank Budweiser and brandy, hung around with Eddie, missed Dianne, cried and kept writing. I listened to my Patti Smith and Lou Reed LPs over and over. I read Sylvia Plath's *The Bell Jar* again. Probably not the best therapy for a nearly suicidal person, but that's what I did.

Jellyroll gigged: Gemini's on the Drag, GG's on South Lamar, one or two clubs owned by coke dealers, an officers' club on Tank Destroyer Boulevard at Fort Hood, clubs in Dallas, Fort Worth, Temple, San Marcos, San Antonio, San Angelo. Disco had insinuated itself, even at Mother Earth, formerly the flagship of the Austin rock scene. With rare exceptions, the only rock bands who played there now played the Top 40 hits. That left us out.

All the best bands Dianne and I used to see—Krackerjack, Queen of Hearts, Franklin's Mast and Slip of the Wrist—were no more. Most had broken up. The Werewolves, among the best of the lot, had moved to L.A. Most of the clubs they used to play were gone, too.

Antone's was blues heaven. Clifford Antone brought in Muddy Waters, Otis Rush, Jimmy Reed, Willie Dixon and almost all the legendary greats who were still alive. There was a large population of expatriate blues musicians from Dallas and Fort Worth who always seemed to be gigging—Stevie and Jimmie Vaughan, Lou Ann Barton, Doyle Bramhall, Paul Ray and Alex Napier. We dug all those people. Unfortunately, their scene had no place for us. Too rock 'n' roll for the blues clubs and not squirrelly enough for Top 40, we needed a whole new scene.

Eddie and I kept jamming and hanging out through the fall, trying to figure out what to do next. Three girls ended up giving us the inspiration we needed. One was Eddie's girlfriend, Carla, and the other two were strangers until they walked into Mother Earth one night.

"Hey, aren't you guys in Jellyroll?" the redhead said.

"Yes we are," Eddie said. "I'm Fazz Eddie, and this is Jesse."

The redhead introduced herself as Kathy Valentine. The one with black hair and milky skin was Marilyn Dean. Kathy was young, too young to be in the club legally, and Marilyn looked even younger, though it didn't really take a Mata Hari to fool the doormen at Mother Earth. Both girls had rock 'n' roll shags and hip clothes. They reeked of practiced cool and potential mischief. Kathy asked what year my Precision was, and I told her it was a '63.

"Cool. Pre-CBS," she said.

"Yeah," I said. I was impressed. CBS had purchased the Fender company in 1964. Ever since then the guitars and basses didn't seem up to the old standard. This was common knowledge among rock musicians, and Kathy's comment was practically code for "Yeah, I'm a musician." But it seemed unlikely that this young chick was one. Carla notwithstanding, female rock musicians were rare in 1976.

"You know a lot about guitars?" Eddie said.

"Well, I play guitar," Kathy said.

"No kidding," I said. "What kind?"

"I got a '63 Strat."

You could've knocked us over with a guitar pick. "Wow, cool," I said.

"Yeah, man, that's cool," Eddie said. "But can you play it?"

"Yeah, I can play it," Kathy said with a defiant giggle. "I'm still learning, but I've been playing for a while."

"I got a drum kit for my birthday," Marilyn said. "We're starting a band, an all-girl band."

"And how old are you now?" Eddie said.

"Sixteen," she said, with that sly smile.

Eddie and I would've been less surprised to meet a couple of movie stars or international spies. We bought Kathy and Marilyn drinks, bummed cigarettes from each other and talked. Kathy had a tomboy toughness and wicked sense of humor. Keith Richards' kid sister. Marilyn reminded me of a black-haired Ann-Margaret as the beatnik noir babe in *Kitten with a Whip*.

The four of us became close friends. As it turned out, Kathy and Marilyn could play their instruments. They needed a little seasoning and practical experience, but they were deadly serious about starting a band, and that was the only way to get it. A few months later their band, going by the name Lickitysplitz, opened for Jellyroll at a gig in San Marcos. Their set was a little shaky, but only because the other members didn't carry their own weight. Kathy and Marilyn definitely rocked.

In early 1977, Kathy moved to London for a few months. Carla flew to London to visit her and check out the punk scene. One day they ran into Tony Laumer, a mutual friend of ours. Tony was there with her friend Lois Richwine. Both girls were originally from San Antonio. Tony, an artist and clothing designer, was engaged to Jake Riviera, the head of the maverick label Stiff Records, which was home to Nick Lowe, Elvis Costello, the Damned and a slew of other great bands at the forefront of the U.K. punk/new wave scene. Lois was in London for the style and excitement. She and Kathy hit it off right away. In the small but intense punk scene, finding a friend—from Texas no less—who shared your enthusiasms was exciting.

That summer Kathy moved back to Austin and started scheming with

Carla and Marilyn about starting an all-girl punk band called the Violators. The three Violators were itching to play, but they couldn't find a girl bass player. They approached me about helping them get started. Jellyroll, having recently lost our lead guitarist and drummer, was on hiatus—maybe even kaput—so why the hell not?

The four of us started rehearsing in October. Kathy had a couple of original tunes, and I started writing some songs, too. The rest of our repertoire consisted of covers, specifically, songs by old bands who we thought were still relevant—Stones, Yardbirds, Kinks, 13th Floor Elevators, the Velvet Underground—combined with some of our favorite punk/new wave bands—the Sex Pistols, the Damned, Elvis Costello and Nick Lowe. Carla and Kathy did most of the singing. The band was rough but way ahead of its time for Austin. Playing with the girls was a blast; there weren't many guys who were as fun to hang out with.

Eddie and I had been preparing ourselves for this route ever since we'd met. We'd get together and sample the latest Pebbles garage rock compilation or our obscure sixties LPs and 45's, rockabilly and early Stones, Eddie Cochrane, the early Sun records by Howlin' Wolf, Elvis and Jerry Lee Lewis. Weird gems like "Flying Saucers Rock 'n' roll " and "My Gal Is Red Hot." When that sonic blast of pure sex and bad juju hit you in the face, you just wanted to stand in front of your amp and slam out an E chord as if your life depended on it.

Then you turned on the radio and wondered, Jesus Christ, what the hell happened? Disco and limp-weight dreck from Foreigner and Peter Frampton ruled. "Muskrat Love" by Captain & Tennille was a huge hit. Led Zeppelin had gone from slash-and-burn mojo to loopy ditties about fairies and hobbits. The nasal whine of "Hotel California" was as pervasive as wallpaper. Whatever happened to two-minute scorchers about cars and girls?

The masses had been hypnotized. But when they got a taste of the rude, raw, three-chord racket we were making, some would be confused, others pissed and, we hoped, some thrilled. People needed to be slapped in the face by this stuff, at 120 decibels. I needed it, too.

Lois had moved back to San Antonio, and she and Kathy stayed in touch. Kathy kept trying to convince her to move to Austin. One night after a rehearsal Kathy phoned and said, "Hey, there's this guy I want you to meet. I think you'd like him. He's a bass player."

9. KNOCKOUT KISS

Almost every time the Violators rehearsed, Eddie would drop by. He made himself useful, changing guitar strings, running the PA, arguing with Carla about the solo on a Yardbirds song or the lyrics to a Stones song. Being on the sidelines must have been tough for a guy like Eddie.

One night during a break, Eddie picked up Kathy's Strat and started playing Iggy Pop's "Search and Destroy." I cranked my Precision and picked up the bass line while Marilyn pounded out her best. I was surprised at how full-throated the song sounded with just the three of us. The next night, we jammed on a couple of other songs. Whoever knew the lyrics stepped up to the mic and belted them out. It was so good I didn't know whether to crack up laughing or feel frightened.

Eddie and I had never considered the sound and fury we could create with a trio. Once we had a taste, we were hopelessly addicted. Most of the songs were ones he and I had been jamming on at rehearsals and sound checks—we were just playing them a little faster than before, and it felt right. We could see the future. Our singing was rough but good enough. Who needed a lead singer and second guitarist? A good drummer would do it. Eddie knew a guy named Billy Blackmon who might be perfect. A little Keith Moon, a whole lot of Charlie Watts, he said. Sounded good to me.

Billy managed a sandwich shop on Congress Avenue, next door to the Continental Club. He gave us free iced tea and cracked a lot of jokes. He was from Beeville, a small town in South Texas. He drove an old black Chrysler Le Baron he called the "Batmobile" and idolized the Kinks and Rodney Dangerfield. He said he was interested, but we'd have to play a few Kinks songs. Eddie and I had no problem with that.

The next night, the three of us played for an hour after the Violators rehearsal. The sound was even better than we'd hoped. Between songs we drank Budweisers and told jokes. It was the most fun I could remember having in a long time. We probably drank too much beer.

The next day, I was splashing water on my face when it hit me: Did we really decide to name our band the Skunks?

Lois had long rock 'n' roll hair, huge brown eyes and sexy lips. She wore stylish clothes from London, including purple pointy-toed boots with stiletto heels. That was good, because at five feet, three inches, she was a foot shorter than me. Kathy introduced us at a crowded party she'd made me promise to attend. I was usually attracted to taller girls, but Lois intrigued me right away.

I started by talking up the Violators and the Skunks, but Kathy had already told her a lot about those things. Then I learned that she'd lived in London and New York, and she'd been to CBGB's to see cool bands I'd only read about in *CREEM* magazine. In London, she'd gotten to be good pals with Jake Riviera.

Lois had seen a lot of the bands from the Stiff label. She'd seen Nick Lowe, Elvis Costello, Ian Drury, the Damned, Wreckless Eric and several others at a huge Stiff show. I started rattling off all my favorite Stiff singles and learned she owned every one. Not just every one I owned, but every one in the catalogue.

Lois was so cool and good-looking, she was a little intimidating. On the other hand, I was cool and good-looking too, and I was in two bands on the cutting edge of a new underground scene. Lois seemed interested in me, so I turned on the charm. I said I'd grown up in Johnson City, population 1,000, with eighteen kids in my senior class, and wasn't that funny? She smiled. Her story wasn't so simple. Born in Tucson, Air Force brat, only child. When her dad was transferred to Strategic Air Command, they moved every three years—Sacramento, Iceland, Germany, San Antonio, Panama, San Antonio again, where her dad had retired and now managed the golf course at Kelly Air Force Base.

Iceland? Wow. What a contrast to my own life: except for a few trips to Mexican border towns, I'd never even been out of Texas, though I wouldn't admit that until I knew Lois much better.

Just when I thought we were hitting it off, she said, "Why don't you cut your hair and wear straight-leg jeans? You'd look great, you know."

I laughed. "I'll think about it," I said. Not because I was considering it but because I wanted to keep her talking long enough to entice her into bed.

"I wouldn't tell you if I didn't think you had the looks for it," she said. "I mean, if you're going to be in a cool band, you've gotta have the right look. If you're playing cool music you don't want to look like a hippie."

I laughed again. Was she serious? I thought I looked like a rock star, not remotely like a hippie. Surely she was teasing. "You really think I should cut my hair?"

"Yeah. It would frame your face a lot better, not to mention making you look more up-to-date."

What an attitude problem she had. I excused myself and began checking my other options for female companionship. I had lots of girlfriends but none at the party. Kathy had made sure they weren't invited.

I decided to give the girl with the attitude problem another chance. After another round of small talk, I popped my question: "How about if I give you a ride?"

"Thanks, but I think Kathy's leaving in a few minutes anyway."

"You were planning on spending the night at her place?"

"Uh-huh," Lois said, smiling. It was a nervy smile. Beguiling.

"What about spending the night with me?"

"Uh-uh." Same nervy smile.

"No? Come on."

"No."

I don't remember saying good-bye, but I do know I walked out in disbelief. I didn't get it. Did Lois like me or not? She acted like she did, so why was she criticizing me and refusing to sleep with me? I wasn't used to that. In the wee hours of the morning, I pulled out my notebook and wrote a poem. It described her as pretty and bewitching but cold.

The next day I drove over to Kathy's house. Lois was getting ready to drive back to San Antonio. I walked her out to her car. We talked a few minutes. I found out she'd attended San Antonio College for a couple of years. She had an office job at a hospital, but her heart belonged to rock 'n' roll. She'd done some band interviews for a rock magazine in San Antonio. She had an electric guitar, too, but didn't know how to play it yet. Kathy was going to give her lessons.

Then it was time to go, so I gave her the poem. I don't know whether I'd expected her to pick a fight or fall into my arms, begging my forgiveness. What she did was thank me, fold the page and put it in her purse. She gave me another one of those smiles.

We kissed. It was a hell of a good-bye kiss.

"Would you like my phone number?" she said.

I sure would. She gave it to me, then drove away in her green Mustang. A piece of my heart went with her.

Lois came up to Austin again on New Year's Eve. My hair was cut short and spiky, and my jeans were pegged. "Wow, you look great," she said. "What an improvement. Not that you didn't look good before. You just look better."

She looked great, too, and I told her so. Our destination was Soap Creek Saloon, an Austin-style cosmic cowboy and blues honky-tonk. Eddie and Billy and I were playing the opening set in a one-night-only band we'd thrown together for the occasion with a guitarist friend named Charlie Ray. The crowd response was lukewarm at best but we didn't care. We got free drinks and fifty bucks apiece.

We partied at Kathy's house after the gig. I asked Lois if she'd come home with me. She smiled and shook her head. I got pissed off again, although I wasn't as mad as the first time. Midnight was approaching, and at the stroke of twelve, we kissed. Lois was a great kisser. She had supple, expressive lips, and when they parted and our tongues met, I felt transported. For a fine moment, nothing existed but the two of us. I felt an ache when it finally ended. I liked her a lot, but I couldn't take any more rejection.

We talked a while, kissed some more, and then she suggested that next time we could go on an actual date. Just the two of us.

"That would be a better chance for us to, you know, get together," she said. "What do you think?"

I told her I liked that idea, and we sealed the deal with a kiss. Looked like the new year was starting with a big boom.

My next opportunity to get close to Lois wasn't exactly intimate, but the occaison promised to be memorable. On January 9, I rode down to San Antonio with the whole Skunks/Violators gang and met up with Lois at the entrance to a redneck honky-tonk called Randy's Rodeo, where the Sex Pistols were about to play. Malcolm McLaren, the Pistols' twisted Svengali, had gambled that a hostile reception from shitkickers in Texas cowboy joints and equivalent places in the band's swing through the South would garner gobs of publicity and add an element of cinema verité to Johnny Rotten's vow to destroy rock 'n' roll.

The Violators had actually tried to snag the opening slot. After getting our demo tape and band photo, the concert promoter called back to say that we could have the gig if he could fuck Marilyn, the drummer. We told him to fuck himself instead. Local band the Vamps got the gig. They were pretty good—lots of Iggy Pop and New York Dolls covers.

Mayhem erupted when the Sex Pistols took the stage. Johnny Rotten shouted, "All cowboys are faggots!" as the band launched into "God Save the Queen." He was wearing ridiculous plaid pants and a matching jacket, and a T-shirt with a picture of two cowboys jerking each other off. The crowd began throwing beer cups and cans (empty and full), coasters, pizza and tomatoes at the band, which sounded like a pack of howling coyotes let loose in a chicken pen—blowtorch guitar, snarling vocals, bass rumble, snare drum cracking like a nail gun. They were half rock 'n' roll messiahs, half sideshow freaks.

Johnny Rotten sneered the vocals, spitting and baring his teeth. Steve Jones and Paul Cook anchored their whirlwind of sound with napalm-drenched Eddie Cochran riffs and a rock-steady backbeat. Sid Vicious, who could hardly play a lick, made horrible faces and underscored Johnny Rotten's attempts to keep everyone pissed off about everything—

including the notion that something significant might be taking place. All this for the bargain price of three bucks admission.

Lots of people hated the show and didn't get it at all. Did this punk stuff signal the end of rock music as they knew it? Others just figured the Pistols were a freak show buzzing through town on its way to oblivion. *This band sucks. Their music stinks!* No, you frat boys and cosmic cowpokes, that's the scent of history in the air.

There was one disappointment. Lois was sorry, she said, but we couldn't spend the night together. Turned out her mom and dad weren't keen on her having a male guest. How about if she came to Austin next Friday and spent the weekend with me? That way we could definitely get together.

I liked that idea. Friday was the night of the Skunks/Violators premiere at Raul's. Big weekend.

Small wonder I got pneumonia. Playing in two bands required a massive amount of energy. The Violators needed a lot of work, and I put in many nights in a drafty rehearsal studio. The Skunks didn't rehearse much, but we played hard and drank hard. Everyone except Carla smoked cigarettes.

For eighteen months I'd been adding pills to the mix, too. Whenever I wasn't performing or rehearsing or in some girl's arms, I went through the same cycles of misery. Beating yourself up with guilt and thinking that you deserve to be dead won't kill you right away, but it'll push you in that direction.

My pneumonia wasn't serious enough for hospitalization, but it kept me in bed for almost two weeks and gave me a taste of what slow death might be like. Everybody was unhappy with me, since we'd had to postpone the Violators' debut gig a whole two weeks. I was disappointed because the promised overnight weekend with Lois had to be put off, too.

I really couldn't promise to be much better the following weekend, but she wanted to come up. By Thursday, I was still pretty weak. When she arrived on Saturday afternoon, I saw that she'd brought an overnight bag and a big dish of eggplant lasagna. Both were welcome sights.

That night I told her my story, the one I told every girl, and cried as usual. I couldn't help myself. You're in my arms now, kissing me. Listen to my heartbeat. This is who I am, a wounded, bleeding guy. Shattered and incomplete. I'll never love anyone else again, but spend the night with me anyway.

Nothing about Lois had been routine. I hadn't thought ahead about us. I liked her, but for all I knew this might be a one-night fling. I'd been with other girls until pneumonia struck, but Lois and I had been talking on the phone every couple of days. I liked hearing her voice, pitched a little lower than other girls, sexy and self-assured. And she was a great kisser.

When I told her my story, she listened but didn't say anything. Nor did she say anything about the framed 8 x 10 of Dianne and me on the nightstand. I cried on her shoulder; we kissed and made love. I didn't mind that she didn't say anything. What could she say? Nothing ever helped anyway.

Afterward, I couldn't stop talking. The moonlight streamed in and tinted her features in silver and shadows. At one point she looked like Heddy Lamar. Then she became a young Elizabeth Taylor. I saw images from Italian paintings and marble statues, and her Italianness became more apparent. I was in an ecstatic hallucinatory delirium, playfully babbling stream-of-consciousness poetry, musing on her beauty and the way she made me feel. I never wanted to let go of her again.

I hadn't done anything like this since Dianne. I didn't worry about Lois thinking I was a lunatic. I was totally uninhibited, a raving romantic poet. In retrospect, I'm surprised she didn't pack up and drive back to San Antonio during the middle of the night. Next morning, she was still there, trapped in my arms.

Lois' eggplant lasagna was the best thing I'd ever eaten. The herbs and spices and fresh garlic, lots of it, worked magic on me. I felt something good happening.

Lois said she knew the seasonings would be good for me. I needed to take better care of myself, she said. More food like this, more herbs and spices, and vitamins and supplements. Did I take any of those? Not unless you count Librium and Valium, I said. She smiled but didn't think it was funny. She'd been right about my hair and clothes, and the arguments for a lifestyle change were pretty hard to beat.

Another unusual thing about Lois was the loving way she spoke about her parents, without irony or bitterness. She had nothing bad to say about them. I didn't know anybody like that. She could be kind of bossy, but she seemed to have strong nurturing instincts. Being an only child seemed to have forged her confidence and self-assurance. She had great personal style.

Her favorite home was Panama. Cheap rum, exotic scenery, and the possibility of going swimming in the Atlantic in the morning and the Pacific in the afternoon. Surfers, dune buggies, blue water and fresh seafood. The privileged existence Americans enjoyed in the canal zone. That's when she had a Corvair. She liked Mustangs a lot, too. The green one was her third. Her favorite designer was Betsey Johnson, and although she was a Stones fanatic like me, she considered Debbie Harry of Blondie the most exciting pop icon since Mick and Keith had come along. She'd only been back in San Antonio a few months, but she was bored already. The Alamo City was a heavy metal town, and it didn't look like it was going to change any time soon.

"By the way," she said, "you looked good onstage on New Year's. You look like you belong up there."

"Are you coming back to see our first gig?" I said.

"Definitely. I wouldn't miss it for the world, but you'd better take care of yourself so you're up for it. You know what I mean?"

Her smile underscored the double entendre. I kissed her then in a way that left no doubt that I knew what she meant, and that I took it for a promise, too.

Later on I stood in the driveway, watching her Mustang disappear down the street. I thought about that promise, with her perfume in my nose, her taste on my lips. The taste of a knockout kiss.

10. GIMME SOME

The first beer can landed at my feet during the first song. A plastic cup followed. No more than half a dozen cups and cans by the end of the third song, and they rarely came close to hitting anybody. It was a gentle plinking compared to the Sex Pistols, but I still hoped this fad would die soon. I doubted I'd ever get used it.

Count Five's "Psychotic Reaction" kicked off our show with a spiky burst of energy. Next we plowed into "Heart of the City," a pub rocker by Nick Lowe with an urgent bass line. A few dancers tried it and decided they liked it. From there we shifted into power chord rock for "Adolph Hitler Was a Closet Queen," one of Eddie's songs. The lyrics were sick, but the song seemed to energize the crowd. Like a lot of our more disposable early material, it was very much in the room, as the jazz guys liked to say.

Maybe a hundred people in the club, fantastic for a first gig. Maybe canceling the first date had worked in our favor. More time had passed since the Sex Pistols, more publicity on this punk phenomenon. Who were these bands, the Skunks and Violators?

Some just stood there, mystified and uneasy. Others were visibly thrilled or deeply offended. A few yelled insults. Some yelled, "You stink!" The first time I heard it, I was taken aback. It may be hard to believe, but even when we named the band, it didn't occur to me that people might yell that at us, even in jest.

I didn't think of the Skunks as a punk band at all. I saw us as a glorified garage band with ambitions for greatness. We played those songs because they were great fucking songs. We put the same snarl and bombast in everything we played. But that didn't make me a punk rocker or the Skunks a punk rock band. The important thing was that we'd struck a nerve and found our audience.

I had on a white shirt and skinny tie, spiky hair. Eddie had on a black T-shirt, his hair in an early Beatles cut. Billy's hair would've fit right in with the sixties Brit invasion, and he wore a Hawaiian shirt. In 1978 this look was radical enough to piss people off. Frats would hurl insults and beer bottles at us when we walked down the Drag. People in restaurants stared.

"Play some Zeppelin, you faggots!"

"Shut the fuck up," I said to the longhair. A dude with a narrow face, a body with all the muscular bulges and contours of a No. 2 pencil. "This is called 'Heroin,' and it's dedicated to you."

Oddly enough, Pencil Dude knew every word of the Velvet Underground song and proved it by shouting out each line just before I sang it. He did it again on another Velvets song and one by Iggy, too. He did it again at an outdoor show two weeks later. He was sporting a short, spiky haircut. Flash forward two months: Pencil Dude is onstage at Raul's with his own band, the Ideals. His name turns out to be Davy Jones and he's a hellacious guitar player.

There were at least a dozen other future bandleaders in the room. Each of these early gigs was like a recruiting rally, spreading the punk ethos and spawning a gaggle of spiky-haired bands—the Next, the Standing Waves, the Mistakes, the Explosives, the SKPs, Eddie & the Inm8s, the Chickadiesels. Students at the University of Texas spread the word. They were looking for something new. There were oddballs rejects, metal heads who couldn't get gigs anywhere else, art students who would start their first band tonight and buy their first guitar tomorrow, left-wing folkies wanting to give it one last shot, fusion geeks with a superiority complex, and oddballs and outcasts of all stripes: Gator Family, the Delinquents, Sharon Tate's Baby, Terminal Mind, the Blame, the Re*Cords, the Shades, Radio Planets.

They crowded into this funky Tex-Mex joint with cheap wall

paneling and plastic plants in baskets hanging from the ceiling. Three amiable if skeptical Hispanic men ran the place: Raul, Joseph and Bobby. They were stout, round and refrigerator big, but they proved to be gentle, generous and open-minded. If provoked, however, there was no bullshitting around. Bobby could toss out a troublemaker by walking into the guy like a bulldozer. Joseph carried a gun.

They called me Chuy, a common Chicano nickname for Jesse, which made me think of my high school buddies, the Reyes brothers. And they were fond of Lois. She ran the door for us and made sure everybody paid to get in, even so-called friends of the band we'd never laid eyes on.

Fortunately, the fusillades of debris and mock insults would fade quickly, once people learned you didn't have to feign anger or madness to show your appreciation. Clapping, words of encouragement and regular dancing would do nicely, thank you very much.

We finished off the set with "Earthquake Shake," the first song I'd written that was a keeper, revamped for the Skunks. I had notched up the tempo from a grinding blues rocker to bullet-train punk metal.

We ended with pummeling power chords, cymbal smashing and feedback, and ducked into the vest-pocket dressing room backstage. After a minute or so it occurred to me that people were still clapping, whistling and hollering. Holy shit, that wasn't bad. Eddie was smiling, Billy shaking his head, sopping wet with sweat. We did high fives and the soul brother shake, then went back and played a quick encore of "Thigh High," the second song I'd written and not thrown away, and the Who's "My Generation."

Thank-you-very-much-good-night-the-Violators-are-up-next!

The Violators turned lots of regular guys into mouth breathers. Three girls onstage with a guy on bass, playing loud and fast—the fetching young Marilyn pounding the drums like a bratty disciple of Charlie Watts, the thin girl with the waterfall of blonde hair slashing sharp hooks on a '58 Les Paul, and the leather jacket rooster-top redhead sneering as she sang: "You call me on the telephone/You say you don't like being alone/So I say I'm going home/Hey, boy, you wanna come?/Gimme gimme gimme gimme/Gimme gimme gimme some!" A hot song that came on strong, "Gimme Some" either killed 'em or chilled 'em. I was happy with the reaction; it was one of mine. I'd written it after hearing Kathy and Marilyn talking about the sexual attributes of certain guys in local bands.

I should've expected it after the Skunks' set, but there were a lot of freaky reactions to the Violators. You'd have thought the girls were naked. From the opening chords of the Pistols' "Pretty Vacant," people clustered around the stage. Fights broke out for no reason. Things got weirder. We turned in serviceable covers of "Mystery Dance" by Elvis Costello, "Problem Child" by the Damned, and some of the sixties rockers. The people who hated us didn't care if we were playing Sex Pistols or Chuck Berry. They insulted us just as loudly. "You guys suck! Show us your tits!"

I caught Lois' eye when we were playing "Search and Destroy," the last song. Eddie came up to sing, and we blasted out the music as he hammed it up. I looked over at Lois again as we clanged out the final chords, and she was nodding at me with a curious smile. I wondered what it meant.

Several guys were already hanging by the dressing room. Before the night was over, we'd have to enlist Joseph and Bobby to expel the wannabe male groupies who didn't seem to understand the word "no," or even the more explicit "Get the fuck outta here." Apparently some guys assumed that any girl who played in a rock band would jump at the chance to have sex with anything on two legs, any time, any place. The girls were amazingly good sports. The more tasteless and naive the proposition, the more they laughed.

Every night I played with the Violators, some dude would come around and say to one of my bandmates, "Hey, y'all play pretty good for girls."

Singing and playing bass at the same time can be a little tricky, and that's why Eddie sang more songs than I did at the beginning. I was looking for new cover songs that would suit me, but then I decided it would be better all the way around if I concentrated on writing new ones. Some of my songs were failed attempts to learn songs from records. "Gimme Some" came from "Gimme Some Lovin'" by the Spencer Davis Group.

Once I figured out the chords, I realized that the vocal (by fifteen-year-old Stevie Winwood) was too high for me. I couldn't figure out the chords to the Stones' "Stupid Girl," so I wrote "Cheap Girl." The lyrics originated from the trash talk Eddie and I used to banter around with the wild girls at Mother Earth. None of it was meant to be taken seriously. Some people were offended by the tackier lyrics, though, and accused the Skunks of misogyny. I had to look up *misogyny* in the dictionary. I was dismayed to find that anyone thought I might be hateful toward women.

I wrote several other new songs in quick order: "Desperation," which combined a hard-driving beat with a melodic reggae chorus, "6th Street Peggy," a Stonesy rocker about a downtown hooker, and "Something About You Scares Me," a Who-inspired song about Bela Lugosi. Eddie helped me learn some of the tricks of songwriting. He opened my eyes to the fact that the best songs were usually pretty simple. They were just verse/chorus/verse/chorus/bridge/verse/chorus. All you really needed were three chords, some verses, a chorus and a bridge. The bridge holds the parts together. If the other parts are a little tense, you might need a bridge that slows it down for eight bars and gives a sense of release. A bridge can add a ray of hope to a sad song, inject sophisticated melancholy into a brainlessly happy one or turn a handful of fragments into a tune you can't get out of your head.

A really great bridge makes sense of the other parts and creates a feeling of wholeness to the melody and narrative. That's what Lois did for me. She helped me bridge the gap between dreaming about something and doing it. She helped me make sense of my ambitions.

Eddie taught me about song structure and inspired me to put more kick-ass into my playing. That was damned important too, but I was never gonna kiss him for it.

"You ought to concentrate on the Skunks," Lois said. "You're really good. You guys could make it, get a record deal and everything."

We had this conversation two weeks or so after the first gig. Lois was living in Austin now, sharing an apartment with Carla, Kathy and Marilyn.

105

"You think so?" I said. Her opinion took me by surprise. "The Violators are really hot, though."

"They are now, but the Skunks are getting better by leaps and bounds. You're already better than the Violators. You're better musicians, and you write great songs."

"Thanks. I didn't know you felt that way."

She smiled. "There's one other thing you ought to think about."

"What's that?"

"The Violators can get another bass player, but the Skunks are your band."

I assumed she meant mine and Eddie's, though I wasn't sure. I just nodded.

"I like your songs a lot better than Eddie's," she said.

I was vain enough to assume she wasn't saying that because she was my girlfriend. It made me feel good. But I was taken aback that she'd weigh in on important decisions about my music career. She hardly even knew me.

I thought about the things she said, and in the middle of the next Skunks gig, I realized she was right. The Violators were fun, but the Skunks were getting a lot better, and fast. The novelty of having three girls in the band would give us a better shot at a record deal. On the other hand, being the guy who put the "almost" in almost-all-girl-band wasn't a burning ambition of mine.

I needed a band that could become an extension of me. Kathy, Marilyn, Carla and I were crazy about each other, but I didn't think they wanted to be one of my appendages, nor I one of theirs. The girls were surprised when I gave notice, but they got over it quickly. No hard feelings.

Two years later, Kathy would be playing bass in a band called Go-Go's, collecting royalties on a platinum-selling record and living the life of a genuine pop star in Los Angeles. Pretty good for a girl, yeah.

All of a sudden I had a new life. Besides having a band that was making headlines, I had a new girlfriend and we were serious about each other. Lois made sense of the dissonant melodies of my life which, to date, had been working at unproductive counterpoints to each other. She helped me realize that if I wanted this new life, I had to shed some of the old. Start taking vitamins and supplements, eat plenty of garlic, take care of my body. Otherwise I'd crash and burn the way I had in January. The pneumonia was a wake-up call, she said.

I didn't argue with her. I knew I'd have to stay in good shape to make a go of the Skunks. Lois' father Harry was a self-taught expert on vitamins, herbal extracts and other dietary supplements and natural remedies. She got Harry to recommend specific things, and some of the effects were noticeable immediately. A shot of apple cider vinegar and honey every day, for example, prevented cramps in my bass-plucking hand.

Changing the way I dealt with my grief and memories was the hardest part. The subject was so contentious that I came close to walking away from Lois. Her position came out in deadly barbs: "Why do you still have that picture on your nightstand?" "Are you still in love with her?" "How much longer are you planning to cry about it? It's been over two years!" She wanted me to forget about Dianne, get rid of her stuff, not talk about her. Live in the present, forget the past. "You need to just get over it," she said.

We had two major fights about it. I walked out during the second one. The next day Lois said she was sorry. We made up, but nothing had changed. She wanted to just pretend that Dianne had never existed, that the past had never happened.

She was uncomfortable around Dianne's things. The big surrealist painting in my efficiency apartment, for example. I could tell she didn't like it. Put myself in her shoes, I probably wouldn't, either. I could understand her feelings a little, but what was I supposed to do? Getting rid of that painting would be like cutting off part of my body.

If anyone could expect to cut me off from my past, Lois was the one. She was a lionhearted little Leo, a Napoleon in red lipstick and high-heeled boots. She was the gal with a plan, and when she wanted something she went about it with a fierceness I admired. Maybe adding some of that to my own personality would be a good thing. It also looked like the only way I was going to keep her. I had to be fierce, too.

I couldn't stop loving Dianne. She would always be part of me.

Wherever I might go, she would be right here. The tape loop would continue. The guilt and other psychic wounds would remain. I could try to minimize them, but that's all. I learned to compress my feelings about Dianne. I hardened myself to certain emotions, especially those that would make me prone to too much empathy. I virtually shut down certain parts of myself, cauterized others.

My tears dried up. I wouldn't shed another for almost ten years.

The Skunks started kicking ass. I wrote more songs. My voice got stronger. We rode the punk wave. Our fans were intense. They danced like crazy. A girl who worked at a copy shop ran off our posters for free. Guys volunteered to be roadies. Roadies told people they were the managers of the band. Girls volunteered to be groupies. (Billy and I said no thanks; Eddie rose to the challenge.) Photographers gave us cheap live shots. Other clubs started booking us, and we began to break out of the punk/new wave scene, playing where "normal" bands played. We played opening slots at Mother Earth, a few weekend nights at Soap Creek Saloon, clubs in San Antonio, Killeen, Dallas and Fort Worth, and a beachside concert in McAllen. Almost every time we played, we gave autographs.

A deejay/record producer named Joe Gracey said he'd like to record us at his studio, in the basement of the KOKE-FM building. If you went by stereotypes, you'd think that Gracey and the Skunks would be natural adversaries, since, as a country deejay with a twist, Gracey had been one of the key figures behind the rise of redneck rock. But he had also produced the first Fabulous Thunderbirds single, and it smoked. We told Gracey we'd love to do some recording.

Recording with Joe in his basement studio was fast fun. Nothing fancy; the most sophisticated special effect he used was a spring reverb. After the first night we had a nifty sounding demo. A week later, we figured we had a single. Three more weeks and we had almost an LP's worth of material in the can, with just a few details left to fill. The band had been together less than three months. Man, we were on a roll.

After months of pestering the guys at Armadillo World Headquarters to book us, we finally got a call. Would we be interested in opening for the Dictators? Hell yes, we would. We loved their new album and already had the date marked on our calendars. The Taters, as they were known to fans, belonged to that all-important handful of bands now referred to as proto-punk, bands who were cool before 1977 or so, when punk rock raised its spiky head. The gig was a turning point. We'd cracked open another bulwark of the old guard, and it felt good. We got to play for our biggest audience yet, on the same stage that had hosted Roxy Music, Iggy, Freddie King, Captain Beefheart, the Tubes, and Bruce Springsteen and the E Street Band. We got to play as loud as we wanted, too.

After the Dictators show, we regularly opened for touring acts at the Armadillo and other concert venues, but a lot of our lucky breaks occurred on small stages. The night before the Elvis Costello/Rockpile concert that summer, Elvis and Jake Riviera showed up at our gig at Raul's. Elvis accepted our invitation to play on "Mystery Dance." I expected him to take a bow and leave the stage, but he stood there looking at our set list, which was about half cover songs. So I asked if there was anything else he'd like to play. He nodded and said, "Just keep going." So we played our regular set, and he never left. He knew every cover song—John Lennon's "Cold Turkey," the Velvets' "Waiting for My Man" and "Neat, Neat, Neat" by the Damned. We were playing Nick Lowe's "Heart of the City" when Nick himself walked in, followed by two other members of Rockpile, Dave Edmunds and Terry Williams. Nick looked up at the stage, saw Elvis and cracked up laughing.

After our break, Elvis joined us onstage again. This time we let him call the shots. He led the band in "Honky Tonkin'," "Tonight the Bottle Let Me Down," and a half dozen other C&W songs I'd never played. Eddie and Elvis were digging it, though, and so were the people in the club, so what the hell? I kicked on my fuzz box to keep things interesting and thumped along to the only set of two-steppers this band would ever play.

The jam was written up in all the music columns. It was the first time Elvis had sat in with a band in the States. Attendance swelled at our gigs, and we started seeing more comments about our musicianship than jibes about the name of the band.

Later that summer I found my way into the radio station studio where Patti Smith was giving a poetry reading the day before her Austin concert. After the reading, I introduced myself and gave her a gig poster. "Skunks, huh?" she said. "I've got a poem called 'Skunk Dog,' you know."

"Yeah, I know. I like your poetry a lot," I said. "I'm a huge, huge fan. It would be cool if you came down and jammed with us tonight."

"I'll be there," she said, "but I can only play in the key of E, OK?"

Some fans even pushier than me wedged between us then, so I gave her the OK sign and left. I'd gone down to the station hoping for such an outcome, but when I said I was a fan, it was an understatement.

Word that the High Priestess of Punk was going to jam with the Skunks spread like wildfire (with a little help from me), and by the time we arrived at the club, the place was packed. The room buzzed with anticipation.

We started our set without knowing if she'd really show. But then, as if she'd been waiting outside, she strutted through the door. She was dressed black on black, with a black bowler pulled down so low you couldn't see her face unless she looked straight at you.

We brought her on toward the end of the set, with people yelling "Hey Patti!" and requesting songs until Eddie started making some general racket in the key of E minor. I thumped out a fast loping riff that complemented the guitar, and Billy walloped in with a sufficient dosage of thunder and fury. After a minute or two, we settled back to give Patti room to do her thing. She started plucking the unfretted strings, strumming various combinations, just making noise, and the crowd ate it up. The reason Patti said she could only play in the key of E was that E is the approximate chord you get by playing the open strings of a conventionally tuned guitar. I'd read about Patti's guitar skills in *CREEM* magazine. It quoted her making the same admission about her limitations, word for word.

She began chanting some words. I think the lyrics were essentially free form and meaningless. I used to have a cassette of the performance, and the only thing I could decipher was this refrain: "Have no fear/Tell God the Skunks are here/Have no fear, now, now, now/Go tell God the Skunks are here."

Plugging into Patti's star charisma and the crowd's unqualified affection was revelatory. This was the difference between just being good and playing behind a rock star with a walk-on-water reputation. The jam finally ground to an end fifteen minutes later with a fanfare of feedback howls and a long, whooping roar of deification from the crowd. Patti did a people power salute and hopped offstage. She had ripped all six strings from our spare guitar, which belonged to Lois. It was the same Fender Musicmaster Elvis had used.

Patti joined the paying customers on the dance floor, bopping trance-like during the rest of our set, except when we played "My Generation" and she sang on the chorus. During our break, I tried talking to her. I wanted to tell her how much her music had meant to me during the darkness of the last two years, but she kept avoiding me. Later I saw her on the edge of the stage, drinking a longneck beer. When I walked up, she hunkered down, hiding in the shadow of her hat. I was beginning to get annoyed, so I drummed the top of the crown with my fingers and said, "Nice lid you got there, Patti." That tore it. She flashed me a nasty scowl and skulked off into the crowd.

Lois and I went to the concert the following night. Patti and the band put on a great show. Backstage afterward, we crossed paths with her several times, but she was even meaner than the night before. I suppose, being from Texas, I should know better than to mess with a person's hat. Before visiting these parts, however, she might have looked up the origin of the state's name—*tejas*, an Indian term for "friendly."

The night before Blondie's first concert in Austin, I spotted Debbie Harry and Chris Stein standing in front of Mother Earth. Debbie glowed with an unearthly beauty. Confronted with her tumble of platinum hair, awesome cheekbones, wonderful lips and huge, sexy-sleepy eyes, I felt like I was looking at an image on a movie screen. The pet skunk in my arms proved to be a great gimmick for making an introduction. Debbie and Chris loved animals, they said. They thought Flowers was cute. Funny name, too. I had to warn them about Flowers' tendency to bite and scratch when she got excited. I also explained that I was only Flowers'

master by default. Her real owner asked me to skunk-sit for the weekend, and then she never came back. They loved the story.

"By the way, I'm a Skunk, too," I said, handing them a flyer for our gig that night.

"Hey, cool," Chris said. "Looks like the place to be."

"We'd love to come," Debbie said.

Sure enough, the whole band showed up, Debbie, Chris, guitarist Frank Infante, bassist Nigel Harrison, keyboardist Jimmy Destri and drummer Clem Burke. During our last set, Frank, Jimmy and Clem jammed with us on several songs. It was a real kick. They were all fine musicians, but the real standout was Clem. This was the first of many times I would play with him. He's the best drummer in rock. Also a great guy and a snappy dresser.

The night of the concert, we hung around backstage with the band again. They were all swell. Lois got to meet her idol, Debbie Harry, and there was none of the weirdness that had occurred with Patti Smith.

Years later, after the dawn of the Madonna era, Lois and I saw Debbie at a flea market in Manhattan. She was with Andy Warhol, his odd little face framed by one of his outrageous platinum blond wigs.

Debbie, once upon a time the most famous blonde in pop music, was wearing a hat. I didn't mess with it.

At the end of the summer, Kathy, Marilyn and Carla moved to L.A., where they became the Textones. Marilyn got discouraged right away and came back to Austin. Kathy and Carla stuck it out, though. Developing their own Stonesy sound, the Textones eventually found a bass player and drummer (both male) who would stick around long enough for the band to start releasing records and assert itself on the L.A. scene.

Back when Eddie and I talked about starting a new band, moving to L.A. was a part of our rather fuzzily conceived goals. Once the Skunks started gigging, things were happening at such a fast and rewarding pace that the L.A. scheme became moot, in my opinion. Why go anywhere? We could make it from Austin. Moving to L.A. seemed stupid. Eddie was still for it. "Austin sucks," he said. "L.A. is where it's at. We've got connections there. We'll get a record deal. Nothing's happening here."

"What about the album?" I said. "You don't call that happening?"

"Aw, fuck it," he said.

"Look, man, we got a good thing going here," I said. "We'll go to L.A. on tour and kick ass whenever we feel like it."

"You gotta be there, on the scene, if you wanna make it."

"I don't like L.A.," I said. "*Hotel California* and all that shit. Go there and be one of five hundred bands trying to get a gig? Starve to death or get a busboy job while you're trying to get a record deal? We're stars here already. Record companies will come here to check us out. Fuck L.A."

Eddie didn't say anything. Not to me, anyway.

We weren't hanging around nearly as much as before Lois. Eddie was still going out almost every night and bedding down every second or third chick he ran into. I assumed Carla had to know, that they had some kind of arrangement.

I never thought about it, though, until a friend of Eddie's came to town on business. I think she worked for a record label in L.A. Eddie and I were renting a house in South Austin, and four nights in a row the girl came home with him. My bedroom was down the hall from Eddie's, and the racket she made when they were having sex was incredible. Lois and I had never heard anything like it. But the fact that the girl was also a friend of Carla's made the situation a little weird, even for Eddie. He was my buddy and Carla was my friend, but I didn't say anything to him about it, and I certainly didn't say anything to Carla. Lois didn't either.

Carla found out anyway. The sound of screeching tires one night after band rehearsal was our first clue. Eddie, Billy, Lois and I were standing in the front yard as Carla's Mustang came careening around the corner. Eddie dove out of the way as the car jumped the curb and plowed toward him, lurching to a stop just shy of the house. She jumped out, yelling curses at Eddie for fucking a friend of theirs behind her back and in the blink of an eye, smashed him with a roundhouse right that knocked him sprawling. A few more blistering curses and she took off again, burning rubber around the corner.

So much for my assumptions. I made a mental note never to mess with Carla.

Eddie seemed different after that. I assured him that neither Lois nor I had finked on him, but I got the impression he didn't believe me. There was still the same ferocious spark when we played, but also a new rivalry. When I sang, he jumped around more than ever, posing and doing Pete Townsend leaps and windmilling his power chords. Between gigs, we didn't talk a lot. But things seemed to be going great for the band. The personal stuff, I figured, would sort itself out.

That September a band called the Huns played their first gig at Raul's with a snarling determination to seize the day. From their jagged haircuts, makeup, artfully torn clothes and calculated anger, it was obvious that the band took this punk thing seriously. Not one of them had invested more than six months practice on his instrument, and at times it sounded like much less. But many people in the room seemed to regard the Huns as Austin's Great Punk Hope.

Joseph had pulled me aside and advised me that I might want to check this band out. "A couple of these guys are real assholes, Chuy," he told me. "But I don't know, I think they're gonna put on a really wild show."

One of the first songs they played was "Something About You Bores Me," a parody of my Bela Lugosi ballad, "Something About You Scares Me." In a vitriolic preamble, the singer, Phil Tolstead, snarled, "The Rolling Stones and the Skunks suck, man. They're boring old farts. They're fucking dinosaurs. The Huns are God!"

Lois and I loved hearing the Skunks mentioned in the same sentence with the Stones, but the band's follow-through was laughably inept. The rhythm section was a knock-kneed mess; only drummer Tom Huckabee sounded as if he had any potential. Phil's singing sounded like a whiny kid with a head cold throwing a tantrum.

The band's charm had worn thin by the time they played "Glad He's Dead," about the Kennedy assassination. Was this a desperate attempt to be daring or a truly tasteless joke? We didn't know and didn't care; we were out of there.

Cop cars were pulling into the parking lot as we left. Probably just another noise complaint, we figured. Who could've guessed that history was about to happen? From all accounts, calling it a "riot" was an exaggeration, but "Raul's Riot" made great copy.

As Lois and I drove down the Drag on our way home, Officer Steven Bridgewater sidled up to the stage, waiting for the song "Eat Death Scum" to end so he could tell the band members to turn it down. The song is a violent diatribe against a girl responsible for giving a guy a sexually-transmitted disease, except that Phil seemed to be singing the lyrics to Officer Bridgewater. But the cop wasn't in the mood to be serenaded thusly. He stepped onstage to halt the show and Phil kissed him. That tore it; Bridgewater started to arrest Phil, who began yelling, "Start a riot! Start a riot!"

Bridgewater was calling for backup when the guitarist bonked him on the head. General mayhem ensued. Bobby, the refrigerator-size bouncer, saw two guys with blackjacks beating up punks and sprang to the punks' defense. Turned out the guys were plainclothes cops. Things got worse, but the so-called riot ended before anyone was seriously injured.

The Austin music scene, however, previously known mostly for its long hair and boots and solemn respect for the blues, would never be the same. The Huns were infamous overnight, and so was Raul's. More people started coming to our gigs, too, whether we played at Raul's or other places. Some people were disappointed that the Skunks weren't as outrageous as the band that caused the Raul's riot, but sufficient numbers kept coming back to hear the music and dance and have fun. The Huns later recruited a good guitarist and a fair bass player, released a single, and broke up. Phil became an evangelical missionary. Tom Huckabee became a Hollywood screenwriter/producer and one of my best friends.

The basement demo tapes we'd begun in the spring were sounding so good that Joe Gracey suggested we put out a single. He and his business partner, musician-turned-attorney Bobby Earl Smith, had a small record label. By the fall we had more than an LP's worth of material in the can. Why not an LP? they said.

We thought that was a great idea. The LP was slated for a January 1979 release. KLBJ-FM was already playing the tapes regularly and getting lots of requests. We thought we should insist on having a record contract. Joe and Bobby Earl took it under careful consideration and agreed. Weeks passed; no contract. One night at an after-hours party I bugged them about it. A few minutes later, they herded us into the kitchen. Bobby Earl had drawn up a contract on a cocktail napkin. What could go wrong? We signed it.

However, it had become increasingly clear that all was not well with the Skunks. Eddie's playing was better than ever, but he sometimes sulked onstage and continued trying to upstage me. A rift had developed, and I was pretty sure it went beyond the business with Carla.

Maybe he was jealous. I was becoming more comfortable with my onstage persona, and I was singing and writing more songs. We still played covers, which meant that Eddie still sang a lot, but my originals dominated our LP. Writers mentioned my songs whenever they wrote about the band, and the term cheap girl had entered the lexicon of local slang.

People were asking me a lot of strange questions. *What's the band gonna do next year, Jesse? Are you moving to L.A.? Are the Skunks going to break up?* Rumors hardly ever surprised me, but eventually I started feeling paranoid. Did these people know something I didn't?

The answer was yes. After our New Year's Eve gig, a mutual friend took me aside for one of those I-thought-you-should-know conversations. Eddie, she said, was leaving the band to go on tour with Elvis Costello—as a roadie! Apparently Eddie had told every musician in town except Billy and me.

Billy was furious. He hated Eddie for it. I was crushed. I felt betrayed. How could he do such a thing? We were going places. Why didn't he at least tell me? Richard, our road manager, tried to talk Eddie out of it. Billy and I wouldn't stoop that low. If he's out, he's out. Fuck Eddie.

The local press duly reported the news. *Rumors*, a weekly entertainment rag, quoted me saying, "Maybe he'll start going by Eddie Muñoz now." Music writers seemed gleeful about stripping "Fazz" from his identity. He was "ex-Skunks guitarist Eddie Muñoz" from then on. I wondered if Eddie was embarrassed about his last name. I certainly didn't think he should be, but if he was, I was glad.

Eddie got his quotes, too: "We started the band as a joke. So what's the big deal?"

The following year, after touring with Costello's road crew, Eddie got a phone call from Carla, who felt a twinge of regret for dumping him. She told him about a guy named Peter Case who had auditioned as a rhythm guitarist for the Textones after she and Kathy parted company.

Carla didn't think Case was right for her band, but they got along well and liked all the same records, so when she learned that he was starting his own band, she recommended Eddie. Eddie auditioned and got the job. The band, called the Plimsouls, became one of L.A.'s more successful bands of the era.

I wrote a song about Eddie called "Slander," one of my best to date. My anger fueled a sustained burst of creativity. I became more prolific, more determined, more fierce than ever.

Lois steeled me. "You can do it. Find another guitar player and make Eddie eat his words." Her powerful eyes held me like a vise. "It's your band, you know."

She'd said those words once before, hadn't she? Now it sounded prophetic. I was glad she was on my side.

Richard Luckett, our roadie, put up some flyers for a new guitarist. Billy and I auditioned several. Most of them were so lame, we thought there must be a language barrier. We'd say, "Play aggressively, like Pete Townsend, for example." They thought we said, "Play wimpy, like you took some downers." A few weeks went by and things looked bleak. One afternoon Richard went to see a friend who lived in a co-op dorm off campus. Walking down the hall, he heard some guys jamming. The lead player was good. Richard set up an audition. His name was Jon Dee Graham. He was tall and skinny with tawny hair, good-looking. Only nineteen years old, a freshman at UT, enrolled in the honors program. He played a red semi-hollow-body Gretsch guitar through a punchy little Sunn amplifier he'd borrowed from a friend.

Two songs later he had the job.

He had fantastic energy. He was funny, literate and easy-going. He was a quick learner, although he tended to play some songs his own way. We'd work out the fine points later. I hated the thought of losing any momentum. I didn't want Eddie to think he'd have the last laugh. The Skunks was not a joke.

With a little work, Jon Dee Graham would do fine. He didn't know it yet, but he'd have to quit school. I'd get Richard to break the news later.

Jon Dee learned the songs in a week. We played our first gig two weeks later. "Hey, this guy is pretty good," people said. "But what happened with Eddie?" A month later, they were saying, "This guy is great! What's his name?" Two months later: "Who the fuck is Eddie?"

11. DON'T PUSH ME AROUND

In 1979, it seemed possible that a band like mine could go to New York City, play a few gigs, and get discovered. We had a record and a van and a big live sound. If we could just get on a stage before the right people, we knew we'd kill 'em. Other bands were doing it the same way. The punk/new wave scene was like a resistance movement, and DIY was the route bands like the Skunks had to take if they wanted to get somewhere. Bands did things this way in the early sixties, relying on themselves or going to small independent record companies, using independent promotion and distribution, making things up as they went along. In the late sixties the industry became centralized, monolithic and practically unapproachable. That was the monster most of us blamed for foisting horrible music on everyone.

Now there was a vital, somewhat nebulous network willing to help you get publicity, bookings, airplay, maybe entrée to a major label. You hit the road, built your reputation as a live act, pushed your homemade records and went straight to New York or L.A. to make a frontal assault on the record company hotshots in person.

It sounds a little vague and naive, but DIY had plenty of believers. DIY had made big stars of the Police, for example, or so went the popular legend. Sometimes I wondered if it was just a fairy tale made up by cynical record company executives to make bands like the Police seem more appealing. Most of the time, though, I believed wholeheartedly in the legend and thought it would work for the Skunks.

I felt entitled to some good luck. I guess I thought fate might give me a break after Dianne. I carried the tragedy like a stigmata, a source of inner strength and pain. Maybe it was part of a Jesus complex. At least once a day, the tape loop played, but I never cried, never spoke of it. I made veiled references to my story in my songs. In "Haunted House" the listener might assume that the references to death and ghosts were metaphorical, but they weren't: "I am living in a haunted house/Her memory lives here, but she's checked out." "That's What You Mean," which churned along on a minor key bass riff set to a reggae beat, was more or less about a tragic love affair, but when I wrote the words, I returned to the same well of sadness: "Salty pillows from my tears/ wasted words, wasted years/oh, depression, oh despair/how I wish I did not care." No one had to know where these words came from. People rarely asked about song lyrics anyway.

The stigmata helped me maintain a sense of fearlessness. I never worried about tragic consequences, say, on a road trip. I figured, What's the worst that can happen? I've already been there.

The first Skunks single, *Can't Get Loose b/w Earthquake Shake,* was sweet revenge. I'd gotten fed up with Joe Gracey and Bobby Earl Smith. They kept putting off releasing our LP, each time giving us an excuse that was less credible than the previous one. Finally one afternoon we borrowed a two-track reel-to-reel recorder and recorded the two songs in a friend's garage, then overdubbed the vocals in Richard's kitchen. We mailed the tape and $348 to a pressing plant in Dallas, and two weeks later, we had our record. Our friends the Bodysnatchers were officially the first Austin punk band to release a single, but ours made a lot bigger impact.

The only logical place to have the release party was Inner Sanctum Records, the nerve center for the scene. We spread the word with a small ad in the paper and announcements by our friendly radio deejays, and we plastered the Drag with flyers. Nothing happened without flyers.

The party was a great kickoff. We played for an hour in the parking lot to an enthusiastic crowd. Beer was available for fifteen cents a cup, and the air was charged with excitement. People lined up to get their records signed and showered us with congratulations. The store sold over 300 singles in the first three days. Everyone knew we were leaving for New York two days later to play CBGB's.

Playing club dates in New York didn't mean we'd hit the big time, but it was a giant step. If we never accomplished another thing, having a clipping with our name in a CBGB's ad to paste in my Skunks scrapbook would be very cool. Even the way we'd gotten the booking was cool—John Cale, a founding member of the Velvet Underground and one of the godfathers of punk/new wave, had set it up for us.

Cale was on a roll in 1979, a respected cult figure with a handful of intelligent, quirky solo LPs. His stature was also greatly enhanced by his production work with Nico and Patti Smith's groundbreaking debut, *Horses.* His new music was darker and stranger than ever, with cryptic references to mercenaries and political intrigue. The Skunks opened for Cale at the Armadillo in Austin and again at the Sunken Gardens in San Antonio. His band was made up of the crème of the Manhattan underground scene, and both shows were sensational. We hung around with the band, quite a bit, probably amusing them as much as they impressed us, and after the San Antonio gig I gave Cale a cassette from a recent Skunks gig while I took the opportunity to compliment him profusely. He thanked me for the compliments and for the tape. I entertained a fantasy that he'd call me back a few days later, raving about the songs, saying he wanted to get us signed to a major label so he could produce our record.

A few weeks later, Lois and I flew to New York with a vague but determined plan to book some dates for the band. For the first couple of days, the only good thing that happened was seeing Lou Reed play a fantastic show at the Bottom Line. The third night, we went to the Mudd Club, one of the city's trendiest night spots. Getting the velvet rope parted for us seemed like miracle enough (even with the help of Lois' best friend, Melanie Popkin, who worked for a record company), but that was before we spotted John Cale. I had to elbow Mick Ronson and Ian Hunter aside to get to him.

"Hello, Texas," Cale said in his ominous Welsh baritone. "Thanks for the tape, by the way. We listened to it quite a lot on the road."

I told him how much the compliment meant to me and then went out on a limb and told him why we were in town.

"Call my manager, Jane Friedman," he said. "Tell her I said to help you."

Just like that, we were in. Jane Friedman could open all the doors for us. Besides managing Cale, she'd worked with Television and Patti Smith. Sometimes it paid to read every word on the back of album covers, along with every issue of *Rolling Stone* and *CREEM*.

Friedman didn't even ask Lois and me to have a seat when we were led into her office. She just picked up the phone and called the people who'd been treating us like pesky insects. The first was Hilly Christal, who managed CBGB's. "Hilly, it's Jane," she said. "Listen, you've got John playing there on the 11th and again next month, right? OK, I've got a band here from Texas called the Skunks. . . Yeah, so how about a weekend in August? Yeah, they need a good weekend slot. . . OK, that sounds good." Next she called the managers of Max's Kansas City, Hurrah's, Tier 3, Maxwell's and so on. She never got put on hold, never had to leave a message, never asked if they would book us but when. This was how things could work with DIY when you had a little l-u-c-k on your side.

Because of the high hopes and big stakes, it seems odd that we'd wait until a week before our grand adventure to buy a van. But that's what we did. It was a beat-up '69 GMC Travel-all, a sort of stone-age SUV, for $600.

The truck's original owner was the Texas Highway Department, and it had a lot of rough miles on it. It was official bright yellow with a big blue steel brush guard. The driver's side door bore a crude painting of an armadillo leaping in front of a Texas flag, just the kind of hokey cosmic cowpoke image I despised. We were going to pull into Manhattan looking like the Beverly Hillbillies.

The engine ran, the wheels rolled, the lights lit, but otherwise only Fred Flintstone's car was more primitive. No dashboard lights, no radio, no heater. We used vise grips for window cranks. The doors didn't lock, so we secured them with chains and padlocks. Despite its shortcomings, we had a perverse affection for the ugly yellow truck. It was so uncool it was cool. We thought it might even get us to New York.

The truck had some play in the steering when we first bought it. The second day on the road, the problem went from moderately bad to slapstick bad. Even on a straightaway the driver had to constantly correct the drift, and it swerved so much we got seasick. We were pulled over by every state trooper between New Orleans and New Jersey. They assumed we were drunk. They were often right, but somehow we talked them out of it.

Just a few miles across the Alabama line, the wheel seized up. Manhattan seemed like the other side of the world.

After getting towed to the next town, a mechanic told us the problem was the steering gear. It was dry as a bone. "Don't you boys in Texas believe in grease?" He patched things together and, after charging us a mere $10, sent us on our way, shaking his head.

Next to beer, which we drank like water, our favorite distraction was fireworks. We shot off bottle rockets by the gross at other cars on the road, at each other. Smoke bombs, cigarette loads, M-80s, whatever. If it blew up, smoked, flew or fizzed, we shot it off.

Not all of our pranks involved explosives. Once our roadie Richard made the mistake of falling asleep during a poker game, so we duct-taped him to the bed. When we were done he looked like a silver mummy. The only part of his body left free was his mouth, so he'd be able to scream when he woke up.

And he did.

We were a three-piece band from Texas on a no-budget tour, in a city that ate suckers like us the way a whale feeds on plankton. But we were true believers; in the way that a Christian believes praying and doing the right thing will get you to heaven, we believed that having the guts to come to New York and play our brand of rock 'n' roll would make something happen. Some people might've said we were shooting bottle rockets at the moon by coming here, but with three and a half weeks' worth of gigs, including Friday and Saturday at CBGB's, we had a fighting chance to get noticed.

We arrived in midtown Manhattan at the beginning of rush hour. Assaulted by the city's noise and smells and vertical visual rush, I felt exhilarated and a little scared. My heartbeat kicked up. My teeth showed when I smiled. Richard, so far the only one brave enough to drive in the city, pointed out landmarks when he wasn't shouting curses at traffic. Billy, doing his Rodney Dangerfield routine, kept saying things like, "I hope we don't get robbed and killed on our first day here."

We were stopped in front of the New York Public Library. Forgetting the comic appearance of our vehicle, we tried to affect nonchalance as people pointed and stared. Richard had some previous New York experience, but I could claim only the one trip of a month ago, the first time I'd been out of Texas except for a few border town trips. Nor were the other two Skunks sophisticated travelers. Billy was from Beeville, a South Texas farm town. Jon Dee had grown up in Quemado, a tiny village on the Mexican border. The library's stone lion seemed to have Jon Dee hypnotized now. "We don't belong here," he said in a shaky voice. "Let's just go home."

"Get real, man," I said, trying to project confidence. "This is gonna be fun. Don't worry. What could go wrong?"

With perfect timing, the light turned green and our Flintstone wagon refused to go. We'd been in Manhattan fifteen minutes and our truck had broken down. Honking and insults filled the air.

The mechanical problem was fairly simple; two parts of the clutch had separated. Richard rigged them back together, and we were on our way. Jon Dee looked convinced that we would be eaten alive before sundown.

Down in the Bowery section of Manhattan's Lower East Side, CBGB's was the legendary matrix of the American underground, proto-punk music scene. It was the house of Blondie, the Ramones, Johnny Thunders and the Talking Heads. It was the Los Alamos of rock 'n' roll.

The place is actually a dump, a room a lot narrower than deep, not much larger than Raul's. The most unique thing about it is having to go through the backstage area in order to get to the rest room—neither of which is very nicely appointed. The PA and stage lights, however, are first rate.

By the time we take the stage, I'm speeding on adrenaline. I plug in my bass and step up to the mic as the emcee announces us:

Ladies and gentlemen, from Austin, Texas, the Skunks!

The room was full, front to back, with a mix of spiky hair, rock 'n' roll shags, Lower East Side musicians and other slackers, the bridge-and-tunnel crowd, tourists. Leather jackets on everyone, which was amazing, because back then they cost a lot more, and you had to work to find them.

The applause was polite in a tight-assed way—nothing like the whoops and whistles back home. No free rides in this town, buster.

I swig my beer and thump my bass—loud enough to rattle everything. Perfect. The monitors are nice and loud. Billy thraps on his snare, Jon Dee stabs a couple of licks, then clangs a power chord, teases out some feedback. We're ready. I nod at Billy. He clicks his sticks for the count and we crash in—tight, loud and mean. The first song is a 90-mile-per-hour instrumental called "Wild Rumpus"—the Ventures meet the MC5—and it goes over OK. We bang out the rest of the set: "Out of Style," a bit of vitriol directed at Eddie, then a change-up with the punky verse-reggae chorus of "Desperation," a structure I ripped off from the Police. We get a bit of applause, not much. "Cheap Girl" is next. Because of its tacky, sexist lyrics, this song will cause me more trouble than anything else I'll do during the Skunks' career, but it never fails to go over. Even here, where 99 percent of the audience has never heard it before, people are bopping their heads to the beat, catching on to the hooky melody instantly. Some decent applause now, and the rest of the set goes over OK. We slam out the last chord to "Can't Get Loose," and that's it, we're done.

Applause but no big surge of noise for an encore. We go backstage. Instead of feeling let down we backslap and high five each other, because it feels pretty good. Just to have come this far and survived, and we did better than that. Tomorrow night we'll kill 'em.

John Cale wasn't there, but the rest of his band was, and some other local musicians, too. Our best friend in town was George Scott III, Cale's bass player. A great bass player with a unique sound, George also played with the Ray-Beats and Lydia Lunch's band, 8-Eyed-Spy. We were staying in George's apartment, which was just around the corner from CBGB's.

Saturday night Margaret Moser was at the show. Margaret was going to write up an exciting on-the-scene chronicle of our Manhattan assault. The truth was we didn't kill 'em after all. We just held our own again. No salivating New York rock critics or record company executives, no encore. But we still had more gigs to play. Something exciting could still happen.

George's apartment, barely half a block away, was on the fifth floor, a classic nineteenth-century immigrant's dump with the bathtub in the kitchen and one window facing the street. That window was important to us. We left our truck on the street, with all our gear in back, even my Fender basses, Jon Dee's red Gretsch guitar, and Lois' Fender Musicmaster. We never left guitars and amp heads in the truck, but that night the thought of carrying the stuff up five flights of stairs inspired us to make an exception. One of us would stay by the window at all times, keeping an eye on the street.

That way nothing could happen.

We stayed up all night, listening to records and drinking. We drank too many Budweisers. We got sleepy, less diligent about watching the truck. The next morning, my Fender basses, the two guitars, my powerful Sunn bass amp, Jon Dee's amp and Billy's snare drum were gone. We called the police. They came. They took a report.

Did they think we'd get our gear back? *Oh, sure, absolutely. Ha, ha, ha. You oughta be more careful next time, Tex. This is Manhattan.*

We were devastated. I could have cried about losing those P-basses. Especially the '63, my first Fender. That really hurt. Jon Dee cried. He'd learned Chuck Berry on that Gretsch. It was his first, his only electric guitar. "There's not another guitar like it," he kept saying. "I'll never find another one, never."

It was Sunday morning. We were supposed to play Boston Tuesday. George promised he'd find guitars and amps for us to borrow. That was good enough for me. We could still do it. No need to panic.

Creatively, and usually when it came to business, the Skunks was my band. But Billy and Jon Dee saw this as a matter of survival.

"No, let's go home," Jon Dee said. "We're beat."

"We're in over our heads. Let's go now, before something else happens," Billy said.

Richard was on my side. The roadie.

They didn't give a shit. Let's just go. Now. Cut our losses.

I wanted to stay and slug it out. We had a mission. Drive back to Texas with our tails between our legs? It was unthinkable.

We left Manhattan on a cold, gray dawn, four guys stinking of club grime and clammy desperation. We'd been up the better part of thirty hours. I still had on my polka-dot glitter stage socks, which went so well with my pointy-toed pimp shoes. They looked sad now. The truck was swerving worse than ever, despite our best attempts to make it appear sober. An hour outside Manhattan a New Jersey trooper pulled us over. We told him our sorry tale and asked if he wouldn't just let us continue on our miserable way. He said he'd like for us to step outside the van and asked for permission to search it.

The trooper found Richard's stash of pot. Wrinkling his nose at the dark green flakes, the trooper said, "This looks like homegrown."

"Yes, sir, it is homegrown," Richard said, his head hanging low. "It's pretty bad stuff."

The trooper surveyed our downbeat combo of moppy heads and bleary eyes and said, "You have any more drugs in the van?"

"No, sir," Richard said.

"Then why don't you dump that baggie out on the road here and you fellows try to be careful on your way back to Texas."

Richard then emptied his disreputable stash into the New Jersey ditch and we made ourselves gone from that place. It was a long trip. We were so hangdog we didn't shoot off any fireworks until we crossed the Texas state line.

New York had carved another notch on her belt, having crushed yet another band of struggling rockers beneath her spiky boots. As soon as we got another vehicle, we'd be back. And this time we'd kill 'em.

Back in Austin, the Skunks regrouped, duct-taped our wounds, played harder than ever, wrote new songs. Despite the trip's hardships, the experience made the band tighter emotionally and musically. Every night songs morphed in new directions; every week we evolved a little more. Jon Dee was blossoming as a musician at an astonishing rate. He was constantly finding new chords, new voicings and sounds on his guitar.

The new songs Jon Dee and I wrote more than made up for the ones we dropped from the show, including the covers we used to do with Eddie. Our repertoire could stretch to four sets now, which meant we could play in clubs that would only hire one band for the night. Few other bands in the Raul's scene could handle that kind of gig. Most bands had maybe an hour's worth of material. We also played parties, especially fraternity parties, which paid well. We did it for the money and we enjoyed the work. We were a star band and a bar band, and we were proud that we could do it without compromising our material.

The punk scene, which was still synonymous with Raul's, had moved to the left of the Skunks. The hot bands were punkier, edgier or artier than us, or maybe just new. Some of the fans were put off by our big guitar sound and were going in the direction of minimalist guitars, cheesy organs, quirky stuff.

Mother Earth was by now utterly obsolescent. A funky but chic south Austin joint called the Continental Club became our main hangout, whether or not we were playing there. It was located on Congress Avenue in a laid-back part of town where you were likely to see tire swings in the yards and a great Tex-Mex cafe was never more than a couple of blocks away.

The cheap rents attracted a lot of musicians to the neighborhood, especially blues musicians. The Armadillo and the Austin Opera House (owned by Willie Nelson) were a few blocks away. The Continental opened in 1957 as a private supper club featuring touring acts like Glenn Miller and Tommy Dorsey. The place went burlesque in the sixties, featuring notorious strippers like Bubbles Cash and Candy Barr. In 1979, a bunch of like-minded guys took it over so they'd have a place to drink and hear their favorite bands. Luckily, the Skunks was one of them.

The Continental gave us choice weekend bookings. The stage was just as small as Raul's and the air conditioner was certainly no better, but we had a blast playing there. The audiences were rowdy and loved to dance. The club's partners—Wayne, Roddy, Summer Dog, Robin and Roger One Knite—knew how to have a good time, especially after dark. Wayne Nagel, who booked the club, became a good friend of the band. When the Stones played in Houston, the Continental gang organized a caravan and booked hotel suites for us. Closing time meant nothing to those guys except a bolted door and an open bar for their friends.

I loved those guys. It was like being in the Rat Pack.

Lois and I had been using the word "love" for quite some time, though I wasn't ready to move in with her. She gave me space. I was also getting tight with Lois' parents in suburban San Antonio. I'd relax on their sofa and drink Scotch with Harry while Helen and Lois cooked up sensational meals. I discovered chicken cacciatore, homemade gnocchi, linguini and clam sauce and other Italian dishes from Helen's spicy repertoire. Garlic became like a drug to me. I'd never been in a house with such wonderful smells, where every dinner was a cause for celebration.

I loved the Richwines' Italian traditions. I enjoyed hearing the family lore, including vignettes of life in the Pennsylvania steel towns where Harry and Helen had grown up, Harry's combat experience in the Pacific in World War II and details of their time in California, New York, Arizona, Germany, Panama, Iceland. There was one constant Lois recalled about all the places they lived: walking home and smelling her mother's cooking from blocks away.

Maybe it was the ironic contrast to our rock 'n' roll Bohemian lifestyle in Austin that made weekends with the Richwine family so appealing. Simple pleasures, no worries about band rivalries, hostile rock critics or sociopath agents and club owners.

The future was uncertain, but we didn't worry about it. Rock 'n' roll was what I was about. I loved playing enough that I didn't have to have truckloads of money. On the other hand, failure was not an option.

Lois believed in me. She was certain I would make it.

One day when I was back at my apartment, I took a long, hard look at Dianne's huge purple surrealist painting and a few other large keepsakes. I didn't know what to do with them, but I knew if I kept looking at them, I might start crying again. Finally I swallowed hard, closed my eyes and carried them to the dumpster.

12. WHAT DO YOU WANT

Six months after our first New York trip, we went back for more. On the way up we played New Orleans, Baton Rouge and Atlanta. In New York we did CBGB's, Max's Kansas City, the Eighties, TR3, the U.K. Club and a handful of other places.

Nobody missed the hillbilly wagon. We rode in comfort in a 1974 Open Road RV, playing poker, watching TV, napping, playing guitar and writing songs. This is the life, we said, hoisting cocktails around the table. Theoretically, at least, the RV was a motel room and kitchenette on wheels. Unfortunately, the RV allowed us to experience all the problems of a used car and an old house in one package. The engine broke down frequently, and when we were stationary for any length of time the roof leaked; the toilet overflowed, it was cold and it smelled bad. And it's almost impossible to park a house in Manhattan.

The best of the three southern gigs was Atlanta. We'd be coming back there for sure. New York had its ups and downs. With so many bands gravitating there, it was possible to feel like another generic cluster of starry-eyed naifs, though I was too cocky for that. All it took was one person who could tip the balance in your favor—a deejay, an A&R person, agent, whatever. You never knew.

We trudged through ice and snow to put up gig posters, called rock critics and put them on the guest list, checked in with our contacts at Stiff and IRS Records. Friends like George Scott helped us cultivate other contacts. Some of them came out to see us play. We did radio interviews, especially in the college towns on the way to New York. You do whatever you can to get a buzz going.

We rocked like hell at CBGB's. The room was full both nights, but the response was probably better the first time we played there. Hard to figure. A power pop band called the Colors played before us. They were cool. Great hair. Almost a new wave bubble gum act. We made $150 each night, which wasn't bad, all things considered.

I felt an absolute righteousness in our mission there. Maybe because I'd spent countless hours listening to New York bands and reading about them and Andy Warhol and the avant-garde scene. Maybe because it was the anti-Texas. Just being in New York was like being on speed. No matter which bridge or tunnel took you into the city, whether you drove in or took a train or bus, you could feel your heartbeat and respiration kick up as soon as you got close. The city had that power. It was addictive as hell; the trick was knowing when to stop.

"I love you tall Texas boys," Lydia Lunch said after our gig at Tier 3. "You're so cute."

Lydia was the dark princess of the New York punk scene. In one LP jacket shot, she's wearing a black leather bra studded with metal spikes. Porcupine boobs. Her reputation as a dominatrix and sex addict preceded her, but she was sweet in casual conversation, and I thought she was interesting. She said she'd always wanted to party in a band's RV. I promised to give her the nickel tour.

We slow-danced to a couple of songs later on (no spikes that night). Afterward I went back to my table to fetch my beer. A girl I'd been talking to earlier smiled and said, "Go ahead and fuck her, if that's what you want to do. See what it does for your career."

Wow. Was I that transparent? I thought about some things, including the fact that Lois was back home waiting, taking care of Skunks business and feeding our cats.

"Some other time," I told Lydia, and kissed her good night.

The temptations facing a young musician on the road are mighty, but none of them ever seemed worth the risk of losing what I had at home. I didn't want to have a guilty conscience next time I saw Lois. Billy also remained true to his girlfriend on the road, and so did Jon Dee—most of the time. Sometimes the combination of availability and the convenience of the RV was too much to resist.

Drugs weren't a big part of the Skunks saga, either. Richard smoked pot every day. I constantly harassed him about it or booby-trapped his joints with cigarette loads. I hated the smell and it made my skin feel itchy. I didn't like the way it turned normal people into mouth-breathing zombies or Grateful Dead fans.

Jon Dee was acquiring a taste for methamphetamine, although the rest of us thought it was only an occasional indulgence. Cocaine was abundant, and it was hard to pass up a free toot when it was offered, and it was offered frequently. But it was like caviar to a poor man; sure, I enjoyed it when it was free, but cocaine was the last thing I ever thought about spending money on. I was too high on playing rock 'n' roll to risk screwing it up for a temporary artificial high.

We drank like fish, though, especially Budweiser, the king of beers. At a gig I might have five or six beers, but the effects seemed to be minimized by the adrenaline buzz of playing rock 'n' roll. We also drank while driving between gigs, maintaining the ridiculous fiction that it enhanced our alertness behind the wheel. Fortunately we never received any tragic lessons on how fatally stupid that notion could turn out to be.

Occasionally I had moments of self-doubt. Maybe I had a few details of the Police myth wrong, maybe they had a little more help than they admitted. After three weeks away from home, the cracks began to show. Sometimes we'd play several nights in a row, one day banging into the next; then there'd be several days in between with little to do. Especially with no money and empty stomachs. It was bitterly cold.

Our base of operations was a trailer park on Tonnelle Avenue in North Bergen, New Jersey. We lived on about five bucks a day. We'd go to the diner down the street and order a bagel with cream cheese and onion and drink as much coffee as we could hold. We stole crackers. Our meals in the RV consisted mostly of potatoes and bread, or peanut-butter sandwiches. We drank Wilson's whiskey. It was the cheapest we could find. The label said, "Wilson's—That's all!" The slogan intrigued us. What did it mean? This is all you get, so don't expect anything else?

Twenty years later I would stumble across the secret to this mysterious epigram while researching a documentary on the World War I era. Turns out "Wilson, that's all" was one of Woodrow Wilson's reelection campaign slogans in 1916. "He kept us out of war" is probably better remembered, despite the fact that we declared war against Germany six months after Wilson won the election.

We suffered through a wet, icy, mildewy winter in our RV at the trailer park. The bathroom stank, even though we rarely used it, preferring the park facilities. We mainly used the bathroom as a hiding place for the propane tank whenever we went through one of the inter-borough tunnels, where it was illegal to drive a vehicle with a propane tank. The cops never searched the bathroom, and luckily we never exploded, despite all the fireworks we used.

Outside it looked as though we'd crash-landed on a gray planet. The snow on the asphalt plains around us turned gray from thawing into slush and refreezing. Gray buildings, gray sky. We'd sit on the roof of the RV drinking Wilson's whiskey and belching potato stew and coffee and bagels with cream cheese and onions. We'd toast each other, *Wilson's, by God! That's all!* Laughing and repeating in-jokes until each one had been worn to a nub. Our language was a reflexive code of jokes and expressions, sighs, worn-out cassette tapes ("If you play XTC one more time, Richard, I'm gonna kill you") and riffs from songs we'd been working on.

At some point, Jon Dee mentioned that he'd lost his father to lung cancer just two years ago, when he was seventeen. I knew it affected him deeply, but he never talked about it and I never brought it up. Billy's parents had divorced, and I knew his father was a hard man to get along with but we never talked about that, either.

I'd stopped telling my August 16 story before we started this band.

These days, on the rare occasions it seemed necessary to tell, the listener was invariably a male friend. I could tell the tale in a minute or two, although getting it out was like pulling shards of glass from my throat. My heartbeat would go way up, my muscles as tight as wires on a drum. And then what? What could a guy say to that? "Wow. They ever catch the guy?"

After my answer, nothing. Just silence. Even if they had said something it wouldn't have made any difference.

Lois and I never talked about it. Our unspoken agreement was that I wouldn't bring it up and she would acknowledge that it was always there, part of my consciousness. Lois gave me the support I needed in other ways. She stoked my ambitions for bigger things. She helped me keep the band organization going. She inspired new ideas for promoting and booking the band, and for advancing us toward a deal with a real record label. She also gave me a sense of home and family, as well as her fierce, intuitive, generous, resilient love. I missed her when I was gone, but it wasn't terrible. I was doing what I wanted to do. I never doubted her; I knew she'd be there when I came home.

Being on the road also helped clear my mind. Austin was full of painful landmarks, places Dianne and I used to go—on Town Lake, where we walked; Barton Springs, where we used to go swimming; upstream on Barton Creek, where it was wilder and more secluded. Clubs we swaggered into, decked out in glitter and platform shoes. Gnarled live oak trees in the Travis Heights neighborhood that spilled deep shadows across the streets at night. Streets I rolled down in my faded blue Ghia, wishing I was dead. Police headquarters.

I loved Austin, but when I was gone from there, I was out of the framework, and much of the spell that bound me to my nightmares was relieved. I also loved driving across the country, seeing new landscapes, the sense of possibility and adventure, movement for its own sake. I loved being on the periphery, especially at night, when it looked as though the edge of the world was just beyond the glare of your headlights.

Jon Dee was messing around on his guitar and I was reading *The World According to Garp* when I heard him play something new. Neat chords that pulled you in. I put down the book, pulled out my bass and started fishing around. The first section was a series of inversions in D. Droning on my D string, I could play a roving melodic line on the G string. Cool. "Any lyrics?" I said.

"Some," he said.

By the way he shrugged I didn't expect much, but he had the basic idea for the verses and chorus sketched out. I wrote a few more lines and we banged out the arrangement over the next few days. Billy joined us later on a drum pad, which helped.

The chorus was just four words, "What do you want?," repeated in a plaintively challenging melody. The title was obvious. Great song, melodic and powerful and fun to play. One of our best songs ever.

Back home at the end of February, we socked away as much Mexican food as we could, got reacquainted with our girlfriends and played a dozen gigs. Less than a month later, we were back in New York again, staking our wagon down in the same gray trailer park.

Every couple of days Lois sent me a letter, full of sexy talk and news of the pets and what was happening on the home front. She told us that our friends from Austin, Joe "King" Carrasco & the Crowns, had a gig at a New York club called the Eighties, and we were on the guest list. Cool. The Crowns played retro Tex-Mex rock—songs like Sam the Sham's "Wooly Bully," and ? & the Mysterians' "96 Tears." Extended versions of those songs were the high points of their show.

When we arrived at the club on the night of the gig, people were lined up around the block. Maybe the Crowns were actually opening for someone big, we thought. The band didn't have much of a following in Austin.

The Crowns' manager, Joe Nick Patoski, was a former *Rolling Stone* writer. Before the band came to New York Patoski got together with two rock critic friends and mailed every music biz contact they knew a package that consisted of the new single, some press clippings, and a zip-lock baggie with a tortilla inscribed with the band's name and a note that read, "In order to make it worth your while, here's a little bread."

The gimmick succeeded beyond their wildest expectations. All those people really were lined up to see Joe "King" Carrasco & the Crowns. The band came on like gangbusters, a Tex-Mex version of the B-52's. Although we were shocked and maybe even a little bitter, we cheered raucously as they reaped the encores we'd been denied.

Wooly Bully.

Four weeks later, the Skunks left Manhattan behind again, tossing M-80s and smoke bombs out the windows. An unluckier bunch would've gotten shot on general principle, but not us. We planned to drive straight through without stopping. We almost made it, too.

Abbott, Texas, is 125 miles from Austin and consists primarily of a couple of truck stops. Coincidentally, it happens to be the hometown of Willie Nelson. When we stopped there for gas around midnight, the RV's alternator went out. Home was just two hours down the road, so close we could taste it, but we knew for damn sure we wouldn't be sleeping in our own beds with our girlfriends that night. If we'd broken down 1,000 miles from home, it wouldn't have been half as bad.

I called Lois to let her know. She'd been waiting up, she said. Snacks were ready and everything. We commiserated for a few minutes before saying good night. I left the number of the truck stop as an afterthought.

Back inside the RV, things settled into a kind of surly surrealism. Then Lois called with some good news: we were getting rescued! She'd called the Continental Club and spoken to Wayne, who agreed that the Skunks should not be stranded in a truck stop two hours from Austin. Wayne would ride with Lois, and Roger One Knite would bring his own car, probably with Billy and Jon Dee's girlfriends. Great news!

The four of us ended up waiting inside the truck stop. The guys who worked there turned out to be a friendly bunch. They were chain smokers, serial coffee drinkers, and inquisitive, too. "What's it like to be in a band on the road, anyway?" "What kinda music y'all play?" "How you come up with a name like the Skunks?" "What kinda mileage y'all get on that RV?" "Y'all get many groupies?"

Before long, we were telling stories, drinking their coffee and smoking their cigarettes. One of them said, "Would y'all want a little something besides coffee to help you stay awake?"

Well, sure, we said. He reached into the deep pocket of his sagging pants for a handful of small foil packets and gave a couple to each of us. Each packet, containing two pills, bore printing in Spanish that said: *tabletas de ación prolongara*. We each ingested the contents of one packet, and a little while later took the other one, too. Back in the garage they had big barrels full of the packets. "Help yourself," they said. "It's good for you." The guy with no front teeth said he hadn't slept for three weeks.

Time danced by with a new glow. Our teeth shone under the fluorescent lights as we smiled and chattered and smoked and drank coffee and chewed gum.

Finally Jon Dee and I brought our instruments inside so we could play a couple of songs. They enjoyed the hell out of it. Billy unpacked his snare and high-hat and we played a few more. We kept playing. In the raw hours before dawn, amid the diesel fumes, the whine of the interstate and slap-back concrete reverb, we jammed. It was the ultimate in stripped-down, souped-up rock 'n' roll.

I was impressed by how good some of the songs sounded in that naked format, surprised at how much fun it was playing. When we played "What Do You Want," it gave me chills. It wasn't the speed, either.

Our rescuers arrived at a quarter to three. We were rocking out, wide-eyed and smiling for an audience of three mechanics. Boy were they surprised. The mechanics were sorry to see us go.

As we were driving away, Lois asked, "What was going on back there, anyway?"

Being a passenger in the quiet, intimate space of her Mustang felt odd after the weeks in our mildewy hovel on wheels, but I was happy to be by her side again. She looked good and smelled nice, too. She couldn't possibly have said the same about me.

"It just sort of happened," I said. "See, we were going back and forth to get coffee and cigarettes and, well, one guy kept asking about what kind of music we played. You know that guy with no front teeth? He said he hadn't slept for three weeks."

"Are you on drugs?" she said.

"What? Oh, well, just a little speed," I said.

"That explains it."

"That explains what, playing in the truck stop?" I said.

"No. I mean, yeah," she said. "But I thought there was something a little weird about you guys, too."

"Well, it was fun," I said.

"Uh-huh. I'm sure it was."

"It was different, that's for sure, but it was cool. I know I'll never forget it."

"What about the rest of it?" she said.

"The rest of what?" I said. "The tour?"

She nodded. "Was it worth it? All the time and energy?"

"Worth it? Sure. Absolutely."

"Well, how?" she said. "What did you accomplish?"

"I don't know. Lots of things."

We rode in silence. Where was this coming from?

"At least you didn't get all your stuff ripped off," she said, smiling.

"Yeah, that's something." Talk about below the belt.

"Listen, Jesse, you guys need a manager," Lois said. "You need somebody with clout and connections, and you deserve it, too. I think that's what's holding you back from getting a record deal. You and I can only do so much, and you've got to concentrate on performing and writing songs."

"Yeah, but where are we gonna find this manager?" I said. "They're not exactly growing on trees around here."

"Let's work on it together," she said. "Look, darling, these tours are hard on everybody, and I don't think you should keep doing them unless you're promoting an album. In my opinion, you're not going to get a record deal until you get a manager."

"I guess you're right," I said. Suddenly I felt very tired, even though my eyelids seemed to bounce open again every time I closed them. The Skunks were caught. We needed a manager to get a record deal, but we needed a record deal to attract a decent manager.

The world looked glossy and impenetrable through the windshield, especially against the soft, pale glow of Lois' face in profile. I touched her breast and squeezed her thigh. She smiled and gripped my hand.

My nerves were too jangled to talk about managers and logical approaches to what we were doing. Instead I wanted to talk about how the truck stop jam reminded me of how certain songs pack truth and meaning into three chords, a bass line, a beat and a few simple words. I wanted to say things will work out, because we're onto something.

"I love you, Jesse," she said.

"I love you, too."

"And I'm glad you didn't get all your stuff ripped off again." She was leaning over to get a kiss so I obliged her. Nothing more needed to be said, about music or anything else. We rode the rest of the way in silence.

13. THE RACKET

As we approached the spring of 1980, I was hot to go back to New York. Billy and Jon Dee were somewhere between warm and cool. Occasionally, Jon Dee moped about his decision to quit school. As a one-time English major, I knew the decision to dump that opportunity weighed heavily on his mind at the time, but if he ever made any noises about trading in his guitar-hero status for campus life, I treated them as phantom sounds. We played a lot, up to five nights a week, mostly one-night stands, in Texas and places in the South. Still, it was a tough life and we were barely scraping by. We were drinking hard, driving long, sleeping short. It was a strange life, too. One minute you were supercool; the next minute you were the fool. We all felt the strain.

In February we opened for the Clash at the Armadillo on their London Calling tour. The Clash ran white-hot that night, and we weren't half bad, either. After the concert, there was a full house of rowdy rockers at our own gig at the Continental Club. In the middle of our set, Joe Ely and Clash guitarist Mick Jones and drummer Topper Headon wanted to jam, so we accommodated them. The augmented band launched into Ely's "Fingernails" to great whoops and whistles of approval. Afterward, I led them in "Route 66," "You Keep A Knockin'," "Whole Lotta Shakin' Goin' On," and some Kinks, Stones and Velvets. Jon Dee sang on "The Letter," by the Box Tops. It was garage band heaven, the kind of night that could rekindle your faith in rock 'n' roll.

After the gig, as we were loading out of the club, Richard angrily confronted me about an odd incident that had transpired between Dave the doorman and me during the Clash jam. "Why are you such a hard-nosed bastard?" he said. "Why wouldn't you let Dave give Joe Ely his cowboy hat?"

"Because it's my fucking stage," I said. "No cowboy hats allowed on my stage!"

"You're an asshole, Sublett," Richard said.

I flew into a rage, throwing speakers and mic stands around and hurling curses at anyone who looked at me cross-eyed. Chalk it up to a combination of adrenaline, decibels and too many drinks, but my behavior seemed reasonable to me at the time. Richard and I yelled at each other frequently, yet it was usually just blowing off steam. We remained good pals.

My temper did get me in trouble eventually. One night at the Continental, Jon Dee gave me some bad news about our upcoming three-night stand in Lubbock. Having the weekend off was crucial for him because his sister was getting married. Playing that gig was critical to the band for economic and strategic reasons. The door receipts could be several thousand dollars, and Lubbock was a good chunk of the distance to L.A. To cancel now would piss off the club manager for a long time, maybe forever.

So it was his sister we were talking about. We had arranged special transportation so he'd be able to attend the wedding and play the gig. It wasn't enough. He wanted the whole weekend off. I thought that was unreasonable. Treasonous, actually.

The band had played two hard-rocking sets, and we'd done pretty well for a Tuesday night. Maybe Wayne and Roger and Summer Dog bought us a few extra drinks, maybe something else, too. We were in the office collecting our money after the gig, and surly remarks escalated like sparks caught in an updraft. Jon Dee said something about possibly going back to school.

"You can't go to college now, you idiot," I said.

"I can do anything I fucking want," he said.

"Fuck you, you pussy," I said. I picked up the brace from a broken bar stool and threw it at him, but it missed. We lunged at each other.

Richard and Wayne restrained us before blows were struck, but the damage was done. Jon Dee and I wouldn't speak to each other again for almost a year.

The next day we recruited a new guitarist named Doug Murray, formerly with a three-piece band called Terminal Mind. His twin brother Greg played drums. Terminal Mind was like a reverse image of the Skunks. Despite the power trio format and the fact that the bassist sang lead and wrote the songs, the band was geeky enough to please the Talking Heads fans who thought the Skunks were uncool because we wore our sixties influences on our sleeves and played songs about girls instead of the end of the world. Some of their songs were excellent and their sound was tough. I liked the band, though their attitude was a little too serious and nuevo-wavo for my taste.

Doug was a proficient musician and, sonically at least, could hold his own in a trio. On stage, he was stiff and a little too innocent looking to fill the virtual snakeskin boots left behind by Jon Dee and Eddie. But the band's material acquired a more nuanced sound, and my songwriting began to evolve.

The new lineup premiered a week after the fight with Jon Dee, and for the next two and a half years we played fifteen to twenty nights a month. As one of the top local draws at Club Foot, a massive new club downtown, we could expect to earn several thousand dollars a night. Our touring radius expanded to include reliable stops in the Midwest, the South, the Southwest, and even L.A. A feature story in the *Statesman* by Margaret Moser had the headline "Skunks Helped Put Austin Back On The Rock And Roll Map." Finally, writers were refering to us a rock 'n' roll band instead of leaning on cute clichés like "Skunks Surf the New Wave" and "These Skunks Don't Stink After All."

Gracey and Smith finally released our first LP, more than two years late. We thought the album sounded awful and resented the poor timing of the release. Richard and I hand-delivered letters to retailers headlined "Boycott Bogus Skunks LP," which claimed that Gracey and Smith didn't have the rights to release it. Technically, that wasn't true—we did sign that contract on a cocktail napkin. Morally, however, we believed we were right. Grace and Smith retaliated with a press release titled "Beware Rabid Skunks," but the record stores refused to carry the album. Only a small number of records, branded as the "bootleg Skunks LP," eventually filtered to the public. They were immediately snapped up as collectors' items.

The scene was changing everywhere. The Police, the Cars and a few other new wave bands were at the top of the charts, and even harder edged bands were getting critical attention. College radio had become a vital force in breaking new bands. MTV was just beginning to catch on. At first it was a shot in the arm to the kind of music we played, which was increasingly referred to as "new music," a term I preferred, despite its vagueness. Clubs were featuring new music one or more nights a week or catering to it exclusively. Lots of places played MTV or music videos in bar or lounge areas. Almost all this so-called "new music" was highly danceable. The best new places, like Austin's Club Foot, were dance clubs as well as live music venues. Club Foot's cavernous main rooms gave it a capacity for well over 1,000 people, and numerous underground rooms and dark corners added to its appeal. Touring acts like Nick Lowe, New Order, Billy Idol and U2 played there.

The business end of the band ran a lot more smoothly once Lois took over the managerial duties. She had natural gifts for dealing with people and driving a bargain. Club owners, agents and press people liked her, even the ones who'd been put through their paces to reach an accommodation. We regretted not putting her in charge a lot sooner.

October 1980 was a great month. We opened for Ultravox at the Armadillo, then hit the road for L.A. We had a good crowd for our first gig, opening for the Textones and Werewolves, whose fans loudly showed off their Texas roots with hollers and whistles just like we heard back home.

Dianne Roberts sitting in the black light disco room of Little Italy, the pizza joint in San Marcos I managed for a short time.

Above: The Skunks at Raul's in early 1980, just back from our third trip to NYC—guitarist Jon Dee Graham, drummer Billy Blackmon and me.

Left: Joseph Gonzales and Bobby Morales managed Raul's, the first punk/new wave club in Austin.

The day of my confirmation in 1968. Greeting us from the top of the stairs going down are Luci, Lynda, Lady Bird and President Lyndon Johnson. Rev. Norm Truesdell is at left at the top of the stairs. I'm just below him with a bad haircut.

I'm on the left, next to James and Jake, February 1958. I'm three and a half and James, whose birthday I share, is six and a half.

Jon Dee, Billy and I were reunited for a sold-out show at Liberty Lunch in March, 1985. PHOTO: BILL LEISSNER

A sunny afternoon in the summer of 1973, Dianne and I were 19, attending SWTSU (now Texas State University). She's holding our new baby, Boogie. PHOTO: STAN GILBERT

The original Skunks—Billy, Jazz Eddie and me—replenishing our fluids after a sweaty set at Raul's in the spring of 1978. PHOTO: CHERYL G. SMITH

LR: Myself, Carla Olson, Juke Logan, Mick Taylor, at the Roxy in Los Angeles March 4, 1990. This special eleven-member edition of the Carla Olson/Mick Taylor Band also included Ian McLagen and Barry Goldberg on keyboards and Joe Sublett (my cousin) on saxophone. PHOTO: GARY NICKERMAN

Debbie Harry (right) and her number one fan, Lois, backstage at the Armadillo after the first Blondie concert in Austin, 1978.

Backstage at Club Foot. LR back row: Tim Kerr (Big Boys), Charlie Sexton, Todd Rundgren, Randy "Biscuit" Turner (Big Boys). Front Row: Shona Lay and Larry Seaman (Standing Waves). Lois took this photo in 1985.

Richard Luckett with Ringo Starr. Richard was the Skunks first roadie. Ringo used to play drums for some band from Liverpool.

World's Cutest Killers, 1987. Left to right: myself, Jebin Bruni, Kathy Valentine, Kelly Johnson and Craig Aronson. This was Kathy's first new band after the Go-Go's split. Playing with her was always a blast. PHOTO: CHRIS CUFFARO

Here we are with our old pal Nick Lowe, after his keynote speech at South By Southwest in 1998. I've just finished seven weeks of radiation therapy and chemotherapy. PHOTO: TODD WOLFSON

Patti Smith came to Raul's to jam with the first edition Skunks—Billy, Fazz Eddie and me. Patti couldn't play a lick on guitar but she could make a lot of racket in the key of E, and she could definitely hold a crowd's attention. PHOTO: KEN HOGE

Violators. Clockwise: Myself, Carla Olson, Kathy Valentine (smoking), Marilyn Dean. December 1977, we're sitting on a pile of rubble from the ruins of the old Mother Earth night club. PHOTO: KEN HOGE

Joe Gracey
Benefit

Clockwise from top, Jesse Sublet of The Skunks, steel guitarist for Asleep at the Wheel, Alvin Crow, and Ray Benson of Asleep at the Wheel

Armadillo World Headquarters threw a benefit to defray Joe Gracey's cancer-battling deficit with an eclectic, only-in-Austin bill that featured the Skunks, the Fabulous Thunderbirds, Alvin Crow and Asleep at the Wheel. This photo layout ran in *The Daily Texan*. Clockwise, starting upper left, is Ray Benson of Asleep at the Wheel, myself, Lucky Oceans of Asleep at the Wheel, and the Austin honky tonk fiddler Alvin Crow.

May 23, 2001, James Ellroy, demon dog of American literature, mentor and friend, was in Austin to promote his masterpiece, *The Cold Six Thousand*. I was under a lot of strain at the time and Ellroy's visit gave me a much-needed boost. PHOTO: JACK ANDERSON

That's Dr. Melba Lewis on the left, with Lois and me after the biggest gig of my life—a two-song set at Melba's party celebrating five years of no recurrence of my neck cancer.

Lois and I are posing for an ad for Flipnotics, an espresso bar and clothing store on Barton Springs Road.
PHOTO: TODD WOLFSON

We had ten days off in L.A. Billy, Richard and I camped out at Kathy and Carla's apartment in West Hollywood. It was great hanging out with them again. The Textones had put out a single and were playing area clubs, trying to snag a record deal, like every other band in town. Kathy and Carla had been working day jobs, although Kathy had recently lost hers and was collecting unemployment.

They took us around town, to shows at the Starwood, Palomino and everywhere else they could finagle a spot on the guest list. I loved the cool nights and the palm trees, the canyons and fifties architecture, the large population of hipsters and beautiful people. I'd always heard how laid-back the music biz was in L.A., but from what I saw that appeared to be just another stupid cliché. The people I knew in L.A. were serious about what they were doing.

I still thought of Kathy as Keith Richards' virtual kid sister. One night she took me club-hopping and paid for everything because I was broke and she'd just gotten her unemployment check. After a full night on the town, we stopped at a 7-Eleven where we spent her last two quarters on a video game.

Our impact on the music industry there seemed to be nil, yet I hated to leave L.A. When I called Lois, I said, "We need to come out here sometime, just the two of us. I think you'll like it." She was surprised and a little skeptical, too. New York had always been our favorite city, and we assumed we'd move there if and when we left Austin. Now I wasn't so sure.

After L.A. Billy seemed to be brooding a lot. Doug said he was playing the songs too fast. Billy said Doug was boring. They were both at least half right. We tried to work things out. Billy worked on his tempos; Doug tried to move around more on stage. Billy swallowed his unhappiness, chasing it with a few extra drinks every night, which didn't help his tempo problem, and Doug resumed complaining. Greg was ready to join the band, he said. All we had to do was get rid of Billy. Greg was good and in some ways, better than Billy. I liked Billy a lot and I didn't want to replace him, but he seemed unhappy anyway. Late one night after a gig, we were all drinking and laughing, having a lot of fun.

Then we fired him. He seemed relieved.

Bands do these things. Like some strange organism you might see on a nature documentary, a band will periodically attack itself and gnaw off a limb or two, just so it can grow new ones. Sometimes this gooses the band's creativity and it rises to new heights. Other times the band disintegrates.

Usually the former band member is now a mangy dog, the guy who was holding back the band, the one who always farted in the motel room. When you hear his side of the story, you learn that the old band is a bunch of losers, and they'll last another six months at the most, because he was the guy who wrote all the good parts in their songs, the one who was holding it all together. This backstabbing routine is a hallowed tradition.

Greg pushed us to incorporate new beats in our music, including reggae, funk and disco. The new beats allowed me to explore new bass styles, and our arrangements tightened up. We coordinated more bass and drum fills and worked on making the music more danceable. Greg and Doug also started working out harmonies to some of the songs. Doug wrote a few songs and started singing lead a little, too. I wasn't wild about his songs or his voice, but I went along with it to keep him happy and to add texture to our show. Besides, singing with a loud rock band in a club, sometimes four sets a night, can be awfully hard on your throat.

After blowing up with Jon Dee, I made an effort to be calmer with Doug and Greg. The twins were more reserved than Jon Dee and Billy anyway; they seemed naive and buttoned-down in comparison. They could be fussy. They were way too fond of the Beatles. They were born-again Christians, like their mother.

The band was still fun, just not as much fun as it used to be. Whenever I got frustrated with the twins or discouraged because of a setback, I reminded myself of how far we'd come. When that failed to cheer me up, I paraphrased a favorite saying: This life is like pizza and sex; when it's good, it's great, and when it's bad, it's still pretty good.

On the other hand, I thought back to the night I encountered the aphorism about pizza and sex. It was on a plaque in a girl's bedroom during a night of marathon lovemaking. Even then, I figured, there must inevitably come a time when enough is enough, when you're sick of pizza and worn out by sex, when pretty good just isn't enough.

I saw the future one night when I was putting on my eyeliner before a gig. Our recent photo sessions had yielded disappointing results—not a single shot captured the cool dynamic I wanted. Blending a last dollop of gel in my hair, I slicked it back and let the front bangs fall down across my forehead, just so. I stood back and saw the ideal band image I'd been looking for. My pretty face alone, centered in the mirror. The twins had disappeared. So had the Skunks.

The future was clear. It was mine, alone.

Everything was moving in new directions. After several years of singing full-time, my voice was much improved; I didn't sound like Lou Reed imitating Mick Jagger. I was experimenting with new singing styles and adding more harmonies. I let Doug sing a few songs. My songs were becoming more melodic, and I was exploring more sensitive and empathic themes, including that old standby, unrequited love.

I was wearing baggy suits and slicking back my hair. Doug and Greg adopted the look, too. The image I strove for was part Bryan Ferry, part Austin blues gangster, which meant vintage clothes and some new retro styles that were becoming available.

Film noir and detective novels were a huge influence on everything I did. I'd begun devouring hardboiled detective novels on the road, starting with the classics, Dashiell Hammett and Raymond Chandler, and moving into deeper *Black Mask* pulp fiction territory with Roger Torrey's *42 Days to Murder* and Raoul Whitfield's *Green Ice* and *Death in a Bowl*.

When I wasn't on the road, Lois and I caught every picture in the film noir retrospectives at UT, movies like *Out of the Past*, *The Big Combo*, *Crisscross* and *They Live by Night*. I stayed up all night watching them on TV. I felt myself being sucked into this retro world of deep shadows, murky crosscurrents, no-hope heroes, the lyricism of the lost. Chandler and Hammett became as important to me as Chuck Berry and Howlin' Wolf; Anthony Mann and Robert Mitchum as essential as Lou Reed and Bryan Ferry. Lois was almost as obsessed. She was my noir babe in her jade green Joan Crawford jacket with padded shoulders and giant buttons, and her fake leopard coat. She and I traded dialogue in hardboiled lingo, sipped dry martinis, smoked too much.

My friend Johnny Reno, a jump blues saxophonist/singer from Fort Worth, was a fellow hardboiled fan; he looked the part and played the music, too. John Schmidt, who played bass for the Cincinnati-based funk band Erector Set, was another member of my noir support group. Backstage, John and I would talk books and films, compliment each other's sartorial flair and discuss the virtues of Fender basses at great length.

As with my taste in detective novels and films, the color schemes of my Fender basses were all variations of black and blood red; ironically, however, the future of my band was beginning to look rosier all the time. Our popularity in Texas was steadily growing, along with our touring radius outside the state. Our recording career entered a new phase as well.

Republic Records was founded by a Houston businessman who'd made enough money from his construction company and chain of cineplexes to risk taking a loss in the music business. His Austin partner was in the high-end stereo business. We were the first band they wanted to sign. We had been holding out for a deal with a major label, but we felt the time was right to put out a quality studio album, so after some haggling over terms, we signed with Republic in 1982. The label opened an office on South Congress Avenue and hired Earle Mankey to produce the first LP.

Everyone was excited about Mankey producing, and we expected an awful lot. Mankey produced 20/20's "Yellow Pills," a soaring, psychedelic, perfect pop single. He worked with Sparks, Concrete Blonde, Vivabeat and others. Like a lot of musicians, we went into the studio with big riffs, high hopes and broad streaks of naiveté. We thought our songs were good, and we trusted Mankey to sprinkle fairy dust on them. Radio programmers would be knocked out; critics, too. Record company executives would kick themselves for not signing us sooner and would throw significant sums of money at us to entice us to leave Republic and sign with them. Our biggest problem, we figured, would be finding the right music biz lawyer to get us out of our deal with Republic with a minimum of blood loss.

Preproduction on the LP took almost two weeks. Mankey listened to us play each song, then worked with us to improve our parts, often by significantly paring them down to make the sound tighter, to open up spaces for the melody to breathe and catch the listener's ear. He'd cut up an arrangement and put the song back together in a whole new way. His ideas frequently stunned us. Why didn't we think of that? After rehearsing with Mankey for a week, we recorded a demo version of the LP (including overdubs) at Earth & Sky, a small twenty-four-track studio. Then we moved to Third Coast, a bigger studio, and did everything over for real.

Most of the songs improved dramatically. Working with Mankey changed the way I played and composed forever. The end result was a polished-sounding production, especially for the Skunks. Too polished, actually, for some people, including me.

We arrived in Chicago at about six. I was feeling good. The night before we had played Champaign, Illinois, where one of our songs was number one on the radio. We were touring with our pals Erector Set again. We arrived at the Cubby Bear first, so I walked in ahead of the band to speak to the manager. He was cleaning up, restocking.

"Hey man," I said. "I'm Jesse and we're the Skunks."

He nodded, kept working.

"Hey, do you think there'll be a crowd tonight?"

"No," he growled.

I decided to go for a walk. It was a blustery day outside. The sky was overcast, the air crisp and dry. Over there was Wrigley Field. Someday I'd tell people, "Yeah, I played Chicago. The club was called the Cubby Bear, right next to Wrigley Field."

Big fucking deal. Chicago was an old, big ass town with a colorful story from its glory days for every crack in the sidewalk, but from where I was standing it seemed empty. Not many people on the street. Sky hemmed in by a bunch of buildings, gray and blank overhead.

Why wouldn't people come to see us tonight? Funny thing was, I didn't care much. My voice was in fine shape, the twins weren't getting on my nerves and we were making plans for the next album. I had some good new songs.

Maybe I'd outgrown the Skunks. I was twenty-eight years old. Did I want to be a Skunk when I was thirty years old? Would I always be a

Skunk? I thought about what I would tell my grandkids. *Yep, your grandpa was in a band called the Skunks. Yep, played the Cubby Bear Lounge in Chicago, right next to Wrigley Field. Nobody came.*

I wanted something more. Maybe I should start a new band, with a new concept. Maybe I should be a writer. I could write hardboiled, I was pretty sure of it. A year ago, these thoughts would've been unimaginable, but here they were: I don't have to do this. I've scratched this itch. I know what it's like to be semi-famous. I've heard my songs on the radio. Is this all I want, more of this? No. I've got other ideas.

I walked back to the club feeling like a new man. We had a good crowd at the Cubby Bear. The Skunks rocked. Erector Set rocked. The jam session really rocked. My voice was better than ever. That bar manager didn't know shit.

I didn't tell the band of my decision till Christmas. I called them up and told them the band was over; I was bored. They were surprised, but OK with it. Who knows? Maybe they'd been planning to leave me. We booked a series of farewell shows for February in Austin, Houston and Dallas. We'd be going out with our pockets full of change. The show in Houston went well, and two nights at Club Foot were sold out. Erector Set came down to open the show. We had a massive jam at the end—a medley of "Waiting for My Man," "Sister Ray" and "Louie, Louie."

The last show in Dallas came very close to being the last gig of our lives. We were just south of Waco when a cold front blew in. After crossing a low bridge I felt the van shudder and, assuming it was a blow-out, I hit the brakes. But no, it was ice, and over we went. The van rolled and skipped over the grassy median in a heartbeat. The windshield popped out as we went skating down the other side of the freeway. Upside down, going toward a head-on collision.

I was staring out of the place where the windshield used to be, saying to myself, "Oh man, I sure hope my pretty face doesn't get messed up."

Finally we scraped to a halt. Our road manager, Pat Costigan, had been fast asleep in the passenger seat. Eyes still shut, he stirred and said, "Are we there yet?"

"Wake up, bro, we're upside down," I said.

He opened his eyes and said, "Wow."

The twins were under a pile of guitar cases and speakers. I had a fleeting image of the two of them impaled by a mic stand or perhaps their skulls crushed. I didn't like them very much, but killing them had never entered my mind. Not even Jerry Lee Lewis, the Killer—who had shot his own bass player—would do such a vile thing.

The doors were all jammed shut, so Pat and I slithered out the windows and managed to extricate the twins, who were alive after all. We stood there for a moment, staring in disbelief at the upside down van with its wheels still spinning, and we began to laugh hysterically.

None of us had a scratch. I checked myself in the mirror: my pretty face was just fine.

Maybe I should've found a more suitable pair of coconspirators and persevered with a new band called the Skunks for a few more years. Surely we would have scored more substantial acclaim, made more money, lived larger, left a bigger mark on the history of rock 'n' roll.

Well, so what? Frankly, Scarlett, I didn't give a shit.

That was the end of the Skunks.

PART 3.
anythingcanhappenland

14. ROCK CRITIC MURDERS

I was taking a piss under the Hollywood sign, just underneath the second O, I think it was, and thinking about how much I loved it here above the city of angels. I never got tired of the hills and the houses that were wedged into their nooks and crooks and angles and cliffs in as many imaginative ways as there were denominations of money, desperately trying to hold on to some of that Southern California magic. You could see a long way. You could look down on the landmarks of Hollywood, Beverly Hills, downtown and Culver City, and if you were lucky, the beach communities of Venice and Santa Monica and Malibu, where the blue-brown haze marked the place where the sky made its uneasy merger with the city of dreams.

Jogging up here from Lake Hollywood was one of my favorite routines. As long as the air wasn't too bad, I tried to indulge myself at least once a week. I always paused to take a leak in the shadow of the world's most famous, dream-invested billboard. I'd been coming up here ever since Lois and I had joined the great migration westward in early 1987. The Pacific Ocean marked the end of the trail. I strained to see if I could see it. Not today; too much haze and smog.

Lois and I had gotten married in the fall of 1984, after we'd been together almost seven years. Not long after that, we started talking seriously about uprooting ourselves and moving here. It had all the heat of an illicit affair, the romance of a honeymoon, the mysteries of a first date. Our adventure would kick off my new career with a bang and would end with a beautiful, blue-eyed baby boy.

1984, the year I turned thirty, seemed like a good time to take stock. Looking over my material criteria for success, I didn't appear to be there yet. I had some cool bass guitars and a cool car, but I still had worries about the basics. We lived month to month, no savings in the bank, no insurance, no real assets aside from our good looks, talent and the aforementioned cool stuff.

Things could've been a lot worse. A long way from my old diet of Top Ramen and potpies, Lois and I could afford steak or a modest expedition to the sushi bar and a bottle of single malt Scotch at least once a week, and we almost always paid the rent on time. A few years before I would've been happy with this.

Artistically speaking, I took pride in my recent accomplishments. Three months after folding up the Skunks, I had launched a radically different band, Secret Six. It was my Bryan Ferry turn, and most of the time I was just singing and enjoying the hell out of it. The music was keyboard driven and dance oriented, the lyrics tending toward the melancholy. My songwriting was prolific, and my singing had grown by leaps and bounds.

Major label reps kept in touch with us, listening closely to new demo tapes. Producer Liam Sternberg signed us up for a compilation album on Elektra Records showcasing ten promising Texas bands. The contract for the album, titled *Ten From Texas: Herd It Through the Grapevine*, gave Elektra an option on Secret Six, that gave the record label six months to decide whether or not it would offer the band a lucrative recording contract. Lois and I were betting that Elektra would probably exercise the option.

I was working on a hardboiled detective novel, too. I felt at home with the language of that world and the viewpoints it offered on life, so what the hell, I thought, I'll see if I can pull it off.

My music career wasn't in the dumps by any means, but Secret Six wasn't nearly as popular as the Skunks had been. The band's first few gigs were treated like a hot-ticket premiere, but the buzz tapered off. We played regularly, but we didn't attract the same crowds at our gigs and couldn't demand the same fees. I had to look for an extra source of income. I worked part-time for three months as a skip tracer at a collection agency, then turned to freelance writing, both of which led me to the idea of writing detective novels. My sleuth, named Martin Fender, would be a bass player who occasionally worked part-time as a skip tracer.

Lois was working for the *Austin Chronicle* in advertising sales and making a good living. She was still my biggest ally, biggest fan and most important critic. She was my booking agent; she also booked Charlie Sexton, Lou Ann Barton and others. All these things plus being my lover and sticking by me. Knowing full well I faced a million temptations on the road but trusting me anyway. Carrying on through disappointment and critical backlash.

Wanting to get married someday. Like, yesterday, but not pushing it. When I thought about it, all of the above sounded like the requirements for rock 'n' roll wedding vows, and she'd already lived up to her end of the bargain.

We had the ceremony and reception in the Maximillian ballroom of the Driskill, the oldest hotel in Austin and one of its most famous landmarks besides the capitol. Built in 1886 by cattle baron Jesse Driskill, the majestic limestone Romanesque hotel is a grand monument to the cattle industry and is as Texan as a building can be without being tacky. The building's cornice line is studded with longhorn cow heads and bovine-looking gargoyles, and crowned with busts of Driskill and his two sons.

The guest list included a few rock stars, and a good mix of local musicians, deejays, writers, club owners, fashionistas and a TV reporter or two. The ceremony was performed by a local judge, the Honorable Robert Duran, whom we chose because his name made us think of Duran Duran. Exchanging vows lasted all of five minutes—no prayers to the Almighty, no touchy-feely new age poetry—just simple, elegant pledges of love, loyalty, understanding and patience.

Lois was a vision of loveliness, and a little nervous. Her maid of honor was her good pal from New York Melanie Popkin. Richard, the Skunks original road manager, was my best man. Par for the course, he picked me up in his date's car, which had gotten soaked from rain the night before because someone (most likely Richard) left the windows down. My tux was wet, and Richard smoked a joint on the way to the hotel. It was almost like being on the road with him again, except we weren't shooting off fireworks and at the end of the trip, we weren't trying to sneak five guys and their guitars into a double at the Motel 6.

Our parents were proud and happy, of course. Mom and Dad thought Lois was perfect for me. James and his wife Diane were there, but Kathryn couldn't make it. She was in the army, stationed in Germany. That's one way to get out of Johnson City.

We honeymooned in New York. Our room at the Wellington, next door to Carnegie Hall (where Stevie Ray Vaughan had just played a triumphant concert), was a gift of our generous friend Jake Riviera. Lois' Italian relatives had stuffed our pockets full of cash at the reception, so we proceeded to live it up. We went on quests for Indian cuisine, splurged on single malt scotch, took a carriage ride through Central Park. We even had meetings with a number of record label executives, who showered us with congratulations and good wishes and promised to listen to my demo tape. It was a neat kind of revenge for the hardships and little cruelties that city had inflicted upon us, and a sweet way to kick off this new phase of our union.

Los Angeles was the place to be. The air smelled different. Trees were different, the hills were different. Even the sky and the light seemed to be a special grade. People remade themselves here. They looked in the mirror and saw a new face, a different shadow on the wall. You made a good part of your own luck in a place like this. It didn't hurt that we had a significant support group of Texan friends in the music business, and a few in film, too. Nor did it hurt that one of those friends was Kathy Valentine. L.A. had certainly been a lucky move for her.

A few weeks after the Skunks' L.A. trip in 1980, Kathy and Carla had a fight that ended with Kathy out of the Textones. One night a few weeks before New Year's Eve, Kathy bumped into Charlotte Caffey in the women's room of Whiskey-a-go-go. Charlotte played guitar in a hot all-girl punk band called the Go-Go's. The band, unsigned and almost unknown outside of L.A., wanted to dump their current bass player. Did Kathy know anybody? Any girls, that is? I can play bass, Kathy said (actually, she could play a little, but referring to herself as a bass player was a stretch). Cool.

"I learned the songs on a three-day coke binge," Kathy told me. "We had a couple of rehearsals and then we played three sold-out nights at the Whiskey over New Year's, two shows a night."

The Go-Go's signed with I.R.S. Records in early 1981. The single "We Got the Beat" went platinum, the first album, *Beauty and the Beast,* double platinum. "Vacation," a song Kathy had written in the Textones, mined even more platinum for the second LP. The Go-Go's were a pop sensation, one of the biggest success stories of the punk/new wave scene. They blasted the "men only" sign off the gates to the rock world. Every chick rocker since then struts in the footsteps of my pal Kathy Valentine and crew.

Among other things, Lois pointed to the success of the Go-Go's to convince me to move to L.A. "I know you're worried about having to start over somewhere new," she'd say, "but look what happend for Kathy. The same thing can happen for you." By the time she'd broken down my resistence and psyched me up for the big move, Belinda Carlisle was on her way to becoming a solo superstar, and the other Go-Go's were inking their own solo deals. Kathy was being courted by labels but hadn't signed anything yet. Lois and I were just starting to box up our belongings in Austin when Kathy called and said, "Hey, since you guys are coming out here to live, how would you like to start a new band with me? I think it would be real cool."

"Yeah," I said, "I think it'd be real cool, too."

Kathy's phone call couldn't have come at a better time. I'd been forced to call it a day for Secret Six. Keeping the band fully staffed had been a full-time challenge. My original concept had been myself on vocals plus a core of bass, guitar, keyboards and drums augmented by backing singers and percussion. I settled for a shifting lineup that never exceeded more than six musicians.

I fired four drummers the first year. One was a gun nut. He carried an M-16 in a Les Paul case and always took a pistol on the road. One was agreeable no matter how much bourbon he drank. The best of the bunch was so cheap he used a screwdriver handle for a beater on his bass drum pedal. No one worked out for the long haul.

Gary Guthrie was in the band for a while. We had a great time together until we started arguing again, just like when I was his pusher, except this time he was the one who got fired. Gary had introduced me to a young musician named Jeff Campbell. A wizard with gadgets and equally adept at keyboards and guitar, Jeff turned out to be the most valuable member of the team from the beginning to the bitter end. Apparently he shared that opinion. When Jeff and his girlfriend, Nancy (backup singer and percussionist), decided to quit the band they erased all their parts on our demo tapes. That was a new one.

That was it for Secret Six. I sold the van to an Austin band called the Wild Seeds, who put another 100,000 miles on it. Then I bought a yellow 1970 Karmann Ghia convertible. Driving it was like walking into a party with the coolest pair of shoes in the room.

We were surprised when my option with Elektra expired without the anticipated offer for a big money contract. We should have known when I called Elektra and couldn't find anyone who'd heard of the band. The *Ten From Texas* LP had been released the day before.

I knew I'd have some luck; I just didn't know what it would look like. During our last two years in Austin, I went back to playing bass again, and worked part time on an unlikely project—*The Encyclopedia of the Useful Wild Plants of Texas*. The encyclopedia was the baby of two highly intelligent, dedicated and somewhat eccentric people, Scooter Cheatham and Lynn Marshall. I learned about botany, Indians, pioneers and a million other things, and shook the cobwebs off my grasp of grammar and story construction. The experience was a much-needed tonic for the madness of the music profession.

During all this, I kept writing new songs and tried not to take the music business too seriously. From all I'd learned, it shouldn't have been too difficult.

Kathy flew me out to rehearse with prospective band members. The lineup was impressive. Kathy was on vocals and guitar. The lead guitarist and co-vocalist was Kelly Johnson, a lithe, blonde string-scorcher formerly of Girlschool. Jebin Bruni, on keyboards, had been with John Lydon's (a.k.a. Johnny Rotten) Public Image and Broken Homes. The drummer was Craig Aronson, also from that band. Besides playing bass, I sang lead on a couple of songs, backing vocals on others.

Kathy and Kelly made a great team for fronting the band. Each had her own unique brand of charisma—Kathy the redheaded rocker with a voice somewhere between Debbie Harry and Keith Richards, Kelly the gazelle-like Brit, firing off tracer bullet riffs from her tiger-stripe guitar and striking arena rock poses with glee. Jebin, an elfin L.A. native, was the only formally trained musician among us, yet he rocked with the abandon of a kid in his first garage band. Craig was a fine drummer, a perfectionist, and an amiable companion, though sometimes sensitive and volatile. Not that the rest of us didn't occasionally sulk or fume.

The band felt solid for being so new, but we needed lots practice, so Kathy flew me out several times in the following weeks. The last trip, Lois came along to scout for apartments. On our last day, she found a small apartment building in Studio City with a vacant two-bedroom/two-bath that seemed perfect. The sign out front clearly read "no pets," but the manager, who'd been fortifying himself with chardonnay while painting the apartment, seemed pliable. "What about one little cat?" Lois said, intending to mention the not-so-little one later. He said he guessed that would be OK.

What a piece of luck. The place was spacious and sunny, and the second bedroom was ideal for my creative headquarters. Several of our neighbors were lovable white-haired eccentrics who'd retired from show business, and several others were still in it. A good mix. We liked the place even better after learning that the original owner of the property was the late Robert Ryan, one of the great noir tough guys.

Playing in Kathy's band was fun, but the real reason Lois and I moved to L.A. was so I could become a crime novelist. Before Los Angeles, whatever I knew about fiction writing had been either learned by osmosis or from my mentor, the rock critic Ed Ward. I met Ed soon after he moved from San Francisco to Austin in 1979 to be music editor at the *Statesman*. I went by the office to deliver a Skunks single and press kit. I don't know what I expected, but it wasn't a barrel-chested eccentric with a booming voice. He looked like a biker in his leather cap, with long black hair and a mustache that would've looked perfect on one of Pancho Villa's men.

Ed's laugh was even louder than his voice. He was extremely opinionated, in person and in print. His knowledge of music, as well as hundreds of other subjects, was encyclopedic. Almost every time I spoke to him I learned something interesting. He had some great stories, too.

I didn't know about Ed's interest in mystery fiction until he complimented me on my first short story, published in the *Austin Chronicle* in 1984. "The Hardboiled Highway" was a road essay describing the club circuit in the South and Midwest, albeit thinly disguised as a mystery short story. The narrator was an Austin blues bassist very similar to myself named Martin Fender.

Martin's girlfriend, Ladonna, is strong, smart, soulful and of Italian descent. She often gives Martin a hard time about his impractical life, which creates dramatic and romantic tension, but she loves him and is a beacon of stability in his world. Readers always tend to love Ladonna's character, and are hardly ever surprised when they meet Lois and discover the strong resemblance between the two.

I'd spent a good part of the last ten years in dark clubs and studios, an environment that provided plenty of fodder for plots and characters. I had faith in my protagonist, too. I saw him as a bass-playing Philip Marlowe/Sam Spade, tough and world weary but principled, a romantic at heart. No one else was doing detective novels like these, and the established authors got the details wrong when they wrote about rock 'n' roll.

I wrote about murder without really venturing into the dark parts of myself that had experienced it first hand. But the classic hardboiled detective genre was more about the detective himself, not necessarily about the horror of murder. The detective tries to repair cracks in the universe to staunch outbursts of chaos. The murder case is just the point of inquiry; the detective asks the hard questions about life in a world where everything is fixed against the little guy, the guy with principles. The detective knows the system doesn't work, but the good guys have to go on pretending it does. Otherwise, chaos.

Those were some of the reasons I loved crime novels and film noir. The language was the poetry of shadows and moonlight, with a thumping jukebox in the background. Noir was timeless and universal, like the blues.

I wrote the first draft of *Rock Critic Murders* in three weeks, going through several cases of Tecate beer and quite a few cigars. On my next efforts, I would dispense with the alcohol, but smoking cigars seemed to be essential. Smoking a cigar seemed to stimulate my imagination. Probably just as important, it helped me keep my ass parked in front of my Mac for long periods of time.

On a day when a winter storm paralyzed Austin with freezing rain, Lois and I braved the elements to drive across town and deliver the manuscript to Ed, who had offered to read it and lend some friendly advice. I could tell he was impressed with the big pile of gig posters, the back of each one covered with typescript and Wite-Out.

"You really did it," he said in his booming voice. "Of course, that doesn't mean it's any good."

"No, it doesn't," I said, "but it is."

He called a week later. "We need to work on this," he said. "Maybe we can turn it into a real book. It's very possible that you're a writer, Jesse."

That was music to my ears.

Ed lived in a small white frame house in Clarksville, a neighborhood originally established as one of Austin's first black communities after the Civil War. He was a gourmet cook but a terrible housekeeper. CDs, records, tapes, books and ephemera were crammed into shelves and apple crates, which lined the walls and filled every corner. A broad, low table in the living room held towering stacks of CDs that swayed like living things in the heat of the afternoon.

Ed and I met at his house once a week. I brought the beer and took notes, argued and listened. Ed ripped through my book line by line, pausing to point out the occasional original idea, along with every error, weak spot and outright stupidity I'd committed. He'd chuckle or groan at my jokes and poke fun at each unintentionally humorous passage. Ed could be harsh, but I could take it from him.

In March 1985 the Skunks played a reunion gig at Austin's Liberty Lunch. The lineup was Jon Dee, Billy and myself. A thousand people came, filling the place to capacity. It had taken only an hour and a half for the three of us to relearn the songs, even though we hadn't played together in five years. Like riding a bike at 120 decibels.

The next day, when we came to pick up our gear, we found a sobering sight. From end to end, the edge of the stage was a pattern of dried blood stains, like a message written in a mysterious code. The stains were the color of dried blood. Over the course of the night, some of the fans had cut themselves on glass from broken beer bottles on the edge of the stage. When it happened they apparently didn't notice or didn't care, because they stayed there. Some of them were pounding the stage instead of clapping, which resulted in the dense line of red exclamation points at our feet. It was a moving coda to a memorable experience.

The gig gave me the idea to use a band reunion as a plot device in *Rock Critic Murders.* It also left me enough money to live on while I wrote. The book begins with the reunion of a band, but soon leads Martin onto the trail of greedy developers who are plundering the Austin area's natural environment for profit. Following Ed's input, I did several rewrites in 1986. Ed said we should go to New York and take it to some publishers.

"I've got some business there," he said. "I know a few editors, and they'll get the whole picture if they see the real Martin Fender in the flesh."

Lois and I were all for that idea. She booked the first flight we could get at a reasonable rate, and off we went.

Our hopeful trio delivered the manuscript to editors at Avon, St. Martin's and Viking Penguin. The meeting at Avon was anti-climactic. The editor came out, shook our hands, took the manuscript and excused himself. The meeting at St. Martin's was a bit more exciting. When the cab stopped at the Flatiron Building, Lois and I both let out a long "Wow." We'd been fans of the fabulous cake-wedge shaped building forever.

The last delivery was the coolest of all. The editor at Viking, André Bernard, spent a good thirty minutes talking books and music with us. The meeting seemed to bristle with promise. As we were leaving, Bernard gave me a stack of new crime novels.

This book submission thing wasn't nearly as painful as people made it out to be. What was the big deal?

The answer came in the terse rejection letters that began filling my mailbox. The notes were short and to the point—no chance of misinterpreting their answers. André Bernard, however, wrote a page-long personal letter including criticism and praise for my work. "There is no doubt in my mind that you know how to write, and write well," he said. "You've got a terrific way of narrating your story, and the main character is believable and interesting." He didn't think the story worked as a novel, though, and no still meant no, so his compliments came as cold comfort.

I started sending out copies of the manuscript, sometimes several a day. They came flying back, blunt form letters clipped to the title page.

I refused to be discouraged. The people who didn't like my book were uncool, that's all. I wasn't completely delusive. I knew I wasn't as good as Chandler or Hammett, not as good as John D. McDonald or even Robert B. Parker. But nobody else was me, either. Nobody out there was writing about music and getting it right. The world needed Martin Fender and his hardboiled Austin retro blues groove. The only thing I lacked was a hip, smart editor—a person who was looking for me, even if they didn't know it yet.

Ed said he was sorry about the rejections, but he didn't have any other connections. I was on my own.

We still had moving crates to unpack in Studio City when I started mailing out manuscripts for my second novel, *Tough Baby*, which I'd written in a feverish five weeks. They met with the same boomerang effect as the ones mailed from Austin. Oftentimes, the assistant charged with typing a note for the return package would rub salt in my wounds by getting the book title or my name or gender wrong. Sometimes all three.

Depression was knocking at the door, threatening to move in, but then I had an idea. André Bernard! The editor at Viking, the one who said I was terrific. I'd send him the new book. If he liked *Rock Critic Murders* just a little bit, he'd love *Tough Baby*. Maybe I should call him first, let him know it was coming. That was the professional thing to do anyway.

Good thing I called—Bernard was no longer at Viking. Damn. I moped around for half an hour. Then I had another flash of clarity. Surely Bernard didn't fall off the face of the earth. He was probably at another publishing company. I called back and asked the operator if she could tell me where he'd gone. She put me on hold. After a minute she said she was transferring my call to someone else.

"This is Lisa Kaufman," said a new voice.

Lisa sounded young. Unfortunately, she didn't know where Bernard had gone, but she offered to look into it.

"What was your name again?" she said.

"Jesse Sublett."

"Hmm. Your name sounds awfully familiar."

"Well, I'm a musician. I had a band called the Skunks. We used to play New York clubs. Maybe that's where you heard of me."

"Maybe that's it. Where did you say you're from?"

"I'm living in L.A. now, but I just moved here from Austin and—"

"Austin? That's it. I lived in Austin for a while. I was working with James Michener, helping him on his Texas book. I loved Austin. You're a famous musician down there, aren't you?"

"I guess so. Semi-famous, semi-legendary, I like to say."

"Do you mind telling me what your book is about?"

I told her about both books, plus the short story that launched Martin Fender. Lisa said she loved the idea of a crime novel set in the Austin music scene.

"What do you do at Viking, exactly?" I said.

"I'm an editor," she said.

"Oh!" I said, practically dropping the phone. "I had no idea. I thought I was talking to someone in the mailroom or something."

She thought that was funny. Not only was she an editor, she said, but Viking had put her in charge of developing their new mystery and suspense line. My books sounded like something she'd be interested in publishing. Would I mind sending her copies?

Lisa called back less than a week later. She loved my writing. My books needed some work, though, and she wanted to know if I thought I could stand doing extensive revisions.

"Sure, I can do that," I said. "I've got no problem rewriting. I was just hoping to find someone who thought my books were cool."

"Oh, they're cool, all right," she said. "They're very cool. You need an agent, though. You said you don't have anybody representing you?"

"No. I haven't had any luck with that."

"Well, it just so happens that I just had lunch with an agent named Abby Thomas. She just might be perfect for you. Why don't you call her and let me know what you decide?"

I called Abby. She said she was anxious to read my books. I mailed her the books that afternoon. She called me a week later.

"I would love to represent you," she said. "Your writing is fresh and exciting. You're the real thing. I've been talking to Lisa and I agree, your books need some work, but you already know all the things that can't be taught. You're brilliant."

I told her she had the job.

Abby made some inquiries at other publishing houses, but in the end Viking's offer looked like the best thing going. The contract she negotiated included an option to publish my next two novels. The Martin Fender series would kick off with *Rock Critic Murders*. Contracts would be ready in a few weeks.

I called my mom and dad. They were proud. We were much closer these days. Lois helped me do that.

Lois and I celebrated that night with a four-star spicy Indian dinner and a bottle of single malt scotch. Hadn't she told me moving to L.A. would bring us luck?

15. KICKIN' YOU OUT

Being on the road again with Kathy's band was swell. Besides playing all over L.A., we played a dozen or so cities up and down the coast, as well as Tucson and Phoenix. San Francisco was a revelation. I loved the cool ocean air, Chinatown, Fisherman's Wharf and all the sites I'd read about in Dashiell Hammett novels. I liked the routines of traveling and, in small doses, didn't even mind the drudgery of delayed sound checks and other unique quirks of the business.

We'd named ourselves World's Cutest Killers, after a headline in a *National Enquirer* story Kathy had found about preteen assassins who worked for South American drug lords. Our first gig, the headline slot at a star-studded AIDS benefit, got us glowing reviews in the L.A. press.

Gigs and rehearsals were enlivened by the presence of the famous, infamous and almost-famous. The ex-Blondie boys would pop into rehearsals to jam. Clem Burke was a constant companion since he was Kathy's boyfriend, and it was always a blast when he took a seat behind the drum kit. Ian McLagen played keyboards now and then, treating us to rootsy riffs he'd played with the Stones and the Faces. Baseball players, film and TV actors came backstage to hobnob.

It was a kick to be in a band without having the pressure of being the bandleader, worrying about every detail, knowing that the success of the enterprise depended on you, your talent and your ability to give your all every time you stepped onstage. With that pressure off, I could concentrate on playing. Taking things in instead of taking everything on. Didn't have to set up sound checks and rehearsals, schmooze the club manager. I saw being a bandleader in a whole new light—the necessary vanity and paranoia. The endless worry about whether the other guys are supporting you. Are they talking behind your back? Is the drummer going to quit? The annoyance at bad reviews, looking out at the audience and taking note that several important people ducked out early. I was glad to let go of all that.

I was also recording new songs on my little four-track Fostex cassette recorder. Sometimes I'd write a couple of songs a week. My output amazed the other band members. Kathy was the most prolific after me, but her songs came along more slowly. I was careful to reassure her that I wasn't trying to take over her band by inundating her with material. We collaborated on songs, too, but I wondered if she was doing it because she was trying to make me feel more creatively fulfilled. The first one we worked on together was called "I'm Kickin' You Out." I wrote it with Kathy in mind, just as I'd done with "Gimme Some," almost ten years ago now. A rocker with a propulsive James Jamerson–inspired bass line and mean-spirited lyrics, the song became one of the highlights of our show.

When producer Mike Chapman signed the band to a publishing deal, it felt like we were on our way. Chapman had produced Blondie's big hits, including the platinum single, "Heart of Glass," and we were in awe of him, especially Kathy, the biggest Blondie fan I knew after Lois. We went into the studio to record a classy demo of six songs. In exchange for producing the demo, Chapman would get a percentage of our record deal. We were all banking on the assumption that the label would also hire him to produce our album.

Two of the six songs Chapman chose were mine, "Nails in My Heart" and "We Break Our Own." Things went smoothly until he started mixing the songs. I argued about the way he was mixing "Nails." He thought it sounded like a hit, I thought it sounded like shit. He was thinking Aerosmith/ZZ Top, I was thinking Bryan Ferry/Robert Palmer.

My arguments went nowhere. It was like butting heads with a bull. Kathy tried to calm me down. I yelled at her and kicked my bass case and broke my big toe, then limped out in a huff.

A month later Kathy invited me to join her at a Studio City bar called Residuals and told me I was fired. She treated me to several rounds of expensive single malt scotch before breaking the news, which she dropped between a double Oban and a double Laphroaig. It was for my own good, she said. She knew I wasn't going to be happy playing with her forever and she wanted to take the band in a new direction. I was one of her oldest and best friends, and I'd been a pillar of strength for her, just like ten years ago in the Violators. She loved my songs and thought I should start my own band and get my own publishing deal, because I deserved it.

Then she bought me another round.

I'd never been fired from a band before. I said some mean things. I mentioned hiring a lawyer. I accepted the drink, though.

I was three sheets to the wind when I left, but fortunately I ran out of gas just two blocks from the bar. I managed to coast a block to a liquor store, where I called Lois.

"What's wrong?" she said.

"Kathy kicked me out," I said. "I just ran out of gas, too."

Lois came to rescue me. Again.

After Kathy fired me, I holed up with my four-track and wrote a bunch of new songs. Most of them originated from titles of fictitious songs mentioned in *Tough Baby* and my third novel, *Boiled in Concrete*. I referred to these songs as being the work of a band called Cloud 19.

Cloud 19 was my contemporary ideal of a band, half imaginary/half real, half blues/half garage rock. A flesh and blood version of the band rented a studio and recorded the songs on my birthday, May 15, 1991. Ron Rogers, another Austin expatriate friend, engineered the session and played rhythm guitar. Don Fisher, also from Austin, played drums and Jon Dee Graham played lead guitar.

Jon Dee was living in L.A. and playing with John Doe's (ex-X) band. We had hooked up and were pals again, and his guitar playing on the demo was as hot as five-star curry. The whole thing went so smoothly it was as if Martin Fender had stepped out of one of my books to show me how it's really done.

A few months after Kathy fired me, Carla asked if I'd consider playing in her band. "Sounds like fun," I said, and after rehearsing a few times, we started playing gigs at clubs in L.A., San Diego, Santa Barbara and San Francisco.

In the early eighties, when Kathy Valentine was zooming up the charts with the Go-Go's and doing the usual things rock stars do, Carla Olson persevered with the Textones. Kathy's replacement on guitar was George Callins, Eddie's old pal from San Antonio who'd recruited us for the Queen Bee gig—a fact we never mentioned again. The Textones had evolved as Carla blossomed as a songwriter and performer, but despite a brief run on the Billboard chart with *Midnight Mission*, the band's debut LP, they never found mainstream success like the Go-Go's. They kept releasing CDs, however, and were stars in France and Sweden. A band could do a lot worse. During rehearsals, we frequently jammed on Stones songs. Nobody could mimic those Stones dual-guitar licks like Carla and George.

Then, a few months after I joined the band, ex-Rolling Stones guitarist Mick Taylor came aboard to show us how those licks were really played. I'd seen Mick with the Stones on the Ed Sullivan show. I was just a gangly kid and he was a superstar. Now he was playing on the same song as me, playing riffs I'd heard a million times, sometimes in my dreams. Now and then nodding approval at one of my songs.

Mick is arguably one of the best guitarists in the world. He started out in John Mayall's Bluesbreakers, and replaced the Stones' original guitarist, Brian Jones, in the summer of 1969. The Stones had fired Brian; he'd been so messed up on drugs and alcohol that he'd ceased being a functioning member of the band. Brian died shortly afterward under murky circumstances, probably either in a drug-related accident or murdered by one of his druggie associates.

Mick quit the band in 1974 because he was bored with it, he said, but his five-year tenure with the Stones coincided with a good proportion of their best work. That's Mick Taylor you hear on "Honky Tonk Women,"

"Brown Sugar," "Tumbling Dice," "Moonlight Mile," "Sway" and the albums *Let it Bleed, Sticky Fingers* and the penultimate rock 'n' roll masterpiece, *Exile on Main Street.*

The Carla Olson/Mick Taylor Band recorded a live album at the Roxy on Sunset Boulevard. Five additional venerable musicians were recruited for the show and a series of gigs stretching over the course of a month and a half. The extras made us a twelve-piece band, a very big sound onstage, a rolling caravan of rock.

Carla was at center stage on lead vocals, skinny as a schoolgirl down to her cigarette-leg jeans and pointy-toe boots, with the same long, straight blonde hair flying and the same '58 Les Paul she was playing when I'd met her back in 1975. On her left was George, not much changed over the years, either. At rehearsals or when they were just tuning up, Carla and George riffed on Stones songs the way Christians quote the Bible, the way happy people hum. They appeared to know every song the Stones ever recorded.

The other permanent members of the band were Tom "Junior" Morgan on saxophone and Rick Hemmert on drums. I'd never had such good rapport with a drummer. The melding of our playing gave the band a muscular bottom-end groove.

Ian McLagen, a veteran of many Stones tours, was on the Hammond B-3 organ and electric piano. Barry Goldberg, who had played with Electric Flag and Bob Dylan, doubled on piano and organ. Lisa Bronston sang backing vocals, Juke Logan played harmonica and on sax, we had Phil Kenzie and Joe Sublett. Besides being my fourth cousin, Joe was a former member of the Cobras, one of Austin's premier blues bands. He'd also played with Bonnie Raitt, Taj Mahall and Dennis Quaid.

Mick still had a big mane of dirty blond hair, and his solos still had enough takeoff thrust to astral project an elephant around the world. Sounds issued from his guitar that I'd never heard before. He played blindingly fast leads, beautiful Middle Eastern melodies, the most authentic Delta bottleneck blues this side of Robert Johnson and all those unmistakable trademark sonic blasts for anyone who grew up during the Stones age.

Damn, it was fun.

I was happy just being one of the guys in the band, and one of the songwriters. Two Cloud 19 songs were in our repertoire: "Who Put the

Sting on the Honey Bee" and "World of Pain." With Mick Taylor playing guitar on them, backed by nine other musicians who weren't half bad either, my songs sounded even better than they did in my mystery novels. And Mick liked *Rock Critic Murders* and *Tough Baby*. Turned out he was a big Raymond Chandler fan.

16. TOUGH BABY

It started when I was still playing with Kathy and Lois was working at the *LA Reader*. At first I thought it might be the fact that our days and nights were running on different tracks. When I rehearsed with the band I got home between eleven and midnight. After that I usually stayed up a few more hours, writing or working on songs. Lois was one of those minimum-eight-hours-of-sleep people, and unlike me she had to get up for her nine-to-five job.

One night I came home and the apartment was silent, dimly lit. I put down my bass, went back to the bedroom. Dark in there, but I could tell Lois wasn't asleep. It was the sound of her breathing, the way Kiki and Marlowe, lying next to her in bed, simultaneously looked up at me, their bright eyes saying, *'bout time you got here. It's been rough.*

Her face was buried in the crook of her elbow. I crouched by the bed and kissed the back of her neck. "Hi, sweetie," she said finally, her voice muffled, lips against the pillow. She'd been crying.

"What is it?"

"Oh, nothing."

I turned on the light.

"Don't." Off it went. She sniffled, reached for a Kleenex.

"What'd you do tonight?" I asked. Change the subject, maybe the answer will come.

"Nothing. Watched TV a little."

"What did you watch?"

"I don't remember. What about you? I suppose you had a great time."

"Sure. It was cool. Mac came by and jammed. So did Nigel, Clem and Frankie. Clem played drums for a few songs. Hank Ballard and the Midnighters were rehearsing in the room on one side of us, and L.A. Guns was down the hall. We also worked up one of my new songs."

"You're having a great time out here, aren't you?" she said.

"Yes," I said. "Aren't you?"

No answer.

"Well?"

"No. I hate it."

"Why?"

Silence.

"Why?"

Silence.

"Is it your job?"

She sighed. I knew the answer to that one. She'd recently started working with a rising young photographer, which was a lot cooler than the *LA Reader* job, but it had its frustrations, too.

"Hang in there, sweetie," I said. "You'll get something better. I know you will."

We hugged. Finally she said, "I don't know what it is. I mean, I don't know. I'm just not happy here. I know I should be. You certainly are. But I'm not."

I didn't know what to say. I'd had a sneaking suspicion about this. I was hoping it would resolve itself.

I stretched out next to her and turned on the TV. Smiles lit our faces as a car chase cut to James Garner's face and the *Rockford Files* theme song—harmonica and wheezing synthesizer—came buzzing out of the set. We loved the show. It served up delicious slabs of L.A. scenery, including places that were a stone's throw from where we lived. Rockford's Firebird, gold chains, men in awful plaid suits, women and men in bad wigs, wall-to-wall polyester. As we settled in to watch, Marlowe, the perfect world-weary big striped tabby cat, ambled up Lois' legs and curled up between us.

"Marlowe's old movie star girlfriends keep calling him," she said.

"He's just a gigolo," I said.

Kiki, petite and prim with her pink nose and tuxedo, glanced at us and yawned, showing her tiny, sharp teeth.

"Kiki's been bored with Hollywood ever since talkies came in," Lois said. "Kitties had faces back then."

Our cats had rich fantasy lives. We talked about them as if they were our children, our alter egos. They opened presents every Christmas, and on Thanksgiving we sculpted little turkeys out of dressing for them. Sometimes they looked at us like we were crazy.

"When are we going to have a baby, Jesse?"

So that was it. It rarely reared its giant head, but when it did, it ruled the room.

"We need to wait," I said. "I really want to be more settled, to have more going on before we do that. It's a giant change."

"Yes, I know," she said. "But I can't wait forever."

"I know," I said. "I know."

It became like an old song. She'd raise the question, we'd lapse into the same lines of dialogue. Lois wanted to have a baby. I said we needed to wait. I wanted to reach some definitive point in my art and career. I wanted to be ready to be a father, not overwhelmed by it. These arguments seemed similar to ones I'd used to put off our marriage; I realized that. But then there were the practical reasons. You need a lot of money to have a kid. Especially in L.A.

Besides working on my Martin Fender novels, I was writing spec screenplays and treatments. I also wrote a series of short stories about a hardboiled North Hollywood non-musician P.I. named Clapton. I optioned the stories to a producer at Propaganda Films, who wanted to develop the Clapton stories as a TV series. My agent started sending me out on meetings with other producers. A year later I optioned *Rock Critic Murders* to a film company, who also paid me to write the screenplay. While the deal was peanuts by Hollywood standards, it was more than I'd made on any one project in my life, and it kept us going for a while. It would've been swell if the movie had actually gotten made. At least the option kept getting renewed every year, which made up for the royalty checks that never materialized.

Life wasn't too bad, actually. We were getting by, paying the rent and having fun living in Los Angeles. But where would the money for a kid come from?

I had a hard time getting used to the idea that Lois wasn't happy in L.A. When we first arrived, she was happy, I know. We immersed ourselves in the place. We studied its history and architecture, its myths and mysteries. We sought out places that had been featured in films and books, like the Chemisphere house in *Body Double,* the St. James Hotel in *Murder, My Sweet.* On weekends we'd look up the addresses where Raymond Chandler had lived. Often we drove up to Big Bear Lake reading *Lady in the Lake* or listening to a tape of the radio play. Sometimes we met friends at Boardner's for drinks because Chandler used to drink there or we dined at Musso's, trying to envision the time he and John Houseman got snockered on martinis so Chandler could break his writer's block and start on the screenplay for *The Blue Dahlia.*

We met all the important mystery authors who came out for book signings and struck up lasting friendships with many Los Angeles-based authors at the monthly meetings of the So-Cal chapter of Mystery Writers of America. It was a cool constituency. Some nights, Lois and I would close the bar at the Sportsmen's Lodge in Studio City with Jerry Petievich (*Live and Die in L.A.*), Wendy Hornsby (*77th Street Requiem*) and Terry Baker, owner of the mystery bookstore on the boardwalk in Venice beach. Michael Connelly and I became friends while he was still a crime reporter for the *Los Angeles Times*, anxiously awaiting the release of his first novel, *The Black Echo.* Lunch at the police academy with LAPD detective Paul Bishop (*Citadel Run*) was always fun and informative.

Probably the most remarkable crime novelist we befriended was James Ellroy, a fascinating, charismatic author who earned the title "greatest noir novelist" the old-fashioned way, by being darker than the next ten authors combined and by grounding his diabolically convoluted plots in Los Angeles' twisted psychohistory. A native of L.A., Ellroy was living on the East Coast but frequently returned on book tours. When I met him in 1988, he was promoting his breakthrough novel, *The Black Dahlia.* The story was his fictional take on the most famous unsolved homicide case in L.A. history, the gruesome murder in 1938 of actress/party girl Elizabeth Short.

Ellroy became obsessed with the Black Dahlia story in his youth because of its parallels to the 1958 murder of his own mother, when he was eight years old. She was the victim of a sex murder. The crime was never solved. Ellroy grew up weird, sniffing glue and panties, committing petty crimes and devouring sleazy detective magazines and hard-boiled crime fiction. His bad habits and deviant obsessions nearly killed him before he cleaned up and dedicated himself to his goal of becoming the greatest crime novelist who ever lived.

I'd read about Ellroy's history in the *LA Weekly*. He was infamous for scribbling profane book inscriptions and taking readings to a new level, performing a rap that sounded like a jive deejay hawking books written by a madman. "It's a book for the whole family," he'd intone in his menacing baritone, "if the name of your family is Manson." His fans ate it up.

The day after we first met, he called and invited me to breakfast. He drank lots of coffee. He was a caffeine freak. In contrast to his performance persona, I found him warm, sincere and engaging.

He told me about his youth and a few things about his mother's murder I hadn't heard before. I told him about Dianne's murder. He wanted to know if I was ever going to write about it.

I said I didn't know and changed the subject. "Do you really hate rock music, like your protagonists?"

"Yeah," he said, nodding. "Yeah, I really do. It's all noise to me. I don't get rock music. I like jazz and some classical stuff."

We had other things in common, though, including a murder that wouldn't go away. He seemed to have taken his past and assimilated it into his work. It was the driving force behind his writing. I had thrown myself into music to escape my past. Yet I wasn't obsessed with murder; I turned to crime fiction because I loved the language, the guise of the detective, his sense of righteousness in a crazy world. Writing, like playing music, quieted my mind. It made the flashbacks stop for a while.

I liked Ellroy a lot. I admired his courage, his crazy energy, his turbocharged intelligence. He talked like a bebop solo with a 200 IQ. I was glad he called me for coffee.

He would write the story of his mother's murder and his search for her killer in *My Dark Places*, published in 1996. My estimation of him would soar even higher. After years of writing all around his story, he had confronted the thing that made him James Ellroy. I didn't know if I could do something like that. The idea scared me.

17. ANYTHINGCANHAPPENLAND
DECEMBER 21, 1993

This must be the loneliest place in the world. I'm staring at the whiteness in front of my nose, telling myself this lump in my throat is probably nothing and it'll be nice to get this thing over with, get the hell out of here.

Now they're telling me to be very still and hold my breath. There goes the whirring sound again. The CT scanner's electromagnetic eyes are slicing through me, skin, flesh, bone, soul, past. How long do these things take, anyway?

They say it's probably nothing. That's why I'm here, just to make sure. That's what I keep telling Lois. She worries about cancer a lot, though not nearly as much as my mother, who's always seemed obsessed with doctors, disease and death. Cancer seems to be the thing she fears most.

I don't remember how long I've had the lump. Maybe a year or so, maybe more. I kept putting it off. Finally I went to see my doctor. He said it's probably nothing, but I should see a specialist anyway. An otolaryngologist. A what? Call him an ENT, for ear, nose and throat. I've been to one of those before, when I had nodes on my vocal cords.

Dr. Nixon has a thin face and sharp nose, smells like cigarettes. I just had a cigar. "It's probably nothing, but we should do some tests," he says.

Are my cigars a problem? He shakes his head. Two a day is probably

181

nothing to worry about, he says. Still, I decide I'm definitely going to quit. No use pushing my luck. He sends me for an X ray, and it still looks like nothing. Blood test results look OK, too. Might as well do the CT scan, he says. That way we'll know for sure.

So here I am. A white mummy lying in a white case in a white room. The technician is a black woman, nice looking with purplish lipstick. This is my lunch break. I've been working on history documentaries for TV the last four years. Mostly war documentaries for A&E. I'm doing a mini-series about America's western expansion called *Adventures in the Old West* for the Disney Channel. My third Martin Fender novel, *Boiled in Concrete*, came out last year, but it missed the bestseller list just like the others, so the steady money from low-budget TV is welcome.

I'm sure it's nothing. I had a moment of doubt when I walked into the waiting room and saw people sitting with quiet, serious looks on their faces. Fish hovered in the huge tropical aquarium, mouths miming "Oh, no" as they sucked oxygen from the water, staring at those glum human faces on the other side of the glass.

If it was absolutely nothing I wouldn't be here, but it's gotta be nothing. I just became a father, just figured out what life is really about. I can't leave my wife and son, can't just die on them. When I think about that, this lump in my throat feels like it's the size of a fist.

Be perfectly still. Hold your breath.

I've been immersed in history the last few years. Our documentaries don't pay as well as movies or even the classier docs like Ken Burns' *The Civil War*, but it still beats working. Lewis and Clark are the big story in the first episode of our mini-series about the West. It's occurred to me that crossing the wilderness in 1804–1807 with the Corps of Discovery has a few parallels to life on the road with a band. For one thing, they met a lot of wild women along the trail. The women from some of the tribes just wouldn't leave them alone. The guys grumbled behind the backs of Lewis and Clark, just like the grumbling you'd hear in the dressing rooms of any backup band on the road. One of them accidentally shot Lewis in the ass.

On *Adventures of the Old West*, I'm working for a producer named

Stephen Purvis, originally from Austin. The narrator is Kris Kristofferson, who also sings a few songs for the series, including "Ballad of Lewis & Clark," which I wrote. Who could've predicted that the guy who wrote "Me and Bobby McGee" would someday be singing a folk song by the guy who wrote "Gimme Some" and "Cheap Girl"? The producer for the war series is Monte Markham, a veteran actor in film (*Hour of the Gun, Midway*) and TV (*The Fall Guy, Perry Mason*).

Between the two series, I've been working long hours, actually going in to the production office every morning. It's the first time I've done something like that in years. I rarely get home until seven o'clock.

Lois has been working at *LA Weekly* for the last two years. Ad rep, the same job she had at the *Chronicle*, the best job she's had since we moved here, but less fulfilling than she'd hoped. A mother is what she really wants to be.

Her biological clock finally clobbered me. I always knew Lois was a strong, incredibly persuasive human being, but once her biological imperatives began to assert themselves, I realized she was only toying with me before. Her wants and needs began advancing like the coordinated, pincer movement of army regiments, deployed with ingenious tactical precision. I didn't have a prayer.

Lois accepted my surrender graciously.

Now that we're committed in this new direction, I think more about the future, the safety and prosperity of our family unit. I used to worry about becoming like my parents. I didn't want to lose my identity; it's one of the reasons I wanted to put off having a baby. Now I don't care; the family comes first. *Todo por la familia.*

Naturally, Lois is way ahead of me on all this. She's much better equipped to handle the emotional stresses and complications. The more I see of mothers, the more impressed I am with the female of the species. They're the ones who take the ultimate chance, finding a mate and nurturing a life inside their bodies, then running the gauntlet of dangers ahead, risking the loss of that life and maybe their own as well, at any time between conception and birth. What an awesome bunch of responsibilities. I love and appreciate Lois more than ever.

183

We start trying to have a baby. We learn a few things about life in the process. The way things eventually work out, my sperm homes in on Lois' egg right around the time the fireworks are exploding on New Year's eve 1992. A boy is made. We decide to name him Dashiell.

Because we're going to have a baby, Lois wants to move back to Texas. Our parents are there for one thing. For another, L.A. has been racked by one disaster after another for the past several years—earthquakes, fires, riots and car-jackings, to name a few. Texas has its problems, but it might be a better place to raise our son.

I don't want to leave L.A., but I've decided to trust Lois' maternal instincts. We'll move back to Austin at the beginning of 1994. The mini-series should probably wrap by then, and if it hasn't, we'll leave anyway.

Because I've got a feeling Dashiell Sublett isn't going to wait for anything.

I'm doing double duty today, working on a script on the Battle of Leyte Gulf and taking script meetings on the *West* series. Lois took off early because her maternity leave starts tomorrow, three weeks before Dashiell's due date.

She calls at 3:30 from a nail salon. I'm a little distracted by my work, and at first I think I haven't heard her correctly.

"I'm getting a manicure, and it's time."

"Are you sure, I'll come get you, wait. What do we do, leave your car there?"

"I'm sure, but don't panic. I think I've still got time to finish my manicure."

Luckily, rush-hour traffic cooperates as I race from West L.A. to Studio City to drive my freshly manicured wife through Laurel Canyon to the hospital on the edge of Beverly Hills. The timing works perfectly.

Lois has practically phoned in her epidural ahead of time, so when things get serious, she goes with the flow and when Dashiell Sublett emerges after a mere ninety minutes of labor, Lois is smiling.

The doctor asks me, "Would you like to hold him?"

"Of course I would."

Electrifying. My brand-new son looks up at me with eyes as blue as swimming pools. I've never seen eyes like that, never felt anything like this before.

They say everything's a blur to a newborn, but my son sees me and knows who I am. Knows who he is, too.

Beaming. Taller and broader in the shoulders than I was five minutes ago. I make an announcement: "This is the world's most handsome man, and I'm his dad."

Lois smiling.

I say it again: "This is the world's most handsome man."

No one argues with me, not the doc, not the nurse. Both busy but grinning. Who could possibly disagree? Who would dare?

Later, a giddy kind of sustained ecstasy. Look at those eyes, those lips, that tuft of hair. Look, he clenched his fists!

The nurse says, "You two might want to get some sleep tonight, because this might be the last chance you get for a long while."

Wasted words. Lois and I stay up all night, talking and looking at our baby boy. We're the happiest we've ever been. Why go to sleep? No one's ever been happier.

What a drama this day has been. What happened to my hostile agnosticism, to being on strike against prayer? Did I ever clasp my hands together for an extra-long-distance cellular call and say, *Please, please, please let Dashiell and Lois be OK?*

You bet I did.

If having one child is this dramatic, it's hard to imagine what four or five would be like. I was ten years old when my sister was born. I fed and bathed her and changed her diapers, but over the years certain details faded from memory, and eventually I was under the impression that there was some kind of grace period with newborns. I know they required attention, but I've gotten fuzzy on the proportions. For some reason I'm thinking there'll be a few weeks or months when Dashiell's more or less like an exotic potted plant or tropical fish. You can take care of the basic needs, like feeding and changing, then lay him down and go back to what you were doing, like writing a book or watching TV.

I'm wrong. Dashiell needs much more than food, water and sunlight. The message comes through loud and clear about a minute after he emerges, when I'm holding him in my arms and staring into those swimming-pool blue eyes. This is my son, the World's Most Handsome Man. I'm his dad, and his agenda is my agenda from now on.

Dr. Nixon says the scan doesn't look like cancer. He smiles. I smile. I sigh with relief. "So what is it, then?"

"It's probably nothing, but we should do a biopsy anyway."

"Oh?"

"Just to make sure."

"Do you have to go in the hospital for that?"

"No, not at all. We can do it right here, and it won't take long. You'll probably spend more time signing the forms. If you want me to do it, that is."

Of course I do.

First, Novocaine shots in the neck: hot bee stings from a tiny needle. Be right back, the doctor says. Probably takes a ciggie break. Numbness sets in. He comes back and slowly impales me with the giant needle, probing my neck until he's certain he's found the cyst, pushing the needle in far enough to draw out fluid. He squirts the fluid into several small glass tubes. The nurse comes in while he's labeling each tube and takes them away. They're off to the lab, I'm off to the war in the Pacific again. The Battle of Leyte Gulf was the largest naval battle in history.

"Come back in three days."

Three days pass. Good news. The lab report turned up no cancer cells in the biopsy.

"It seems to be what we call a branchial cleft cyst." Nod, smile. Aroma of Marlboro Lights.

"OK." Hard gulp, tentative sigh. "Is that bad?"

He shrugs. "These things happen. It's nothing to worry about."

"Great."

"But this thing doesn't belong in your neck, so it needs to come out. That's the only way we'll know for sure it isn't cancer. I'd like to do the surgery a few weeks from now. Would that work out for you?"

"Sure. Let's get it over with."

The lump looms over what are otherwise very sunny days in my life. I started on this parade of tests just before Dashiell was born, beginning with my primary care doc, continuing with Nixon the otolaryngologist, getting probed and X-rayed and CT-scanned in the white room. Thanksgiving was full of mixed thoughts—high on fatherhood, new truths about the miracle of life, wondering if this is the beginning of a golden thread or its unraveling.

Lois is at her best during these times. Thanksgiving is a big feast. Harry and Helen come to visit and hold their grandson and help out. We toast the little man landed in our nest like a shining star, but deep down, I'm worried as hell that I might not be his father much longer.

Chances are, it's not going to happen. I don't feel like a guy who has cancer. Not me. I can write all night or play a gig and then drive all night, and the next day do it all over again on two or three hours' sleep. I play hard and work hard. I can't have cancer.

But these things have to happen to somebody. It's a numbers game. On any given day, X number of people will have good luck and Y will have bad luck. That's the way it goes. I've had my share of both. Seventeen years ago, a psychotic killer broke into my house and killed the woman I loved. What else do you need to know about bad possibilities? Here in L.A., city of angels, the best and worst things happen with great regularity. Stars are made, born, destroyed. Fortunes gained, lost, stolen, given away. Tomorrow morning you could win the lottery. You might be discovered by Steven Spielberg, killed in a freeway shooting, buried in an earthquake. The reminders are everywhere. On the same street corner, with Mexican fan palms undulating overhead in the Malibu orange postcard sun, you'll see a clot of homeless people, a stretch limo carrying a rock star, Ernest Borgnine pumping his own gas into his Rolls Royce at a convenience store.

Less than two weeks after we move here, we're at a gas station at the corner of Laurel Canyon and Ventura Boulevard when a black Mercedes swings in and lurches to a halt. The driver is squat, balding, bearded, suit with open-collared silk shirt and gold chains disappearing in a jungle of chest hair. The girl is beautiful. They're fighting. Screams and slapping and fingernails. She opens the door to escape, the guy clutching her leather mini-dress. It snaps open and she pops out of the car naked, like a pea from a pod. The guy drives off clutching the dress, the beautiful girl stomping around the gas station, naked in high heels and big hair, waving her arms and yelling about the guy to bystanders whose mouths hang open like garage doors. After a few minutes of this, my gas tank is full and I'm trying to pay the big-eyed clerk. The Mercedes swings into the parking lot. The beautiful naked girl gets in and they drive away. This is anythingcanhappenland.

Don't think about the worst that can happen, I told myself. Just don't think about it.

The surgery will be on January 12. We sweat out Christmas, trying to concentrate on the great gift we've been given. Babies are supposed to bring good luck. After Christmas we start packing for the big move to Texas.

Another white room, white ceiling, white walls. Black pain. Waking up in the recovery room after surgery is the loneliest place in the world. My neck is on a railroad track with a freight train full of lead rolling over it a thousand times a minute. I hear nurses talking about vacation plans, luxury cruises at great prices, departure times, travel agent recommendations. I can't speak, can't move. Ringing in my ears.

Wait a minute, it's "White Room" by Cream. Goddamn it, I can't move, can't speak.

Then I realize Lois is at my side. Everything's fine, she loves me, everything's OK. I sculpt these words with silent lips as best I can: I'm in pain! She gets a nurse. "We'll take care of it, Mr. Sublett. We'll make you more comfortable in just a second."

Dr. Nixon says the cyst was a lot bigger than he expected. The thing was spread out, extending to the back of my neck, under my ear. The surgery took longer than he'd anticipated. "The good news is the lab reports came in, and it's negative."

"Negative? But does that mean—?"

"Not cancer. It was really ugly, but it wasn't cancer. You can go home and resume your life. Don't worry about it."

"That's great news."

Except my voice sounds like Elmer Fudd. Nixon says not to worry, it's the swelling in my neck and tongue. The effect could last several weeks to a couple of months, but it'll go away.

That night I learn that Demerol makes me vomit. Not good when your neck feels like it's holding your head by a few stitches. They've got a shot for nausea. It stings a little but it's worth it.

After three days in the hospital, home is weird. Our apartment is full of stacked moving boxes and mostly empty bookcases. We left a few of our favorite things on the bookcases. We'll pack them last. These include some of Lois' collectible ceramic vases and some of my favorite rare books, titles by hardboiled pioneer Carroll John Daly, a few first editions by Charles Willeford and *Riata and Spurs* by Charles Siringo, the Texas cowboy, detective and author.

I'm sleeping on the couch because my snoring, caused by the swelling in my throat, keeps Lois awake. She tells me it's very loud.

The Northridge quake hits at 4:31 a.m. and registers 6.7 on the Richter scale. The first jolt nearly tosses me off the couch. I can hear the tectonic plates scraping and growling deep underground. I can hear the building swaying, plaster cracking and beams bending, nails popping. Car alarms screaming, dogs howling.

Must get to Dashiell and Lois. I hoist myself up by tugging on my hair, the only way I can rise without excruciating pain in my neck. I find Lois. We scoop up our sleeping boy and probe the darkness. No electricity.

We decide that outside is best. Let's go. Another jolt rocks the building hard. Going downstairs, we sway like drunks as the structure shakes. Water sloshes out of the pool, instant tidal wave. Palm trees whip back and forth overhead. The neighbors pour out of their apartments, smiling nervously, eyes wide as Frisbees. Dashiell sleeps blissfully.

With Lois and Dashiell in the courtyard, I stagger back up the steps to help our next-door neighbor, Donya. She's old and frail, once a beautiful actress and dancer. She used to date Kirk Douglas and Captain Midnight. "What about Fluffy?" she says, referring to her grossly overfed cat, whose snow-white hair matches that of her mistress.

"Don't worry. She's under the bed, I'm sure, just like our cats. She'll be fine."

Another L.A. crisis. This one is a little grungier than the others. We've got a baby to worry about, for one thing, and I'm not exactly my usual self. And it's a bad earthquake.

I've got an appointment with Dr. Nixon today, but when I finally get through to his office, they say he isn't coming in. His house in the Hollywood hills broke in half.

No electricity or hot water for the next five days. The precious things we saved to pack last have tumbled from the bookshelves. Lois' vintage vases shattered on the carpet. We have to wear shoes in the apartment because we can't clean up the broken shards in the rug. For the next five days we live by candlelight, following the news on a battery-powered TV. I have a sick fascination for the drama and weirdness of it all, even though a lot of the coverage is a sham, a series of cheesy gimmicks to keep people like me glued to their sets.

The epicenter of the quake was under Northridge, several miles to the north of us in the San Fernando Valley. Many apartment buildings pancaked, collapsing several floors down to a short stack of stucco rubble, car grilles flashing death grins from under sandwiched parking garages. A friend who lives in Northridge saw toilets flying through windows. Here's hoping no one was sitting on them.

A man and woman in Van Nuys living in an apartment crammed to capacity, floor to ceiling, after decades of obsessive collecting antique toys and books and assorted ephemera, were crushed in their bed under the weight of their stuff. Death by garage sale.

I'm wearing a large surgical bandage around my neck, and whenever we venture to the bombed-out supermarket on Ventura Boulevard to buy food and batteries (rationed, four to a citizen), I endure the cynical, laughing remarks of strangers. They point at my bandage and laugh, grinning like horses: "What happened, you get a whiplash during the earthquake?"

Two weeks later the moving van comes for our stuff. A flatbed truck takes the Ghia. I drive it up the ramp, just like I did seven years ago, moving from Austin to L.A.

Late that evening we finish cleaning the apartment we've lived in for seven years. Turn in the key, say good-bye, check into a Best Western. We'll leave early in the morning. I'm wistful, hopeful, a proud father, feeling inspired, feeling strange. God, I love L.A., but Texas will be good, too. Babies bring their own bread. Way to go, son; I'm thanking you in advance.

Sometime before dawn a 5.1 aftershock hits, a little farewell kiss on the way out of town. Willie, our skittish tabby, rips a hole in the box spring and crawls inside. He's had it. When it's time to leave we try to coax him out, but he won't budge. I have to take the box spring off the bed, tilt it up and pour him out.

We point our Saab toward Texas and drive. Dashiell's in his car seat, Willie hanging out in back, Marlowe mostly riding on my lap while I drive. Kiki's in a little tin urn they gave us after she was cremated.

Dashiell cries, demands a lot of attention. Happy when he's nursing at Mommy's breast, sleeping beautifully but only for a couple of hours at a time. Always hungry, always needs tending, takes every ounce of love you give him. He's a pain and a joy.

Heading into Texas through El Paso, we hit an ice storm. Slick roads, fierce winds, freezing rain and sleet. The Saab's de-icer goes out, and the windshield grows a thickening skin of frosted ice. We pull over at a dark gas station to wait it out. We're scared; it's predawn darkness and we've got a baby. Everything's heightened, anxieties and joys alike. We're a family unit hurtling through the darkness to a new/old home. Like pioneers. The species must go on. My neck hurts, feels like a clamp is around my throat. Metal hands. A couple of Vicodin and it's better.

Arriving in Austin three days later, I still sound like Elmer Fudd. Hell of a way to greet my old friends. Although it bugs me, Dashiell and Lois don't seem to mind. Nor does it make much difference to Helen and Harry or Jake and Elizabeth. They're ecstatic about our return and having a beautiful new grandson to fawn over.

What a difference it would've made if Dr. Nixon and the pathologists had found cancer in the tumor he removed from my neck. We'd still be in L.A.; I might be in the hospital having some kind of gruesome surgery performed, plus radiation and chemotherapy. I'd lose my hair. I might even have a hole in my throat. Scary to think how close we'd come to disaster.

But everything was cool. Nixon said, Don't worry about it, you don't have cancer. And guys like that don't make mistakes, do they?

PART 4.
FRANKENSTEIN
ROCK

18. HOW TO FLY
THANKSGIVING DAY

Today is Thanksgiving, ten weird days and lots of big changes since that late-evening scan in the white room. "Good luck," the guy said to my back. Well, Mr. CAT scan Man, I woke up this morning with this thought: Five days after I carve our turkey, Dr. Lewis will be carving on me. Maybe I'll end up being a pile of bones and skin and funky gristly parts, too.

The needle biopsy by Dr. Lewis confirmed that there was cancer in my neck, a type called squamous cell carcinoma. The CAT scan led her to believe that it has spread through much of the right side of my neck, metastasized in the lymph nodes, some saliva glands, maybe elsewhere. No wonder no one wanted to look me in the eye. Research on the Internet pegs my five-year survival stats as less than 9 percent. That's 91 dead bass players out of 100.

The numbers give even more black hole weight to the free-falling sensation I felt when Dr. Lewis gave me the news. She was careful not to say anything specific about the staging or severity of the disease, but my instincts told me that this wasn't going to be a simple case of surgery followed by other prescribed procedures. I had that world-screeching-to-a-stop feeling, that game over feeling. If I didn't die, I'd end up a dissected monster, the most appealing parts of me removed or altered beyond recognition.

Cancer is scary shit. A lot of people have nightmare fantasies about it, and at the first sign (no matter how dubious) they see it as an automatic death sentence. I'd never been one of those people until this lump appeared under my jaw, and then reappeared. That's when I started having dark thoughts, suppressing them like I suppressed Dianne's murder.

After Dr. Lewis told me the facts of my diagnosis, I felt myself transported to the front door of 2109 Glendale twenty-one years ago. My world screeching to a halt. Terror, guilt and the absolute zero emptiness of death.

Now I felt like a dead man again. I hated to admit it, considering all I had to be thankful for, but it felt worse the first time.

But as I wrestled with the twin nightmares of my past and apparent future, I began to sort things out. Maybe it hurt worse the first time, I told myself, but I've got to deal with this time. Lois and Dashiell didn't exist for me back then, but they're my everything now. For their sake, I've got to get over this cancer son-of-a-bitch. Maybe I wanted to die the first time, but I sure as hell don't wanna die now. If I made it back from that, maybe, just maybe I can make it through this.

I was forty-three years old, almost twice as old as I was then. Other than having a case of stage four cancer, I was in robust health. That was fairly impressive, considering the recklessness of my youth and the self-destructiveness of my grief. If I survived this thing, maybe it would be possible to find the strength to put that lost and scrambled part of myself back together again. I owed it to myself, I owed it to my wife and son.

I'll tell my parents before dinner. I've managed to keep it secret from them the last twelve days, despite my mother's daily queries. I couldn't tell them because they had my mother's medical crisis to worry about. My mother, who's sixty-six now, had surgery four days ago. I couldn't let her go under the knife worrying about me having cancer. The strain might be too much. This time they operated on her neck, the fifth or sixth time they've gone in to fuse and bolt together the deteriorating vertebrae along the length of her spine. She's always in pain, whether she's recuperating from the last surgery or building up to the next one. It's not easy for us to bear witness to, either. Lois and I were surprised when Mom said they were coming today. She usually takes a lot longer to get up and around. She probably suspects something.

We told Lois' parents several days ago. They took it in stride. Harry and Helen don't dwell on things like illness and death. Maybe it's Harry's military discipline, or something about growing up in the steel towns during the Depression. They're coming for dinner today, too. Two months ago the Richwines moved to a house just three doors down from us. Having a mother-in-law living that close may sound like a recipe for disaster, but I think it's going to work out fine unless Dashiell's grandparents spoil him beyond all hope of salvation.

My brother and sister endorsed my strategy of secrecy, sent their prayers and promised to come for Christmas. James is a short-haired family man running a bank in Okeene, Oklahoma, living in the country with a wife and four kids and horses and cows. Hard to believe this is the guy who took me to my first rock concert and used to run a head shop in Austin. Kathryn, ten years younger than me, works for the U.S. Marshals Service in Savannah, Georgia. She met her husband in the army and has a black belt in karate. They have two kids. I like having a bunch of nieces and nephews.

I know what's going to happen when I tell my mother. That crinkly look will appear around her eyes and mouth, the same look her mother used to get, as if she's resigned herself to the worst. It won't matter what I say to try to convince her that everything will be fine. My dad will be mostly silent, but not because he's as tough as he appears on the surface. I remember the first time I saw him cry. Lois and I had come to visit from L.A. As we were leaving, pulling out of the drive with them standing in the yard, I saw him blinking. Standing there stout as an oak tree, skin tanned from thirty-seven years working on power lines, tears rolling down.

My parents are proud of me and crazy about Lois. They're old and getting fragile. One thing I picked up from Lois over the years: I end phone calls and visits with the words "I love you."

Lois taught me a lot of things like that.

She's been up since the crack of dawn getting everything ready. She's in her element, planning, preparing, being the hostess and taking charge of social events. Like her mom, she's a fantastic cook, a real artist at it. On this Thanksgiving in particular, her responsibilities have come as a welcome diversion.

We bought a three-bedroom fifties ranch house, sitting on a hill less than a mile south of Town Lake and about a mile east of the Continental Club. Our first four months back in Austin, we lived in a duplex three blocks from 2109 Glendale. The market was tight, and when no other options seemed available, Lois asked me if I thought I could handle it. I said yes. Now I took special routes to avoid that haunted street, except for the times I found myself intentionally driving down it, unable to help myself.

The house had a new front and was painted differently, but the sides hadn't changed much and the look of the lot was the same. Sometimes I wondered what would happen if I knocked on the door. Would the person who answered see something in my eyes that betrayed my nightmares?

Otherwise we slipped back into Austin without much trouble. Lois found a position on the *Chronicle* ad staff, and I continued to work on documentaries for the same producers. Telecommuting was rarely a problem. Sometimes I flew to meetings in L.A., San Francisco or New York. My favorite job was a *Biography* episode on Attila the Hun. I started working on a new Martin Fender novel. We resumed old friendships and started new ones. We grew into our role as parents, surviving the dreaded ear infections, toddlerhood and nursery school. Dashiell was bright and curious. Lois and I wondered how we'd survived all those years without him. He was the most amazing thing to happen to us.

I checked in with a doctor about two weeks after our return. I gave him copies of the medical records from Dr. Nixon and told him about the lump. He said my neck seemed to be healing well. Later, after Lois drew attention to it, I realized I was getting colds and other nagging illnesses more than I used to. I complained to the doctor about it and had him examine me again. He said my neck looked fine but on my request referred me to an otolaryngologist. I told the otolaryngologist I thought the lump area felt funny. He said it was just scar tissue, but I wasn't convinced. Later I read a distressing story about this doctor in the paper. He was operating on a patient who had nodes on his vocal cords. Unfortunately, the anesthesiologist had the patient on pure oxygen, and when the doctor attempted to remove the nodes with a laser, it ignited the pure oxygen, shooting flames into the patient's lungs. He died a few weeks later. The doctor blamed the anesthesiologist, but it made me wonder if I should consult with someone else.

By our third year in Austin, I was pretty sure the lump was back. I was even more certain about the smaller ones. The back of my neck felt funny, harder than normal and sore. I went to a new doctor, who ordered some tests, including an ultrasound of the lump area. After viewing the test results, the doctor shrugged and said, "I don't know what it is, but don't worry about it."

"But could it be cancer?" I asked.

"No," he said, smiling and shaking my hand. "Let me know if you have any other problems."

I tried to forget about the whole thing. I told myself the lumps had gone away. Maybe I just stopped looking for them. That worked for a while. Finally I told Lois that the lumps were still there, and were bigger than before. She got mad, then found me a new doctor named Hillary Miller. I liked Dr. Miller immediately. She was attentive and energetic and seemed very proactive. She gave me a thorough physical exam and sent me for X rays and blood and urine tests. After looking over the results and hearing my complaints in greater detail, she agreed that I needed to see an otolaryngologist. She gave me a list of ten otolaryngologists on our insurance plan. But could she recommend one?

Without hesitating, she circled the name Melba Lewis.

My first appointment with Dr. Lewis was in November, three years and ten months after Dr. Nixon removed the first lump. Despite being in the middle of a hectic day, Dr. Lewis took time for pleasantries and laughed or smiled at my jokes, even when they were just goofy asides. She had red hair, a slender figure and a West Texas accent. She was an attractive woman with a great smile and struck me as a warm, intelligent, very hard-working professional.

After a lengthy examination, she asked questions about my previous surgery, the follow-up, how much I smoked (two to three cigars a day), how much I drank (on average, two scotches a day), the history of cancer in my family, allergies. Some of the questions she repeated, including the ones about smoking and drinking.

She arranged for me to have blood tests and a CAT scan. She wanted to see me again the following Monday. "We'll figure this out," she said. "First, we need to eliminate various possibilities. It could be a recurrence of the branchial cleft cyst."

"Does that happen?" I asked.

"It's rare, but not impossible," she said. The other possibilities included a thyroid problem, cat scratch fever, TB and several other medical conditions.

By Monday, the other possibilities had been ruled out.

"I think we need to do a needle biopsy," Dr. Lewis said. "We can do it here in the office. Would it be all right with you if we did it now?"

"Sure," I said, taking off my jacket. "I know the drill."

The drill: swabbed with iodine, numbed by Novocaine, impaled by a giant needle in the neck, several times. Some pain despite the Novocaine because Dr. Lewis had to probe hard into the lump to get a good sample. Four glass slides smeared, labeled, dispatched to the lab. She'd call me as soon as she heard from the lab.

Three days later, at 3:15 p.m., the phone rang.

Dr. Lewis was calling from the airport. That explained the background noise. She said she was sorry it took so long to call, she'd just gotten off the phone with the pathologist. It had been a chaotic day, too. I said I was sorry to hear that. What happened? She explained that she was leaving town on a trip and a lot of things had gone haywire at the last minute. To cap things off, her car battery had died at the airport. She apologized again for taking so long to call.

"That's OK, as long as you've got some good news for me," I said. Mr. Nonchalant Wiseacre, chewing on a cigar.

"Well, I'm sorry, but the news actually isn't good," she said.

"Oh," I said. I put the cigar down.

Airplanes were taking off in the background. I had trouble grasping the details. At first, the way I understood it, the tests indicated that I might have squamous cell carcinoma. I'd heard the term before and I'd never liked the sound of it, though I'd never known what it meant. As I listened, I clung to the hope that the tests were inconclusive, maybe erroneous. Maybe they mixed them up with another patient. Dr. Lewis was talking about ordering more tests and examinations.

I detected a note of urgency in her voice: "And I recommend that you have a surgical procedure called radical neck dissection as soon as possible."

"Oh? But maybe those lab tests will turn out to be wrong and—"

"No. Actually, they're fairly certain."

"Oh, I see. Fairly certain." With those two words, everything changed. I started feeling dizzy.

"This is life threatening." Jet turbines in the background. People going places or coming home. The world turning, sun shining, birds in the sky.

But for me, time stopped. I waited.

She said she could schedule the surgery for December 2, less than two weeks away. "If that's convenient for you. I've checked to make sure an operating room is available."

"Fine," I said. "The sooner the better. Let's get it taken care of." As if we were talking about an ingrown toenail or a brake job. I wanted more details, but I didn't know how to ask. What I really wanted to know was this: Am I going to be turned into a monster with this surgery?

"What's it going to be like?" I finally said.

"This is major surgery." She mentioned some details about the procedure, but I didn't hear them. They were like cloud patterns in the sky above a drowning man. "There's a lot we still need to know."

I wanted her to tell me not to worry, to say that this operation, though it was major surgery, wouldn't entail drastic measures, like the removal of anything I was especially attached to, like my tongue or my throat or my lips. But what could she do? She was at the airport, about to leave town. She'd be able to answer more of my questions next week, she said, after she ran more tests, examined me more closely and studied my old medical records.

"I know this is a lot for you to take in," she said. "I'm so sorry to have given you this news on the phone and then leave town but this trip has been planned for a long time and I—"

"It's OK, really," I said. "I'll be all right. Don't worry about it."

"Do you have access to the Internet?"

"Sure."

"It might be a good idea for you to look up squamous cell carcinoma. That way you can learn a little more about it."

I said that sounded like a good idea. We said good-bye.

I found squamous cell carcinoma on the Internet. The more I learned about it, the worse my odds began to look.

It'll be an hour before our parents arrive. Dashiell's playing with Legos, Lois doesn't need me and I need to walk down to the lake, so off I go. It's a cool, damp day, and the light has a strange quality. Near the lake, the mist and fog blend with the horizon like a gray conspiracy, but the trees are vibrant, the fall colors startlingly bright.

I take special notice of the light, the mist, the colors, the way the air tastes on the breeze, the way it feels on my skin. I don't want to internalize all this just because I'm in a heightened emotional state. I know people tend to do this kind of thing when they're facing their own mortality.

I seem to be seeing symbolism wherever I look, but I'm skeptical about that sort of thinking, so I try to ignore it. Sometimes, though, a particular metaphor seems to be exactly what I need. Like now, as I'm about to walk across the Congress Avenue bridge. The bridge spans the Colorado River where it's impounded to form Town Lake, the jewel of the city. When they roll me into the operating room in five days, that'll be another bridge. I'll cross that bridge just like I'm crossing this one. Don't look down. Don't worry about what might happen—whether I'll die or emerge as a decimated version of myself, minus tongue or larynx or other things I've grown fond of over the years. Just do it, lie on that gurney and go to sleep and I'll emerge on the other side. Then take up my life from there.

Think about the Pilgrims crossing the Atlantic on a stinky little ship. Coming over here, setting up at Plymouth for a long and nasty winter. Many died. The following fall, Thanksgiving dinner was a time of celebration and gratitude, but it was also a way of flipping the bird at the elements and disease and other hardships that almost wiped them out.

If it doesn't kill you, it'll make you stronger. That's what they say, anyway. Sometimes you have to forge ahead, no matter if you hear the predators howling in the woods all around. You keep marching and you grow stronger and wiser by the simple fact that you lived through another day, another mile of the trail.

I'll get through this somehow.

On Monday, Dr. Lewis peered into my throat, looking for clues that might reveal more about my cancer, like why the lump might've returned and if it wasn't malignant then, why was it malignant now? The mystery intrigued her.

I found the perfect doctor. She's professional, literate and pretty, and she gets all my jokes. Her mentor at the University of Arkansas Medical School was Dr. James Suen, who literally wrote the book on head and neck cancer. Dr. Suen was President Bill Clinton's otolaryngologist. Dr. Lewis assisted Dr. Suen on some of Clinton's appointments. This association pleases me a lot since I'm a Clinton fan, but I don't find out about it until much later. Dr. Lewis isn't the type to boast.

Her office is a swirl of activity. When I ask about her weekend trip, she says she and her dancing instructor did well in an amateur ballroom dancing competition. That's her hobby. Lois and I think that's very cool. Something about having a ballroom dancer as my surgeon seems right. I want to call her Melba. Maybe later—depending on how things go.

The type of patient Dr. Lewis would expect to see with squamous cell carcinoma, in this stage of advancement, would be an elderly male, a heavy drinker and chain smoker. She's talking about barflies and alkies. Two Scotches a night and two or three cigars a day isn't the kind of behavior that causes this kind of cancer.

Toward the end of an exhaustive examination, she finds a tiny lesion on my right tonsil. This turns out to be the primary—the place the cancer originated. She practically says "Eureka!" when she finally spots it, and lab tests will confirm that she's correct. From the tonsil the cancer apparently metastasized to my lymph nodes on the right side. Dr. Lewis suspects that other tissues on that side of my neck have also been invaded.

Pathologists have already determined that the lump, or branchial cleft cyst, as it was diagnosed in L.A., is malignant. I was surprised to learn that the first cyst, or parts of it, were in storage in L.A. Dr. Lewis ordered samples to be sent to an Austin pathology lab for study. The Austin pathologists found that the samples also contained SCC. The L.A. pathologists screwed up. This means I've had the cancer for five years, maybe six or more.

Obviously that isn't good, but Dr. Lewis doesn't say what it means for my survival statistics. By the gravity of her tone and the apparent stress she shows while talking about it, I begin to suspect that the outlook is as dire as my research leads me to believe.

I don't ask Dr. Lewis anything about my statistics. I'm not sure if she's computed them or not. Maybe she doesn't feel she knows enough yet to put a number on it. Maybe she just doesn't want to tell me. If that's the case, I'll just play along.

I say that I've done some research on the Internet, and what I found out was pretty scary. She nods. "It's serious, all right," she says.

The cancer experts rate the severity of this disease in stages ranging from one to four, with four being the most serious. Mine appears to be stage four. A site I found devoted to oral pathology has grim things to say about squamous cell carcinoma: "Squamous cell carcinoma is a common oral epithelial malignancy that all too frequently leads to mutilative surgery and death. One study showed that the overall five-year survival rate for all stages of oral SCC is under 50 percent." No sugarcoating here.

Sometimes it's like being on a crazy game show where you're supposed to guess what kind of prize is behind the door, except instead of prizes they're different kinds of bombs. You never know what's going to blow up in your face next. Like whenever I meet a new doctor. He or she will enter the exam room, shut the door, extend a friendly hand and say "Hello, Jesse, my name is Dr. _."

"Nice to meet you," I say.

"You're famous," he or she says, glancing at my chart.

"Oh, well, a few years ago I had this band called the Skunks, and I write crime novels and—"

"No, what I mean is we've all heard of your case. You have a highly unusual case of cancer."

"Oh."

"Normally a person with this type and stage of cancer wouldn't be alive after four years."

Nothing quite makes your day like being told you ought to be dead already.

When I was a kid, a friend of my father's had this kind of cancer. They took out his tongue and voice box. He spoke by making an awful belching sound through a hole in the base of his throat. It scared me. I've seen others use a device that produces a cheesy electronic voice when held against the throat.

I think about Joe Gracey, who produced the first Skunks album. They removed his tongue and voice box, but he was still making music, producing records and writing songs. Happily married to a country singer, raising kids. He seemed to be OK with his fate, communicating with a Magic Slate and body language.

I like my neck the way it is. I like my voice. I'm not as vain as I used to be, but I'd still rather carry a pocket mirror than a Magic Slate. But maybe that's what I'm in for. Maybe something even worse. The unknowns are the scariest part.

On December 2, Dr. Lewis is planning to remove my right tonsil and the soft palate surrounding it. She'll also be taking out, on the same side, my jugular vein, saliva glands, the large tumor and several smaller ones, all of the lymph nodes, the large muscle on the side of my neck and a nerve that controls certain arm movements. Will she stop there, or will she need to keep cutting and cutting and cutting?

I don't know about praying. I've had problems with God. If he's capable of intervening to prevent the loss of life and limb, then where was he on August 16, 1976? Why do we have cancer, AIDS, war, genocide, poverty, child abuse? What about the Inquisition, slavery, ebola, crack babies, Milli Vanilli? With a track record like that, why would you expect God to do you a favor?

"I pray all the time," Lois said.

"That's fine," I said. "For you."

"You're gonna fight this, aren't you?" she said.

"Of course I am."

"Jesse, you don't sound very convincing."

This was right after the phone call from Dr. Lewis. Lois came home from work and asked what I'd found out, so I told her. Dashiell was in the living room watching Cartoon Network.

Lois and I were hugging, our eyes just inches apart. Like many women, she has a built-in lie detector. It even works over the phone.

"Give me a chance to get my attitude screwed on right," I said. "I only found out an hour ago. I'll get it together. I'll start praying, too."

"OK," she said.

I don't want to leave Dashiell and Lois. I don't want to become a monster, either.

The next day, I called the neighborhood Lutheran pastor. Rev. James Linderman had been a chaplain with the Green Berets in Vietnam. Tough guy, tall and broad shouldered. I liked him. He talked to us for a while and prayed with us. Made us feel better. We apologized for Dashiell's behavior; he was running around the room, climbing on the furniture. Linderman laughed and said, "Let him be a kid. It's not bothering me. I've done this when people were shooting at me. This is nothing."

Maybe Linderman wouldn't have approved of it, but we also visited a botanica in our old South First Street neighborhood, where we bought votive candles and crucifixes. I ended up talking to the proprietor's husband. He's also a Vietnam vet and an Aztec *curandero*. He prayed for me, too. He said he was confident that things were going to turn out OK. We left feeling more reassured.

We drove out to Stonewall. We cruised past Trinity Lutheran Church and the LBJ ranch, then into the country, stopping to look at my grandparents' old farmhouse. On the way back to Austin I thought about growing up in the Hill Country, being part of that landscape even when I was thinking of nothing but escape. Now I could see that, for better or worse, I was still a part of it. It helped make me what I am, pushing and pulling me, zapping me with positive and negative ions. So what if there were shitkicker bullies in high school? They told me I was weird. What did I want? To be accepted by them? Their harassment gave me validation and motivated me. I should thank them.

Thank you, dear, sweet funky landscape and small-town people. Now that I'm newly humble, can something out there please save my life? Yes, I'm on my knees, hands folded now.

Is it hypocritical to be praying now, after twenty-one years of snarling agnosticism? That bugged me at first, but not anymore. I'll do anything to fight this evil son-of-a-bitch.

Red leaves, yellow leaves, purple, orange. The lake is a mirror reflecting those brilliant colors against the gray sky. The trees are electric, flashing and pulsing with different flavors of light and tonality.

Down the trail, around the curve downhill to Waller Creek. A fair day for bird watching. Several great blue herons, one green heron, egrets and other wading birds, turtles and squirrels and the same fiery show of leaves. Someone flipped nature's brightness switch.

There's a fine-looking great blue heron standing in the shallows near the mouth of Waller Creek. I was crossing the pedestrian bridge over the creek when I first saw him. He's almost four feet tall. Neither of us moves. What's he thinking? Every fall color seems to be in the reflected fan of water surrounding him, as if it's an artist's palette and he's the brush.

His chest feathers ruffle and he leans forward and launches into the air, his powerful, broad wings taking three or four leisurely strokes to carry him across the lake. A voice whispers in my ear: *It's going to be as hard for you to learn to live again as it would be to learn to fly like a bird.*

The thought comes to me just like that, a voice in my ear, a note slid under a door.

Maybe nature's trying to get my attention, letting me know it's here to help. Is that what Henry David Thoreau would think? Thoreau and the transcendentalists believed you saw God through nature. That's always seemed reasonable to me, whether there is a god or not. Thoreau was cool.

Maybe it's a miracle. I feel for the lump. Nope, it's still there. A miracle would be nice right about now. I actually do believe in them, more or less. I used to believe that I deserved to make a living playing rock 'n' roll . A pretty far-fetched wish, but I got it. I didn't get super famous and filthy rich, but I didn't exactly wish for that. The next big thing I wanted was to be a writer and to make my living doing that. I got that wish, too.

Lois would agree with me that Dashiell is a miracle.

Now and then I get lucky.

We tell Mom and Dad the news before dinner. My father, the toughest guy I've ever known, cries a little. My mother says she's known all along.

I carve the turkey and we eat. It's good.

19. UNDER THE KNIFE

Check-in time at Seton Medical Center is nine a.m., so we take Dashiell to preschool at the same time we go every other morning, pretending to be unrushed and unworried for his sake. Lying like dogs, in other words, but it's good therapy. Like an acting job, you become the character. Who knows? Maybe you'll achieve alchemy, turn make-believe into reality.

We remind Dashiell about what's going to happen today. That Daddy's going to the doctor to get his neck fixed, that I'll be spending a few nights there. I'll be fine again very soon. He and Mommy will come visit. Don't worry about a thing, OK?

"OK," he says. His eyes, big and clear, betray no troubled thoughts.

He seems to be taking it all in stride, but what do I know? I've been walking around five years or more with cancer taking over my neck, thinking everything's just fine. More kisses and hugs and then we're gone.

Surgery patients get one day's free parking. Nice to know. You sign your name at the surgery center check-in and wait. When it's your turn, a nurse takes you to the room across the hall where they get you prepped and ready to roll.

The room has reclining chairs, reading lamps, art prints. Seems like all the medical offices we visit are heavy on Impressionism, a style I have not yet learned to love. No Bosch or Dalí. Lots of Monet. A nurse greets us and hands me a hospital gown, disposable booties and a plastic bag for my clothes. Over there's the changing booth. Strip off everything, she says, even your wedding ring. Once I'm naked, it's starting to get real. The gown sucks. Like the hood of a car, its primary purpose is to allow the surgeons access with minimum interference; embarrassment prevention is not a priority.

We sit and wait and try to think of anything except why we're here. Lois brought *Vogue* and *Metropolitan Home*. I've got *National Geographic*—polar explorers and arctic birds. I've become a bird nut. Just looking at pictures of birds, especially large wading birds and sea birds, gives me a cool feeling. It's a lot like the feeling I used to get from Dianne's rabbit trick. In fact, the rabbit trick still works for me.

I've got a new writing journal, a virgin. I write the date on the first page, underline it. Underline it again. Two seconds later I realize I have nothing to say. Away goes the journal.

Lois and I talk. She reads her magazines. I look at pictures of men and birds on the ice and the cold, pitiless ocean. They take my vitals. More forms to fill out and sign. Is this just busy work? The activity seems to continue right up until you go under the knife. This looks important: Do you have a power of attorney on file? Are you aware that the surgical procedure about to be performed upon your body might not necessarily make you better? Are you aware you might lapse into a coma and never wake up? Or that you might suffer paralysis, blindness or death?

This form doesn't say anything about cures, but I hold out hope that miracles do happen. Even in this place, where you have no legal right to expect them. What the hell, I sign everything.

I wonder what Melba's doing. That's what we've been calling Dr. Lewis among ourselves. I wonder if she goes jogging on a morning like this.

They give me Valium. I give them a urine sample. "Your doctor is in the building," says the nurse. I wonder what kind of things they do right before a big job. They must have certain personal rituals they do to psyche themselves up and for good luck.

Like before a gig, when we'd get into our groovy stage clothes, put on some eyeliner and mousse up our hair, warm up our instruments. Maybe shadow box a little. Sing some scales, tell some jokes. What does a surgeon do to get in the groove? Lois and I talk about it a little. I say I'm sure Melba isn't listening to the Sex Pistols and telling dirty jokes, doing high fives right up until the last minute. Lois laughs. Sure, but how can you know?

Finally they come to get me. I hop aboard the gurney and they wheel me into another room. There are half a dozen gurneys in there, most of them occupied, like airplanes on the tarmac awaiting take-off. It's cold in here. They bring a blanket. They take my vitals again. Every new person who comes along tells me their name, like a waiter at a restaurant. At least two or three more times, I'm asked to verify my name, and do I know what kind of surgery I'm having today? I'll have the special, please. Right or left side? I think about the guy in Florida who went in to get his right leg amputated and they mistakenly cut off the left. Shit happens. Probably not a good time to be making dumb jokes, like telling the nurse I'm here to have a sex-change operation.

The assistant anesthesiologist is about to start my IV. You're about to feel a little sting, he says. Sting, pause, bang, I'm hooked up. What about the other gurneys? Where are they headed? Probably some are here for minor things, like an oil change. Kids' stuff, like a nose job or appendectomy. Maybe one or two are in worse shape than I am. Maybe one of us won't make it out of here alive.

You're up, they say. I kiss Lois good-bye. We've talked this through before, and by this time it's condensed down to a private language, a handful of simple words and phrases: *I love you. . . Don't worry. . . Everything's gonna be OK. . .* Doesn't sound like much, but the combination of words and feelings behind them says everything.

A nurse tells Lois where she'll be able to find me after surgery, and I'm rolling on, leaving her behind, through the automatic doors into the hospital's inner maze, corridors of green scrubs and shiny stainless-steel carts and bright lights. The gurney slows a bit as the last pair of white doors pop open like an Easter blossom and admit us, the gurney quickly swings into a parking place under the big lights. Not a cozy place, it's all function in here. There's not a lot to see. Instruments and gadgets are tucked safely out of your line of sight. Wonder where they hide the chainsaw. High ceiling, extra-bright lights. It's going to be like time travel. I'm going to be in here for a long time, but I won't remember a thing about it, maybe not even this very moment. I don't know many details about the procedure, like what they do first. Draw a dotted line where they'll make the first incision? I look around for Dr. Lewis and they tell me that the drug that's gonna knock me out has begun flowing into my veins. The next thing I know I don't know anything at all.

I'm writing on my Mac with my eyes closed, writing hard because I've got a deadline and the ideas are flowing. It's a nice groove but it's just a Demerol dream. I'm actually in a bed in the Surgery Intensive Care Unit, my hands tied down and a web of tubes and wires attached to me. I just woke up. Wednesday morning, December 3. The operation took over twelve and a half hours.

Pinned down and trussed up. Tubes and lines everywhere, a Frankenstein monster waiting for a jump-start.

There's a face, close enough to kiss me, talking to me: "Mr. Sublett. You're in surgery intensive care. You've got a breathing tube in your throat. That's where you're getting your oxygen right now. You'll have that tube—now, don't try to push it out—for the next twenty-four hours or so. When you can breathe on your own again, we'll take the tube out and move you to a room."

She's gotta be kidding. I never counted on this. To have those fire hoses in my throat for twenty-four hours, that's inconceivable.

There's a feeding tube, too. In through the left nostril, all the way to the stomach. The usual IVs, catheter, EKG cables. Lois is here. "Hi, sweetheart. How do you feel?" Not a great thing to ask at this time. Freaky and helpless, I want to say, but I can't talk. Maybe a simple word or two. Can't she see that? I just shrug.

Lois squeezes my hand. "Dr. Lewis says everything went just fine. Don't worry, everything's gonna be all right." I squeeze her hand. So this must mean my worst nightmares haven't come to pass. I've still got my tongue and voice box and all that.

What if my nightmare had happened? How could she tell me? Probably could've seen it on her face.

"I love you," she says.

I squeeze her hand.

Breathing is hard work. My mouth fills up with blood and mucus, and I'm drowning. My nurse sees me struggling and reminds me to breathe through the tube. It seems impossible. Just when it feels like I'm going down for the last time, fingertips sinking below the bubbling surface of that lake of blood and mucus, I pass out again.

Writing again. Trying to put it all into words, finding some nice phrases, searching for those command and save keys. But they're not there, which means I'm conscious again, which means choking on blood and mucus. "Don't do that, Mr. Sublett. Take it easy, just breathe through the tube, don't try to push the tube out. No, don't do that, take it easy, just breathe through the tube." I shake my head: I can't, I can't, I can't do it. I'm drowning.

Going down again. This is it, I'm gonna die, oh damn it. I think about Dashiell and Lois and realize I've gotta fight, gotta hold on, try harder. Somehow I gulp some air through the tube, gulp a little more and a little more, pass out again.

Dr. Lewis spent the entire twelve and a half hours operating on me—no relief pitcher, no Starbucks breaks, no ducking outside for air, slipping away to check email, trips to the lounge to see who's on *Oprah*. Later on I asked her, "Don't you get hungry or tired?"

"Dr Pepper's my secret," she said. "Sometimes I have one of my assistants rig a tube under my mask so I can sip it for energy."

"So that's all you had?"

She thought about it. "No, actually, this time I didn't have anything. Not even Dr Pepper."

The only time she sat down during my surgery was for the extended tonsillectomy, which she performed sitting at a stool opposite the top of my head. This position makes it a lot easier for the surgeon to look deep into the throat. The bulk of the surgery time, however, was taken up by the radical neck dissection procedure, a complex and time-consuming job. During that procedure, Dr. Lewis, the otolaryngologist who specializes in head and neck cancer, who takes a special interest in pediatric cases, a frequent champion in amateur ballroom dancing competitions, was on her feet. No Dr Pepper.

Lois and my parents were in the waiting room the whole time. After six hours, my mother started freaking out. "Something's gone wrong," she'd say. "I just know it."

This didn't make things any easier on Lois. All those hours went by in a narcotic wink for me. But Lois and my parents felt the tick and tock of every second and minute.

The pathologists also put in a full day. All day and deep into the night, Dr. Lewis and her assisting surgeon, Dr. Leary, were sending down batches of tissue she'd removed from my throat—tonsil, tonsil bed, jugular vein, muscle, tumors, lymph tissue and so forth. The pathologists had to log in every sample they received, then examine it for cancer. They would confer to see if their analyses concurred and then call the OR with their report, then start on the next batch, and on and on. Dr. Lewis depended on these battle assessments to determine how far she needed to go with the surgery.

The pathologists spent a great deal of time taking inventory of my lymph nodes. Lymph nodes are supposed to filter out poisons; when cancer cells clog them up, they become swollen—encapsulated—and eventually can be replaced by the cancer. If even one lymph node is found to be "positive," meaning cancer has invaded, it means the cancer may have spread to other areas of the body. Out of eighty lymph nodes checked by our pathologists, forty-eight tested positive. This represented a serious invasion.

The pathology reports, which I obtained later on, make repulsively fascinating reading. They make me feel like Yosemite Sam in an old Loony Tunes cartoon. He gets blasted with a hail of point-blank gunfire, but when the smoke clears he's still standing, apparently untouched. "Ha, ha, ha! You missed me!" Sam says, howling with laughter. Then he takes a drink of water and it squirts out from a dozen holes in his body.

OK, so you didn't miss me, Big C, but I'm still standing here, alive and kicking.

The next morning the respiratory therapist clears the goo out of my mouth (which has to be done every half hour or so) and, with little finesse or gentleness, pulls the breathing tube out. It's painful and a little scary, and it's the only time someone handles me roughly, at least while I'm conscious. Being set free from the damned breathing tube is a relief of gigantic proportions, however, and it means I am leaving SICU.

From SICU they take me to a small room in Intermediate Care. I'm still heavily sedated and my vision is fuzzy. Lois comes to visit a couple of times, but everything's a blur. I sleep a lot and the day passes quickly.

They're moving me to another room when I finally realize those two colored smudges on the walls are art prints. My vision was that fuzzy. Both turn out to be Monet. To my right is a seascape. The nurse pushing my wheelchair pauses for a minute when I'm next to the other print, so I get a good look at it. As the image comes into focus, a painful laugh escapes from my reconfigured throat.

It's a bridge. Yes, a bridge, but it's a dinky little thing. Instead of being the massive metaphorical span of my imagination, it's a small decorative wooden arch over a stream full of purple water lilies. The message is clear: You crossed a bridge, all right, but just a small one. There'll be plenty more down the road.

Lois brings Dashiell to visit every day in the new room, but he isn't keen on seeing me in that condition. I'm sure the feeding tube bothers him the most. He pays little or no attention to the IVs and suture staples that zip back and forth the length of my neck like a punk rock zipper, but that feeding tube, coming out my left nostril and taped just above my ear, really bugs him. I hate it too.

By the fourth day I really want to go home. During the night I developed a case of thrush, an eruptive oral infection that makes your mouth feel like it's on fire. Combined with the pain in my overhauled tonsil bed, it's an exquisite hell until Dr. Lewis comes by for her daily check-up. She prescribes an antibiotic that cures the infection with amazing rapidity.

I use the opportunity to plead with her to let me go home early. Previously, eight days was the shortest length of time Dr. Lewis planned on keeping me, but after thinking it over, she says that, if everything else is cool, I might be able to go home tomorrow, the sixth day after surgery. The only hitch is that we have to master using the feeding tube.

The feeding tube is necessary because my throat won't be sufficiently healed to allow the passage of food for another week or so. The technique is fairly simple: pour the contents of a can of Ensure into a plastic syringe, attach the syringe to the tube and depress the plunger on the syringe. You had to be very careful, however, to make certain the tube was still in position. If it accidentally came out a few inches, the Ensure would get pumped into my lungs. It would be like drowning in a high-vitamin milkshake.

Lois aces the feeding course, and the next night she takes me home.

Fortunately, Dr. Lewis says I'm healing fast and lets us ditch the tube ahead of schedule. Until further notice, my diet will consist of yogurt, pureed vegetables, broth and lots of Ensure—a product I soon realize I loathe almost as much as the feeding tube.

On the fourth day after my discharge, Dr. Lewis says the wound looks good. Everything seems to be going well, and I won't need to see her again for two weeks. That's after Christmas.

"I want you to go home and relax and have a merry Christmas with your family," she says. "Enjoy life, get your strength back and get ready for chemotherapy and radiation. Because all that is going to be a whole lot harder on you than anything I've done."

"You're kidding," I say.

"No, I'm not," she says.

I don't believe her. Could it possibly be any harder than having your neck dissected, the back of your throat retooled? She's got to be joking.

20. CHEMO LOUNGE BLUES

Depending on how you look at it, chemotherapy and radiation is either a great way to start off your new year or a rotten one. I've decided to assume it's going to save my life, so it's a damn good way to kick off 1998, starting at eight a.m. on the first Monday of the year.

Lois drove me here. I can't drive yet, and she wants to get a feel for what's going to be happening. The place is called South Austin Cancer Center, a no-bullshit name, but when you first walk in you might wonder if you're in the right place. The waiting room has low lights, dark woods and deep greens, lending it the feel of a cozy living room. Nice aquarium. You start to notice the large number of women wearing head coverings, scarves and hats, wigs or nothing at all on their bald heads. Now you know, this is the place where all the brave bald-headed women go. Maybe some of their courage will rub off on you as you learn how to swallow all over again, your own tongue a stranger in your mouth.

We sign in. Everyone here seems profoundly good at their jobs, and they turn out to be warm and cheerful and empathetic, though not in a Hallmark sort of way. An oncology nurse takes us to the place I dub the Chemo Lounge, a room with a dozen stations for patients to receive IV infusions of chemotherapy drugs and other medications. Each station has a comfortable reclining chair and its own entertainment center: TV, VCR, radio, headphones, magazine rack and reading lamps. My station is in the corner by a window. A large tropical aquarium occupies a central position on the opposite wall like a wide-screen TV. Plenty of chairs for visitors.

News flash: Dr. Kasper, my chemotherapy oncologist, says it's very unlikely I'll lose my hair. This makes Lois and me exceptionally happy. There is a good possibility, however, that I'll experience some nausea, but how bad can that be? I definitely don't want to lose my hair, so it strikes me as a fair trade-off.

My treatment plan is controversial. There's no proof that chemotherapy works on my type of cancer. Dr. Lewis, however, believes it's worth taking the chance. Lois and I agree.

In a meeting with another doctor, I say, "What do you think the chances are that I'll be cured?"

"Well, pretty slim, actually," he says.

At first we're stunned; then we get mad. After the doctor leaves the room, Lois takes my hand and says, "You're not gonna let that bother you, are you?"

"Hell, no. Fuck that slim-chance shit. I'll show 'em."

Dr. Fein, my radiation oncologist, was encouraging in his own straightforward, cynical way. He's a fast-talker with a knack for dark comedy, even when he isn't kidding. Lois and I like him, despite what he promised to do to me at our first appointment.

"The first two weeks won't be so bad," he said. "Pretty soon, though, you'll start feeling tired all the time. By the third week, the side effects will really kick in. Your saliva will dry up completely, maybe permanently. It'll be hard to swallow, much less eat. You'll lose your sense of taste. You might lose your voice. Your tongue and throat will be, basically, uh, you know, burned. During the last couple of weeks—well, no doubt about it, you'll pretty much hate my guts."

We'd already discussed some of the other effects, like damage to my gums and teeth and possibly even the bone structure of my jaw. Future dental work will be a potential nightmare. No saliva? Burned tongue? Too much to absorb. It reminded me of an old lawyer joke. Satan promises to make a young law school graduate into the greatest, richest criminal lawyer in the world; all he has to do is sell Satan his soul. When Dr. Fein asked if we had any questions, I replied with the punch line: "This deal sounds great, but what's the down side?"

"Excuse me?" He looked slightly alarmed, as if he suspected I might be mentally deficient.

"That was supposed to be a joke."

Lois smiled. She's been dealing with my sense of humor forever.

"Oh, yeah," he said, laughing nervously. "Don't worry, you'll be fine, really. You'll do just fine."

Lois wanted to know one thing: "Do you think the radiation will get rid of the cancer that's left?"

Pathology reports confirm that I have positive margins, meaning there was still plenty of cancerous tissue left after the operation. I suppose Dr. Lewis could've removed every bit of malignant tissue, but we probably wouldn't have been on speaking terms afterward. If I still had the ability to speak.

"We've had good success with this kind of treatment," he said. "It's one of the worst things we do to people here. Don't get me wrong, because it can get pretty rough. But we've had good success."

Lois and I liked his positive spin and his dark sense of humor, too.

"Your case is really weird," he said. "It's pretty amazing, in fact. Dr. Lewis has obviously decided to treat you very aggressively, and I think that's the right way to go. Even though you're gonna end up hating some of us for what we're going to do to you."

Here in the corner recliner, I'm hooked up to the IV, watching Turner Classic Movies. My itinerary includes blood tests, forms to fill out, IV infusion with drugs to flush out my kidneys, then the chemo infusion, a trip to the radiation wing to get radiated, then back for the rest of the chemo, more flushing drugs and other stuff. This thing is like an eight-to-five job. Lois hangs out for about an hour. A good-bye kiss and hug, good luck wishes. "This is gonna work," she says.

"I know." Thumbs up, wink, one more kiss, a boob squeeze, she's gone.

The kidney-flushing drug, dextrose sodium magnesium potassium chloride, feels like a hot poker in my arm. I'll get two bags of this stuff and then cisplatin.

Gillian, one of the two chemotherapy nurses, comes over to check on me every few minutes. The room is filling up, and she and Cheryl, the other nurse, are constantly on the go. When Gillian learns I'm a writer, she tells me about *Buns,* a children's book she co-wrote with her husband. It's a chronicle of famous American landmarks, like the Grand Canyon and Statue of Liberty, which were all visited by Gillian's photogenic pet rabbit, Buns. There's a photo of Buns at every site.

"I saw it when it came out," I tell her. "Congratulations. What a neat book."

"Why, thank you," she says. "That's quite a compliment, coming from a real writer."

For the next hour, I have to read something that's a little less pleasant: the info sheet on cisplatin. It's definitely not a recreational drug. Years from now, after I think I'm cured and I have all this behind me, I might experience new side effects, out of the blue. Screw it, can't think about that now. What about nausea? There it is, page one, but everybody knows about that. So I might get a queasy stomach and have to throw up, what's the big deal?

The list of possible side effects seems endless. What am I supposed to do, pick my favorite five, or run screaming out of here? Ringing in ears, dizziness, trouble walking, numbness, loss of taste, loss of reflexes, black, tarry stools. Spontaneous human combustion seems to be the only thing they left out. Maybe I missed it.

"Well, any questions, Jesse?" Gillian asks. She's Irish, and her voice has a pleasant lilt.

"It says here that this drug can also cause certain types of cancer, such as leukemia."

"Yes, it is rather disturbing." Gillian nods. "But we're trying to save your life."

I sign the release.

I'll be coming here for a cisplatin infusion once every three weeks for nine weeks. Three weeks after the third dose, there will be another drug, same schedule. I'll also come in mornings to get blasted with gamma rays five days a week for seven and a half weeks, for a total of thirty-five doses.

There will also be periodic appointments with Drs. Fein, Kasper and Lewis. Gillian says I may also need to come in periodically for "hydration or something."

I don't plan on coming here any more than is absolutely necessary, so I don't take much note of remarks like that.

Ingesting food is very difficult since surgery. Swallowing is difficult, my jaw is weak, my mouth and tongue seem retarded. Even pureed foods are still a chore to get down.

Christmas was full of good mood elevators, like watching Lois put up the tree and going with her to Toys R Us to fulfill the wish list in Dashiell's letter to Santa. Then I'd dip down again, looking around at my wife and son and mentally screening my own version of the angel's cautionary tale in *It's a Wonderful Life,* when he shows Jimmy Stewart how things would turn out if he really jumped off that bridge.

I usually managed to steer away from maudlin negativity and concentrated on the good stuff, like Dashiell opening his presents on Christmas morning, walks at the lake, Lois' cooking (I couldn't eat much of it, but I still enjoyed the smell), listening to music (lots of blues and Roxy music) and playing my bass. It's been a while since I played a gig, but I always have my bass guitar next to my desk so I can play whenever I feel like it. I appreciate it now. James and Kathryn came to visit, too, and it was great to see all the nieces and nephews together with Dashiell. Mom and Dad call every day. They always want to know what they can do to help out. Sometimes I have to invent chores for them.

Three times a day, I meditate and practice the visualization program I've been learning from a book called *Getting Well Again: A Step-by-Step, Self-Help Guide to Overcoming Cancer for Patients and Their Families.* The authors combined oncology, psychology, meditation, spirituality and a few other disciplines to come up with a program that has achieved positive results in large numbers of cancer patients, many of whom had been relegated to a veritable cancer death row.

The book explains how to rally the body's immune system and natural disease-fighting resources to fight cancer by using a focused regimen of meditation and visualization. I was skeptical at first, but at Dr. Lewis' urging I decided to give it a shot. After reading the book for several days, I've learned enough to start the program.

Each session begins with meditation to relax your body and mind. The next step is a sequence of mental images which you employ to visualize your body's natural immune system battling the cancer. After each battle (naturally, you visualize your side winning), you concentrate on personal goals and positive imagery, seeing yourself healthy and happy at various times in the future, six months, a year, two years. Each session takes thirty minutes, but it makes me feel like I'm doing everything I can to win this fight, and I trust Dr. Lewis' judgment.

I've also been going to physical therapy twice a week. The loss of muscle and the trapezius nerve in my neck has left me with stiffness, loss of motion, weakness and pain in my neck and right shoulder. Physical therapy helps a little, and the massages are nice. I've been writing in my journal every day and working on some book reviews for the *Chronicle*, and every two weeks, I turn in a Texas history essay for the online edition of *Texas Monthly.*

All in all, I've been busy.

Christmas scene #1: Dashiell wants me to build the Ferris wheel with his plastic Junior Erector Set. I warn him that I don't have a lot of energy, so the project will take a couple of days at least.

"That's OK, Daddy," he says. "I'll help you build it."

Smiling at me, face full of sunshine, he helps me up and I think to myself, this is what they mean by lightning in a bottle. How could the cancer number crunchers ever factor in a miracle like this?

Christmas scene #2: The World's Most Handsome Man runs into the living room, a zillion-dollar smile on his face. "I want to tell you something very important I read in the paper," he says.

"Really? What did you read?"

"There's a Gumby concert tonight. We have to find it. Socks (his current pet name for Lois) is gonna meet us there. I'm gonna get onstage with Gumby and play in his band."

"That's great, Dashiell."

"I'm gonna ride Pokey onto the stage. Then I'll tell all the guys in his band where to stand and what songs to play."

That's my boy. A born band leader.

Lois asks him about the songs he's going to play. He says he'll play them for us. He sits on the couch with his guitar and plays several songs with a fantastic, tuneless enthusiasm. So far they all seem to be instrumentals.

"Do any of these songs have words?"

"Yes."

"Well, why don't you sing us some?"

He plays and sings.

Each song is as unique as a snowflake and just as fragile. The lyrics are little miracles of free association, like transcripts of dreams. At least one song is about what it's like to be a genius. That's my boy.

When the concert ends, Lois and I are awed, like explorers who've just stumbled into a pharaoh's tomb or some other indescribable wonder.

There's a new plastic bag hooked up to my IV, flowing in concert with the first one. Gillian says it's called Decadron, an anti-nausea drug. After the second bag of kidney flusher, she starts the cisplatin. The spigot is on low. Haven't felt a thing yet. I don't know what I expected. The sound of muffled cannon fire? The crackling of gamma-fried cells?

I watch a Greta Garbo documentary on TCM. The combination of Garbo's magical alchemy and her mysterious life is a nice distraction.

Around eleven, they escort me back to the radiotherapy section. Calvin and Jennifer are the radiation technicians. Calvin is a gregarious African American who towers over me. Jennifer is a pale, pretty, soft-voiced brunette. An odd couple, a great team. Calvin takes me into a windowless room through what looks like the door to a bank vault. A foot thick. This stuff is that deadly.

I peel off my shirt. Calvin helps me lie down on the narrow gurney. He asks if I'd like a blanket even before I realize it's cold in here. Sure, I'll take a blanket. He drapes it over me.

"Ready, Mr. Sublett?"

Calvin is holding my radiation mask. It's a white mesh model of the frontal hemisphere of my head. Fashioned on my first visit here, a week ago, it was a flat square of metal when I first saw it. The metal has a very low melting point, and simply soaking it in hot water makes it as soft as a slice of warmed American cheese. When its frame was clamped in place behind my head, the mesh settled onto the contours of my face, and within a few minutes it had hardened and cooled to room temperature. Now it's got my name on it. It will fit so snugly that I'll barely be able to blink my eyes. Calibration markings for the gamma ray accelerator can be made on the mask instead of my skin.

"Ready," I say.

Calvin puts the mask on my face and locks it in place to the bracket behind my head. "How does that feel? Are you comfortable, or is it too tight?"

I tell him I'm fine, and he laughs because the mask fits so snugly the words come out sounding like *Mm-fnn*. I can barely manage to smile in answer to Calvin's calming, morale-boosting repartee.

Soon I'm alone. Calvin and Jennifer are on the other side of the vault door. The gamma ray machine being moved into position over my face by remote control is a state-of-the-art Varian 2100 Dual Photon/Electron Linear Accelerator. The giant aperture can be swiveled to any position like a giant robot eye. It comes so close to my face or the side of it that I can't see the thing, but I can hear the clicking of its multi-leaf collimator, a sort of shutter for shaping the beam for each angle of attack on my neck and jaw. It sounds like metal teeth, the teeth of a robot eye that reaches inside me to blast every fast-growing cell in its path.

The doses are quick, a few seconds on each side. I don't feel anything. I have to take the technicians' word that something has happened. Each time the calibration is changed, Jennifer and Calvin explain what they're doing and apologize for taking so long. They have to double-check each new setting. After the last angle, they take an X ray for quality assurance.

"Sorry, it'll just take a minute," Calvin apologizes. As if I've got somewhere else I need to be.

Back at the Chemo Lounge, *Camille* is starting. That one's too tragic for me just now. I mute the sound and start writing in my journal.

My stomach feels a little queasy. I suppose this is the nausea part. Gillian gives me another dose of the anti-nausea drug. It seems to help.

Lois arrives and waits with me. Drip-drip-drip. Finally the last bag collapses, empty. All done at 5:30 p.m. Long day.

I sit in my recliner and eat my dinner with my family, a tired dad after a full day at the Chemo Lounge. Even with my crippled mouth and throat, I manage to devour two large helpings of a mildly spicy eggplant dish Lois whipped up.

After dinner, my friend Tom Garner calls. Am I still up for barbecue on Wednesday? Hitting the barbecue trail with my buddies is one of my favorite rituals. Tom is a criminal defense lawyer and book collector. For our ritual barbecue lunches, he and I usually round up another friend or two and drive south on Highway 183 to Lockhart or Luling, which have some of the best barbecue in the state and probably the whole world. It's a great ritual—the jokes, the book talk, the women talk, the drive itself, the eating of smoked meat off brown butcher paper.

I tell Tom I wouldn't miss it for anything, especially after today. We banter with jokes and small talk a few minutes. I suppose the main reason he called was to see how things went, but it's easier to talk about barbecue than chemotherapy.

After the phone call, I realize how tired I am. My bones ache, my chest feels heavy. Both cats, Willie and Marlowe, are curled up next to me, a pair of furry apostrophes.

Damn, I'm tired. I drink another big glass of water to help flush the chemo out of my system. Be sure to flush twice after you pee, a friend advised; that stuff is poison.

I tell Lois about seeing the hazardous materials emergency clean-up kit on Cheryl's cart today.

"What the heck do you need that for?" I asked her.

"These are toxic chemicals," Cheryl said. "There's one we call Red Devil. If it gets on your skin or in your eyes or your lungs, you're basically screwed."

Around 3:30 a.m. my stomach is churning. I stumble into the bathroom just as all that eggplant starts to gush out of my mouth and nose. I go back to bed, but I'm up again a minute later. This time everything since breakfast comes up. Lying down is impossible. If my head hits the pillow, the bile burns the back of my throat. I vomit dozens more times. The anti-nausea pills don't help at all.

At eight Lois takes me back to SACC. I'm beyond miserable. Everybody crosses their fingers when Calvin eases me down on the table for my radiation treatment. It seems a sure bet the second they snap on my mask I'll throw up in it. Calvin tells me how to sound the panic alarm and promises to throw open the vault door and rip the mask off if I give the signal. By some miracle, I get through the treatment. But a few seconds later, the heaves are back again.

They take me back to the Chemo Lounge for IV fluids and some additional anti-nausea drugs. My stomach finally settles down.

Like a fool, I try eating some soft scrambled eggs around noon. Less than five minutes later, I see the eggs all over again. The rest of the day is like that. Nothing will stay down, not even water. Nothing helps.

So this is what they meant by nausea.

Dr. Lewis writes a prescription for Nembutal suppositories. I try one. At first I just feel relaxed, then everything shuts down. I sink into a black pillow and go away for awhile. Far away.

The next morning I can barely get out of bed. I'm trashed. I don't vomit until around noon, and only a couple of times later on. But I obviously can't be taking Nembutal every day. I'm not about to become a junkie, especially not one that's addicted to suppositories. It would lack the inherent glamour of the needle.

By the end of the following week the vomiting has tapered off, which means I'm throwing up less than ten times a day, and once in a while some form of nourishment stays down. The most likely reason for the drop-off at the Sublett vomitorium is that the cisplatin is pretty much out of my system.

Next Monday, I'll go in for another dose of that evil potion and the vomit volcano will erupt all over again. As an alternative to Nembutal, I'll try a shotgun approach, taking a daily combination of compazine, lorazepam and a highly touted anti-nausea drug called Zophran.

Zophran costs $400 for a two-week supply. I take it religiously, even though its effectiveness, in my case, seems minimal. That's just one prescription out of half a dozen I'm taking right now. Our insurance policy has a limit of $800 in copaid prescriptions per year. This is frightening. We'll have to start pawning things to survive.

My weight is plummeting. I weighed 175 before surgery, and at 6 foot 3 I usually passed for skinny. Surgery peeled off 15 pounds. Each cisplatin treatment will be more devastating, especially with the compounded effects of radiation. Eating will become all but impossible. My mouth and throat and nose will become sources of frustration and torture.

I have my family and friends and a fantastic group of medical professionals all working to help me emerge from this darkness. But even so, I feel like I'm cut off from the world of life and sunshine. Cancer never seems to attack something you could afford to take a hit on, like your little toe, your earlobe, a small rib. It's always breasts, prostate, testicles, lungs, brain, throat and mouth. It's like Satan has singled you out in the most insidious, most personally devastating way.

I wasn't able to make the barbecue run with Tom on Wednesday. A week later, the idea of going on the trip is still sadly laughable, despite my attempt to sound regretful when Tom calls again.

He comes over in the afternoon. He's got Neal Barrett Jr. and Dick Holland with him. Neal is a great comic novelist, one of the funniest guys I know, and Dick is a hip academic guy, music fanatic, devotee of hardboiled, beat and other groovy lit. They've been to City Market, our favorite joint in Luling. They take up positions in the living room, having bestowed on me a big brown bag of goodies. They're all smiles as I take inventory of the hefty portions of brisket, sausage and ribs.

"You guys are swell," I tell them. "Home delivery and everything."

"Well, if you're too lazy to come to us, we figured we might as well come to you," Tom says.

I pick out a nice-looking rib, dab it in some sauce and take a small bite. It takes several minutes to chew and swallow. I take another bite and struggle with it for a minute or two. It's still a dense lump of beef tissue when I give up and wash it down with half a glass of water. I hate to tell them, but the meat tastes like old tires soaked in battery acid, and it smells like burnt hair and laundry soap.

"You're not full already, are you?" Neal says.

I think I'm going to throw up. "You guys are real friends," I tell them. "I really appreciate your bringing me this barbecue, but that's about all I can eat right now. Maybe I'll have some more later on."

I can't believe how sad they look.

Jon Dee is living in Austin again and is well on his way to being one of the city's most popular singer-songwriters. When he comes over, he brings votive candles. He says he knows I'm going to come out on the other side of this thing because he can't imagine his life without me in it. Our friends in L.A., Tom and Barbara, send a box of books and stay in constant touch.

Some people shun us, as if we're lepers in a primitive society. Even when they see Lois in public, they avoid mentioning my illness. They just can't handle it. It's remarkably similar to some of the reactions I experienced after Dianne's murder. Some people will do almost anything other than attempt a simple humane interaction.

There's no sense asking why it had to happen or moaning about how life isn't fair. Fair doesn't have anything to do with it and never did. Bad things like murder and cancer have to happen to somebody, so there's no use taking it personally. The world is a trick garden of Eden, rigged with land mines and cruel traps that can spring without notice, without rhyme or reason or divine justification. We're not entitled to happiness and love and beauty, but if you're lucky you might find them in spite of everything.

I've been thinking about Dianne. Most of the time I'm so busy trying to stay afloat that the tape loop doesn't run. But sometimes I can't help wondering about my throat being the site of the cancer's attack, the strangling pain, the choking sensation I feel when I can't swallow. Why my neck and throat, the same site where a monster's hands choked the life out of her?

It's a pretty nasty coincidence.

Most days I want to kick ass. The *Getting Well Again* program makes me feel confident and upbeat. I manage to wake up in time to sit in my recliner while Dashiell gets ready for preschool. It's important for him to see me up and around and dressed, for me to give him a good-bye hug and kiss before he and Lois leave for the day. I don't want my son to go off to school thinking of his father lying in bed, wondering if he's always going to be that way. I get up, put on my pants and a shirt, spend a few minutes with him before he leaves. Some days that's my biggest accomplishment.

21. ZOMBIE ALIEN
CHEMO-RADIATION BLUES

D r. Lewis is sympathetic when I relate the story of my pals' barbecue delivery. I run down a list of other symptoms and episodes, rounding off the number of times I vomited a day to the nearest hundred.

"I'm sorry," she says. "I'll see what we can do to make things a little easier for you. I'll call Dr. Kasper and see what ideas he has on his end."

"Well, actually," I say, "I've been having second thoughts on continuing the chemo, you know, and—"

"No," she says. "No, no, no." Her voice is solemn and firm.

I gulp and stutter, "Uh, well, it was just an idea because—"

"No."

I guess she's heard it before: My sense of taste and smell are completely haywire. They're supersensitive and super perverted. Almost all foods have lost their natural flavors and acquired demonically deranged new ones. Some of the milder taste sensations: wet cardboard and straw. Some extremes: spoiled milk, rancid grease, crankcase oil. Fruit juices taste like toxic chemicals, risotto like sun-baked road kill.

Every human who comes within ten feet reeks of body odor and sour breath. Our house is a smorgasbord of foul smells. Each room has a specific odor: kitchen, compost heap; bedroom, locker room; hallway, sewer. Coffee is rancid bacon grease. Several times an accidental whiff of Lois' hazelnut latte has caused instant projectile vomiting.

My throat was just recovering from the trauma of the surgery when the radiation made my tongue feel as though it had been run over by a car. My saliva began drying up during the third week. I lost the saliva gland on the right to surgery, and radiation is frying the rest of them. Dr. Fein warned me not to expect them to recover. My mouth might be as dry as paper for the rest of my life. Without saliva, certain foods are impossible to eat. Chips, crackers and bread are out of the question, and even soft vegetables, fruit and other foods simply won't break down without saliva. If you're having trouble chewing and swallowing, which I am, it's close to impossible to ingest solid food without the lubrication and digestive power of spit.

My weight plummets. By summer, I'm down to 125. At that weight I'm pretty scary looking. It should come as no surprise that some head and neck cancer patients die of malnutrition, mostly because eating is so torturous. Some patients, especially the elderly, just give up and starve themselves to death.

For many people in my situation, Ensure is often the mainstay of their diet. By my second week of treatment, Ensure tasted like sour milk and caustic chemicals. You couldn't get me to drink a can of the stuff if you held a gun to my head. Sometimes just thinking about opening a can makes me vomit.

My metabolism is running like a furnace, trying to repair the damage from the surgery plus the cells that are being killed off by chemo and radiation. The calories I can get down are like drops of water on a hot griddle. We roam the aisles of the supermarket searching for things that might work. I feel like an alien on a planet where everything is toxic to my species. We're desperate. If things don't improve, Dr. Lewis says hospitalization will be next. I'm already going down to the Chemo Lounge several days a week to get saline infusions to replace all the fluids and electrolytes I'm losing. My spot there has become my spare living room and writing office.

I could move my neck enough to drive a car again after my third week of chemo. I took Dashiell for a ride in the Ghia with the top down. It seemed like the first time in months he and I had done something together, but it had only been since the surgery. It's a good thing we did it, because the next chemo dose wiped me out. Now I'm just driving once in a while. Lois usually takes me to my doctor visits, but Harry takes me to my daily radiation treatments and triweekly chemo infusions.

Mom and Dad come by several times a week, to do chores around the house and bring things they hope I might be able to eat. For their sake I pretend that my mother's chicken soup is going down just fine.

Friends recommended smoking pot for nausea and to improve my appetite. Even my doctors said I should try it. Like everything except Nembutal, its effects on my nausea are barely noticeable, and it makes me uncomfortable, paranoid and depressed, which I really don't need. Cancer makes me paranoid enough.

Richard gives me a hard time about smoking pot. He thinks it's hilarious since I used to give him so much grief about being a pot head. He calls me up and says things like, "Hey, man, are you gonna go see the Grateful Dead when they come to town?"

Cisplatin is ototoxic, which means it can damage your hearing. Radiation isn't kind to your inner ear, either. A hearing test at Dr. Lewis' office confirmed that I'd suffered significant hearing loss. I have tinnitus in both ears. The left sounds like shattering glass, the right like an orchestra of chain saws and buzz saws. It's quite a show.

There are lots of weird sensations, including various aches from chemo, surgery wounds, radiation pain and the prickly numbness that comes from the combination of radiation and chemo. The most consistent pain I have is in my neck and shoulder, ostensibly from the removal of tissue, muscle and nerves on the right side of my neck. Probably the biggest single chunk of tissue removed during surgery was the muscle connecting the clavicle to the side of the neck, just under the lower jaw. Radiation has turned one of the surviving neck muscles to fiber. This aggravates the pain problem.

There are lots of medical explanations. My symptoms aren't unusual, but their severity and persistence might be. I keep taking Vicodin and Tylenol, assuming that someday the pain will go away. There's no reason to suspect any other explanation for this pain. How could there be a logical explanation for the similarity of the pain in my neck to the sensation of being strangled? Sometimes I can't help but wonder.

I find myself looking forward to seeing my pals at the cancer center. At first I assumed they'd been trained to be caring and friendly, but experience has melted away my cynicism. They understand what I'm going through better than anyone else. They know hundreds of people with cancer, and quite a few with cancer similar to mine.

I've never heard them utter a false note, an insincere word. Never a sullen Monday morning greeting, never a short attention span. They're like best friends or a mother, except they never let you down, never get mad, never give you a guilt trip or try to make you go to church.

One afternoon as I'm watching the cisplatin drip into my arm I ask Gillian if she and her husband are going to write a sequel to *Buns*. I'm disappointed to hear that not only are they divorced, but her husband got custody of Buns, who passed on soon after the divorce. I give her my condolences. "Well," Gillian says in her lilting voice, "she had a good life."

22. LESS THAN NINE

Just after breakfast this morning, our Volvo station wagon is rolling down to the coastal bend. We're hell bent on seeing the only migrating colony of whooping cranes in the world. Getting Dashiell excited about the idea wasn't easy. He hates car trips that last more than five minutes and is not terribly interested in birds. Touting the whoopers as being "almost as tall as Mommy" seemed to perk him up. Buying him the red binoculars was a smart move, too, although he isn't satisfied unless he's got my pair around his neck as well.

The drive takes a little over three hours, a damn long trip for a guy in my physical condition. The last few weeks have not been fun. This trip is one of my first *Getting Well Again* goals, though, so wimping out is not an option.

At the halfway mark, we pull into a Dairy Queen for lunch. I order the chicken fingers. Lois crosses her fingers. "Do you seriously think you'll be able to eat that?" she asks.

Thinking positive despite any real evidence to support it, I answer, "Yes."

As usual, Dashiell looks unconcerned, although sometimes we suspect he's faking it. I begin my battle with the chicken tenders. It takes well over an hour, several refills of Diet Coke, dozens of gulps of a medicinal mouthwash called Triple Mix and extra cream gravy, but I eat the whole

235

thing, French fries and all. Even better, I do not vomit. My first meal of solid food since surgery. It's a good omen for the weekend.

I graduated from radiation treatment two weeks ago. A Valentine's Day present. As I exited the radiation vault, Calvin and Jennifer shouted "Congratulations!" and showered me with confetti. They also presented me with an official certificate and a plaque that reads: "Courage is being scared to death but saddling up anyway"—a quote from John Wayne.

Dashiell keeps amazing me. It's a struggle to keep him and Lois in sight. As we reach each new wildlife viewing platform, catwalk or observation tower, he asks, "When are they going to show us to our hotel room?" He's gotten it into his head that the Aransas Wildlife Refuge is a hotel. No explanation will convince him otherwise. He's always loved staying in hotels. Maybe, instead of hyping the tall birds and alligators, I should've given him a picture of a Best Western.

Standing up to five feet high, the whooping crane is the tallest flying bird in North America. Their wing span ranges up to seven and a half feet. Normally, during migration, a whooper's average speed is about 53 kilometers per hour, but if the wind is right they can go much faster. Boosted by a stiff tailwind, a whooping crane was once clocked going 107.5 kilometers per hour.

The whoopers start touching down at Aransas around October every year after completing the 2,500-mile flight from their spring-summer home at Wood Buffalo National Park in northern Canada. They return north in late March and early April. The ladies at the visitor center told us that a record number of 187 whooping cranes had returned to Texas this year. Very impressive, especially when you consider that the flock was down to only 16 surviving birds in 1940.

Now, thanks to preservation efforts such as the establishment of the 100,000-acre Aransas National Wildlife Refuge in 1937, the migrating flock has continued to rebound. As a result of experimental breeding programs, small numbers of wild whooping cranes exist in other locations, while researchers have made gradual progress toward developing other migrating flocks. It'll be a great day when their efforts succeed, but as long as the Aransas flock survives, they will always represent a very special kind of miracle.

Here I am at the top of the observation tower, watching a family of three whoopers feeding in the estuarial marsh at the tip of the refuge, facing Matagorda Bay. I'm very proud of having made the three-hour drive. It's a pretty historic trip.

A gregarious snowbird from Seattle offers the use of his high-powered telescope. The view is so good I can almost tell what the cranes are eating in their long, daggerlike beaks.

I thank the man for the use of his telescope. "We're celebrating my last radiation treatment for stage-four neck cancer," I say.

He gives me a congratulatory grin.

"I figure if they can make it, I can make it."

He shakes my hand firmly, then gazes out toward the bay, where the whooping cranes are. Everyone else on the tower is looking out there, too. Lost in thought, their faces serene.

Lois takes me to get a tube called a groshong catheter installed in my chest. While I'm under a local anesthetic, a Dr. McFarland sticks this thing into an artery a few inches from the heart, leaving a valve dangling at the end of a plastic tube on the outside. Feels pretty weird, but it'll save me from getting new pokes in the arm when I start up chemo again this week.

The catheter is a must for the new drug, 5FU (fluorouracil), because it has to be infused over the course of five days via a battery-powered pump I'll carry in a fanny pack. After the fifth day I return it to the cancer center like an empty beer keg after a party.

In recovery after the procedure, a male nurse comes to check my blood pressure. His name is Rene. I notice he's got a scar on the left side of his neck that's almost a mirror image of mine. Turns out he had the same kind of cancer, same surgery, same radiation treatment, though the dosage wasn't as high. I ask him if his sense of taste and saliva came back. He says, "Sure, everything came back." I ask him again, just to be sure. He says it again: "Everything's back to normal, no problem. Five years, too."

Cool. If my luck will hold out. . .

Lois takes me home afterward and makes pan-fried catfish. Catfish is relatively easy for me to chew and swallow, and I can almost taste it. It'll be great to taste Lois' cooking again. Her kisses, too.

I'd be nowhere without her.

In May my red blood cell count is way down. Besides making me weak, it means they have to keep putting off my next chemo. Which is great news the first time, but eventually, I get anxious to get back on track. I can't plan anything, my life is still on hold and I don't know when I'm going to get better. It's depressing.

Lois takes me down to the Chemo Lounge on my birthday to check my red cell count. I can either get hooked up with a nifty fanny pack or sent home because my count is too low. I don't know which one makes me more bummed out. Turns out it's the second option.

When we get home I get a strange phone call. Wayne Nagel wants to know if Jon Dee and I can do a short set at the Continental Club the following week. The gig is a Rolling Stones tribute benefit. The proceeds will go to the SIMS Foundation, which provides mental health counseling services to needy musicians. It's hard enough to drag my ass out of bed, much less think about getting onstage, but I have always hated to turn down a good gig. I say yes. I also give Wayne a few caveats related to my condition, but he knows all those things already, since he regularly drops by to visit.

The night of the gig rolls around. Lois can't go. Dashiell has school the next day. I drive to the club by myself. Full house. I greet a lot of old friends backstage and at the bar. A good number of Austin's best rockers are on the bill, all of them happy to do the SIMS Foundation a favor. Doug Sahm is backstage talking up a storm as usual. Charlie Sexton, Ian Moore and Alejandro Escovedo play dynamite sets, but I think ours will be even better. Jon Dee and I put our heads together, tune our instruments and take the stage with David Green, the drummer in his solo band. There's some applause as we're announced as the Skunks, and after David clicks a four-count on his sticks, we launch into "Under My Thumb."

My fingers are numb and tingly from chemo, but I can play and the thumping thunder coming out of the bass amp gives me strength. The lights are hot and people are smiling as I step up to the mic. Listen to that voice! It's got a new gravel and grit, thanks to all the things my throat has been subjected to in the last six months. Sure, I'm missing a few notes off the top end of my range, but that edge makes up for it. Besides, it makes me sound more like I feel, a skinny white boy who has the right to sing the blues.

Jon Dee's guitar is ripping out monster chunks of sound, and David's drumming is just right, powerful and rock steady. The crowd likes us. We segue to "Route 66," "Walkin' the Dog" and "Little Red Rooster." We're rattling the rafters. The songs suit our style, raw and loud and mean, and that sound gives me a gigantic shot in the arm.

As I sing, my hair falls in my eyes. The Austin blues singer Lou Ann Barton always used to tell me I had "that good fallin' hair." She's been bringing me her homemade potato soup, trying to put some pounds on this skeleton of mine. Besides being the best female blues singer around, she's a fantastic cook. I'll gain some weight some day. I'm happy to realize, after all this, at least I haven't lost my good fallin' hair.

I know I'll make it back. I'll get strong enough to take my last doses of chemo. I'll rebuild myself. If I can get up onstage and play rock 'n' roll, I can do just about anything. Rock 'n' roll just saved my ass again.

In June we went to the Grand Canyon. Again, it seemed touch-and-go whether I'd be able to handle the trip, but it was one of my recovery goals and it seemed that the act of planning and actually going on the trip might give me the momentum to be well enough to do it. Apparently it worked. We had an amazing time. The canyon worked its magic on us.

When we came back, I had my last dose of 5FU. I bottomed out at 125 pounds. Two weeks later, I had another CAT scan. Dr. Lewis smiled as she wrote "N.E.D." in the appropriate blank on the report—no evidence of disease. So far so good.

By summer's end my appetite was returning and my sense of taste and smell were slowly recovering. Lois would fill the house with great smells, like rosemary and roasted garlic or linguini and clam sauce, and haul me around to restaurants where she urged me to order everything on the menu that sounded appealing.

I could finally kiss her. Tasting her lips and mouth, smelling her hair and biting her on the neck were pleasurable again. Being able to do that again was one of the best reminders that life was worth living. I was human again.

In the spring of 1999, Evan Smith, the editor of *Texas Monthly*, sent me a contract for a 2,000-word piece about my cancer experience. The essay I turned in was centered around the Continental Club gig with Jon Dee and was about the importance of rock 'n' roll and imagination to my recovery.

I showed the first draft to Dr. Lewis and asked if she could fact-check it for me. I said I especially wanted her to double-check the information I'd gotten on the Internet, the staging of my disease and the survival stats.

As she read that particular page she said, "Hmm."

"Is it accurate?" I asked. The site had referred to a study on squamous cell carcinoma that was more than thirty years old. Surely the survival odds were better than 9 percent by now.

"Actually, you're barking up the wrong tree here," she said. "Cancer of the tonsil falls into the category of what we call oropharyngeal cancer. It has some different characteristics from the cancers cited in this particular study."

"And the survival rates," I said. "They're higher?"

"No, they're actually lower."

I felt myself stumble backward into the deep shadows of my film noir, *The Big C*. I'd gotten used to the idea that my chances were low, but less than 9 sounded to me like 100 people in a bus going over a cliff. Might as well be zero.

Now that the cat was out of the bag, Dr. Lewis seemed relieved for the chance to talk more freely.

"Your cancer was really bad," she said. "I didn't think you should know how bad it was. I was afraid if you knew, you might give up, you might not have the will to fight."

She'd done the right thing. I almost asked her to tell me what my actual survival figure was. But I didn't. I didn't want to know. Nine percent was close enough to zero.

240

PART 5.
LOVE & DEATH

23. OUT OF THE PAST

The deco building has dark wood trim, high ceilings, wrought iron balustrades. In the foyer is a photo exhibit of old Austin, with bulbous 1930s sedans on wide downtown streets, men in baggy suits, everybody wearing hats. I feel like a private detective on a case.

But the only pay I get is information, because I'm the detective and the client, too. Inside the windowless room with the newspaper archives, my hands are shaking, my heart is racing. I can do this, I tell myself. I can do this.

> SUSPECT JAILED IN WOMAN'S STRANGLING
>
> Jesse Sublett knew something was wrong when he walked inside the small house at 2109 Glendale Place and noticed the cats were missing.
>
> In a back bedroom, he found his girlfriend Diane K. Roberts, sprawled nude and facedown on her bed, a pillowcase wrapped around her neck.
>
> Sublett, 22, who lived with Roberts and her brother, discovered the slaying at 3:37 P.M. Monday when he came home from an out-of-town trip.
>
> He told police his 22-year old girlfriend's four cats were always inside the house, but police only found one. Officers theorized the other cats may have gotten out when the killer left.

By 1:49 A.M. today, police had arrested a 19-year-old suspect in connection with the slaying, which police said they believe to have been sexually motivated.

However, early this afternoon, the suspect still was being questioned. No charges had been filed.

According to police, Roberts, an unemployed secretary whose father lives in Houston, died of manual strangulation. Tests are being conducted to determine if she had been raped.

Sublett's parents live in Johnson City.

Mrs. J.E. Sublett, Jr. said her son called her this morning to tell her of his girlfriend's death.

"He was crying and was so broken up, I could hardly understand him," she said. "He said he was going to Houston. I told him I wanted to go with him, but he said he already had somebody to go."

Mrs. Sublett said she had met the victim many times. She described her as "friendly and pretty."

Sublett, she said, is a musician, and the couple's hobby was music. They had been friends since 1972, according to Justice of the Peace Bob Perkins, who examined the body at the slaying scene.

"All I can think of is my son," Mrs. Sublett said. "I just want to put my arms around him and make sure he's all right."

Investigators said they believed an intruder entered Roberts' residence early Monday morning through a window.

Police would not say which window, but a reporter Tuesday saw a pane missing from a back window. The window screen was on the ground nearby.

The woman was found in a small back bedroom of the white, stuccoed house, lying on a mattress on the floor, surrounded by pillows. Rock music posters had been used to decorate the walls of the room.

Neighbors said they frequently were disturbed by loud, hard rock music coming from the Glendale residence.

One neighbor said she had complained to police about the noise.

Roberts was described as an attractive, tall, slender woman by neighbors, who had set out food in case the dead woman's cats come back.

Capt. Bob Parsons of the police criminal investigation detail said the suspect in the case may have been an

acquaintance of Roberts, but would not elaborate.
Roberts' body was taken to Wilke-Clay Funeral Home,
where services were pending.

It's the lead story of the day, page one above the logo, Tuesday, August 17, 1976. The printout is dark but legible. I keep it as far from me as possible while reading. It's a rattlesnake, waiting here to bite me these past twenty-six years. Dry mouth, can't swallow, but I haven't lost it yet.

One of the archivists helps me clear the jam on the microfilm printer. She can tell something's wrong with me, but she pretends she hasn't noticed. My neck hurts like hell, like it's in a vise. No surprise. Pop a pain pill.

They used Dianne's driver's license photo. Almost looks like a mug shot, but you can see she's pretty. Misspelled her name, using only one n.

The story says she lived with her brother? Oh yeah, people used to say we looked alike. "Are you brother and sister?" Right. The reporter obviously got the idea from a neighbor, probably the one who admitted calling the cops because of that frequent "loud, hard rock music." Is the mention of rock music posters on the walls supposed to mean something seedy or significant? Guess it did in 1976. That "mattress on the floor, surrounded by pillows" was our luxurious love nest.

Overall I'm surprised the story isn't more sensational and ugly. No mentions of the noose "wall hanging," the dagger-in-the-head portrait, the other weird art, Dianne's pagan trinkets and candles. I'd always thought there'd be insinuations of devil worship, drugs and other innuendo. Maybe in the follow-up stories. Plus, I'll never know what they said on TV.

Twist the scroll knob, headlines blur past. Only a year since we pulled out of Vietnam. The big Bicentennial. Gerald Ford was president, running for reelection in November. "Disco Duck" was a big hit that year. Captain & Tenille were so hot they had their own TV show.

"Teen Held in Slaying" tops the story Wednesday morning. There's a photo of the house, with our overgrown yard and the toilet flowerpot. A cat at the end of the sidewalk, looking to one side. The caption reads, "Slain woman's body was found in house at 2109 Glendale. The victim's house cats outside were the first clue that something was amiss." I don't recognize this cat. I don't think it's one of ours. Makes a good caption, though. According to the story, Brummett was an electrician, with an apartment just a few blocks from our house. Never realized he was so close. He was awaiting trial on rape charges filed in Kerr County the previous November. Moved here from Kerrville in March. He was "an acquaintance of the victim."

> *Police said they filed a capital murder charge in the case, which allows prosecutors to seek the death penalty because they believe the murder was committed during the course of a rape.*

Death penalty? Limey told me there was no death penalty in 1976. Was he lying? I'll definitely be checking into that, but I don't dwell on it now because the evening edition seizes my attention: "Suspect Shows Police 2 More Slaying Victims." On Wednesday I was in Houston getting ready for the funeral. Look at what I missed. Beth Pearson was a newlywed, only fifteen. Carol Ann London, eighteen, had just graduated from Kerrville's Tivy High. These are the murdered girls Limey mentioned, the leverage in Brummett's plea.

Now I know why I'm in this windowless room, peering into the past. This has been messing me up for twenty-six years now. Maybe it even gave me cancer. There are important things I never knew. Finding them now is like walking through a minefield, stepping on one bomb after another.

It's two days before Halloween 2002. I've known for a long time I'd have to do this, but it wasn't until now that I managed to find the time and courage. Lois urged me on. "Get to the bottom of it," she said. "Figure out what's been bugging you so you can get on with the rest of your life."

I knew I'd write about Dianne someday. I was scared about what might happen when I did, but I could feel in my bones that it was the right thing. First I wrote some essays about hanging out with Eddie, our low-rent rock-star lifestyles in Jellyroll, how the Skunks and Violators got started. Then I wrote about how Dianne and I met. The day I wrote about the Queen Bee gig and finding Dianne the next day, I stayed glued to the keyboard until I'd covered the police interrogation, Brummett's arrest and telephoning Earl Roberts in the middle of the night.

The account ran almost forty pages. After printing it out, I lay down and cried, loudly, for a long time. Both cats, Willie and Kiki #2, came into the room looking alarmed, then jumped on the couch and cuddled next to me. Marlowe had died the previous November.

I couldn't look at those words again for months. I clamped the pages together, top and bottom, so they wouldn't spill open and provide unwanted captions to my flashbacks. I was upset and depressed. A colleague called with an offer to write a promotional film for a hip technology firm. After that, when I wasn't working on documentaries I wrote about other, more pleasant things. Like chemo and radiation and the time I tried to quit my pain medication cold turkey.

In the summer of 2001 my fifteen-year-old nephew's best friend died in a gruesome accident, and it was only by a quirk of fate that my nephew hadn't died with him. Willie the cat died of lymphoma. A drummer friend named Mambo John Treanor died of neck cancer. His case was similar to mine, but his survival statistics were higher. "Hang in there. You'll make it," I kept telling him. "If I can make it, you'll make it." I was wrong. A friend was murdered by drug dealers. They used a flamethrower. They made her and her husband beg for their lives before burning them up, along with all their cats and their house, too. The world is such a goddamn meat grinder.

I couldn't sleep. The tinnitus in my ears, courtesy of cisplatin and radiation, buzzed louder than ever. Twice I scared the hell out of Dashiell when I couldn't stifle a crying fit. I tried to work through it. I went to yoga three times a week, wrote poems, took long walks at Town Lake, thinking and watching birds. Thought how lucky I was to have Lois and Dashiell and the life we'd made.

I decided to try a new tack and confront the thing head-on. Stop hiding from those murder pages. Show them around, say, *Look, this is my story*. On a dark whim, I e-mailed a pitch for an essay-length version to the *New York Times Magazine*. The editor called me the next morning and bought it. My story would run in late August, in the back-of-the-book section called *Lives*, which is often about death. It was a good fit.

Writing the essay for the *Times* was more difficult and disturbing than I had anticipated. Condensing the story uncovered new facets of my guilt and grief. I could look back on my twenty-two-year-old self as a different person, one who was reckless and selfish and not all that likeable. The editor, Cat St. Louis, was gifted at milking me for painful details and crystallizing the story for maximum dramatic punch.

It was almost like therapy, except I felt much worse afterward.

Why didn't I just take Dianne with me to the gig? Because I thought I might get lucky with some slinky groupie afterward? Why was I such a shithead (i.e., a typical musician)? I ended the story by saying how unbearable I found the possibility that Brummett could go free in two years. Readers would probably assume that I'd been doing everything I could in the last twenty-five years to block his parole. The truth was, I had not been able bring myself to do anything about it until now. Before this I just could not think about it.

When I finally made the call to the Texas Department of Criminal Justice, I learned that the procedures were fairly straightforward. I started with a short protest letter, intending to do much more later, but I did nothing until the story for the *New York Times Magazine*. Having done nothing in the past year made me feel like an asshole. What if the monster got out because I just didn't have the guts to fight it? I called the Victims Services line at TDCJ and found out that I'd already missed three reviews. The first was in 1996. Twenty years? That was sick. The other reviews were in 1998 and 2000. Denied all three times. I promised myself that Brummett wasn't going to make it in 2003, or any other year of this millennium. From now on, every time his case came down for review, there'd be a freight train of evidence roaring at him from the other end of the tunnel.

To do the job right, I needed to present the parole board with a concise, accurate summary of Brummett's twisted life. That meant I had to know about the other killings and charges, which meant research and confronting more hideous reality.

But I wasn't in shape to do any of this. I was a mess. Lois told me I needed to see a therapist. She was right, as usual.

Dr. Catherine Daniel, my psychologist, has a pleasant face, a soothing voice. She appears to be moved by my story, not surprised at all that I've come seeking help. Good, I don't feel like a faker. When I tell her the most severe chronic neck pain I suffer due to cancer surgery is the strangling sensation at my throat, there's a sharp intake of breath. "Oh," she says, nodding. "Like Dianne."

She pauses for a beat and says, "I think you have post traumatic stress disorder."

Never occured to me before, but now that she says it, it makes sense. "I think you're right."

"There's a treatment called EMDR. It stands for Eye Movement Desensitization Reprocessing, and it's been very effective for people who have PTSD. Would you be interested in trying it?"

"Absolutely."

The brain mechanics believe that traumatic memories are encoded differently than regular memories. Normally the brain files away new information during REM (rapid eye movement) sleep, but a traumatic event can jam up the filing system. The memory becomes hard-wired in the brain by the limbic system, which controls basic emotions and operates outside of conscious awareness. It's also encoded with a fear response to dangers. As we experience threats and dangers, such as being accosted in a dark alley, we learn to avoid alleys instinctively. If we do find ourselves in a dark alley, the limbic system initiates its flight-or-fight response and floods the body with adrenaline. But if the alley encounter is especially traumatic, memories of the event, accompanied by other intense reactions, might be triggered by the thought of a dark alley or a place with a similar feel or smell. That's why I still frequently hallucinated scenes of murder and mutilation when I unlocked the front door and why these other recent deaths had me caught in a vortex of depression.

Dr. Daniel compiles a list of troubling thoughts I have. I tell her about the tape loop. We zero in on the moment I walked into the bedroom, knelt beside Dianne and saw her face.

"OK," she says, "when you found her." Makes a note. Next she asks me to rate the distress the memory makes me feel on a scale of 0 (no distress) to 7 (extreme distress). I give it a solid 7.

"Now I want you to concentrate on that memory. Just that part of it, when you found her. While you're doing that, I want you to keep your eyes softly focused on my hand." She demonstrates, moving her hand back and forth horizontally.

Then we do it for real. I start concentrating, reliving the experience. I can feel tears, my heartbeat kicking up, a hyperawareness as I see the bedroom, the oak trees outside the windows, Dianne's face, bruised and bloodied. I'm watching Dr. Daniel's hand. I'm crying hard.

She stops. I'm not aware of how much time has passed. A minute? Two minutes? It's like a cloud passed overhead. My breathing has slowed; I'm no longer crying.

Quiet voiced, as always, she says, "OK, Jesse, how do you feel about that memory now? Better, worse or the same?"

I pause and think. I want to be sure. "I don't feel quite as bad."

"On a scale of 1 to 7, how would you rate it?

"Guess I'd give it a 5. Maybe even a 4. I'm surprised."

She nods, makes a notation. "Jesse, when you were thinking about when you found Dianne, did any new memories occur to you?"

Definitely. I tell her something I had completely forgotten. A disturbing detail in the bedroom. We work on it. During the remainder of the session, we treat five or six bad memories. Each ends with a lower rating. More than half the memories trigger other memories. Some are painful, though some are not, like remembering Dianne's red baseball cap with the strawberry patch on it. I'd forgotten about that.

Before I leave, Dr. Daniel cautions me that I may have other memories and thoughts between now and the next session. If they're painful, she says, remember that we'll work on them next time.

The next few days were strange. The relief was genuine. The memory of seeing Dianne dead wasn't erased, but it wasn't triggered every time I thought of her, and when I examined the memory, it didn't have the same power. My thoughts about Dianne tended to be less painful. I began seeing her in life again. Still, the doctor's warning that other painful memories might surface turned out to be true. So I cried a lot between sessions, too. And I reminded myself how lucky I was. Lucky to have Lois and Dashiell. Here I was, though, obsessed with a dead girlfriend from twenty-five years ago. At times it must have seemed pretty unfair, even crazy. If Lois were to suddenly demand that I choose between her and a ghost, how could I blame her? To her credit, she never did. I don't know if I could be that understanding and patient myself.

Progress continued roughly along the same track over the first three sessions with Dr. Daniel. Sometimes the treatments unearthed painful memories, and I continued to have some black days, but there was always a little net forward movement. I was sleeping better, working more.

My fourth appointment was on September 11, the day of the terrorist attacks on the World Trade Center and the Pentagon. Lois came home and we stayed glued to the TV. It was impossible not to take the attacks personally. People were being interviewed on the street. Some mentioned Pearl Harbor. A woman said, "It's horrible, I can't believe it. Nothing will ever be the same again." Other people said it, too. Things will never be the same again.

I wanted to say to them, *Brother, sister, I know what you mean.*

The world had become a darker place. As I saw it, the shock people described was the realization that the world wasn't the one we thought we lived in, with its illusion of stability and basic goodness. Your next step could be through a trapdoor to hell.

My heart went out to the victims, survivors and shell-shocked masses, and to the city itself. I was bitter and sad. Like a lot of people, we felt that New York was our city, too; it was a part of us. But I also felt relief, as if some of the terrible burden of my grief had been taken up by others or dispersed by the explosions.

Things will never be the same again.

24. CYPHERS CREEK

B eth Pearson and Carol Ann London lived next door to each other. Best friends, both reported missing September 17, 1975. Back then the information seemed abstract. Now they're real people, with names, faces, lives. The photos in the articles are grainy. Two dark-haired girls, looking like schoolgirls used to look in Johnson City when I left. I feel ashamed for never trying to find out who they were. It never occurred to me. I was too shattered.

In Kerrville Brummett was known as Lyle Stone, while some records have him identified as Lyle Richard. Brummett was the name of his birth father, long out of the picture by 1976. Brummett told Curly Beck about the girls Tuesday evening. Lieutenant Jordan and Sergeant Beck hauled him down to Kerrville that night, meeting up with a search team that totaled twelve men.

They searched a cow pasture on the Salvaggio ranch a few miles off I-10 near Cypress Creek Road. It took most of the night. When the bodies were located, Kerrville authorities arrested Brummett's best friend, Allen Ladd Woody. Woody was a twenty-year-old construction worker from Center Point, a small town of barely 600 people ten miles south of Kerrville.

Carol Ann London worked at Doyle Kindergarten. Beth Pearson had only been in Kerrville for five months, having moved there from Irving.

Her father was a Baptist preacher. She and Jim Pearson had gotten married three weeks before she disappeared. Both girls sang in church.

Beth and Carol Ann went driving in Jim's car on the afternoon of September 17. Jim found the car the next morning in the courthouse parking lot. Several days later, a grass-cutting crew found the girls' clothing scattered on the side of I-10 just a few miles from the cow pasture. That discovery, said Sheriff E. A. Schreiber, prompted a search that involved fifty law enforcement officials who combed the area "for hours" but found "no other signs of foul play." In another account the sheriff said, "It had been raining real hard so we presumed they had run away from home and maybe changed clothes."

Runaways? This is so depressing, stupid and sad I feel the urge to slap the sheriff in the face, even though he's dead now. Those monsters might have been caught. Brummett could have been stopped before he murdered again.

Thursday's *Statesman* says Brummett was under indictment for two counts of rape in Kerr County and one count of credit card abuse—three felonies. Add two counts of capital murder, one in Travis County for Dianne, another in Kerr County for Carol Ann London. A story in the morning edition of the *Kerrville Times* says that he was also charged with murder in the death of Beth Pearson. Kerr County charged Allen Woody with capital murder in the death of Beth and murder in the death of Carol Ann.

The final edition quoted the assistant manager of Wolfe's Nursery in Kerrville, where Brummett worked part-time as a laborer: "There were no smooth edges on Lyle. He was tough, but he was polite and courteous to our customers." The story also quoted Brummett's landlord, who claimed that he and his pregnant wife, Laurie, were model tenants. "He was never intoxicated, never out of line," she said. "All of his neighbors liked him."

I remember cold eyes and a weird sneer.

No one seemed to be calling anyone in Kerr County to task for screwing up. No mention of whether Brummett had been questioned regarding the girls' disappearance. In a small town like Kerrville, where everyone knows everyone else's business, this seems bizarre. A rapist, a long-hair druggie fuckup in a little redneck town. How could the cops not wonder about him?

The newspaper made at least a nominal attempt to sketch Brummett, mentioning his pregnant wife and his various jobs, obtaining quotes from various acquaintances. They made an effort to let people glimpse more than yearbook photos of Carol Ann and Beth. But they didn't seem to try very hard to say who Dianne Roberts was, other than "an unemployed secretary," a pretty girl who had four cats and whose "hobby" was music. In follow-up stories they mentioned only the essentials, i.e., in what position and state she was found, how she was killed.

Apparently newspaper readers in 1976 needed lurid details more than they needed to know Dianne was an artist, a poet, a funny and sensitive girl. By the weekend, Dianne's murder was mentioned as an adjunct to the main story, pending identification of the Kerrville girls. On Sunday the cases were mentioned in a humorous police beat column on the op-ed page. Jordan had to get his squad car sprayed for ticks after it was parked all night at the Cypress Creek pasture. A wacky end to a long week for the homicide chief.

I was relieved to find out that Woody was still in prison. His case, I learned, was also due for parole review in 2003. Woody had only been found guilty of first-degree murder and sentenced to ninety-nine years. Under state sentencing guidelines, he had a mandatory release date of 2009, by which time he would have served one-third of his sentence.

A lot of murderers and rapist-murderers are released after serving shorter sentences, I realized, but that did me no good at all. The possibility that Brummett would be set free filled me with bitterness. The fact that the Kerrville cops botched the case so spectacularly brought back my feelings of resentment against small-town cowboy cops. Why was a monster like Brummett still running around free ten months after these girls disappeared?

I started trying to find out how I could get my hands on the Brummett files from the Austin Police Department and Kerr County. I did Internet searches on all the names I had so far, starting with Beck and Jordan of APD, plus all the names from the *Statesman*. I called two lawyer friends for advice on how to get the murder files on the three cases.

My music attorney, Rick Triplett, suggested I request copies of the files under the Freedom of Information Act. He told me how to make the request. Police departments and district attorney's offices would be legally obligated to fulfill the request. Tom Garner, my book collector/attorney pal, had a different take. "Some of these people might go out of their way to help if you just ask instead of forcing them to give you the information through open records," he said. "Lawyers and cops love to talk about old cases. The trick is finding the right person." Tom knew some people in Kerrville. He'd call me back, he said.

Mike Cox called me back that afternoon. Mike was a former public information officer for the Texas Department of Public Safety, a state agency that administers various branches of law enforcement, including the legendary Texas Rangers. In addition, Mike was a former crime reporter and true crime author, and he was acquainted with quite a few people who'd been involved in the cases. Several were deceased; some were missing in action. He shared the phone numbers of the rest.

"You should probably call a Kerrville attorney named Ilse Bailey," he said. "She used to be with the district clerk's office, and I don't think she was in Kerrville before 1976, but she's a nice gal and she'd probably be able to help. She knows a lot of people in law enforcement."

I already knew Ilse Bailey was a nice lady, because she was married to Dr. Al Graham, Jon Dee's older brother. The last time I saw her was at Jon Dee's second wedding, three years ago. She'd probably mentioned that she worked for the county clerk, but I'd forgotten all about it.

Ilse said she'd be glad to help. I sent her a summary of the information I had plus a list of questions. She promised to get back to me soon.

I got busy tracking down old Austin cops. Number one on my list, Curly Beck, was dead. Lt. Colon Jordan was alive, but suffering from Alzheimer's and diabetes. His son, Paul, promised to ask him about the case but warned me not to get my hopes up. Colon Jordan died not long after that.

Former APD Capt. Bob Parsons, deceased. Sgt. Manley Stephens, lead detective on the case, nowhere to be found.

George Phifer, APD captain of detectives in 1976, answered his phone on the third ring. He remembered the case. Manley Stephens was the man to talk to, he said, but he didn't know how to find him. Burch Biggerstaff might be able to help. He was head of APD Criminal Investigation Division in 1976. Phifer gave me his number and wished me luck. Biggerstaff returned my call that night. He was sure sorry, he said, but his memory of that time was completely gone. I tried dropping some names and facts to see if that would help. Not a thing. Gone. Sorry.

Former Justice of the Peace Bob Perkins was now a Travis County district judge. He did remember the case. Even though I didn't learn anything new, I liked talking to him. He couldn't do anything about the file, he said, but he suggested I check with the county clerk's office.

"You want to keep these guys in prison, right?"

"Absolutely," I said.

"Then you should get in touch with People Against Violent Crime. They're a victim rights group. They wrote Texas' victim rights law and got it passed, too."

Perkins assured me that PAVC could definitely make a difference. He also urged me to check out their Tree of Angels service, which was held at the Christian Church downtown every Christmas for victims of violent crimes.

"From what I gather, Jesse," he said, "it might be a very good thing for you to do. Might give you some peace of mind."

That sounded like a lot to hope for, but I said I just might take his advice.

Kerrville is 104 miles west of Austin. I drove west on Highway 290, passing through Johnson City, where I grew up; Stonewall, where I went to church; and Fredericksburg, where I was born, just 16 miles from Kerrville, where Lyle Brummett grew up.

In 1976 Kerrville was a town of 16,000 people; now it's up to 20,000. Still a small town. The courthouse square is bordered by a cluster of retro-looking businesses, that old Main Street U.S.A. look that brings a smile to tourists and junk-store junketeers who flock here from the city.

Deer hunting is a very big deal here, as it is everywhere in the Hill Country. Coming into town, a banner over the main drag reads: "Hunters Welcome." The Tivy High School football team is called the Antlers. I don't think Lyle Brummett ever played football. He did, however, play Little League, according to Carol Ann's brother, Bill. Carol used to go to Bill's games. So although they never knew Brummett well, they'd known him since he was eight or nine years old. That may explain why Carol Ann and Beth accepted a ride from Brummett and Woody after their car broke down.

Ilse gave me a thick folder with documents on Brummett and Woody's cases from the county clerk's office. What did I owe her? Just $27 for the printing, she said. A bargain. She rattled off more information, including the names of some cops who might talk to me and others who wouldn't because they were dead. Sheriff Shreiber, Deputy Sheriff Paul Fields and their immediate successors were all deceased. Then we met with Joe Davis, a retired Texas Ranger who worked the case in 1976.

Davis was president of the Former Texas Rangers Association, and his office was decorated with memorabilia related to that elite crime-fighting organization and his other big passion, deer hunting. An affable guy with an easy-going manner.

"He was always a troublemaker," Davis said of Brummett. It's a comment I would hear repeatedly. Not a sicko, a bastard, a rapist. I suppose it's part of that Old West habit of dramatic understatement.

Brummett was an eleventh-grade dropout. He had several older siblings, including two sisters in the Navy. Lived with his mother and stepfather.

"Lyle was very cooperative," Davis said about the search for the bodies. "He had absolutely no remorse. Whenever we asked him to show us how something happened or where, he was up for it."

Only bones were left, scattered under a sprawling oak tree.

"One of the girls wore a ring. Beth, I think, or maybe both of them. Lyle said they threw the rings toward the creek. One of the other Rangers, Henry Ligon, picked up a little rock, gave it to him and told him, 'Just throw this rock the way you threw that ring.' Threw the rock and we took the metal detectors over there in the weeds and grass, and about ten minutes later we had the rings."

I told him that guilt is one of the reasons I'm doing this: "I should've kept this guy away from us, especially once I found out about the rape charges. I should've done more. I should've fixed that window—"

"You can't think that way," Davis said. "A guy like this is going to do these things on his own. The missing pane of glass, whatever, he is just gonna do it. That's the kind of guy he was. Dangerous. Sadistic."

Did he know anything about Brummett or Woody's background that might have made them that way? He offered some basic Freudian conjecture. Probably hated his mother, took it out on girls.

But did he know of anything specific? Any rumors about it?

"Nope."

What about when the girls disappeared? Why did everyone assume they ran away, even after their clothes and underwear turned up?

"I don't remember too well. Far as I recall, they'd run away before, hadn't they?"

The leaves have turned and the air is crisp. The holidays are coming. Lois is happy, planning tomorrow's Thanksgiving dinner and a big party soon after. Dashiell is usually a great mood elevator, too, starting off at breakfast and on the way to school. He's been updating me on the roster of Yu Gi Oh cards he's acquiring in booster packs, listing the special powers of each monster and the damage they can inflict on an opponent's cards. It's impossible to sort out more than a small percentage of this information (especially before my third espresso), but the sound of his voice is music, his handsome face a tiny sun.

Next week I'll mark five years cancer-free. Last week, the producer who holds the option on my Martin Fender novels called to say that a TV network is interested in developing a pilot script for a series. Even if nothing comes of it, and most likely nothing will, it's fun to think about. Lois is writing a hip cookbook. Great idea. She might end up being the hot writer in the house.

Thanksgiving—it was a smart man or woman who came up with the idea of a holiday devoted to expressing our appreciation for the important things in life, including the fact that somehow we've survived another year.

It takes time to get the hang of all the legal jargon in the file Ilse gave me. After a quick inventory of the indictments, Miranda warnings, motions and other documents, the first thing I read is a report from a mental exam Brummett was given in February 1976. His attorney, Charlie Strauss, filed the motion, claiming his client appeared to have "a mental disease or defect" rendering him incompetent to stand trial. The examining doctors found that, while Brummett had serious psychological problems, he was fit to stand trial. Brummett appeared to have "no autistic or psychotic trends. . . obsessions or phobias;" however, he exhibited "total lack of feeling for others, and he shows no significant loyalty to any person, group, code of ethics or conduct. Subject is hedonistic and pleasure oriented." Based on the results of psychological tests and interviews, the examiners concluded that Brummett suffered from antisocial personality disorder. Such individuals, they stated, not only know what they're doing, but how to get away with it. "[They] feel no guilt or remorse, and they may lie or play whatever role is expedient in gaining their own immediate desires." The examiner noted that Brummett appeared to have "many sexual problems and poor emotional adjustment." On IQ tests, Brummett's scores averaged out to 86, classified as "dull normal."

Before Brummett was indicted for the rape of Lyn Burke on November 16, a judge took testimony from Burke and some other witnesses about the events of that night. Lyne Burke testified that she was at a nightclub called the Chalet and needed a ride home. She saw Brummett, Woody and Charlie Harris (Woody's stepbrother) there. They were acquainted but not friends. Woody said they would give her a ride. Brummett drove, but instead of taking Burke home, he took her to a secluded area and after tricking her into getting out of the car, he raped her. Burke stated that Woody and Harris tried to stop Brummett, but apparently they were unsuccessful. Brummett made her promise not to tell anyone about it before he'd take her home.

I wonder if Harris knew that Brummett and Woody had already murdered two girls. Is that why Woody tried to stop the rape, to prevent another murder? I'm curious about the chronology of these crimes. A date on a bail bondsman's receipt catches my eye: September 17, 1975. That seems significant, but I can't figure it out. I start writing down dates and work up a timeline. A few minutes later, I've got it.

Brummett was arrested and charged with raping Susan Taylor on September 2. He remained in jail for fifteen days. He made bail on September 17 and was released that afternoon. September 17 is the day Carol Ann London and Beth Pearson disappeared. The same goddamn day this monster was bailed out on one rape charge, he struck again. This time two girls were murdered. Two months later, he was charged with raping Lynn Burke. Rape, murder, rape—where would his spree have ended if it hadn't been halted in August 1976? He was a serial-rapist-murderer with nowhere to go but hell.

The folder holds at least one more awful surprise. Brummett was jailed on November 16, 1975, and remained there until he made bail on March 12, 1976. The court set a date for a jury trial on all three indictments—July 6, 1976. On June 10, however, Brummett's court-appointed attorney, Charlie Strauss, filed a motion for continuance, stating that he would not be in the country: "Defendant's Attorney is being married on July 3, 1976, in Kerrville, Kerr County, Texas, and immediately following said marriage, will leave the country for a period of one week, and will not return until July 10, 1976."

If Brummett had stood trial on the original date, he might have been convicted and sent to prison. Instead, he remained free on bail. Thirty-five days later, he murdered Dianne Roberts.

Brummett had confessed to his role in the Kerrville murders soon after he was taken into custody by APD in 1976 . Even before I knew his name, I had assumed that Woody had done the same. Wrong. Apparently he did, in fact, make a confession after taking a lie detector test, but then, on the advice of an attorney, he stopped talking and went to trial on a plea of not guilty. The important thing here is that without Lyle Brummett's cooperation, Kerr County probably would have had to drop its murder charges against Allen Woody.

It took two more trips to Kerrville, during which I interviewed more Texas Rangers and other sources, and located many more documents and newspaper clippings related to Brummett and Woody. With this information I finally got a clearer picture of the events of fall 1975 through May 1977, when Brummett and Woody were each transferred to prison to begin their terms.

Woody's trial was transferred to Fort Stockton on a change of venue due to adverse pretrial publicity. Small wonder there. The prosecution called sixteen witnesses, including various law enforcement officers, the victims' dentists, who had identified the girls' remains through dental records, and Beth and Carol Ann's parents; but without Lyle Brummett, the prosecution had no case at all. On the stand Brummett testified that September 17 was the day he made bail on the previous rape charge. That evening he and Woody went driving and saw Carol Ann London and Beth Pearson in the courthouse parking lot by their car. The engine was smoking. The girls needed a ride, Brummett said, but he and Woody asked them if they wanted to get high and the girls said yes. (Family members denied that either girl used marijuana or any other drug.)

They drove out of town, turning onto Cypress Creek road. They pulled over and hiked deep into the deserted cow pasture. The girls came willingly, Brummett said, because he and Woody said their pot was stashed out there. He testified that at one point they started having intercourse with the girls. Brummett claimed that he was with Carol Ann London and Woody was with Beth Pearson. Pearson began struggling, Brummett said, and Woody choked her to death. Brummett said, "Something took control of my mind, and I then strangled the London girl." He claimed that Woody made sure the girls were dead by bashing one in the head with a rock and clubbing the other with a stick.

At least one witness had seen Beth and Carol Ann get into Woody and Brummett's car, but aside from that, only Woody could corroborate Brummett's account of the murders. Woody claimed he'd spent the evening at his mother's trailer, watching TV and eating a sandwich with her before bed. The confession Woddy had made to Ranger Henry Ligon was ruled inadmissable.

Brummett made a skuzzy main witness, but what could the Kerr County prosecutors do? With only skeletal remains, there was no forensic proof of the rape charges. Even proving death by violence was difficult.

And as far as physical appearances go, Woody was probably even less attractive on the stand than Brummett. In the *Kerrville Daily Times* photos, his dark, shoulder-length hair is wavy and fluffed out, like a girl's. He's got a putty nose, big teeth, big eyelashes and a tiny, almost girlish waistline. He'd been on probation for a charge of graveyard desecration.

A witness named David Hensley testified that he had accompanied Brummett and Woody on a trip to Del Rio on September 22, five days after the murders. Hensley stated that during the trip, Woody said he and Brummett had murdered two girls. The threesome financed the trip with the stolen credit card that was the subject of Brummett's third felony indictment. When they ran out of cash, Hensley said, Woody suggested they kidnap a whore and then kill her when they were done with her.

The jury voted to convict Woody of murder, rejecting the more serious charge of capital murder, and sentenced him to 99 years. The maximum sentence available to the jury was life imprisonment, the minimum, ten years. Unfortunately, Texas did not and still does not have a provision for life without parole.

On April 22, one week after Woody's trial ended, Brummett pled guilty to the reduced charge of murder in the death of Carol Ann London and received a life sentence. The murder charge against him in the death of Beth Pearson had already been dropped, as part of his agreement to testify against Woody.

The last surprise fact my research unearthed was that, up until the end of April, Brummett was scheduled to stand trial for murdering Dianne. I had always thought he'd entered a guilty plea soon after giving his confession. Instead his attorney, Charles Craig, kept pushing for a better deal.

After two postponements, Brummett's trial date was set for May 9. From my newspaper research I learned that in the months between Brummett's arrest and the two weeks after Woody's trial, capital punishment was a frequent topic of discussion. The moratorium on U.S. executions, which began with the 1968 Supreme Court ruling that all existing death penalty statutes were unconstitutional, came to an end in Texas, Florida and Georgia in May 1976, when the Supreme Court ruled that the newly written statutes in those states were constitutional, clearing the way for legal executions.

Challenges were in the air, but technically capital punishment was legal again in Texas, despite what the D.A.'s office told me. Maybe their man just wanted to give me a simple answer to a complex legal issue. This was only conjecture on my part; he never replied to any of my letters, never returned my calls.

Gary Gilmore had been executed by firing squad in Utah on January 17, 1977. Ernest Smith, convicted of capital murder in an armed robbery, was set to be the first Texan executed under the new law. His date was set for April 26. On April 27, the *Statesman* reported that Brummett had confessed to the reduced charge of murder in the death of Dianne Roberts, and was given a life sentence to run concurrent with the term imposed in the Kerr County murder. All other pending charges were dropped.

Maybe Charles Craig had reason to think he might be able to bargain for a better deal than that, but surely the Travis County D.A. was able to counter Craig's arguments by reminding him that the electric chair at Huntsville, affectionately known as Old Sparky, was back in business and ready to take new customers. It seems logical.

As it turned out, Texas would not kill its first death-row inmate until December 7, 1982, when Charles Brooks was executed by lethal injection. I can't help wishing that Brummett had been the first to die.

Two shitbird murderers went to prison for a long, long time. Society was a little safer with them off the streets. Woody will serve at least thirty-three years, and with any luck Brummett will be locked up until he dies. Sometimes, I guess, that's as close to justice as you can get.

An awkward, delicate friendship has developed between Bill London, Jim Pearson and me. After the murders happened, none of us could face the grim reality—no newspapers, no TV reports. I didn't know about them, and they didn't know about me. None of us thought to consult a lawyer or to visit the district attorney to make sure justice was done. When Jim testified at Woody's trial, he wasn't allowed in the courtroom, so he never heard any of the testimony. He still has trouble believing what he has learned.

Bill London still feels guilty because Carol Ann asked if she could borrow his car that night and he said no. He can't help thinking that if he'd said yes, his sister might be alive. He's had nightmares, flashbacks and panic attacks. His parents have never been able to talk about it.

On my last visit to Kerrville, Jim took me out Cypress Creek Road. We stood next to the sprawling live oak tree where the girls' bodies were found. Jim, a fifth-generation stonemason, is a compact man with thin, floppy hair and hard lines etched on his face. His hands are callused and scarred.

Beth was two months pregnant. They'd planned to buy a trailer and put it behind his parents' house. Why did the cops say the girls ran away? They left all their belongings in the car, even their shoes. Why would Beth leave her diary behind for Jim to read, talking about how happy she was?

Bill and Jim are now actively protesting the possibility of paroles for Brummett and Woody. Working through TDCJ Victim Services, Jim has arranged face-to-face meetings with Brummett and Woody. Beth's sister, Renee, is also going to be there. Jim says they want to hear exactly what happened that night. I hope they know what they're doing.

This pasture is like a thousand other places I've been in the Hill Country. I can almost imagine I'm a kid again, deer hunting or prowling with a BB gun near Johnson City, Stonewall or Willow City. I know the smell of the trees and rocks, the sound of the wind pushing through the cedar breaks and a mockingbird's rapid-fire medley. Except for what happened here, this feels the same as those other places, but now it can never be the same. Not for Jim, not for Bill, not for me.

Ranger Ligon told me about staying here hours after the others left, scouring the ground for bones. "I was on my hands and knees, picking up little finger bones and whatever was left. I didn't want to leave anything of them behind."

Later on, in the cold of February and March 1977, Ligon was scouring the hillsides and riverbanks near the state hospital. That's where Brummett said he raped and murdered another girl, a hitchhiker passing through town. Brummett led investigators to the place, but they never found anything. Ligon kept going back, searching. "First little flood of the year and the body would be long gone from there," he said. "Did he really do it or did he make it up? That one still haunts me."

Bill London said people always knew Brummett was weird. "He was always cruel to animals. He tortured cats and dogs. But no one ever thought it would lead to murder."

In Brummett's confession to the Kerrville case, all the references to Cypress Creek Road were typed out as Cyphers Creek Road. For clarification, a short addendum at the bottom of the last page, signed by Brummett, stated that "the word Cyphers is spelled wrong and should be spelled Cypress." Whether it was the result of a lisp or Brummett's low I.Q., I don't know, but the word sticks in my mind. It seems fitting that cypher, a variant spelling of cipher, is the mathematical symbol for zero.

It also refers to a person or thing without influence or value, a nonentity.

25. HOUSTON & BACK

Fortified with hugs and kisses from Lois and Dashiell, I left for Houston early Saturday morning. Dianne's brother, Gary, was in town to take care of his mother's estate. We could talk while he was packing things at her condo. He had some pictures of Dianne for me, and he promised to see if Earl could meet us there.

The information I got in Kerrville was important, but it had become a black hole, sucking me in. It also distracted me from my search for cops who'd worked on the Austin case. Limey wouldn't call me back; maybe someone else could tell me if the D.A.'s office had told me any other falsehoods. But I wasn't making any progress. Nor had I made any progress finding Dianne's father, mother or brother. Nothing in Houston information, no hits on the Internet.

Then I received an e-mail from someone named Daniel Norton. He explained that his late father, Joseph Norton, had married Dianne's mother in 1978. Did I know that she had died recently? No, I did not. His message had a link to her obituary.

Daniel wanted to thank me for what I'd written about Dianne in *The New York Times Magazine* and in *Texas Monthly*. His father and Mary Ann were friends for years before they married. Though Daniel had only met Dianne once, he remembered her as "a lovely and expressive young girl."

I couldn't help thinking of the time when Mary Ann guilt-tripped Dianne into coming to Houston to spend Thanksgiving with her, instead of going skiing with Earl in Vail—her first choice by a mile. Yet when Dianne arrived at her mother's house, there was a note saying she'd changed her plans and left town with a friend. Probably Daniel's father. That's the divorce wars for you.

Gary lives in San Diego now, Daniel said. Earl was still in Houston, remarried, still in the oil business. Daniel gave me Gary's e-mail address and Earl's phone number.

I'd gotten it into my head that Earl probably blamed me for Dianne's death. I hoped I was wrong. I wanted to talk to him, but I was reluctant to call him out of the blue. I e-mailed Gary first, reintroducing myself. I also mentioned Brummett's pending parole review.

Driving to Houston, the memories flashed by like road signs. Passing through Rosenberg on I-10 just before the sprawling humongopolis, I remembered those times in college when we would pull off on a certain county road to pick mushrooms. I remember thinking Donovan's *Cosmic Wheels* LP had satanic overtones and hearing ominous sounds buzz through the air on giant insect wings.

Seeing Mary McGee was great. She and her partner, Paul, were going on nine years. He was a Brit, smart, funny, modest. He owned a T-shirt printing shop. Mary worked at home doing the specialty items. She looked great, trim and pretty as always. That classic smirk was still there, neatly set off by her bright green eyes. Mary told me that for years she was angry with Dianne for abandoning her. Of course it didn't make sense. She still had dreams about Dianne, and the smallest memory could still bring on tears.

Mary came along to see Gary. He was in his mother's condo, drinking beer, watching the football game. Glad to see us. "You're my link to my sister," he told me. "I've got a picture of you and Dianne next to my computer at work. I look at it all the time. You guys were so pretty together."

He was incredibly thin. His face was long and narrow, framed by shaggy brownish-blond hair. I reminded him about the parole hearing and asked him if he'd talked with the victim rights people yet.

"No, not yet, but I want to talk to the parole board myself, in person," he said. "Do you know how to do that?"

"No, I don't. I'm not sure if it's possible," I said.

"I wish I could call my sister. I wish I could call her and say, 'Hey Sis, I had a bad day, what do you think I should do?' I miss having a sister. There's a hole in my life and always will be because of that sick son-of-a-bitch."

Gary was a computer programmer. For a while he managed a jazz club in Albuquerque. He was still tending a defunct relationship with a woman living in Europe. He'd just sent her some money even though she wasn't coming back.

Earl couldn't make it, he said. I said I'd try calling later.

There was hardly space to walk in the condo. The colors seemed off. Stale greens, faded gold, tan. An occasional artifact from South America or China, but mostly middle-class American home furnishings and accessories from several decades ago.

"This is all stuff from the divorce, isn't it?" Mary said.

Gary nodded. "Mom got the house and everything. Dad was very generous. She kept everything and, you know, just hung onto it."

That was it. We were in a time capsule, circa 1971. Spooky. There was a stack of moving boxes in the hall, but at the rate Gary was going he'd still be packing a year from now.

"Here, I want you to have these," he said, handing me a manila envelope.

I opened it gingerly and out slid Dianne's school pictures—first grade, second, fourth, sixth, tenth and eleventh; even the multiple copies. I'd never seen any of them before. She was always a pretty girl, even when she was six and had her new teeth. This was worth the trip.

Gary asked me if I wanted a painting. It was Dianne's first, an oil still life, flowers in a vase, next to an empty vase. Blue and yellow daisies, they looked like, and some others with drooping yellow blooms. Signed "Dianne Roberts, 12-13-68."

"It's the only painting of hers I have," he said, "but I want you to have it."

I thanked him for his generosity. We hugged and promised to keep in touch.

Mary and Paul and I went out for sushi. Next morning, Mary drove us around Meyerland and Bellaire, past the Presbyterian church where she and Dianne met at Sunday school, Bellaire High, shopping centers where they used to go shoplifting just for grins, and the bayou trails and remaining strips of woodland notched between the 1950s houses. Mary pointed out places where they used to ride their bikes, where they'd sneak off to get high. Teenage stuff.

"We used to make up all these games," she said. "There was one called TV dinner roulette. We'd set four or five places at the table, however many people there were, and at each place we'd put a TV dinner or a bowl of ice cream or something really hideous, like canned beets. Then we'd sit down and start eating until someone called "move," and we'd have to move on to the next spot and eat some of that food. God, the things we'd think up when we were high."

We drove past the house on Beechnut Boulevard where the Roberts family lived until Dianne was eleven. A modest 1950s ranch style home. The house they lived in on Loch Lomond had been replaced by a much larger one, but Dianne's favorite willow tree, just down the street, was still standing.

When we first met, Dianne and Mary seemed so exotic. Big city excitement and sophistication. An army of colorful friends. Whenever I came home with her, Houston's vast freeways made me dizzy. They had neighborhoods serviced by streets longer than the roads connecting Johnson City and the next three towns like it.

Now I saw Houston in a whole new light. Presumably, in all the years that had passed, I had acquired a bit of sophistication of my own. I'd been to some even bigger cities, and lived in L.A. for seven years. Now, in this part of Houston, I sensed a quietness I'd never noticed before. Things felt safe and contained, almost like a small town.

I thought about the funny smirks I used to see on Dianne and Mary whenever they talked about Meyerland and Bellaire. Despite the monstrous size of their high school, they were living in a small town unto itself, an island of white, middle-class safety and tranquility in big, badass Houston. The only outsized things here were the trees. No wonder, for all their quirks, Dianne and Mary were fairly down-to-earth girls.

Swaths of surviving bayou and forest and scattered stands of towering evergreens helped humanize the Big H for me—especially in Memorial Park, Dianne and Mary's favorite stomping grounds. They offered an escape from that suburban ideal when it became too suffocating. They gave you a sense of refuge, a sense that the grownups couldn't control everything in your life. You feel the presence of the trees even when you aren't looking at them. They block the sky in places, and even when you aren't directly in their shade they give the light a special quality. They scent the air and mute the noise, and the bayou pulls you along.

Even the streets where Dianne and Mary grew up are named after trees: Oak, Cypress, Spruce, Magnolia, Pine and one of the longer ones, Willow. No wonder Dianne would get that Mona Lisa smile when she talked about going down to the bayou and hanging out under the trees. Many of those trees are still here, gripping the sloping banks with their knuckled roots and evoking a cool, benevolent presence.

I phoned Earl when we got back to Mary's house. His wife answered. I could hear his voice in the background. "Tell him I'm on my way out the door. Tell him to call around twelve." She repeated the message word for word.

His machine picked up when I called at noon. I left a message. Sincere, fairly succinct, not terribly hopeful that he'd call me back. After twenty-six years, what would I mean to him?

Mary and I hugged before I left. "It's getting better," I said. "Isn't it?"

"Yeah," she said. "It's good."

Finally, out of frustration, I went to the Travis County Courthouse, dug into the felony index, found the file number and requested the microfilm reel that contained the court records on Lyle Brummett. It took half a day, but I read every word and printed out about $50 worth of it.

What I learned was this: Brummett's confession confirms Dean Morley's version of the events on the evening before the murder. The two of them came to our house, hung out, went to Mother Earth until about midnight. After that, he says, Dean went to his girlfriend's place. His statement does not mention Dean's name again. Brummett returned to our house around two a.m. He parked across the street and left his shoes and shirt in the car, unlocked the window via the loose pane of glass, crawled inside, snuck back to our bedroom. He claims that Dianne did not resist, but the caustic remarks he attributes to her afterward do not sound like the comments of a consensual participant. That's when he murdered her.

In an affidavit, Detective Manley Stephens states that the first time he looked at Brummett he noticed deep scratches on his arms. Brummett claimed he'd gotten the wounds while installing electrical wiring. Stephens' skepticism leaches from his lines of dry, unemotional prose like blood soaking through a thin bandage. Stephens and other investigators determined that Brummett had a long history of violence and mental and sexual problems. He'd been subjected to psychological tests numerous times—in school, during an abbreviated stint in the Navy and after getting in trouble with the law.

I found the statements given by Dean Morley and Eddie Muñoz and myself. I also read the affidavits given by defense attorneys Charles Craig and Delmar Cain. I read the documents from an appeal that an attorney for Brummett filed in the late 1980s, based on claims of inadequate counsel from his court-appointed attorney (Craig) and a supposedly tainted confession. The appeal was denied. There were no real surprises. There wasn't even anything particularly grisly, like an autopsy report, crime scene photos or the cops' notes. Those would be in the police file.

The only surprise was that before Brummett pled guilty at the end of April 1977, Craig made a last-ditch attempt to get the remaining charges dropped, even though his client had admitted his role in all three murders on the witness stand at Woody's trial.

When I was finished with the file I paid my bill and walked out into the sunshine. Even though I'd been crying a lot lately and sleeping little, I didn't feel upset. Nor did I feel a sense of release. I just felt numb. After dinner, Dashiell and I played a game of Yu Gi Oh cards. He trounced me once, and the second time I let him win. It felt good.

Earl Roberts answered on the second ring. "Hello, Earl," I said. "This is Jesse," and we began talking. His reassuring baritone seemed to reach across the miles and the years like a sympathetic pat on the back. He asked how I'd been doing.

I spoke quickly, with the nervous energy of a caffeinated phone solicitor. I told him about having finally sought therapy after so many years of nightmares and flashbacks, and that I realized now how culpable I was for letting this monster come near us, how Earl probably blamed me and I didn't hold it against him if he did.

"Don't let this ruin your life, Jesse," Earl said. "Don't feel guilty. We all feel guilty, Gary, myself, you, Mary Ann, Mary. We all felt responsible to some degree. But the only person responsible for Dianne's death is Brummett. Don't make this your cross to bear."

"I guess you're right," I said, just to fill the space, like a grace note. "Dianne loved you," he said. "You'll always have that. That's something no one can ever take away from you, or any of us she loved."

"Yeah, I'll remember that," I said. It was a good thing for him to say. I told him that it meant a lot to get to talk to him, then I told him about the parole situation. The information seemed to take him by surprise, as if he'd trained himself not to think about it. I promised to send him information on how to file protests, how to get on the automatic notification list, things like that.

"Let's me and you have a cup of coffee sometime," he said. "What do you say?"

"That'd be great," I said. "I'd really like that." I said something about coming down to Houston in the next week or two, though I had no plans in the works.

"Well, take care of yourself, then, Jesse."

"You, too."

I'm going to stop this investigation business. I've gone as far as I want to go. There's nothing to be gained from going deeper into that black hole. I don't care about the killers' hearts or souls, and I've been as close to the inside of their minds as I can stand. I don't need to know a single new detail about August 16, 1976. I know who murdered Dianne. There's nothing more to solve.

Was my suppressed trauma from Dianne's murder the thing that gave me cancer? Maybe, maybe not, but I do believe that this quest was an essential part of my five-year recovery. It wouldn't have been complete without it.

I'm glad I finally talked to Earl. It was a big relief. I wonder how it was for him. Seeing Gary was good. Seeing Bellaire and Meyerland through Mary's eyes was important, too. I missed Mary Ann, but at least I saw her condo. That odd time capsule from 1971 was a cautionary tale: don't get trapped by the past.

I have also recently decided that I am opposed to capital punishment. There's too much risk that innocent people might be executed. If you suspected that my discovery of the arbitrary and cynical deals that are made in our judicial system swayed my opinion, you would be correct.

I'm taking a break from all of it. I need to put some distance between me and this wilderness. I'm going back to my life, my wife and son and cats and guitars.

I wish I felt convinced that Brummett couldn't have gotten a harsher sentence, but I'll keep the pressure on the parole board. Hopefully they'll keep him in prison forever. But if they don't, then what? How would I react, knowing he's free to walk on the green grass, under the big blue sky, breathing the same free air I breathe? If this was the Old West, it wouldn't be that outrageous for me to hunt him down and blow him away. Back then, a guy had to look out for the safety of his family and the community.

I'm still a good shot with a rifle or pistol, but this isn't the Old West. We can afford to be more sensitive and humane now; in fact, we're obliged to be. We can't let people who've become monsters turn us into monsters.

If I saw Lyle Brummett on the street, I'd just have to have the moral strength to let him walk on by. God, I hope I never have to, but people have survived worse things.

The Tree of Angels service was right after Thanksgiving, before I'd decided to quit my research. I was in a dark state, not sleeping much, rarely smiling. The star of the service was Raven Kazen, the director of TDCJ Victim Services. She was a tall, broad-shouldered woman in a red dress, red lipstick and shiny earrings, black hair pulled back. She spoke in sermon-like cadences about grief, loss, strength, redemption, sin and why Christmas is her favorite time of year. She also spoke about a meeting the previous night with a group called Parents of Murdered Children. It would take guts to meet with a group like that. She's got 'em.

I'd been curious about this woman ever since I started communicating with Victim Services and PAVC about keeping Lyle Brummett behind bars. Her name was on all the correspondence I've seen. Raven Kazen sounds like the name of one tough cookie, an avenging angel. Yet her speech was all about support, sympathy, God, caring, redemption.

The church was full, front to back. I heard only a few sniffles during the service. In every pew, at least one person held an angel ornament representing a victim of a violent crime. In addition to the new crime victims, there were hundreds of ornaments from past ceremonies with no representative to hang them. Later, people from PAVC would make sure they all found a place on the tree. The usher gave the nod for our row to walk up the aisle. I had three angels, for Dianne, Carol Ann and Beth, each with a name tag on a little string. They kept getting tangled together.

The Carol Ann and Beth angels were rosy-cheeked cherubs, and the Dianne angel looked Germanic. The ritual was bound to serve a lot of other people better than it would me, but I was glad I was doing it.

Taking advantage of my height, I found a spot for each angel near the top of the tree. It was just a gesture, but it felt like more. Somehow I felt lighter inside.

26. GIG

Even though I was the guest of honor, I couldn't help feeling detached and a little distracted at my party. The real drama seemed long past, and I felt a little like a con artist for being the center of attention. On the other hand a party is a party, and we owed it to ourselves to commemorate my survival and thank all the people who'd helped make it possible, particularly our lovely and brilliant host, Dr. Melba Lewis. Actually, she was the one who reminded me that I had ended my "Staying Alive" essay in *Texas Monthly* with a vow to rock out on the Continental Club stage with Jon Dee and Billy on this date. When I told her it wouldn't be possible because Jon Dee was on the road and Billy was stuck with obligations in New York City, she seemed disappointed.

"OK, but we've got to have a party," she said. "Let me take care of it."

So here we were. At least I'd had the good sense to get diagnosed with cancer in time for the holiday season. Christmas puts an extra glow on just about everything.

Melba lives in the hills west of Austin just around the bend from Lake LBJ. The hills are pretty at night, and Austin looks a little like toy town all lit up for Christmas. Her house is large but not ostentatious. Her two kids are good-looking, intelligent overachievers. Jessica, seventeen, is one of the top French students in the country. Joey, a freshman National Merit Scholar, was off at Vanderbilt. A champion wrestler in high school, going into neuroscience.

Melba, looking pretty with her long red hair and a bright blue dress, greeted us with big hugs and kisses. I felt a little awkward at first, talking to her in the middle of the large room where she practices her ballroom dancing. After spending countless hours with her over the last five years in tiny examination rooms, it was disorienting to share a large, open space with her.

The guests were split about evenly between her office employees and a few colleagues, and our friends, including musicians, writers and other associates. There was a full bar with a bartender and a nice spread of food, including a chocolate mousse dessert served from a giant martini glass. The whole affair, Melba said, was subsidized by drug companies. I'd been to some parties thrown by drug dealers, but they weren't the same.

When Melba first came up with the idea for the party, she said, "Hey, you could play. I've got a ballroom in my house. It'd be perfect."

I liked the idea, even though a loud rock band in a house has been known to ruin a lot of parties. Jon Dee and Billy still weren't available, though, and I was too busy with my own road trips and research to put something else together. As the date approached, Lois and I realized that not to play at all wouldn't be right. I brought my Fender bass and small amp.

Toward the end of the evening, everyone gathered in Melba's ballroom. She made a short speech, thanking her employees for sticking together and doing such a great job all year. Then Melba described how I had come into their lives. I was a little embarrassed, but it reminded me how many different people—besides family and friends—had contributed to the restoration of my health. Not just Melba and the people in that room, but hundreds of others.

Then I gave my side of the story, starting with the diagnosis. "Before I knew it," I said, "I began to realize what a swell piece of luck it was that Lois and I found Dr. Lewis.

"There's no doubt in my mind that she saved my life—along with Lois. Whatever parts one of them didn't save, the other did. To have these two women, plus all the great people who worked for Dr. Lewis and all my great friends, I know I'm a really lucky guy."

As I strapped on my bass, I said, "This is a song about an angel, and I'm dedicating it to Dr. Lewis. When I wrote it I was thinking it's interesting that when a male angel, Lucifer, was kicked out of heaven for having an attitude problem, he became a big pain in the ass for mankind. But it's always different when the angel is a woman. They're always wonderful and magical.

"Not that Dr. Lewis has ever been kicked out of anywhere, but this song is about an angel who gets kicked out of heaven and a guy who's lucky enough to be in love with her. It's called 'That Love Thing.'"

I suppose I was thinking either of sixties Atlantic soul or Al Green when I wrote the song. I'd picked it because of its full, melodic bass lines, and I was pleased that the room's acoustics complimented the bass and my unamplified voice with natural reverb. The first verse contains some of my favorite lines.

> *It was a sad day in heaven*
> *When they had to let her go*
> *The sun went dim as an old bulb*
> *Wind refused to blow*
> *The stars, they just wouldn't come out*
> *Birds fell from the sky*
> *But now she's in a better place*
> *And I'm a lucky guy*
>
> *She's got that love thing going*
> *She's like a big wheel rolling*
> *She's got that love thing going tonight*

When the song ended, there was boisterous applause, though I realized that I was playing to a captive audience. Next up was "Waiting for My Man," the Velvet Underground tune about a New York City junkie going to his dealer for a fix. "Maybe this is a risky choice," I said, "since there are a lot of health professionals in the room, but since this party is sponsored by drug companies, why not at least one drug song?"

I've been playing this song since around 1973, so I know it pretty well. I felt assured that it would sound good with just bass and vocal. Melba, all smiles, danced. The Fender sounded full and evocative, and my voice rang out nicely. The song is about a desperate addict waiting for his drug dealer, then scoring and hurrying back home to shoot up, and vowing to "work it all out" someday. Despite the bleak message, it's an oddly uplifting song in a way—or at least it's always felt that way to me.

"Thank you very, very much," I said when I was finished. "I really appreciate it. I'd love to play longer, but I don't want to wear out my welcome. Lois always tells me, 'Always leave 'em wanting more, not less,' and she's right.

"You ever notice that in movies, the nightclub singer will play one or two really cool songs, and that's it? Then the singer hangs out for the rest of the night. I mean, isn't that cool? A two-song set and then you're done. I always wanted a gig like that. I guess tonight I finally got one."

My friends and saviors laughed generously, and I took a bow.

Life is good; no major disasters lately. Sometimes it takes stormy weather to make you appreciate the sun coming out. Now that the word *recurrence* doesn't hold as much terror as it used to, Lois and I get a kick out of the various recurring cycles and themes in our lives. The Rolling Stones made us bigger fans than ever when we saw them on their fortieth anniversary tour, rocking as ferociously as a bunch of teenagers. Skunks reunions are fun, too. But so are the Cub Scouts Pinewood Derby races. Dashiell's car is always the coolest.

"Fazz" Eddie Muñoz got in touch recently and we're pals again. The next time we do a Skunks reunion we'll have to do three sets—one with Eddie, one with Jon Dee and, for the finale, a quartet featuring Eddie, Jon Dee, Billy and me. That's gonna be a hell of a show.

Jon Dee's been giving his son, Roy, guitar lessons; I've been giving Dashiell bass lessons. During a Sublett-Graham get-together after Christmas, Dashiell played a new song for us on piano, and Roy's eyes suddenly lit up. "Hey, Dash and I should start a band!" he said. "Wouldn't that be cool?"

Yeah, we agreed. That would be cool. That would be supercool.

Acknowledgements

This book would not exist if not for my incredible wife, Lois. As with all my other artistic endeavors, she's been my inspiration, foundation and tireless promoter. I want all my readers and the entire world to know how much I love and admire her. The same goes for our son, Dashiell, the World's Most Handsome Man—and possibly, the coolest and smartest. Dashiell's favorite saying these days is, "You're cool. . . But you're still in trouble!" I feel that way often.

I thank my mom and dad for being who they are, for giving me my moral compass and for the influence of their faith and amazing integrity. Thanks to my brother James for taking me to my first rock concerts and for building my first fuzztone pedal, and to Kathryn Woods for being my amazing sister. Thanks also to Helen and Harry Richwine for bringing me into their family and enriching my life experience.

I wish to thank my publisher, Tom Southern, for rescuing this book from chaos, and for having the enthusiasm, wisdom and good taste needed to shape it into its final form. Tom put me in the hands of editor John Paine, copyeditor Sarah Nawrocki and proofreader Judy Bloch. Together their impressive talents and eye for detail helped me bring the book into fighting trim. Thanks to Elizabeth Vahlsing for envisioning and executing the dust jacket and book design. None of it would've happened, however, if David Wilkinson and Bonnie Bratton hadn't urged me to send Tom the manuscript in the first place. Able assistance was also provided by Ann Theis, Karen Rheudasil and Doug St. Ament.

What a stroke of luck it was that hip photographers were around to document some of the events in this book and have graciously allowed me to use their work—Todd Wolfson, Ken Hoge, Jack Kinslow, Tracy Hart,

Will Van Overbeek, Jack Anderson, Chris Cuffaro, Bill Leissner, Gary Nickerman, Kathy Murray, Glenn Chase and John Carrico—thank you. Thank you, all band members from my loud, loud past, including especially Skunks alumni Eddie Muñoz, Billy Blackmon, Jon Dee Graham and Doug and Greg Murray. It would have been much duller without our premier roadie/poster artist/political provocateur, the inimitable Richard Luckett. Road managers deluxe Pat Costigan and David Fox performed above and beyond.

My fellow Violators were Kathy Valentine, Carla Olson and Marilyn Dean. The Jellyroll gang included Eddie Muñoz, Danny Coulson, Robin and Ron Dixon, plus, briefly, Mark Evans and the late David Dare. Thanks also to Stan Gilbert and the guys who played with me in the beginning, the late Dan Gersbach and Skip Hiatt. Secret Six members who deserve singling out include Jeff Campbell, Nancy Reynolds, Kevin Tubb, O.T. Loflin, Bruce Hughes and the late Gary Guthrie. Gary, I'm sorry this book didn't come out before you died. It would've been fun arguing with you about all the parts you'd say I got wrong.

World's Cutest Killers included Kathy Valentine, Kelly Johnson, Craig Aronson and Jebin Bruni. The Carla Olson/Mick Taylor Band also featured Ian McLagen, Barry Goldberg, George Callins, Rick Hemmert, Tom Junior Morgan, Juke Logan and Joe Sublett. Manager Saul Davis was the dogged genius behind the scenes. Thanks also to all the other musicians, writers and fans who made and continue to make the music scene in Austin and elsewhere such a fertile, mysterious and vibrant entity.

If not for the love and support of Pattie Hadley, Melissa Marshall, Mary McGee, Kathy Valentine, Carla Olson, Karen Grotefen, Jeannie Harris, Danny Coulson and Eddie Muñoz, I don't know if I could've survived 1976. Thank you.

If not for Melba Lewis, M.D., I don't know if I could've survived 1997. I have Dr. Hillary Miller to thank for referring me to Dr. Lewis. I also owe a giant debt of gratitude to all the other doctors and medical professionals who played a part in the massive efforts to save my life and make my recovery more bearable. These include especially Dr. Michael Kasper, Dr. Douglas Fein, Dr. Timothy Dziuk, Dr. Joseph Leary, Dr. Mark White, Dr. Catherine Daniel, Dr. Greg Edson and all the respective staff members of the aforementioned. Extra gratitude is extended with love to Gillian, Cheryl, Calvin and Jennifer at South Austin Cancer Center and Bobbie and Kathy at Texas Oncology.

Evan Smith, editor of *Texas Monthly*, was one of the first people to urge me to write about these experiences. He kept the pressure on by keeping his promise to publish the first account of my cancer battle and an expanded version of my original account of Dianne's murder. Evan is cool. Thanks also to publisher Mike Levy. Thanks to Jim Hornfischer for his early efforts to shape and promote this book, and to Nat Sobel for his encouragement and advice.

Appreciation and acknowledgement of the inspiration and support they've given me are due my great writing pals who are scattered from Berlin to L.A. These include Ed Ward, Michael Connelly, James Ellroy, James Carlos Blake, Terry Baker, Wendy Hornsby, Les Roberts, Gar Anthony Haywood, Gary Phillips, James Crumley, Jon Jackson and Betsy Willeford.

In Austin, you can't throw a guitar pick without hitting a musician or writer, and I'm lucky to be able to call a good number of the best of both groups my friends. I've already listed many of the former, and among the best of the latter, Margaret Moser deserves special thanks. The same goes for Louis Black and Nick Barbaro, editor and publisher, respectively, of the *Austin Chronicle*. Thanks also to John Morthland, Joe Nick Patoski, Turk Pipkin, Mike Cox, Sarah Bird, Carol Dawson, Elizabeth Crook, Jim Shahin and Robert Draper. Scooter Cheatham and Lynn Marshall deserve more credit than I can detail here.

Cyndi Hughes, director of the Texas Book Festival, along with Bill Wittliff, Connie Todd and Steve Davis of the Southwest Writers Collection at Texas State University, have been good to me and all Texas writers. Among other important and curious literary artifacts, SWC is the repository of my old manuscripts and my retired Skunks mod two-tone creepers.

Wayne Nagel, the world's number one Rolling Stones fan, is supercool. Rick Triplett is Austin's hippest attorney. Tad Smalley called me every day during chemo and made me laugh. Sometimes that was no small feat.

Special acknowledgement must be extended to my fellow members of the Manly Men Lunch Group, a fine group of writers and aficionados of hardboiled lit and Texas barbecue: Tom Garner, David Wilkinson, Kip Stratton, Dick Holland, Neal Barrett, Jr. and Jan Reid. Thanks to Dennis McMillan, Esq., for being a unique and tireless promoter of fine hard-boiled literature as well as a highly eccentric 21st-century dandy.

Thanks also to my great friends Saul Davis, Tom Huckabee, Barbara

Cohen, Rocky Schenck, Abby Levine, Tony and Hunt Sales, Allison Brush, Monte Markham, Lee Fulkerson and Joe Uliano. Richard Linklater lent his support. My old pals Jake Riviera and Nick Lowe are nothing but cool.

In Kerrville, I appreciate the assistance of Ilse Bailey, Henry Ligon, Joe Davis, Bill London and Jim Pearson. Thanks also to People Against Violent Crime, Texans for Equal Justice and the Victim Rights division of Texas Department of Criminal Justice for their work to aid victims of violent crime and to ensure that the public is protected from violent criminals for as long as they are a threat to society.

Thanks to Eddie Wilson for being Eddie Wilson (no one does it better) and my friend. Thanks to Johnny Reno for turning me on to Rauol Whitfield and "Telephone Call from Istanbul." Thanks, Christina Patoski.

Lou Ann Barton, you're still blues diva number one.

To all of you whose names I've unintentionally left off (including my memory consultant), thank you, and I apologize.

The Skunks

Can't Get Loose/Earthquake Shake, released summer 1979 on our label, Skunks Records, SR1: Our first release, recorded on a two-track reel-to-reel in a garage on a Friday afternoon. Both songs by Jesse Sublett. First pressing: 1,000. Second pressing: 1,000. Personnel: Sublett/Graham/Blackmon.

The Skunks Double EP, released 1980, SR2/3. Includes a seven-inch, 33-1/3 RPM EP (SR2) with "Gimme Some"/"Promises" b/w "Hello Heartbreaker"/"Top Ten" and a seven-inch 45 RPM single (SR3): "Cheap Girl" b/w "Something About You Scares Me." Personnel: Sublett/Graham/Blackmon. All songs by Jesse Sublett except "Gimme Some," co-written with Eddie Muñoz. That's Lois on the cover. First pressing: 2,000. Second pressing: 2,000.

Live at Raul's, a compilation with four other bands, released in 1980 on Raul's Records as RR1. Our songs, "Cheap Girl" and "Don't Push Me Around," were among the top ten most requested songs at KLBJ-FM for two years running, right alongside "Stairway to Heaven." Personnel: Sublett/Graham/Blackmon. The CD version, released in 1995 (DejaDisc DJD3216), includes two tracks by Roky Erickson.

"What Do You Want"/"The Racket," released October 1980, SR4. Personnel: Sublett /Blackmon/Murray. Our worst record. Jon Dee co-wrote the A-side (also covered by the Gator Family); I wrote the flip.

The Skunks [usually called "The Black Album"], was recorded in the summer of 1978 but Rude Records didn't get around to releasing it until 1980. "Something About You Scares Me," "Gimme Some," "Memphis," "6th Street Peggy," "Top Ten," "Television Lover," "Cheap Girl," "That's The Kind of Girl I love," "Desperation," "I Smell

Trouble." Personnel: Sublett/Munoz/Blackmon. Produced by Joe Gracey, recorded in the basement of the KOKE-FM building. This is the record that caused all the trouble.

The Skunks [usually called "The Purple Album"], released in 1982 on Republic Records, RR8201. "Questions for Laura," "Hurt," "Quiet Girl," "Let's Get Twisted," "For Your Love," "Pressure," "Telewoman," "Still the Same," "Jesse's Not Like the Other Boys," "Gimme Some." Produced by Earle Mankey. Personnel: Sublett/Doug Murray/Greg Murray.

Earthquake Shake: Live, a 20-song CD culled from two performances in early 1980, one at Max's Kansas City in New York, the other at the Back Room in Austin. Cassette recordings of these shows surfaced in late 1999. We collected the best tracks and released this CD December 2000. Listed as one of the top ten local releases of the year by the *Austin-American Statesman*.

Earthquake Shake, released as a limited edition vinyl LP by Rave Up, an Italian punk label, is very different from the aforementioned CD. The record features many selections from the Skunks' previous records, plus some live recordings not included in the CD, such as the slam-metal ballad "All Tied Up."

SECRET SIX
Ten From Texas: Herd It Through the Grapevine, compilation of ten bands selected and produced by Liam Sternberg, was released in 1984 by Elektra, EA 60373-1. Our song, "No More Weekends in Warsaw," is quite good.

FLEX
This short-lived trio released two recordings in the mid 1980s, a five-song 12-inch record produced by Dave McNair and a five-song cassette produced by Ron Rogers and distributed exclusively to the registrants of the New Music Seminar in 1986. Both works were eponymously titled. Not my best work.

CARLA OLSON AND MICK TAYLOR
A live CD was recorded at the Roxy in Los Angeles on March 4, 1990, and released under various titles, including *Too Hot for Snakes* in the

U.S. and *Live at the Roxy* in Japan. The CD kicks off with my song, "Who Put the Sting on the Honey Bee," which I originally wrote for Lou Ann Barton.

CARLA OLSON BAND

Within An Ace was released in the U.S. by Watermelon Records in 1993. The CD features guest performances by Mick Taylor, Ian McLagen and others, and includes my blues ballad "World of Pain," one of the bleakest songs I've ever written.

CLOUD 19

A five-song cassette was recorded by this band on my birthday in 1991 and given away to the first 150 buyers of my third novel, *Boiled in Concrete*. It's pretty cool. Check these titles: "Walking Through the Boneyard," "Sabertooth Tiger (In a Little Kitten Suit)," "Rained All Night," "S.O.L." Jon Dee Graham plays guitar.

PHIL SEYMOUR

Precious to Me, released by Shelter in 1996, includes two songs I played on along with George Callins and Rick Hemmert. It was fun but sad. Phil was recovering from treatment for lymphoma at the time, but he sang his heart out.

Other bands who have recorded my songs include Splash City (from France), the Delphines, Sons of Hercules and Kris Kristofferson. The best of these is probably the Delphines' (Kathy Valentine's band) version of "Pissin' in the Wind."

For more detailed information on the Skunks and salacious tidbits about my life in music, plus info on my books and signing events visit www.jessesublett.com.